"*A man that is born falls* [...] *into the sea. If he tries to c* [...] *people endeavor to do, he drown* [...]

"*No! I tell you! The way is to the destructive element submit yourself, and with the exertions of your hands and feet in the water make the deep, deep sea keep you up . . .*"

Stein to Marlow in
LORD JIM by Joseph Conrad

IN SEARCH OF PARADISE
The Nordhoff-Hall Story
by Paul Briand, Jr.

For James Norman Hall the drama of Conrad's *Lord Jim* was a touchstone. In his own life of adventure and trial he found himself returning again and again to Stein's admonition and he learned, at length, to submit himself to life's destructive elements and to triumph over them. It was a lesson which his friend and colleague, Charles Bernard Nordhoff, was never to master, and it marked the decisive difference in the lives of these two famous writers. Together they created one of the great historical novels of the sea, *Mutiny on the Bounty*. Singly and together they wrote thirty-six books — but few of their works are as dramatic as the story of their own lives and the fates that shaped their end.

For James Hall, Iowa born and bred, World War I and the Escadrille Lafayette offered a stunning opportunity. He came to the War early, flew brilliantly, wrote even more brilliantly about his flying, and was captured and held prisoner by the Germans. It was not until the end of the war that he met the haughty Californian, Charles Nordhoff, and joined with him to write the history of the Escadrille in which they had both served with distinction.

Their mutual disgust with the postwar world, their common experience and interest in writing, their longing for escape and adventure, inspired them to strike out for Tahiti to write a travel book about the South Seas. It was a trip to an edge of the world from which they never really returned.

In *Search of Paradise* tells a story that combines the mud of warfare with the sparkling color of the South Seas — the struggle for success with the ultimate defeat of a romantic ideal — and contrasts Hall's success in love, marriage, and the realization of his powers as a writer with Nordhoff's ultimate and tragic end. Between them was a great talent which, when melded, produced books of tremendous strength and vitality. What lay behind that talent is the thread that binds this brilliant dual biography.

IN SEARCH OF
PARADISE
The Nordhoff-Hall Story

PAUL L. BRIAND, JR.

Centennial Edition

Mutual Publishing Paperback Series
Tales of the Pacific
Honolulu · Hawaii

*The author wishes to thank the following publishers for permission to
quote from their publications: Atlantic Monthly Press–Little, Brown and
Company, My Island Home, by James Norman Hall, copyright 1952 by
the estate of James Norman Hall; The Forgotten One, by James Norman
Hall, copyright 1949 by James Norman Hall; The Hurricane, by Charles
Nordhoff and James Norman Hall, copyright 1936 by Charles Nordhoff
and James Norman Hall. Harper & Row, Publishers, Faery Lands of the
South Seas, by James Norman Hall and Charles Bernard Nordhoff,
copyright 1921 by Harper & Brothers. Houghton Mifflin Company, The
Fledgling, by Charles Bernard Nordhoff, copyright 1919 by Charles
Bernard Nordhoff; Kitchener's Mob, by James Norman Hall, copyright
1916 by James Norman Hall; High Adventure, by James Norman Hall,
copyright 1918 by James Norman Hall; On the Stream of Travel, by James
Norman Hall, copyright 1926 by James Norman Hall; Mid-Pacific, by
James Norman Hall, copyright 1928 by James Norman Hall; Flying with
Chaucer, by James Norman Hall, copyright 1930 by James Norman Hall;
Under a Thatched Roof, by James Norman Hall, copyright 1942 by James
Norman Hall; The Lafayette Flying Corps, edited by James Norman Hall
and Charles Bernard Nordhoff, copyright 1920 by James Norman Hall and
Charles Bernard Nordhoff.*

Cover design by Momi Cazimero

Printed in Australia by The Book Printer, Victoria

For a completing listing of other books in the "Tales
of the Pacific" series and ordering information,
write to: Mutual Publishing Company
2055 N. King Street
Honolulu, Hawaii 96819
Phone: (808) 924-7732

THIS BOOK CONTAINS THE COMPLETE TEXT OF THE ORIGINAL HARDBOUND EDITION

Reader's Note: Chapter divider pages appearing in the original
edition have been omitted to allow inclusion of additional material.
This may cause gaps in page numbering.

For my sons
Paul L., III
Robert Bruce
and David Joseph

And for my daughters
Mary Katherine
Anne Marie
Margaret Mary
and Ella Elizabeth

A Tale of Paradise Postponed

"I will tell you a story which was told to me when I was a little boy. Every time I thought of it, it seemed to me to become more and more charming, for it is with stories, as it is with people — they become better as they grow older."
Hans Christian Andersen
What the Good Men Will Teach You

And so it is with the true-life story of *In Search of Paradise*. Now, after it has been out of print for over fifteen years, Mutual Publishing is honored by playing a role in giving a new beginning, a new life, to a book which never reached the audience it deserved.

With the 1960 publication of his first biography, the critically acclaimed and best-selling *Daughter of the Sky: The Amelia Earhart Story*, Lt. Col. Paul Briand, Jr. was on his way to becoming one of the finest biographers of our time. There were no forebodings to predict otherwise.

It was in 1961, while flying high on his first success, that it was suggested to Briand that his next biography concern the lives of Nordhoff and Hall. These two World War I heroes later went on to become one of the greatest writing teams in history, names synonymous with some of the best fiction from the Pacific Islands. Their adventures in collaborating on *Mutiny on the "Bounty"* rival those in flying on the Western Front.

As if it wasn't difficult enough to write about one man's life, the pitfalls of a dual biography can be almost insurmountable, but Briand faced these the way he did life — head-on. In 1966, after five years of arduous work, *In Search of Paradise: The Nordhoff-Hall Story* was published. Expectations were great. From across the country, critics unanimously praised the book, but this is where Briand's cinderella story was shot down.

In 1966, the Vietnam war was in the headlines every day, leaving a bitter aftertaste in the mouths of nearly all Americans. The Nordhoff-Hall story was about two great war heroes: the last thing anyone was concerned with during this dark time in American history.

As if this was not bad enough, 1966 was the year of one of

the last major newspaper strikes; nearly all the planned advertising was lost.

Things got even worse when the issuing publisher of *In Search of Paradise* was the victim of a corporate take-over. The book never received the marketing and distribution required to bring it into the library of readers' hearts.

After quickly selling out its initial printing of five thousand copies, *In Search of Paradise* fell out of print, and most unfortunately, Lt. Col. Paul Briand, Jr. would never write another biography.

With this edition, a new generation of readers can enjoy the adventures and exploits of James Norman Hall and Charles Bernard Nordhoff.

Paul Briand, Jr. was born and raised in Cambridge, Massachusetts. After Pearl Harbor, he volunteered for service, and later, with the 9th Air Force in the European Theatre, flew combat cargo missions to Normandy, Bastogne, and Arnhem, earning the Air Medal. From the University of New Hampshire, as a distinguished military graduate of Air Force ROTC and as a bachelor of arts in English *cum laude,* he served as an information officer in Texas and Tennessee. Later he was an instructor at the Military Academy at West Point and at the new Air Force Academy in Colorado. He earned a master's degree in English literature from Columbia and a Ph.D. in creative writing from Denver University. He retired as a lieutenant colonel, to teach literature and writing at SUNY Oswego. Author of the biographies of Amelia Earhart *(Daughter of the Sky)* and of Nordhoff and Hall *(In Search of Paradise)* and also numerous popular and scholarly articles, as well as serving as co-editor of *The Sound of Wings,* a collection of flight-inspired literature, he was a member of the writing/editorial/research team for The National Commission on the Causes and Prevention of Violence.

After bringing life to those he wrote about, and joy to those he lived with, Lieut. Col. Paul Briand, Jr. passed away in the summer of 1986, only one year before the rebirth of *In Search of Paradise.*

STEVEN CRAYNE

Preface

Each man *is* an island. There is in every man an islandic core of inner self which no other man can fully explore or know. It is the part of man known completely only to God; and when a man says, "I," he is undoubtedly reaffirming the "I" of his Island Self. Yet, if a man gives thought to others, he will see that he is involved in the human predicament as other men are, that he is, ideally, a part of the mainland of mankind, as John Donne says. But, unless a man can in some way come to know his essential self, his individual identity as a person, and this amid the ocean of human loneliness that surrounds him, he cannot truly build the isthmus of love and consideration that can join him to the island selves of other human beings.

Curiously, the island of Tahiti in the South Seas, where James Norman Hall and Charles Bernard Nordhoff finally settled, after several years of spiritual and physical wandering, is in fact an island and a *presque* isle joined by an isthmus. One was somewhat civilized, the other almost primitive; on Tahiti, Nordhoff and Hall discovered their identities, like

Conrad's Lord Jim in Patusan. But only one found and kept his paradise; the other lost it. Because in the search of paradise it—as in the quest of truth—can be found only if it is recognized for what it is when it is found.

Nordhoff and Hall were the most dissimilar of men, of entirely different backgrounds, educations, families, characters, personalities, motivations, and talents; yet they merged in a kind of fusion, which radiated some of the most famous adventure stories ever told. But the most adventurous story of them all is the story, separate and together, of their own lives.

For the traditional reasons of unity, coherence, and emphasis, I have decided to present the story of Nordhoff and Hall largely from Hall's point of view. Fortunately for the biographer, Hall, with an eye to posterity, saved everything, leaving behind thousands of documents to build a life from; Nordhoff, unfortunately, with an eye to waste and destruction, saved nothing, but what was left in the rubble proved valuable indeed.

For five years I have studied the tertiary, secondary, and primary materials; I have written hundreds of letters of inquiry; and I have traveled more than twenty thousand miles in the United States and to the South Seas to capture firsthand impressions: these were the romance and excitement of research. But the adventure was in the writing, in the attempt to translate, by means of narrative, two fascinating men from literary terms into human terms.

PAUL L. BRIAND, JR.
Lt. Colonel, USAF

U. S. Air Force Academy
Colorado

Acknowledgments

In his research a biographer with luck may uncover hundreds of scenes, events, episodes, and incidents to illustrate the lives of his characters; but it is only how he selects and re-creates from those at his disposal that decides at last the portrait he has drawn, the story he has told, the theme he has revealed. Another biographer at another time might choose other illustrations depending on what he has found and on his point of view; this explains why in some cases there are many biographies of the same person. Accordingly, my insight into the lives of Nordhoff and Hall is revealed in the scenes I have attempted to re-create from those—sometimes many, sometimes few—at my disposal.

For most of the basic events in the life of James Norman Hall I had to select carefully from the many available to me— in his many autobiographical works, in his voluminous letters, in the abundance of anecdotes told to me by his family and friends (he had no enemies that I could find), in the trunks and file cases full of memorabilia at Grinnell College and in Tahiti;

for those events in the life of Charles Nordhoff, however, I had to build assiduously from the few scenes available to me—in his one biographical book, which was in fact a compilation by his mother of his letters from the front, in his few available letters to his family, to Hall and other friends, in his few scattered remnants of notes, unfinished manuscripts and memorabilia left behind in Tahiti, and in the material dug up by me in the relentless correspondence and interviews.

Diligently for five years have I tried to keep a list of the people and organizations who have helped me in my project; I owe my profoundest gratitude to the following:

M. Thomas Ackerland, Ida E. Ainsworth, Paul H. Appleby, Crolyn C. Atkin; Clyde Balsley, Carl Beecher, Peggy W. Best, George Biddle, Dr. Roy D. Biddle, G. Clifford Blake, Carl D. Brandt, Tom B. Buffum; Mr. and Mrs. Cyril T. Carney, Anna Benedicta Carolan, Mrs. John Emmett Chadwick, Donald Barr Chidsey, Mrs. Henry Gray Clark, Carroll Coleman, Barnaby Conrad, Charis Crockett, Thomas E. Cornwall, Mrs. Roy M. Cushman; Chester C. Davis, George Dock, Jr.; Arthur B. Epperson; H. Bradley Fairchild, Mrs. Tod Ford, Henry Forster; Mrs. Harold B. Gardner, Reeve Gartzmann, Leslie R. Gay, Martin Gilder, Mrs. Charles Glaser, Mrs. James Clark Graham, Christian de Guigne, Caroline Guild; Donald P. Hemingway, Mrs. Horace L. Hill, Ruth Hill, Mrs. Clare D. Horner; Ernest Jacoby; Charles W. Kerwood, Charles M. Kinsolving, C. A. Klein; Joseph D. Leland, R. A. Lindsay, Kenneth Littauer, Lawrence K. Lunt; John C. MacFarland, Donald S. Marshall, James McConnaughey, Mrs. Hugh McKean, Fred W. McNear, Jr., Mrs. Rosalie McShane, Richard Miller, Dr. and Mrs. David C. F. Monsen, B. T. Moore, F. P. Morrison, Mrs. Laurence S. Morrison, Don Moss, Mrs. John F. Murphy; Mrs. Charles B. Nordhoff, Charlie Nordhoff, Mrs. Franklin W. Nordhoff, James Nordhoff, Vahine Nordhoff; Eugene Overton; Ina C. Payne, Charles A. Pearce, Major Thomas E. Pearsall, Professor George L. Pierce, Gifford B. Pinchot, Mrs. Henry W. Poett, Jr., Dr. Walter B. Power, Willard Price; William M. Rand, Roy Ray Roberts, Leland L. Rounds; Mrs. Ellery Sedgwick, W. R. Severance, Odell Shepard, Reginald Sinclair, Priscilla C. Smith,

E. T. Springer, Walter G. de Steiguer, Philip W. Stocker, William S. Stone, Professor and Mrs. John D. Stoops, James E. Stronks; Andy Thomson; Murray D. Welch, Marjorie Sutherland Wheeler, Charles A. Whipple, D. Wright Wilson, Edna E. Winship, Irby F. Wood; William A. Ziegler; Betty Fogler, Mrs. E. C. Forsyth, and Major John R. Galt.

Others meriting special acknowledgment are: Ben Benjamin, who helped me get the project started in the first place; Mrs. Allen H. Williams, who prevailed on so many others to help; Major and Mrs. Albert J. Britton, who provided the jumping-off place, down and back; L. L. Winship, one of the first and last of Hall's many friends; Captain William Morgan, for his brilliant assistance in the art of interviewing; Captain Phil Flammer, for his help on the Lafayette Escadrille section; Conrad Lafcadio Hall, for the loan of those precious first editions; Lester J. Briand and the Briand Studio, for expert work; David C. Mearns, Chief, Manuscript Division, The Library of Congress; Henry Alden, Librarian, and Mary E. Klausner, Archivist, Grinnell College; Sargent Kennedy, Registrar, Harvard University; The Book-of-the-Month Club; The Dictaphone Corporation; Robert and his staff, The Arahiri Hotel, Arué, Tahiti; Dave Cave and the Hertz U-Driv-It Agency, Papeete, Tahiti; John Monks, Jr., who made me write that all-important first paragraph at his home in California; Colonel George V. Fagan, Donald J. Barrett, and Gilbert L. Campbell, of the Air Force Academy Library, who are the best in the business; Brigadier General Robert F. McDermott and Colonel Peter R. Moody, whose questions about the manuscript were spurs to its completion; and Edward Weeks, for access to and use of the files of *The Atlantic Monthly*. To Nicholas G. Rutgers, his wife Nancy Ella Hall, and Mrs. James Norman Hall, for their incomparable hospitality, devoted cooperation, and unstinting help through all stages of the project, my enduring thanks; and a special accolade, and my undying love and eternal gratitude, to my wife Margaret, who is willing to accept what is left over from the teacher-writer who is also her husband and the father of her seven children.

Contents

LA RECHERCHE

Dans les profondeurs de son coeur
Mi-vu, peu connu,
L'homme est un enfant, sans soeurs, sans frères,
Qui cherche . . .
Pendant le crépuscule, et en pleurant sa mère . . .
La maison lointaine de son père.

—Charles Nordhoff
Written upon awakening
from a dream, in Tahiti

TO THE NORTHWARD

Look to the northward, stranger,
Just over the hillside, there.
Have you in your travels seen
A land more passing fair?

—James Norman Hall
Written as a boy, on a
barn wall in Iowa

SHELLEY AT LERICI

What blind decision led you to confuse
Your only life with art on that last day?
Nothing was promised by your mindless muse,
And clouds deceived, though mirrored in the bay.

Those lost Ionian sailors you were seeking
Were proof of sudden violence: stinging spray
Blinding the eyes, south wind shrieking;
The swift, dark squall in a bright day.

Imposed on nature, there at Lerici,
Your intuition proved itself unsound.
Insentient winds, a nonmalignant sea,
Met without purpose; being there you drowned.

—John R. Galt

from LORD JIM

STEIN to MARLOW:

A man that is born falls into a dream like a man
who falls into the sea. If he tries to climb out
into the air as inexperienced people endeavor to
do, he drowns—*nicht wahr?* . . . No! I tell you!
The way is to the destructive element submit yourself,
and with the exertions of your hands and feet in the
water make the deep, deep sea keep you up. . . .

—Joseph Conrad

JAMES NORMAN HALL

1
Kitchener's Army

All along the Western Front in the fall of the year 1915, the rain fell, hard and unremitting. In the British sector the roads had become streams of mud; and as the men slogged in columns on either side, they slipped and fell and cursed. One of them, a machine gunner, stopped to shift the weight of the weapon digging into his shoulder. He shivered in his greatcoat, wet and heavy against the cold. Briefly, he looked across the ditch to a hollow farmhouse. The roof, doors, and windows had been blown out; its brick walls were bare and stark. Next to the house stood a blasted poplar tree, its trunk jagged and stripped. Both were cadaverous silhouettes against a gray and darkening sky. In the distance the soldier heard the thunder of guns; it had grown louder and more frequent as they moved forward.

The sergeant came up. "Come on, Jamie boy," he said. "Let's move." Despite the grimness of the September day and the misery of the march, the sergeant was bright and talkative. "Lissen to them guns barkin'! We're in for it this time!" He turned to the men filing by. " 'Ave you got yer wills made out, lads? You're a-go'n' to see a scrap presently, an' it ain't a-go'n' to be no flea bite, I give you my word!" *

The soldiers started to sing. They were led by a ringing Irish tenor voice. The gunner fell in behind the tenor, a tall, hulking Irishman named O'Brien with whom he had often sung in two-part harmony in the barracks, and raised his second tenor to O'Brien's lead. "Wite," the sergeant shouted, "just wite to the end o' this 'ere march! You'll be a-singin' that song out o' the other side o' yer face."

"Strike me pink, Sergeant!" Gardner said. He was a smiling red-faced corporal who liked to tease at any opportunity. "You gettin' cold feet?"

"I'm leavin' me razor to 'is Majesty," said Preston, a sallow-faced Welsh miner, who had been the best gambler at Aldershot. "I 'ope 'e'll tyke the 'int."

Lance Corporal James Norman Hall smiled over the bantering as he waited for O'Brien in front of him to start another song. The only American in the unit, Hall was proud to be a British soldier, one of many hundreds of thousands in Lord Kitchener's volunteer army. In the summer of the year before, he had left his job as a social worker in Boston and sailed to Liverpool, to make a bicycle tour of Scotland, Wales, and England and visit the homes of Britain's famous authors. At one point, he had pedaled to the home of Joseph Conrad, his favorite writer. He came to the door and was about to knock when he lost heart, turned around, and left. He did not want to disturb the master, who must be at work on another novel.

Hall gripped his machine gun more firmly. In July, in London, he had seen the war posters. On three successive occasions he had joined the line that filed slowly up to the recruiting sergeant's station to "see how it felt." On the third morning he enlisted. After almost a year of training and drilling they had been sent to France. Now they were moving up. And, like the others, Hall knew, despite the singing and joking, that a big battle was at hand.

---

* All dialogue quoted, except for a few transitional words in some places, is taken from book, article, letter, diary, notebook, interview, or other documented source—Author.

That evening they came into a small mining village, where they dispersed and bunked down for the night. With twelve of his group Hall sprawled out on the kitchen floor of a cottage. Through the night, as he tried, exhausted and fitful, to sleep, he could hear the rumble of trucks, the march of feet, and the boom of the big guns. When they had fallen out the next morning, one of the officers told them of their fate. The rain still fell, and it was dark, two hours before dawn.

"Listen carefully, men," the officer said. "We are moving off in a few moments, to take over captured German trenches on the left of Loos. No one knows yet just how the land lies there. The reports we have had are confused and rather conflicting." He bent the riding crop between his hands. The tone of his voice became very serious. "The boys you are going to relieve have been having a hard time. The trenches are full of dead. Those who are left are worn out with the strain, and they need sleep. They won't care to stop long after you come in, so you must not expect much information from them. You will have to find out things for yourself. But I know you well enough to feel certain that you will."

He reset the cap upon his head, and smacked the top of his boot with the crop. "From now on you'll not have it easy. You will have to sit tight under a heavy fire from the German batteries. You will have to repulse counterattacks, for they will make every effort to retake those trenches. But remember! You're British soldiers! Whatever happens, you've got to hang on!"

They started down the road again and sloshed through the mud, now more than a foot thick, viscous as ooze. Ahead flashes from gun batteries cracked against black overhanging clouds. Now and again the files of soldiers would have to take to the ditch to make way for the traffic—for ambulances full of wounded, for trucks full of supplies, for staff cars, and for artillery pieces and caissons.

At the village of Vermelles they halted to wait for guides through the trenches. The men lay down in the mud to rest. Hall propped his knapsack under his head and tilted his helmet forward over his eyes. Suddenly he felt a cold, wet nose sniffing at his ear. It was a dog, a skinny wretch, cold and quivering. Hall patted him, then reached into his gear and pulled out a can of biscuits. The dog quickly munched them up.

Sitting next to Hall, Bert Powell poured some water from his canteen into his tin cup and held it for the dog to drink. "I've got a pointer back 'ome," he said, wistfully. "I 'ope me kid brother is feedin' 'im proper like."

Charlie Harrison, who had been a clerk for a beer company, opened a can of beef, broke off a piece, and held it out. "Bert," he said, "you won't need any pointer for 'untin' the 'un." Then he added: "I wish I 'ad an 'alf pint o' mild an' bitter to go wi' this beef."

One of the privates, Walter Bryant, a boy of nineteen, sat up suddenly. He took off his helmet and brushed back his long golden hair with the palm of his hand. "No beer for me," he said. "I got to stay in trainin' for the mile. Someday, God willin', I'll be the best runner in England."

"You'll run more than a mile wi' the Germans shootin' at ya," O'Brien said to him. "Jus' remember to run forward all the time."

"Until you find yourself all alone," Hall added. "Then you can drop back and wait for the rest of us." Hall stood up and looked out over the countryside. It was covered with trenches and shell holes, desolate and forsaken like a no-man's-land. Freddy Azlett walked over to Hall. They were gun mates. "Ain't pretty, is it?" Freddy said.

The order was given to fall in. They now marched off the road into barren fields through wet and slippery clay. The men could not keep their balance, and some fell into the mud. They started across the trenches. Hall could see in the half-light what the officer had been talking about. Broken corpses littered the ground everywhere, some splayed face down in the mud, others lay on their backs, their faces contorted cavities; some were hunched together one on top of the other, others hung from a tangle of barbed wire, weird and grotesque. Hall tried to dodge them, but he fell over them, walked on and over them. When they finally reached their assigned trench, he slumped to the ground, weary, tired, and sick from the smell of death.

Hall unshouldered his machine gun and bandoliers of ammunition, and leaned against the slippery wall of the trench. He pulled out his canteen and took a drink of water, then lit a cigarette. The relieved troops started to file by. They were covered with mud, their thick beards caked with it. They spoke in short, quick, animated bursts, their eyes glinting hard and wild, answering questions as they moved out, happy at last that their particular hell was over for a while.

"Wot sort of week you 'ad, mate?" Freddy Azlett asked.

"It ain't been a week, son. It's been a lifetime!"

"Lucky fer us you blokes come in just w'en you did. We've about reached the limit."

"You blokes want any souvenirs, all you got to do is pick 'em up. 'Elmets, revolvers, rifles, German di'ries. You wite till mornin'. You'll see plenty."

Hall stopped one of them. "Is this the last line of their trenches?" he asked.

The Tommy grinned. "A Yank, eh? Good for you for j'inin' us. Can't tell you, mate. All we know is, we got 'ere some'ow an' we been a-'oldin' on. My Gawd! It's been awful! They calmed down a bit tonight. You blokes is lucky comin' in just w'en you did."

The soldier who spoke was joined by a sergeant. "I ain't got a pal left o' my section," he said. "You'll see some of 'em. We ain't 'ad time to bury 'em."

They rejoined the column of soldiers and left the trenches. Hall pitied them for their horror, but knew that he too would soon have to know it for himself. He remembered Conrad's *Lord Jim* and how Stein had advised Marlow about Jim. Hall could see the page; it swam up before him as he had read it on the park bench of the Boston Common:

"Yes! Very funny this terrible thing is. [Stein said] A man that is born falls into a dream like a man who falls into the sea. If he tries to climb out into the air as inexperienced people endeavor to do, he drowns—*nicht wahr?* . . . No! I tell you! The way is to the destructive element submit yourself, and with the exertions of your hands and feet in the water make the deep, deep sea keep you up. . . ."

Hall knew that he could not become the adventurer he imagined himself to be—his idealized self—unless he could survive the actualities, sometimes brutal and tragic, of adventure. He knew he would have to submit himself to the destructive element. But, Hall asked himself, had he, like Jim, jumped ship? As Jim had left hundreds of Moslems abandoned on what he thought was a doomed ship, had he not left hundreds of people in Boston who needed him? Later, at the court of inquiry, Jim's only defense was: "I had jumped . . . it seems." Similarly, Hall felt that his body had taken him to the harbor and boarded the ship. His mind, throbbing with a sense of responsibility abandoned, said only: ". . . it seems."

Shortly after daybreak the sergeant called them into a dugout and briefed them on the general situation. They were holding a line only a mile away from the enemy. The day before, the British had advanced along the open country that lay before them now, but at the slope of the forward hill they had been stopped, did not have time to entrench, and had to fall back on the position they presently held. Because of the heavy fire the casualties had been high. There was no time to carry in the dead. They still lay out in the open, unburied.

Rifle and machine-gun fire interrupted the briefing. Someone outside poked his head inside the room and yelled: "Counterattack!" Everyone scrambled and rushed out to his place on the parapet. Hall climbed to where his machine gun was set up on its tripod. Freddy Azlett, his mate, joined him at the gun. From his vantage point Hall could see a solid row of rifles down the long curve of the trenches, firing into the advancing enemy. The Tommy artillery opened up and, zeroing in, drove shells into the attack, tearing big holes in the lines. Firing his machine gun, Hall sprayed bullets in a wide arc, stopping the advance in front of him. Except for one German, who somehow got through. The German rose to his feet and extended his arm to hurl a grenade. But he stopped in midmotion, arched back, and fell to the ground. A rifleman next to Hall had killed the man with one sure shot. All along the line the enemy now stopped, turned, and ran back. The attack was over.

"Counterattack against the Royal Fusiliers, would they?" the rifleman said. "We jolly well beat them off."

Later that afternoon Hall and his gun crew went looking for a dugout of their own. They found several but wanted a better one, one that had belonged to German officers. They located their choice at a dead end of the main trench, fifteen feet underground. It was still intact. The roof and walls were solidly built with heavy logs that enclosed a room six feet wide and thirty feet long. Carpets were on the floor and pictures hung on the wall, and off to one side stood a pot-bellied stove. McDonald started to build a fire and put on some water to boil for tea. A great store of equipment had been left behind by the Germans in their rush to get out. Hall started looking through it, stacking rifles and entrenching tools, opening haversacks for food, and emptying pockets of greatcoats. He picked up a bayonet that had been especially prepared by its owner.

"Look at this!" Hall said. "How would you like to be run through with *it?*" He lunged toward the wall with the weapon. The bayonet had been filed down on either side into sharp saw teeth.

Mac finished off his cup of tea, and went out to relieve the guard. As he passed out the passageway, Hall noticed another saw-tooth bayonet over the doorway. On it was inscribed, *"Gott tret' herein. Bring' glück herein."* Hall thought it a presumptuous assertion, but if God did in fact walk in, he hoped He would bring luck—to the present occupants.

A sound of steps came down the stairs. Mac was back. "Jamie," he said, "take my place at sentry for a few minutes, will you? I've lost my canteen and I'll need it. It's 'ere in the dugout some'ere. I'll be only a minute or two."

Hall agreed and stepped out to the post, down the trench only a few yards away. When he took his position behind the machine gun, the Germans started to fire artillery into the line of trenches. Hall could tell by the whistle of the first shells that they were coming in wide and off the target. But another one came, this time screaming in close. Hall immediately jumped from the parapet and fell face down on the floor of the trench. The shell hit, exploded, and covered him with loose earth. He got up, saw that he was unhurt, and groped about, half-blind in a cloud of lyddite. When it cleared, Hall rushed to the dugout. It was a wreck of rubble and splintered poles; the passageway was choked with dirt.

Hall had seven friends inside. He took his spade and began to dig, frantically. When he had made a hole big enough to crawl through, one of the men inside pulled himself toward him on one arm. It was O'Brien, the Irish tenor. His other arm was smashed and bleeding, and behind him he dragged a leg hanging by a tendon and a strip of flesh.

"My God, boys!" O'Brien said. "Look wot they did to me!" He moaned in pain and kept repeating the same words. Hall cut the ties from his bandoliers and wrapped them tightly above the wounds in the arm and leg. The Irishman lay on the ground; his face blanched, then it turned gray. "My God," he said; he raised his head, his eyes suddenly brightened. Then he fell back, dead.

Up and down the line shells continued to burst, breaking the earth and showering the trench with dirt and smoke. Desperate human calls reverberated off the walls. "Picks and shovels!" someone begged. Then from the other side came a voice, loud and pleading: "Stretcher-bearers! Stretcher-bearers, this way, for God's sake, quick!"

The sergeant came up to help Hall. They made a bigger hole to get into the dugout more easily. An oil lamp, hanging from the center rafter, still burned. In the far corner under a splintered section of the roof lay McDonald. His head had been split in half. In a heap along the wall was Gardner, his head severed from his body. Preston sat upright against a post, trying to nurse, with a blood-stained handkerchief, a hole in his side. Bert Powell bled from several injuries; Hall, seeing that Bert seemed most in need, applied bandages and tourniquets until he ran out. Charlie Harrison sat on a stool and groaned pityingly as he looked down at a mangled foot. In another corner the sergeant started throwing off debris; a partly exposed body was buried underneath. It was Walter Bryant. Incredibly, he was still alive.

"Good old boys," Walter said. "I was about done for." As he spoke, another pile of earth broke loose from above and fell over his legs. Cursing, the sergeant started again to clear away the rubble. Hall rushed over to help. "Easy now!" Walter said to them. "Can't feel anything below me waist. I think I'm 'urt down there. That's bad for a miler."

Hall, sick at what was finally revealed, wanted to turn away. The legs were broken and mashed in blood. Walter fell into unconsciousness. As Hall and the sergeant lifted him to put him on a stretcher, he died. Hall looked about him, incredulous at the wretched toll of dead and dying. He could not understand what act of fate had determined that he should have changed places with Mac only a few minutes earlier.

Fortunately for him, there was little time for further thinking on the subject. There was too much work to be done. The damage was immense. Filled-up parts of the trenches had to be dug out again, sandbags filled and stacked, parapet rebuilt, shell holes filled and leveled, gun positions reestablished. The Germans might soon follow on the artillery barrage with a reclaiming counterattack for their trenches. Hall swung his pick and shovel up on his shoulder and hurried down along the trench. Everywhere he looked the sights were horrific. Jutting out from piles of wreckage were arms and legs, like so many broken sticks; here a head protruded, agonized and stopped in death; there a body torn and dismembered beyond recognition. Along either side of the trench the wounded lay in stretchers waiting to be carried out. One of them, caked in blood and mud, called up to Hall:

"I'm shot through the stomach, matey! Can't you get me back to the ambulance? Ain't they some way you can get me back out o' this?"

Hall looked down at him; the soldier was young and frightened. "Stick it out, son," Hall said. "You won't have to wait long. The Red Cross will be here in a minute."

Hall came upon another, hobbling along with a piece of plank for a crutch. "Give me a lift, man, can't you?" he pleaded. "Look at my leg! Do you think it'll have to come off? Maybe they could save it if I could get to 'ospital in time! Won't you give me a lift? I can 'obble along better with a little 'elp."

Hall, not wanting to compound the confusion, did not wish

to explain about the possible counterattack. "Don't you fret," he said, trying to reassure. "You'll ride out in a stretcher presently. Just keep your courage up a little while longer." He rushed on.

"Eeeeeeeeeeeh!" A high cry went up behind him. Hall turned. A soldier in a sudden frenzy had torn one of the arms from a pile of earth. He began to swing it around, then flung it high and forward over the top of the trench. Then, as if he realized what he had done, he sat down on the ground and cried. Tears streamed from his eyes; then he stopped and screamed, loud piercing damning cries. He shook from head to foot with rage, until some of his friends came to comfort him.

Despite all the work of repairing the trench and readying the line, the counterattack never came. The Germans could not have known the opportunity they had missed. That night Hall took his place behind the machine gun. Beyond the trench he could see dark mounds lying on the ground; they were the bodies of the dead, swollen and putrefying, still unburied. He closed his eyes against the night and tried not to smell the stink. Thoughts of home crowded in on his consciousness; imaginative flights were the only temporary escape. He indulged his fancy, thinking of the days of boyhood and the times without number he had lugged water up from the cellar for the family, or the hard coal which he had poured into the stove, watching the blue tongues of flame shoot up, giving a warm bright glow to the kitchen; and the times he had sat at his mother's feet while she sat in the rocking chair, knitting a sweater, and she would comb her fingers through his hair and ask him what he would be when he grew up. He had never said "soldier." But he had often said "writer." Or "teacher."

On the parapet, hugging his greatcoat against the night chill, he thought that some day he would like to rewrite all the verses he had written as a boy. He wanted to make the writing still and sacred, like the G-Note Road near home, and also run with life like the water in the river along the valley below the railroad tracks.

"Hey, Jamie," a voice called quietly. Hall awoke from his

reverie. It was Freddy Azlett, who had come to relieve him of his watch. "You can go in now. The tea is ready for you." Hall climbed down and dropped along the trench wall to the ground. As he felt his way in the dark, he noticed men crouched along the sides. He neared a platform of planks that covered a deep hole, and skirted along the edge. As he came to the entrance to the passageway into the dugout, another soldier passed by, apparently a stranger to the area. He missed his step on the boards over the hole and fell in.

"Na, then, matey!" a voice called to him among the crouched figures. "Bathin' in our private pool without a permit?"

Another added: "Grease aht of it, son! That's our tea water you're a-standin' in."

The soldier stood waist deep in the muddy pool of water, exasperated, but not without comic presence. "One 'o you fetch me a bit of soap," he answered. "Don't talk about tea water to a bloke ain't had a bawth in seven weeks."

Thank God for the English sense of humor, Hall thought; it relieved the terror of the trenches. He went inside and poured himself a cup of tea. Then he went to the table, under the light hanging from the ceiling, and sat down. He pulled out from inside his tunic a small brown notebook and wrote a letter. It was to Bill Ziegler, his old college Glee Club friend, now a teacher at St. Mark's School in Massachusetts. Ziegler had suggested that there would be a position open for him if he decided to leave the service and come home. For Hall, the offer had reawakened interests he had once had in Boston of going to Harvard, working for an M.A. and Ph.D., and becoming a teacher, as Professor Payne at Grinnell had so strongly recommended.

"Your suggestion," Hall wrote in pencil along the squared blue lines, "does appeal to me mightily. After several years of uncertainty, during which time I have considered the question of a life work from every possible angle, I have reached the conclusion that there is no work more worthwhile than that which you are doing. What splendid opportunities for genuine service it offers! William, there is no satisfaction like that which comes from giving and I believe that earnest clean-minded men who love their work and have the ability to incite a love for it in others are rewarded thrice over in the teaching profession. They have their discouragements, naturally, but their rewards are truly satisfying as well.

"If my life is spared," he concluded, "I shall spend the remainder of it in educational work. I have fully decided upon this. But, of course, it is futile for me to make definite plans now. I am glad to be alive and can only hope that I may go through the months to come safely." He dated the letter October 27, signed it, and sealed it in an envelope.

He finished the last sip of tea and returned to his post on sentry duty. He was greeted softly by Azlett as he reached the parapet. They remained on the firing bench together for the rest of the night. At dawn they saw the Red Cross and burial details coming in, before the snipers and artillery began. One Tommy who had been left for dead by his scouting party was brought in. The detail told them the soldier had been out on the battlefield for six days and nights, and had been so badly wounded he could not crawl. A German patrol had found him, had given him water, but refused to take him prisoner because he was wounded. He would have died if the detail had not found him. Another was carried in on a stretcher. He had been shot in the jaw and had lain unattended in the open for five days. His eyes had swollen shut and his face had turned to greenish blue, apparently from blood poisoning. It did not seem that he could last another day.

Hall turned to Freddy Azlett. "What about the ones they can't find out there, still alive, but too weak to call out for help?" he asked. The possibility struck him as unbearable. "What about the wounded they can't find?"

"They be poor blokes," Azlett answered. He shook his head. "Poor blokes."

For almost a month attacks and counterattacks, destruction and repair of trenches and dugouts, the carrying out of the wounded, and the burial of the dead—when possible—continued. For Hall there had been no chance to change clothing or do a laundry. A bath or an uninterrupted sleep were worth a month's pay. Hall and his gun crew had been constantly changed from position to position, then ordered to attack, only to have the order revoked. Or they were told they would not attack, only to be ordered again to attack, then have that order changed once more at the last minute. Up and down the line, they all grew impatient for the big push. At the end of the month, Hall received a letter from his mother. The news was bad. His father had contracted Parkinson's disease and he wanted to see Norman before he died. Could he get emergency leave and come home? his mother pleaded.

Hall wondered if his father would live long enough to see him again, and if he would live long enough to see his father again. He decided to submit his leave papers immediately. The latest order for a full-scale attack looked as if it would not be countermanded.

Several days later the signs of a great engagement became portentous and undeniable. British planes had patrolled the front for several hours, reserve battalions had come up from the rear, and the initial probes from the artillery had started. Hall climbed to the parapet and looked out over the top. The British batteries concentrated their fire on the enemy trenches directly ahead. In their own trenches thousands of soldiers stood poised, rifles ready, waiting for the end of the artillery fire. It would be the signal to go over the top. About him Hall noticed the faces of the men. Most of the first wave smoked, some casually, as if they were waiting for girl friends at Piccadilly Circus; some intently, as if it were the last smoke of condemned men. Others secured their gear, checked their rifles, adjusted the straps of their steel helmets.

Hall looked on at the proceedings, but felt like a split personality in the scene, one part of him saying, "This can't be true. I have never been a soldier. There isn't any European war," and another part of him, quite distinct from the brain, doing the things a machine gunner should in preparation for an attack—checking the bandoliers of ammunition, working the moving parts of the gun to see that they functioned properly, swabbing out the barrel.

The artillery blasted at the enemy trenches for more than

two hours. Then, abruptly, it ceased. An officer near Hall shouted: "Now, men! Follow me!" And he climbed over the top, waving his men forward. The men followed.

The German guns, which had till now held their fire, opened up and started breaking the advance of the first wave of the attack. A second and a third wave of soldiers climbed over the parapet and joined them; heads down, rifles forward, bayonets gleaming, they rushed ahead. Many fell before they had gone a few yards. Others gained the hole through the barbed wire, and started to file through in two's and three's. One private, who had been badly hit, crept back to his own lines, reached the edge of the parapet, and as he was being pulled into safety, was killed by a stray bullet. Then a runner came in with a report. The first two waves of infantry had captured the forward line, and with the help of the third were holding it.

Now the engineers followed the riflemen. They had to re-build the German parapets to face in the other direction, to make them ready for a counterattack. Signalmen strung their wires, establishing connection between the new and the old trenches. The attack continued until early evening, when at last Hall and his crew received orders to move up through the communication trenches to the new line. Although the distance was only three miles, they needed nine hours to make it. The way through was clogged with stretcher-bearers carrying out the wounded. As he held to the wall to make room, Hall could hear some of the accounts.

"They was a big Dutchman comin' at me from the other side," one said. "Lucky fer me that I 'ad a round in me breach. He'd a got me if it 'adn't 'a' been fer that ca'tridge. I let 'im 'ave it an' 'e crumpled up like a wet blanket."

"Seeven of them, abn' that dazed like, they wasna good for onything," recounted a Scotsman. "Mon, it would ha' been fair murder to kill 'em. They wasna wantin' to fight."

Another, pale and shaking, his eyes popping from deep sockets, spoke excitedly and haltingly. "I couldn't get me bayonet out," he said. "W'en 'e fell—'e pulled me over—on top of 'im. I 'ad to put me foot against 'im—an' pull—an' then—it came out—with a jerk."

The success of the attack was not measurable, so charged with rumor was any bit of fact. Some reports were that two lines of trenches had been captured; others that the Germans had fled to the rear in full retreat. Hall decided that he would have to see for himself.

When they got to their new position on the new parapet, Hall and his crew set up the tripod and mounted the machine gun. Hall, fearful and respectful of snipers, peered over the top. The lights in the distance were not at all those of Berlin. They were the flashes from German rifles in yet another line, the object of yet another attack, in yet another battle, in the same interminable war.

The battle of Loos, which would not end until the war itself would end, would cost sixty thousand dead, for a one-mile gain on a four-mile front. But for Hall, the war was over. Although his request for leave had been turned down, he could, because he was an American, apply immediately for a discharge, which would be granted. Hall knew that if he wanted to see his father again, he had but one choice to make.

Getting his gear together, he packed it hastily. He swung his knapsack up on his back and put his arms through the shoulder loops. Then he went to find Freddy Azlett. "Yer a lucky Yank, Jamie," he said. "Be sure not to forget us Tommies."

The sergeant had just returned from inspecting the line. "Count yer lucky stars, Hall," he said. "I wonder if we'll ever see the end o' this bloody dirty war."

Hall hated farewells. They were never any good. He started to leave, then stopped, turned, and looked up at the gun position on the parapet. Freddy stood poised behind it, alone, his eyes straight ahead. Hall stepped out quickly and marched through the trenches to the rear. Directly overhead he heard a plane and looked up. It was British. He wished he had volunteered for the Royal Flying Corps. If the aviators got back to base, they at least could have a clean bed to sleep in and perhaps even a hot soapy bath.

From the training camp in Aldershot he had seen a whole division of them, up in the air at all times. He envied them. To his friend, Larry Winship of *The Boston Globe,* he had written shortly after his enlistment: "If I had the thing to do all over again I would enlist in the air service. But it's too late I'm afraid."

For James Norman Hall it was not too late. There would be time, time to train and to fly for the French and the Americans, time to shoot down five German planes and to be shot down twice, time to become a prisoner of war and to escape, time even to write a book before he returned to France.

It was a slow war.

2

A Volunteer Airman

The trip from Liverpool to Boston took eight days, and for Hall it was a period of dazed unbelief. He could not believe that he was going home, that he was discharged, that the next morning he would not have to take his place again on the parapet in the trenches. He had served 1 year and 99 days, 172 days in France. It was not until he met his Boston friends at the dock that he knew for certain he was not in a dream. Larry Winship, Roy Cushman, and George Greener dispelled all his doubts; they greeted him coming off the gangway, packed him into a cab, and together they drove down Atlantic Avenue, up State Street to Tremont, to the Parker House. To Hall, Boston seemed serenely peaceful, bustling, and noncombatant. He felt he could slip with ease into his old life as a special agent for the Massachusetts Society for the Prevention of Cruelty to Children; simply by wearing his old civilian clothes, he could walk into the office on Mount Vernon Street and ask for his next assignment to the South End.

But Boston had other plans for James Norman Hall. Larry

Winship had paved the way by writing articles in *The Boston Globe* about his friend's experiences at the front, and he had quoted at length from Jim's letters. Headline stories about "Jamaica Plain Boy's Trench Experiences" and a touching firsthand account about sudden death had caught the attention of the city's foremost editor, Ellery Sedgwick of the *Atlantic Monthly*. When Sedgwick learned that Hall had returned, he sent a note over to the Parker House asking him to drop in at his office. Hall was elated. For three years he had sent pieces to the *Atlantic* and had received nothing but printed rejection slips in return. Now the editor wanted to see him. Hall had walked by the office on Park Street many times in the past, and now as he turned the corner by the church and bucked into the cold December wind sweeping down from Beacon Hill, he felt suddenly overcome with fear and diffidence. Fortunately, Sedgwick proved to be genial, warm, and encouraging.

"Have you ever done any writing?" he asked, as Hall sat down on a high stiff-backed chair.

Hall locked his long thin legs at the knee and ankle. He did not want to tell the editor how often he had tried to be published in his magazine. "Yes, a little," he said. "At least, I've always wanted to write."

Sedgwick sought out Hall's shy, deep, brown eyes. "We have just had published by Houghton Mifflin a book by a British officer," he said. "It is called *The First Hundred Thousand,* about Lord Kitchener's volunteer army. It is an excellent story and is certain to have great success in America where we know so little thus far of the actual battle experience of British soldiers in France."

Hall straightened up in his seat and tightened his tie. He sensed what was coming. Sedgwick continued: "I want you to write some articles for the *Atlantic* about the experiences of a private in the British Army. The fact that you are an American will make them all the more interesting to readers over here. And you will be doing a real service for the Allied cause. I can assure you of that. Except for a few towns and cities on the Atlantic seaboard, America is not awake to the significance of this war. Most people still believe that it is merely another of Europe's perpetual squabbles to be settled by Europe alone. They think it is none of our business and are strongly back of President Wilson who believes we should keep out of it."

"Would you want me to stress the fact that we should be in it?" Hall asked.

"No," Sedgwick came back quickly. "No preaching, or exhorting, or reproving the American people for their neutrality." A wry smile broke through. "After all," he added, "who are you? A young American known to no one except your friends, who joined the British Army and has now returned direct from the battlefields of France. I want you to write a simple, straightforward narrative of your experiences. Your day-to-day life in the trenches, the kind of men you served with, the hardships and dangers you shared together—the kind of thing you had in the *Globe*. Don't try to be 'literary.' Write as you would if you were telling of your experiences in letters to a friend. And don't leave out any touches of humor. Life in the trenches cannot be all sheer tragedy, and readers will want to know the lighter side of it as well."

Hall recrossed his legs. "How many articles would you want?" he asked.

"One to start with. I can speak more definitely about others when I've seen what you can do." Sedgwick got up to lead Hall to the door. "If you do this well," he said to Hall as they stepped out to the vestibule, "it will mark the beginning of a literary career for you."

Hall thanked him and started down the stairs to the street. What had been elation now turned sourly to depression. What if he couldn't do it? How could he meet the *Atlantic*'s high standards? Just another rejection slip. He didn't even know how he would begin the first paragraph. But he did have a title. He would call it *Kitchener's Mob*.

"Of course you can do it," Larry Winship said that night at the hotel, trying to encourage him. "When you wrote before in Boston, you never had anything to write about. Now you are a writer who has something to write about. Go to it."

When Hall left on the train for Iowa two days later, these

words from his friend sustained him. He had made up his mind. After seeing his father and spending Christmas at home, he would go upstairs to his room and write as he never had before. Now he had a publisher, the very one he had always wanted.

Riding home on the train he could not join the festive holiday mood of the other passengers; he sat at his window seat, stared blankly at the passing of the scenery, and tried to sort his conflicting emotions. Listening to the exultant college students, he could only think: "How can they be so happy when the young men of Europe are dying in tens of thousands?" But then another thought struck him: "Thank God that one great peaceful nation has refused to be drawn into all that bloodshed and horror!"

When he arrived in Colfax, however, he had decided what his own course would be, although he could not bring himself to tell his parents what it was. He would go back overseas and reenlist, so intolerable was the idea of German domination of Europe. This theme, he was convinced, would underscore every line he would write.

He found his father better than he had hoped. Parkinson's disease, he knew, was incurable, and when he went to his father's bedside he had to force himself to look closely. Arthur Wright Hall lay under the covers with only his face showing and his arms lying on top. The father's face was like a gray mask, the eyes glazed and unblinking, and the hands, turned down on the coverlet, shook in little tremors. Hall blinked his eyes quickly against the welling that began. "I'm glad to see you, Dad," he said, his throat constricting as he spoke. "Mom tells me the doctors think you'll make it all right." After a long interval of silence, Arthur Hall, as if from a tremendous effort of the will, blinked his eye in response. Hall forced a smile. It was a small consolation, but his father was alive only.

That Christmas was not a happy one. After two days of celebration, muted, and more in thanksgiving for his homecoming than anything else, Hall addressed himself to the first chapter of his book. He sat at the table in his old room upstairs and after many false starts at writing and rewriting the first and second paragraphs of introduction, he moved into the narrative itself. In less than a month he had finished the chapter and sent it off to Boston. Sedgwick immediately wired back encouragement: "First article excellent. Send more." But Hall was not encouraged; he wanted to answer: "Very sorry, but must return to service in France. May be able to send further articles from there." Fortunately, however, he did not send that reply. Instead he went down to Grinnell to talk to Professor Charles E. Payne, his mentor and advisor of college days.

"Norman," Professor Payne told him, "this is a decision you must make for yourself. No one can help you with it."

"I feel that too," Hall answered. "I merely wish to know what you would do in my place. You can help me to that extent."

"I don't think you should ask me to," Professor Payne replied. He smiled cautiously. "Do you realize that you might be placing your life quite literally in my hands? Supposing I should advise you to return to England at once, to reenlist, and supposing you were to accept my advice? You might be killed before the winter is ended. How do you think I would feel in that case?"

Hall was overcome by his imprudence. "I'm sorry, Professor Payne," he said. "I had not seen the matter in that light. I will say no more." Hall rose to leave.

Professor Payne placed his hands firmly against the arms of his chair and pushed himself up onto the floor. He thumped on his artificial legs around to the front of the desk. "Wait a bit, Norman," he said. "Let's come back to your problem. . . . I see that you are still an incurable romanticist, which prevents you from taking a common-sense view of things. You believe that because you resolved to return to service after a month of leave, you are bound to do so. . . . How long do you think the war will last?"

"Two or three years more, at least." Hall resettled himself in his seat.

"That is my own opinion," Professor Payne agreed. "Furthermore, I believe that it cannot be won without the help of the U.S.A. and that we are bound to come in. Well, then, the articles the *Atlantic Monthly* wishes you to write may be of real service in making America more conscious of what English soldiers are enduring in a cause that is ours as well. I think you should stay here and finish them. What will it matter if you miss two or three months of service with your battalion, particularly in the wintertime, when fighting has again come to a standstill?"

"That is your honest opinion?" Hall asked.

"Yes. You will have plenty of time to be killed before the war ends. Being a romanticist, you, I suppose, think of that as the most fitting end to a soldier's career in the greatest war in history?"

Hall smiled quickly. "I am not a romanticist to that extent."

Hall returned home, heartened now with Professor Payne's good advice. But the buoyancy did not last. Throughout that winter as he wrote the succeeding chapters, his conscience grated, thought against thought. When he tried to call up the particular circumstantial details to re-create a scene, event, or character, or when he heard from one of his old friends at the front, he yearned to be back with the Royal Fusiliers.

One night, against his will, Hall was prevailed upon to give a talk at the Methodist church about his war experiences. The presentation was a total failure. The response of the audience, Iowa stubborn and midwestern isolationist, was one of amused condescension. Hall was deeply hurt and embittered. He held back his feelings through a brief question period, then rushed out of the building and down the road, alone, depressed, and defiant. He came to the railroad station, went into the men's room, and sat by the stove waiting for his bitternesss to pass. Several hours later he went home and stole quietly up to his room. He sat down at his table, cleared away loose pages of manuscript, pulled out a clean sheet of paper, and wrote quickly. The result, a poem, was an effortless fusion of thought and feeling.

Hall folded the poem and placed it in his notebook. He did not think it would be anything to interest the editors or the readers of the *Atlantic,* not at that time anyway. They probably would have thought it was some morbid necrophilic wish.

On his own part and as of old, there were few things whose meaning Hall could uncover unless he could first put them to rhyme.

The manuscript for *Kitchener's Mob* was not finished until spring. It was a small book of eleven chapters and Hall fretted about its success, hoping it was better than competent; but when it was published in May, it won praise for its straightforward simplicity and vivid readability. And to Hall's disbelief and delight, it sold in ten printings nearly fifty thousand copies. He was now a writer with credentials, the very best recommendations he had ever hoped for. He had not only "made" the *Atlantic* but had been serialized in it, and Houghton Mifflin of Boston was "his" publisher. He had never dreamed such success was possible when he had worked alone and anxious in his walk-up room overlooking Louisburg Square in Boston; indeed, after so many discouraging rejections, he had decided to become a teacher. Larry Winship must have been right: he needed something to write about.

Five months had passed since his discharge from the British Army. Hall resolved to return to England and reenlist. When he told his family of his intention, they were bitterly disappointed; for they thought he had been discharged for good. Hall tried to explain his reasons, but it only made matters worse. He wanted to leave as soon as possible; he could not bear to see the hurt in his mother's eyes. Having packed, he walked up the hill behind the house to have one final view of the surrounding hills north and west. The hepaticas had broken through the blanket of dead leaves on the ground. Hall breathed deeply of their scent; it was a fragrance he wanted to remember. In the distance beyond the barn he heard the call of a meadowlark, a mellow deep-throated song that thrilled him now as it always had. Perhaps his family was right in insisting he stay, for he loved his home. But he had to go.

In Boston, while Hall waited for his sailing date, Ellery Sedgwick invited him to his home for dinner. Again, as if in a dream realized, Hall felt he was entering a sanctum sanctorum. Many times before, when he had first come to Boston and had walked up and down the streets on Beacon Hill, a frustrated aspirant to literary fame and perhaps fortune, he had stopped before the Sedgwick house on Walnut Street and had looked up the steep slope to the elm and maple trees which stood like sentries to keep out the unwanted. Now he stood before the house, not only wanted but invited.

After dinner Ellery Sedgwick led Hall into the garden and they sat down to talk. Sedgwick had another writing project in mind for him and spoke about it now with animation. He wanted Hall to return to Europe, not as a soldier, but as a correspondent for the *Atlantic Monthly*. There was a squadron of American volunteers flying with the French, and he wanted Hall to write a number of pieces about them.

"It would not take you long to write these articles," Sedgwick said. "And they would be invaluable in further arousing American interest in the Allied cause. If you accept the commission I will furnish you with letters of introduction which will smooth the way for you when you arrive in France."

Hall had not heard of the Escadrille Lafayette before, but the unit sounded like a splendid subject to write about. He readily accepted the assignment. He would spend several months on it; then he would reenlist in the British Army. Hall sailed in August.

After arriving in England, Hall took the channel boat to France, then boarded the train to Paris; he had to call on Dr. Edmund L. Gros, the American who acted unofficially as the liaison officer for all American volunteers who wanted to serve with France. Hall explained to Gros in detail his plans for the *Atlantic* assignment and his plans thereafter.

"Do you feel obliged to reenlist as an infantryman in the British Army?" Gros asked. "Why not join up as an airman with your compatriots over here?"

The suddenness of this proposal left Hall dumbfounded. A minute passed before he could articulate an answer. "As an airman! . . . You mean, it would be possible to do this?" I . . . don't understand!?"

"Why not?" Gros answered, opened the top drawer of his desk, and placed a form before Hall. "Just fill this out," he said.

Hall looked at the paper. There were only a few blanks to be filled in—name, age, nationality. It seemed too easy, like a trick. "You won't need any references," Dr. Gros added. "My name is enough."

"Dr. Gros," Hall said, looking for a position of temporary retreat, "I know nothing whatever about flying."

Gros was undaunted. "Neither did the other men who are now *pilotes de chasse* with the Escadrille Lafayette," he said.

Hall tried again. "And I know nothing about internal-combustion engines."

"That isn't necessary," Gros countered. "Both in the aviation schools and at the front there are expert mechanics to take care of the planes and engines. Your only duty would be to learn to fly and fight in the air."

Not wishing to test his good luck any further, Hall filled in the blanks and signed his name. Unlike his previous enlistment, he had volunteered this time for the duration of the war. Three days later, Hall left Paris for the École Bleriot at Buc, near Versailles. With him were two other American volunteers, Douglas MacMonagle from San Francisco, and Leland L. Rounds from New York. It was in September of 1916.

From the station at Buc the three Americans took a taxi to the airfield. As they paid the driver at the headquarters building, a window flew open in one of the barracks and a voice sang out: "Oh, say, can you see by the dawn's early light . . ." A young man smiled from the window. "Spotted you *toute suite,*" he said. "You can tell Americans at six hundred yards by their hats. How's things in the States?"

At Buc the fledglings began their flight training mostly by themselves. They would rise every morning before dawn, have a cup of chickory-flavored hot water for coffee, dress up in black leather pants and long jacket, boots, gloves, goggles, and crash helmet, and go out to the field to wait their turn in one of the Bleriot Penguins. For Hall his first sight of a Penguin was a disappointment. The plane was a high blunt-winged skeleton with two long steel tusks protruding from under the motor to prevent nosing over. The student pilots would simply race this monster back and forth across the field, trying to keep it in a straight line. That was all. It seemed to Hall a simple-minded approach—to learn how to fly by not flying. Until he tried.

The wings of the Penguin were sawed off at five feet and covered with patches of fabric. Also covered was the area about the cockpit in the fuselage; but the rest of the plane, perched on a landing gear of bicycle wheels, was mere frame. When his turn came, Hall swung a leg up over the edge of the cockpit and settled himself inside. He sat high on the seat, half of his body projecting above the fuselage. The crash helmet, a tower of cork and springs and padded leather, held by a tight chin strap, seemed to sit rather than fit on his head. The mechanic started the small three-cylinder engine.

"*Coupe, plein gaz,*" the mechanic said.

"*Coupe, plein gaz,*" Hall answered.

The mechanic turned the propeller until the gasoline was sucked into the carburetor. Then he called: "*Contact, réduisez.*"

Hall repeated: "*Contact, réduisez.*"

The mechanic spun the propeller and the motor sprang to life.

Quickly Hall pulled back on the *manet,* then gradually he eased it to full throttle, the propeller blasting back in response. Then the prop wash knocked the helmet off his head. The strap choking at his head, Hall gripped the triangular top of the stick, but as he did he accidentally tripped the contact button on one side. The motor stopped.

Hall replaced the helmet on his head and tightened the strap more firmly. The motor was started again, but as soon as the plane began to move forward, the torque of the engine pulled the plane to the right; Hall tried to correct it with the opposite rudder, but he applied the pressure too late and too gently. The Penguin started to whirl around and around, like a swinging ball at the end of a string. Hall was in a ground loop, and again he was forced to cut the motor. He would have to try once more.

Finally started again, Hall felt ashamed of his clumsiness; but this time, rushing across the width of the field, he managed stick, throttle, and rudder, brought the tail up and parallel to the ground, and held to a straight line. Suddenly a light breeze caught the tail and the wheels hit a bump on the ground. The plane abruptly started to take off. Again Hall cut the motor. The plane quickly dropped down and smacked back to the ground. Damning his luck, Hall knew he would have to try yet again.

It was not for several more days that Hall could tame the Penguin to his will and keep it steadily in *lignes droites* before the *moniteur*—the instructor—would pass him and send him on to the next stage. With that transition, however, Hall knew he could become an aviator.

The standard-winged Bleriots with fifty-horsepower engines offered far more excitement. At first these had to be crow-hopped up and down the field in a straight line like the Bleriots, but then they were lifted off the ground to ten or twenty feet, and finally brought down in a flat thump by blipping off the motor. After several of these one day Hall, so intrigued by actually being in the air, decided that, rather than blip and come down, he would stay up and make a *tour de piste*—a circle of the field. Hall had heard the others talk in the barracks about using the stick to warp the wing and make flat turns without skidding. Why not try?

Hall raced across the field. He held to a straight line, felt the wheels leave the ground and the controls respond, and kept on flying. The plane bumped over the thermals coming up from the ground and quivered in the wind, but the Bleriot almost flew itself. Hall watched the wheels leave the ground and stop spinning as he angled into the air. He loved the feeling of freedom and immediately tagged it; he felt like a disembodied spirit.

He flew over the old abandoned reservoir at the end of the field and looked down into its brown and murky bottom, then he lifted the nose gently to climb over the trees beyond. Carefully, he eased the stick over to warp into a right turn with the wind. Downwind, he seemed to soar as the ground rushed by. He was now at thirty feet. He gently warped the wing to turn into the wind, but it took him a long time to get around. Be-

low he could see the airfield's graveyard of broken and irrepa-
rable Bleriots that others had crashed. He was now close to the
hangars. To land, he knew, he would have to nurse the throttle back and the nose down so the motor would not *panne*
(stall). Hall wiped the sweat from his brow. If he stalled from
too high up, he would wreck the plane and possibly himself.
He would try to make a long shallow glide. As he nosed down
with reduced throttle he seemed to be floating. The plane was
not settling fast enough. And the reservoir would soon meet
him at the edge of the field. Hall pointed his plane down further to what seemed like a few feet off the ground and blipped
off the motor. The plane pancaked, rattling the struts and jar-
ring the bicycle wheels, rolled a few feet, and stopped.

Hall sat in the plane, happy he was down safely, but waiting
for the bawling-out from the moniteur that was sure to come.
It came, running.

"Pourquoi? Nom de Dieu!" the instructor asked. *"Qu'est-ce-
que je vous ai dit? Jamais faire comme ça! Jamais monter avec
le vent en arrière! Jamais! Jamais!!"*

Hall was incredulous. *"Le vent en arrière?"* he answered.
"You mean I took off downwind? Did I do that?"

The moniteur started to explain again, but quickly softened, then smiled and reached over to shake Hall's hand.

For his daring Hall was immediately promoted to the next
stage—the one he had just entered without benefit of instruction. It was the *pique,* the final class in the Bleriots, but with
the larger sixty-horsepower motors that could hurtle the Penguin through the air at almost sixty miles an hour—if there
was a tail wind and all the cylinders were firing.

Now, the instructor told him, he could make his *tour de
piste* at three or four hundred feet and widen his circumfer-
ence to at least five miles. But, to Hall's dismay, these flights
were not as thrilling as the unauthorized first, and after several
circuits of the field, he enjoyed only the view from the greater
height.

After three months of instruction Hall earned his first leave
and went to Paris. On a November afternoon toward dusk he
strolled down the Champs Élysées. Away from the camp, and

feeling free and expansive, he walked with a spring. Life, for
the moment, was "good to the core." The boulevard, wet from
the morning rain, reflected the lights from the cafés. Taxis
chugged by, tooting as they passed. At the sidewalk tables
couples sat tête-à-tête, and older men sipping their drinks
watched the passersby. The rain started to fall again, and Hall
turned into a doorway to wait for it to stop. Happily, he noted,
he had paused at a bookstore. It was Brentano's. He went inside and idly started looking at titles on the tables and along
the shelves. He came to a series of small books in blue cloth
cover, and his eyes settled on one in particular. He pulled the
book out to examine it more closely.

It was *The Mutiny of the Bounty* by Sir John Barrow. The
book had been first published in 1831; it was being issued
again, now as a classic. For Hall the book reawakened vague
memories he had of a part of British naval history. He flipped
the pages and recognized the names of Bligh and Christian
and of Pitcairn Island. As a boy, landlocked in the Midwest, he
had often read of "the great South Sea" and had made imaginative visits to the islands. He sat down at one of the tables,
and coming to the quote from Byron's poem he started to read
about "Otaheite." It was a narrative of the search for breadfruit, the long stay on the island of Tahiti, the mutiny on the
way home, the open-boat voyage of Bligh, the court-martial.
Hall was entranced. Here was a life completely different from
what he had ever known. He stopped reading, turned the book
over face down, stared along the length of the spine, and made
a promise to himself. If he ever survived the war, someday he
would actualize his boyhood dreams and roam, lonely as
Wordsworth's cloud, among these islands under the wind. Hall
picked up the book, closed it, and went to the clerk to pay her.
As he walked out the door, he saw that the rain had stopped.
He breathed deeply of the clean washed air, slipped the book
into his side pocket, and patted it.

In April Hall, now ready for more advanced training, was
transferred to the École Militaire d'Aviation at Avord. It was
in central France, near Bourges. Douglas MacMonagle joined

him in the move. Together they would undergo the final tests before winning their wings. First in the program came an hour's flight at an altitude of 6,500 feet, then two short hops of 60 kilometers, and finally two triangular flights of three separate legs 100 kilometers apart, in which they would have to land twice, refuel, and fly home. To both Hall and Doug the shorter flights came easy, making the entire program seem easy. It seemed.

When the moniteur announced the day for the triangles, MacMonagle and Hall were ready at five in the morning, eager to make an early start. But the weather held them up—that day, the next, the day after that, and in fact for two weeks. The day of the flight at last arrived, began with a fresh wind from the northeast and a clear sky. The air was very calm at 2,500 feet, the instructor reported, and they could start, he said, at any time. It was the twenty-first of April.

MacMonagle was elated, as was Hall. Mac hugged the old lady who served coffee in one of the hangars and Hall danced a two-step with one of the mechanics. Each student had studied the maps, carefully locating the important landmarks along the route, until they thought there was no possibility of getting lost. Preparations finished, Hall helped MacMonagle into his fur-lined flying togs, eased him into his seat and fastened the belt, then walked to the front of the plane and spun the prop. A few moments later Doug had sped down the field, zoomed into the air, circled the aerodrome, and had headed off toward the east. Hall soon followed.

At 1,500 feet Hall looked down as he passed over the peaks of the Bourges cathedral, turned, and following a straight road leading to the southwest he climbed to 5,000 feet. Below, village and town gave way to farm and château, which in turn gave way to quilted farmland of green and brown. Hall looked above and below and to either side. He envied the birds their view. "Small wonder," he thought, "that they sing."

The single-seater Caudron biplane seemed to fly itself. Hall ran his eye from revolution counter to altimeter to speed dial. Each held steady, the motor at 1,200 revolutions per minute, the altitude at 5,000 feet, the speed at 125 miles per hour. Soon the red-topped houses of the town of Châteauroux came into view, and at the edge of the town he could see the aerodrome. Hall reduced throttle and nosed down for a long glide to the field.

MacMonagle had already landed and came out to meet Hall's plane as it taxied in from landing. The two fliers greeted one another as if it were their first meeting in years. "It was lonely!" Mac exclaimed, pacing up and down in front of the hangars as the planes were being refueled. "Yes, by Jove! that it was. A glorious thing, one's isolation up there. But it was too profound to be pleasant. A relief to get down again, to hear people talk, to feel solid earth under one's feet. How did it impress you?"

"Doug!" Hall said, sharing his exuberance, "I can see, by 1950 at least, nurses flying Voisins filled with babies, old men having after-dinner naps in Nieuports, and families taking off for picnics, Mother cautioning Father not to fly too fast."

MacMonagle looked at Hall disapprovingly, until accountably and with complete absurdity each fell into a fit of laughter. "But, master," said Hall, "there is, after all, color in words. Don't you remember how delighted you were with the name of a little town we passed through on the way to Orléans? Romorantin? You were haunted by it and said it was like the purple note of an organ."

"Whaaaaaaaaaat?" Doug cried out.

"Nothing. It's just the name of our next town for landing. And I bet I'll get there before you do."

MacMonagle agreed. "It's a bet. I'll beat you there and I still plan a little side trip to the east to see some villages on the way." He went over to his plane and climbed into the cockpit.

Hall followed. He wanted to fly completely by compass, ignoring the map. He climbed to 5,000 feet, eased off on the throttle, and listened for the reassuring purr of the motor. He looked over the side, enjoying the unrolling countryside; then, relaxing, he let his mind lie fallow for whatever seed of thought that memory could sow. Perhaps prompted by MacMonagle's remarks about the lonely and helpless feeling that flying gave him, Hall thought contrary thoughts about the friendliness of the skies, and how, as his mother had told him when he was a boy, there were two sainted janitors in charge of the sky—one who kept it clean and blue, and the other who neglected his responsibilities and let it rain and snow.

Suddenly Hall woke up from his reverie. He checked his compass, then looked over the side for a bearing on the ground. He could see from the instrument that the plane was pointed north; but the wind, which was leaning to the left against the tops of trees and bending smoke again to the left from chimneys, obviously paid no attention to compasses. Hall came to a quick conclusion. He had drifted far to the west and wandered off course, just as the moniteur had warned if he did not pay attention to wind direction. To correct his mistake—for how long it had gone on he could not guess—Hall changed his heading by crabbing northeast into the wind, held the new course, and started looking for landmarks—and for possible sites for an emergency landing.

He soon had to make a decision. What had been mere wisps of cloud now built up into solid banks that enshrouded him, cutting off his visibility completely. Determined not to come down yet, he nosed up through the clouds, topping them by a hundred feet, then rechecked his northeast heading. Now the sun was shining against the cloud tops, brightly detailing the shapes and contours in dabs of gold. Hall was exhilarated. The sense of isolation between the ceiling of blue sky and the floor of white-gold cloud, endless and unbroken above and below, made him feel strangely disembodied, a blithe spirit at one with the grandeur of God. But the clouds, deaf and unreciprocate, would not accommodate the fantasy. They started building up higher, into billowing mountains and ugly anvil-topped thunderheads. Hall was soon surrounded by mist again, this time without a way up, over, or around. As he looked for a way down and out, he hit a thick bank of cloud which shrouded the tips of the wings and the tail assembly, then started to cover him with a blanket of cold mist. At the same moment a sickening realization came over him. He had, he knew, no point of reference whatever from either earth or sky, plane or instruments. He would have to fly by the seat of his pants. He heard the air whistle through the wing-support wires, and he quickly checked his speed dial and altitude indicator. The plane, from the sound and the instrument, was speeding toward the ground.

Hall pulled up quickly, rolled to the left, and broke out of the cloud. Through the whir of the propeller he saw the rim of the horizon: giddily, it was tipped up on its side. Hall righted his plane to a *ligne de vol* and looked below for a landmark he might recognize on the map. He could find none. He knew now, with certainty, that he was lost.

Although he still had enough fuel to continue flying, Hall now throttled down to find a place to land. At a thousand feet he passed over what seemed a level field. He reduced power further to glide in; then, as he came down, he saw that the level land had changed to undulating hills and valleys. Surprised but still determined, he continued down. Hall eased back on the stick. As the wheels of the Caudron touched the ground, the right wing tips clipped the edge of a row of trees but not enough to turn the plane. It clattered straight on down a long bumpy hill, and came to a stop just in front of a rushing stream.

Hall lifted off his goggles, pulled off his crash helmet, and wiped his brow with the back of his gloved hand. From behind the plane and beyond the ridge of a hill came the shout of an excited voice. It was from a young boy who came running, waving to others to follow. The boy, gat-toothed and bushy-haired, stopped at the wing and stared at Hall. *"Bonjour, mon petit,"* Hall said to him. The boy remained silent. Other people now appeared, more children, women, and old men. It looked like a whole village. They stood in a large circle around the plane, then one of the men came forward. It was the mayor. Hall tried to explain to him in French what had happened, but the man did not understand. At last the mayor said: *"Vous êtes anglais, monsieur?"* And Hall quickly answered: *"Non, monsieur, je suis américain."*

At the sound of those words, everyone broke into happy smiles. Hall became the hero of the hour. Magically, he was to the villagers more than an English flier, even more than a

French aviator; he was, to the wondrous delight of all, an American! Through slow and labored talking with the mayor, Hall learned that the town he had been looking for was not more than twenty kilometers away. After showing the boys the inside of his cockpit, Hall asked them to help him move the plane to level ground, where he might be able to take off. Three on each side pushed the plane down a gentle slope, then one boy spun the prop. Hall roared up the incline and into the air. Fifteen minutes later he found the large wide circle that marked the lost aerodrome. After he landed he learned, despite his own lateness, that MacMonagle had not yet arrived.

After refueling, Hall saw that the weather had cleared completely and decided to leave without waiting for his friend. The flight home was uneventful, and having learned his lesson, Hall paid close attention to his instruments, particularly his compass, and closely followed the landmarks indicated on his map. Seeing the cathedral of Bourges and then the rows of barracks, the hangars, and the machine shops beyond, he knew he was home. When he had landed and taxied to a stop in front of one of the hangars, Hall felt proud of his first cross-country flight.

But the feeling did not last long. As Hall climbed out of the plane, the moniteur walked over to greet him. *"Alors, ça va?"* the officer said, flatly and completely without approbation. Hall was surprised by the tone. "Where's your biograph?" the instructor asked.

"My biograph?" Hall answered. "My God! . . . I forgot all about it. . . . *J'ai oublié,"* he started to explain in French, then decided not to continue. Better, he now thought, to present the incriminating evidence. The biograph was an instrument to record altitude and also to mark the time taken for each leg of the flight. Hall had started the instrument just before leaving Avord and had forgotten to turn it off at any time, even when the plane had been sitting on the ground at his first stop and later for the emergency landing. Instead of recording four neat markings, one for each of the three legs and one for the unexpected landing, the instrument recorded what looked like the skyline of the French Alps. The moniteur looked at the instrument, then at Hall. The officer did not speak, but the look on his face spoke more eloquently than his voice. For Hall the look said: "You poor simple prune! You choice sample of moldy American cheese."

Chastened and subdued, Hall walked back to the barracks. He knew his next triangle would have to be executed without a flaw; it would be his last chance to redeem himself. A few days later he did. He flew the three legs perfectly, kept his attention glued to his instruments and map, and paid particular attention to the biograph.

And so did MacMonagle, who had not returned from his first attempt until a day later. He had lost two spark plugs and like Hall had had to make a forced landing. Hall and his friend now passed from *élève pilotes* to *pilotes aviateurs,* from the military rank of second-class soldier to that of corporal, and from wearing bare tunics to sporting the star and wings of fully breveted military pilots.

By June 3, 1917, Hall could boast of even further conquests. "I have learned to fly five different types of avions," he wrote home. To his sisters Dorothy and Marjorie, he said: "I could take you from home to Des Moines in eleven minutes. How would you like it!" He had now been transferred to Plessis-Belleville for operational training, the last before being assigned to a front-line unit. He wrote to Marjorie: "I am leaving on Friday or Saturday of this week, I think, having finished all of my training, including aerial acrobacy, group flying, machine gunnery, and combat. . . . Acrobacy was a very thrilling experience the first time I did it. We have to do all sorts of 'stunts' in the air: looping the loop, falling nose-down, turning flip-flops in the air, turning vertically, tipped up at an angle of ninety degrees."

James Norman Hall was now thirty years old, older than most of his fellow pilots, but much younger in spirit than many others who aged too quickly in that big adventure.

3

The Escadrille Lafayette

On the fourteenth of June, Hall and MacMonagle reported for duty to the airfield at Chaudun, near Soissons, on the Arne, to the Nieuport—later Spad—124th Squadron, the famous Escadrille Lafayette. The squadron was composed entirely of American volunteers, except for the French commanders. The Lafayette was but one of four pursuit squadrons assigned to the same field; together they formed a *groupe de combat*. Their mission was to patrol a particular part of the front and to protect reconnaissance planes taking photographs and directing artillery.

Normally, Hall was quick to learn, the individual sorties were two a day, one in the morning and another in the afternoon, each of two hours' duration; and rarely in one day were there more than six hours of flying. To many of the new pilots, this schedule seemed one of slothful ease, particularly to MacMonagle.

That night at the mess room MacMonagle eagerly sought answers from the older pilots. Hall chose to listen. Having heard about only two patrols a day, Mac asked: "What about voluntary patrols? I don't suppose there is any objection, is there?"

Harold Willis, from Boston, slapped another pilot sitting next to him on the back. "What did I tell you!! Do I win?" Then he explained. "We asked the same question when we came out, and every other new pilot before us. This voluntary-patrol business is a kind of standing joke. You think, now, that four hours a day over the lines is a light program. For the first month or so you will go out on your own between times. After that, no. Of course, when they call for a voluntary patrol for some necessary piece of work, you will volunteer out of a sense of duty. As I say, you may do as much flying as you like. But wait. After a month, or we'll give you six weeks, you will do no more than you have to."

MacMonagle was not impressed. Nor was Hall. "What do you do with the rest of your time?" Doug asked.

"Sleep," said Willis. "Read a good deal. Play some poker or bridge. Walk. But sleep is the chief amusement. Eight hours used to be enough for me. Now I can do with ten or twelve."

"That's all rot," MacMonagle rejoined. "You fellows are having it too soft. They ought to put you on the school regime again."

Willis seemed resigned. "Well," he said, "you'll soon see for yourself."

Hall wanted to know about the artillery activity over the front. Willis, as one of the flight leaders, was happier to take this new tack. "Think down to the gunners," he said. "That will help a lot. It's a game after that. Your skill against theirs. I couldn't do it at first, and shellfire seemed absolutely damnable."

Steve Bigelow, another Bostonian, came to the aid of Willis. "You want to remember," he said, "that a *chasse* machine is almost never brought down by antiaircraft fire. You are too fast for them. You can fool 'em in a thousand ways."

Willis continued. "I had been flying for two weeks before I saw a Boche. They are not scarce on this sector, don't worry. I simply couldn't see them. The others would have scraps. I

IN SEARCH OF PARADISE 40

spent most of my time trying to keep track of them." He now addressed himself directly to MacMonagle. "Take my tip, Doug," he said to him, almost paternally, "don't be too anxious to mix it with the first German you see, because very likely he will be a Frenchman, and if he isn't, if he is a good Hun pilot, you'll simply be meat for him—at first, I mean."

"And," Bigelow added, "they say that all the Boche aviators on this front have had several months' experience in Russia and the Balkans. They train them there before they send them to the Western Front." He paused. "As a matter of fact, your best chance of being brought down will come in the first two weeks."

MacMonagle slumped down in his chair. "That's comforting," he said.

"No, *sans blague,*" Willis said. "Honestly, you'll be almost helpless. You don't see anything, and you don't know what it is that you do see. Here's an example." He stopped to light a cork-tipped French cigarette. "On one of my first sorties I happened to look over my shoulder and I saw five or six Germans in the most beautiful alignment. And they were all slanting up to dive on me. I was scared out of my life: went down full motor, then cut and fell into a *vrille.* Came out of that and had another look. There they were in the same position, only farther away. I didn't tumble even then, except farther down. Next time I looked, the five Boches, or six, whichever it was, had all been raveled out by the wind. They left and I was safe for that day."

Hall and MacMonagle were incredulous. "Just remember," Bigelow said, "your job is to patrol the lines. But if a man is built that way, he can loaf on the job."

"Now, don't let's get personal," Willis enjoined.

"No, I'm not," Bigelow replied. "It's a matter of temperament. In *chasse,* a man need never have a fight. At two hundred kilometers an hour, it won't take him very long to get out of danger. He stays out his two hours and comes in with some framed-up tale to account for his disappearance. 'Got lost. Went off by myself into Germany. Had motor trouble. Gun jammed, and went back to arm it.' He may even spray a few bullets toward Germany and call it a combat. Oh, he can find plenty of excuses, and he can get away with them."

Presently the French commanding officer, Captain Georges Thénault, entered the room. He seemed in a sociable frame of mind, and came over to join the pilots. Willis filled him in on their conversation. Captain Thénault considered the malingering question for several moments before he spoke. Hall never forgot his words, for they were the best he had ever heard on the subject. Captain Thénault spoke slowly, carefully enunciating each word: "Let your record be as fine as it is in your power to make it, so that later in life, those of you who live through the war, will have no regrets for the parts you have played."

Hall flushed at the applicability of the remark; slowly he rose, walked out the door, and went back to the barracks. He considered his place in such an assignment, his trench life and flight training, "the blood of his forebears—the confused strains—the consciousness that it was pulling in different ways; he envied other men he had known, men who were 'all of a piece,' whose great-grandsons would be as like them as they were like their grandfathers." He wondered if he would be the man to match the new responsibilities and the new dangers he would have to assume and meet. Diffidence, his old enemy, he had stalked into a remote corner of his consciousness. He knew he would have to defeat it again, as he had in the past, with a giant effort of the will. And this time, he would have to do it before morning.

It was well before dawn the next day when Tiffin, the mess steward, stood by Hall's bed to wake him up. He held a candle in his hand, and his bald head shone in the light. *"Beau temps, monsieur,"* he said, left the candle on the table, and left. Hall's eyes smarted as he sat up and looked out the oil-cloth window to the blackness outside. He dressed quickly, washed, and walked to the mess room.

The other pilots sat eating breakfast and discussing the mission for that morning. Two patrols had been ordered, both to leave at the same time, one to cover from three thousand meters, the other from five thousand. MacMonagle and Hall drew the higher one. After finishing the simple meal of buttered bread and hot chocolate, Douglas MacMonagle walked out the door to check the weather. Banks of clouds hung against the east, a band of blue broadened on the horizon, and from the west a fresh breeze blew. Doug yawned. "We'll go up—ho, hum!" Then he yawned again. "We'll go up through a hole before we reach the river. It's going to clear presently, so the higher we go, the better."

Two of the other pilots got up from the table. They yawned too. "I don't feel very pugnacious this morning," one said, adjusting his white silk scarf under his tunic. The other tucked his leather gloves under his arm. "It's a crime to send men out at this time of the day," he said. "I mean at this time of night." It was ten minutes before takeoff time.

Hall and MacMonagle walked out to the field, to where the Spads were parked in two long rows in front of the canvas-covered hangars. The wind had grown stronger, causing the canvas to fill up, then flap, creaking the wooden frames. From the distance came the sound of the big guns. Some of the Spads were new, but Hall knew they were for the old pilots; conversely, the old planes were for the new pilots. Hall went over to his plane. The painted insignia of the American Indian head on the side of the fuselage was cracked and peeling, the wings were everywhere patched and repatched, and the engine and nacelle were black and streaked with oil.

Cartier, the mechanic, finished arming the machine gun and started to wipe clean the windshield. *"Bonjour, mon vieux,"* Hall said to him, climbed into the cockpit, and settled himself in the seat.

"Alors! Ça y est?" Cartier said. His teeth were yellow from tobacco juice. *"Bonne chance aujourd'hui. C'est votre première fois, n'est-ce-pas?"* The mechanic mounted the step, pulled up Hall's fur collar, and wrapped the muffler tightly about his neck. Hall pulled on in turn his silk, paper, and fur-lined gloves. *"Oui. Merci,"* Hall said to Cartier.

Hall gripped the stick and placed his feet on the rudder bar. The mechanic helped to buckle him in, went to the wheels to pull the chocks, then went around to the front of the plane to pull through the propeller. Hall adjusted his goggles, craned his neck over the side of the cockpit, and tested the ailerons, elevator, and rudder.

At contact the motor spurted to life, and Cartier ran to hold the wings before Hall taxied the plane. Presently Willis, the flight leader, ran over and climbed up on the step of Hall's plane. Hall suddenly remembered that he had forgotten the rendezvous point. "Rendezvous . . . two thousand . . . over . . . field," Willis shouted. Over the blast of the propeller Hall did not catch all the words. Willis continued: "Know me . . . Big T . . . wings . . . fuselage . . . I'll . . . turning right. You and others left. When . . . see me start . . . lines, fall in behind . . . left. Remember stick close . . . patrol. If . . . get lost, better . . . home. Compass southwest. Look carefully . . . landmarks going out. Got . . . straight?"

Hall nodded his head and Willis rushed back to his own plane. A line of Spads started to taxi out to the takeoff point on the other side of the field. Cartier held on to the spar of the wing as Hall turned into the wind and applied his brakes. Hall advanced the throttle and the mechanic waved him off. Hall raced his Spad down the field and eased the stick forward, bringing up the tail. The plane flew itself off the ground. Soon Hall was high over the hangars and started climbing northeast to the rendezvous point, as Willis had directed.

As he nosed up and added more throttle, Hall noticed that the revolutions per minute, instead of increasing, were starting to fall off. Willis and the others in the flight, noticing Hall's difficulty with his motor, started to dive under him and climb up again so they would not lose him. Together they broke through a cloud bank and came out on top. As if in greeting, the sun rose and splashed the cloud floor in pink and gold and violet.

The flight joined up into a tighter formation and flew over the cloud cover. As the clouds started to break and disperse, Hall could see the crisscross of lines that marked the trenches, and just above them the flashing lights of artillery fire. The Spads turned west along and just inside the French lines until they came to the town of Soissons. As Hall flew over the town, he thought of the life he had lived in the trenches and how he had once envied the people who did what he was now doing—flying, clean, with almost godlike detachment from the ground war. He wondered what soldier had taken over his place on the parapet behind the machine gun, and he thought how he had relieved McDonald for only a few minutes and how that act had saved his life. The plane suddenly pitched up from a thermal current, and Hall awoke to his present surroundings. He looked about him. The rest of the flight had vanished. He was alone.

Achingly, he thought: What if I should be trapped, a sitting duck, by a German patrol? He kept scanning the air, wing to wing, nose to tail, above and below, when, under his tail he saw a plane quickly turn and dive. Hall throttled down, jammed the stick forward, and started after him. As he dived he saw white pencil lines of smoke crossing and recrossing in front of him. They meant only one thing: tracer bullets from machine guns. He now bent stick and rudder into a tight spiraling turn, continuing down, until the tracers disappeared. Then he leveled off and advanced his throttle to cruising speed. Suddenly a shell shot up alongside the plane. Hall watched it in horrific fascination as it reached the top of its arc and then began to fall. "Lord!" he thought to himself, "I have seen a live shell, and yet I cannot find my patrol!"

Hall checked his altimeter: He had lost 2,500 meters coming down. He could see the trenches clearly now and the plane began to buffet from the concussion of exploding shells. He remembered what Willis had said about evasive action: "Never fly in a straight line for more than fifteen seconds. Keep changing your direction constantly, but be careful not to fly in a regularly irregular fashion. The German gunners may let you alone at first, hoping that you will become careless, or they may be plotting out your style of flight. Then they make their calculations and they let you have it. If you have been careless, they'll put 'em so close, they'll be no question about the kind of scare you will have."

Trying to fly irregularly irregular and to find his flight at the same time, Hall was having no luck. The accuracy of the shells got better. One burst so close to the nose of the plane that it knocked Hall's hands and feet from the controls. Three more quickly followed, one on either side and one just behind at the tail. Puffs of black smoke swelled and dispersed, clearly marking where he had just been. Fear began to turn to despair. One of the other pilots had recommended: "Think down to the gunners!" but Hall could not do this. The French captain had said he would talk to the shells: *"Bonjour, mon vieux! Tiens! Comment ça va, toi! Ah, non! Je suis pressé!"* Hall felt he could not do this either. In his livid loneliness, he felt the need for friends.

Again he remembered Willis' advice: "If you get lost, go home." Hall tried to orient himself. He knew that the way back was southwest, and it should be a simple matter to turn in that direction. But when he looked at his compass it spun lazily in every direction because of his evasive action. To get a proper reading from it he would have to fly straight and level for a few minutes; that, however, would give the German gunners time enough to zero in on him. He could not do such a stupid thing. Now, in fact, the artillery was increasing. He must be flying, he suddenly realized, not toward home, but further into enemy territory.

Hall kept on looking. From above and behind to his left, he saw a plane swoop down and suddenly turn into a position abreast of him. Seeing concentric circles of red, white, and blue, Hall sighed deeply in relief, and as he looked at the pilot he could see the familiar face, now smiling reassuringly, of Steve Bigelow. Hall knew now, as Bigelow danced his plane through the sky to escape the shell bursts and to lead him home, that he would not have to land at a place like Karlsruhe or Cologne.

When they had landed, Bigelow was full of good-natured ribbing. "And if I had been a Hun!" he said to Hall, who felt guilty and defenseless. "Oh, man! You were fruit salad! Fruit salad, I tell you! I could have speared you with my eyes shut."

"But I was keeping my eyes open," Hall answered as they walked toward the barracks. "If *you* had been the Hun, the fruit salad would not have been as palatable as you thought."

"Tell me this: Did you see me?"

Hall reflected, then replied: "Yes!"

"When?"

"When you passed."

"And twenty seconds before that you would have been a sieve, if I had been a Boche."

Hall did not want to argue the point any further. He was too grateful to be alive and safely home. As he went to his cot and started to take off his leather jacket, MacMonagle, obviously excited and full of news, rushed over to him from the other side of the barracks. Mac had not even bothered to finish undressing; he carried one boot in his hand and still wore the other. "Now keep this quiet," he said, subduing his enthusiasm, "I don't want the others to know it. I've just had the adventure of my life. I attacked a German. Great Scott! What an opportunity! And I bungled it by being too eager!"

Hall sat down on his cot. "When was this?" he asked.

"Just after the others dove. You remember."

"All of a sudden I lost my flight," Hall admitted to his friend. "And I didn't know there was a German in sight until I saw the smoke of the tracer bullets."

"Neither did I," MacMonagle confessed on his part, "only I didn't see even the smoke."

Hall felt better. "What! You didn't . . ."

"No," Mac continued now more calmly. "I saw nothing but sky where the others had disappeared. I was looking for them when I saw the German. He was about four hundred meters below me. He couldn't have seen me, I think, because he kept straight on. I dove, but didn't open fire until I could have a nearer view of his black crosses. I wanted to be sure. I had no idea that I was going so much faster. The first thing I knew I was right on him. Had to pull back on my stick to keep from crashing into him. Up I went and fell into a nose dive. When I came out of it, there was not a sign of the German, and I hadn't fired a shot!"

Hall wanted to know how his friend got back after all this. "Did you come home alone?" he asked.

"No. I had the luck to meet the others just afterward. Now, not a word of this to anyone!"

Hall promised he would not, but that night at the mess

room the need for the secrecy was obviously unnecessary. Mac-Monagle's engagement with the enemy had been seen by two others and by Willis, the flight commander. "There was Mac-Monagle," Willis said, "going down on that biplane we were chasing. I've been trying to think of one wrong thing he might have done which he didn't do. First, he dove with the sun in his face, when he might have had it at his back. Then he came all the way in full view, instead of getting under his tail. Good thing the machine gunner was firing at us. After that, when he had the chance of a lifetime, he fell into a *vrille* and scared the life out of the rest of us. I thought the gunner had turned on him. And while we were following him down to see where he was going to splash, the Boche got away."

The other pilots about the table began to laugh at Mac's expense. Doug flushed in embarrassment; he honestly had not known that anyone else had seen him. Bigelow, still laughing, got up to leave. "Well," he said, looking at Hall and Mac-Monagle, "the Lord has certainly protected the innocent today!" It was the perfect exit line.

During the next week the two patrols which followed the first were comparatively unexciting, for they were missions to find, then try to shoot down, German observation balloons. The task was never as easy as it seemed. The patrol had to get to the balloons before the Germans could pull them down; then the rockets which armed the planes, because of the difficulty in maneuvering and firing, never could seem to hit even such a large target.

One morning, two hours after the second mission, Hall and MacMonagle were pitching pennies against the hangar wall when Willis walked across the field, followed by Whiskey and Soda, the two tame lion mascots of the Lafayette squadron. Willis seemed not of his usual casual manner; in fact, he seemed distinctly mad. And although his words were specifically intended for MacMonagle, both Mac and Hall had been guilty of disobeying orders—leaving the patrol and going off to find Huns to attack.

"Both of you have been lucky," Willis said angrily. "But don't get it into your heads that this sort of thing happens often. Now I'm going to give you a standing order. You are not going to attack again; neither of you is to think of attacking during your first month here. As likely as not it would be your luck the next time to meet an old pilot. If you did, I wouldn't give much for your chances. He would outmaneuver you in a minute. You will go out on patrol with the others, of course; it's the only way to learn to fight. But if you get lost, go back to our balloons and stay there until it is time to go home."

Hall and MacMonagle agreed that they would obey the order, that they understood the good sense it made. Then, on the very next mission, Hall disobeyed, and it almost cost him his life. It was June 26, 1917, a Tuesday. Hall had been assigned to a sunset patrol with Lufbery, Dugan, Bridgman, and Parsons. Lieutenant Bill Thaw, of Pittsburgh, was leading. Before takeoff Thaw had told his flight to rendezvous at thirteen thousand feet over an old reservoir which was close to the lines, where they would form up, then climb to sixteen, and finally move in together. As Willis had, so Thaw cautioned Hall to stay close to the patrol and not to stray.

Unfortunately, however, just before takeoff Hall had motor trouble and could not leave with the rest of the flight. But this time he remembered well the rendezvous point and did not worry about being late. Ten minutes later, when Cartier had found and corrected the trouble, Hall got back into his plane and took off. As he climbed at full throttle, Hall noticed that his revolutions per minute started to fall off. He would have to reduce his rate of climb. By the time he got to four thousand feet above the reservoir, he saw that the others had gone off without him. He tried to catch up, but determined that he was too far behind. Remembering Willis' advice, he knew that he would have to find the balloons, stay with them, and wait for the others to come across the sector. but Hall decided he didn't want to wait around. He saw the lines come up below, turned, and followed them toward Rheims. Off to the right were the French balloons, but there were no signs of any Spads, not in any direction. Hall now headed across the German lines.

Remembering to stay constantly on the alert, and by all means not to fly with his head in the clouds, which to date had cost him two embarrassments, Hall scanned the sky, wing to wing, nose to tail, from above to below. Below! Five black specks were moving across the top of the ground, and another —Lufbery no doubt—slightly higher, flitted about like a fly, doing acrobatics. It must be his patrol! Hall nosed down into a steep dive to join them.

Pulling up to level off, Hall moved against the slanting rays of the setting sun, into the formation of planes. As he joined up, he started to wiggle his wings in greeting, then squinted at the other planes. Strange, he thought, but they were not the kind of Spads he knew. The wings were longer and set lower on the fuselage, and there were V-struts supporting the stabilizers. Drawing abreast in their midst, and seeing the insignia on the sides for the first time, he swallowed hard. Instead of cockades, he saw black crosses. German Fokkers! For a moment nothing happened. The Huns were as surprised as Hall. Chilled with fright, Hall now tried to escape. He pulled up into a tight loop, and coming out on the bottom he rolled, then cut now left, now right, zoomed into a steep dive, pulled up into another loop, and on the top kicked over into an Immelmann. But the acrobatics were all to no avail. Everywhere he looked there was a black cross. He was trapped.

Suddenly, a Fokker loomed up in front of him, coming straight on like an express train, and firing a steady stream of bullets all the way in. Hall felt the slugs pouring into his motor, and he could see behind the windshield of the oncoming plane the square-cut goggles of the German pilot. Hall kicked rudder and slammed the stick over in a hard right turn, and as he started to cut the motor and nose into a dive, he felt a smashing blow in his left shoulder. He thought it had come from behind. As he turned his head to look, a tracer creased his forehead, and from another attacking plane on the left came another shell which struck him in the groin. Now, from every direction, slugs poured into his wings, fuselage, motor, and tail. Hall tried again to reduce throttle and dive out of trouble, but his left hand would not move on the handle and his left leg would not move his foot on the rudder bar. Hall reached around with his right hand. Blood was streaming from his head and over his goggles, and more blood squished into his shirt and pants. Hall fell forward on his stick. The plane, motor roaring at full throttle, nosed over into a vertical dive. The Spad was out of control, plunging fourteen thousand feet headlong to the ground. Hall had passed out.

Motor roared, struts shook, wires shrieked, and as the plane neared the ground, barely a hundred and fifty meters away, Hall momentarily regained consciousness. "Am I on fire?" he shouted at himself. "I'm going to be killed! This is my last flight!" He reached across his body with his right hand and jerked back the throttle; then gripping the stick again with his right hand, he yanked back with all his strength. The plane pulled out, and incredibly, though shuddering, the wings held. Then from the loss and drain of blood, Hall fainted again.

The plane, like a fallen angel drunk or possessed, fell, staggered, turned, then slipped, floated, fluttered, and finally crashed, exploding a cloud of brown dust and a clap of broken wood. Miraculously, the fuselage had fallen into a trench; the wings, resting above on the parapets on either side, had broken off but had also broken the plane's fall; and in his cockpit, wafted down like an autumn leaf, sat Hall, bleeding and hurt, but alive.

When he came to, Hall realized he was being carried on a stretcher. He remembered the crash, then tried moving arm, leg, body, head, in turn. All worked, except on the left side. suddenly, looking mistily forward to the hands gripping the stretcher, he wondered: "Whose hands are they—French or German?" He opened his eyes wide but saw only a red blur; he wiped them with his sleeve, then looked again. The back of the stretcher-bearer was caked in mud. Hall raised his eyes to the helmet. It was ridged on top—the hat of a French *poilu*. *"Bonjour, messieurs!"* Hall blurted happily.

The stretcher-bearer in front turned his head. *"Tiens! Ça va, monsieur l'aviateur?"* he said.

"Ah, mon vieux," the one carrying in back said, *"vous avez eu bonne chance!"* Then they explained how just before the final turn of the plane, he had been heading straight for Germany; and if he had been fifty meters higher when he had come down, he would have crashed in no-man's-land.

The stretcher-bearers carried Hall down into a deep dugout. It was a first-aid station, and in the light of the candles Hall could see a doctor operating on a soldier's leg. Others were waiting to be treated, but as soon as the forward stretcher-bearer announced, *"Aviateur américain, docteur,"* Hall was placed on the table. Other than the wounds from the aerial combat, there were apparently no injuries from the crash. The doctor sutured and dressed the wounds in the shoulder and head. Then he told the orderly to cut off Hall's pants so he could look at the wound in the groin. As he examined it, he said: *"Levez lui un peu."* As Hall sat up, the doctor held a mirror between his legs and said: *"Regardez, sergent. Vous avez de la chance."* Hall looked. The skin of his scrotum had been creased by a bullet. Although he had bled a lot, it was— and he was eternally thankful—only a surface wound.

Despite the fact that he was only a sergeant but again because he was an American, Hall was taken to the hospital and given a bed in the officers' ward. In the bed on his left lay a *capitaine* who had a grenade explode in his face; his head was completely wrapped in bandages. On the right lay a priest who had taken some machine gun bullets in the hip. *"Ou, là là!"* the priest said uncomfortably, the only admission of his pain.

Meanwhile, back at the Lafayette aerodrome, the French officers, having heard of Hall's crash, had learned that Hall had survived and though wounded was recuperating in the hospital. Capitaine Thénault and Bill Thaw, commander and flight leader, jumped in a car and rushed to see Hall. They arrived in time to see Hall being decorated with the Médaille militaire and the Croix de guerre. Later, when the rest of the escadrille learned of these rewards, they were depressed. For such decorations to be pinned on so quickly, the ceremony could only mean one thing. The doctors and generals did not expect Hall to live long, and they wanted him to enjoy, however briefly, the honors befitting a hero.

But Hall fooled everyone. He not only survived, but lived to tell the tale, which, while he was recuperating, he started to write as a manuscript called *High Adventure*. Inexplicably, but perhaps out of modesty and pride—modesty over his successes and shame for his failures—Hall in his book camouflaged most of his own adventures and ascribed them to a fictional but clearly autobiographical character, a person named "Drew." Also, while in hospital, Hall wrote another piece which sold tens of thousand of dollars' worth of liberty bonds. A friend had written him for a souvenir from the front, to help sell bonds, Hall sent him a poem, called "The Airman's Rendezvous," which was an instant success with the public. Boston's hero of the British trenches had now become the hero of the French skies. And although Hall later would have yet another rendezvous with death, death would again forget the time and place.

At the end of September, 1917, the Escadrille Lafayette had been ordered back to Chaudun, near Soissons, on the Aisne. Hall was still in the hospital through July and most of August. On the twenty-sixth he was released and sent to Lyons, in the south of France, to a depot for aviators who had been wounded and were returning to the front; then, through a mistake in orders, Hall was assigned, not back to his Lafayette squadron as he expected, but to another French squadron, Spad 112, at Plessis-Belleville, his old base. There was only one other American in the unit, his friend with whom he had joined up on the same day in Paris, Leland L. Rounds. They rejoiced at their good fortune and flew several patrols together, one an escort mission out of Belfort, near the Swiss border, for the king of Italy, which Hall enjoyed—not because of the royalty but because of the glorious view of the snow-capped Alps. Then, after returning to the Verdun sector, they went on another patrol together, but Hall became separated from his friend in a build-up of clouds over the Vosges Mountains, where, inexplicably, his motor started to misfire.

Quickly checking his instruments, Hall could see that his fuel pressure was falling off; somehow, the fuel pump had stopped working. He reached down to the side of his seat and started to work by hand the auxiliary pump, but it too stopped working. Thinking of the jagged peaks below, Hall immediately reached forward to the gravity-fed tank and turned on the valve. With luck he could fly for fifteen minutes on the emergency tank. When the engine coughed dead after the final drop, the reserve proved enough to carry him over the peaks; but how, he wondered, as he nosed into a flat glide, could he stretch the glide over the foothills to a landing place?

Seeing nothing but hills and stretches of trees, Hall despaired of finding anything to land on, when, off to the left of a village, he saw a sugarloaf mountain and on its top what looked like a broad field for grazing. He noted the wind direction from the smoking chimneys and turned into the wind, flattening his glide to get over the treetops. As he came in, the slope of the land proved more steep than what had seemed at two thousand meters, and cows, which had been invisible from above, now obstructed the landing path ahead. Hall worked his rudder bar left and right, then pulled up abruptly on the stick and stalled out. The plane slammed against the rise of the hill and at the top sped over and down the other side, through a wire fence, straight on between two stout apple trees, shearing the wings clean from the fuselage, through a thick clump of bushes, and finally crashed against a stone wall. On impact Hall struck his head against the instrument panel and broke his nose. Dazed from the blow, he sat in the cockpit holding his handkerchief against the flow of blood. Through the brush he heard someone running toward his plane. It was a short fat man. "Now, my boy," the man said, "what can I do for you?" It was the mayor—always, it seemed to Hall, the first to appear on the scene of crashes and emergency landings. The mayor placed a guard of young boys around the plane, then took Hall to his home. Hall, embarrassed at his lack of funds—he had only eighty centimes in his pocket—had to borrow enough money to get home to Verdun. The mayor, happy to have such an interesting visitor, and an American to boot, wanted to let him have twice the amount asked for.

Early in October, Hall was reassigned to Spad 124, the Escadrille Lafayette, and to Groupe de Combat 13, which was now stationed near the Argonne Forest, at Senard. As he reported to the field, Hall noticed a flight of planes coming in from patrol, landing, and taxiing up to the hangars; he went over to meet them. As they climbed out of their planes, his old friends greeted him warmly. They had just tangled with

Richthofen's Flying Circus, they told him. One plane had been lost on each side of the encounter. "Who did they get of ours?" Hall asked.

The reply was short, but it struck Hall like a fist to the face. "MacMonagle," someone said.

Hall turned, walked quickly away, and started to cry. His old friend, that he and Rounds had joined up with—so gay, talkative, and ebullient—with whom he had trained and flown his first flights together, was dead. To compound his sorrow, Hall learned from the others that Doug's mother, through some administrative miracle, had come to the aerodrome that morning to visit her son, but had arrived too late. Doug had already taken off for patrol. And, he learned further, the night before, Mac had returned from a leave to Paris, still drunk and full of gaiety, and had awakened the barracks with his singing and stumbling. In punishment, Capitaine Thénault, ignoring the fact that the pilots on leave were granted another day of *repos* upon returning, ordered MacMonagle on patrol for the next morning.

Later that month, through the efforts of Dr. Gros, an American delegation of Army officers came to visit the Lafayette squadron. The group wanted to examine the pilots to see if they were fit for duty with the United States Air Service. The findings of the committee astounded everyone. Despite hundreds of hours of combat experience, a number of aces and double-aces, and a great amount of victories, the squadron was pronounced unfit. In desperation Bill Thaw, who had just flunked the physical examination because of a bent elbow, pointed to the doctor's bag, and raised his voice so all could hear: "Doc," he said, "you have everything in that bag but an instrument that measures guts!"

Nevertheless, the examiners remained adamant. Dud Hill had a blind eye, Dolan had infected tonsils, Hank Jones had flat feet, and Raoul Lufbery, regardless of his impressive string of sixteen victories, could not walk a straight line backward. In the end, there was barely a pilot among them who did not have to be granted a waiver on some physical, mental, or even moral, count.

On his first flight after rejoining the squadron, Hall had decided that now more than ever he wanted to prove his ability as a pursuit pilot. And furthermore he wanted to avenge the death of Douglas MacMonagle. But autumn passed and winter began, and although by the first of November the squadron had bagged more observation balloons and brought down more enemy planes, Hall had had only one opportunity, but as he came in on the Hun from behind, the sun at his back, and taking the enemy completely by surprise, his gun jammed and his motor quit just as he closed in for the kill. To miss ramming the enemy plane, he had had to pull up and over, and as he did, his plane fell off into a spin. Difficulties compounded. As he straightened the wings and pulled out of the *vrille,* the tip of one wing bent, a rib in the fuselage broke, and the fabric from one side of the cockpit stripped off and back to the tail. Hall felt extraordinarily lucky to have made it safely back to the field. "I have seven more lives to lose before I'm through with this good old earth," he wrote home, thinking that this last encounter had not counted as one of them.

It was on Christmas day that Hall had another similar opportunity, and although his gun did not jam, nor did his motor quit, his reason for not taking his victim was as believable as it was original. He had taken his plane off to sport among the clouds. He had cavorted among the cumulus clouds, like a kitten playing with balls of cotton, and he had flown into enemy territory. Shooting out from the bottom of a cloud, the sun at his back, unexpectedly he found himself behind a lone German observation plane. Rather than pounce on his prey, Hall slid alongside the German and cut his motor. The Hun was shaken with surprise. Hall shouted across to him as loud as he could: "Merry Christmas!" The German pilot nodded his head, Hall waved his hand, and both planes sped off in opposite directions. It was a gesture on the part of Hall which would not be forgotten, for the German pilot reported the incident and the news spread up and down the line of the German Air Force. It was a gesture which would serve Hall in good stead when his turn would come.

On New Year's Day, 1918, another fateful Tuesday, Hall

had his first kill. It was a very cold day, snow covered the ground, making it difficult to find check points from the air, and motors were difficult to start. Nevertheless, Bill Thaw was restless to seek out and destroy the Hun, regardless of the holidays. "Jimmie," he said to Hall, "let's go out to the lines and have a look around." Hall agreed. It might be easier to stay in formation with only one other plane than with a group of others. Cartier got the engine started and got it to turn over at 1,900 revolutions. Thaw and Hall got into their planes, rolled over the crusted ground and into the air; then, with Thaw only a hundred meters in front of him, Hall lost his leader. But presently he saw him again, happily doing loops and barrel rolls, and Hall, thinking he would surprise his friend by sneaking up on him from above and behind, climbed to catch him. As he swooped in, however, Hall saw that this plane was not Thaw at all. Again unexpectedly, Hall had found the black crosses of the Hun. It was a single-seater, oblivious as before that an enemy was on his tail. Hall thought: "Here is a man who loves flying as much as I do, and who has forgotten, as I sometimes do, what he's up here for." But, Hall decided, this was no time for another season's greeting—and MacMonagle had still not been avenged. From five hundred meters above and behind, Hall, at full throttle, closed in. At one hundred yards he pressed the trigger and tracers and bullets streamed into the Hun's tail and fuselage and caromed off the motor. The German pulled up into a turn, then fell off into a spin. Hall followed him, watched a wing break off, and saw him crash to the ground. Hall turned his plane for home.

When Hall returned to the field, Lieutenant Verdier, the second in command, was waiting for him. Verdier was mad. "Where have you been?" he asked Hall abruptly as he entered the headquarters building.

"Out to the lines with Lieutenant Thaw," Hall answered.

"I know. But where have you been since you lost him?" The lieutenant was becoming exasperated. "Thaw returned twenty minutes ago."

"I met a German pursuit plane," Hall replied simply. He had remembered the exact location of the combat and the spot where the German went down. He walked over to the map on the wall and pointed to the place. Verdier picked up the field phone and called the headquarters of the Fourth Army.

"Bon! Merci!" The lieutenant hung up the phone. He turned to Hall and spoke quickly. "You got him."

"I thought I had," Hall said, casually.

"Headquarters have just received word from the Infantry. There's no doubt about confirmation. One of his wings came off in the air and fell in our lines. The rest of the plane crashed in no-man's-land." Verdier offered his hand. "Congratulations on your first victory. That's the way to begin the New Year."

Hall, however, felt no joy over the victory. Quietly he walked toward the door. He had simply done his duty, and he had avenged MacMonagle's death. He turned his head. "Thank you," he said, and walked out.

It was Hall's first and only kill while serving with the Escadrille Lafayette.

4

The 94th U. S. Aero Squadron

On February 7, 1918, James Norman Hall was commissioned as a captain in the United States Air Service, and on the eighteenth, the Escadrille Lafayette was transferred en masse to the American air forces as the 103rd Aero Squadron. Hall was reluctant to leave the French service, but he wrote home: "It will be a joy to serve as an American in the American Army." And it was a joy too for him to wear over his left breast pocket two French decorations: the Médaille militaire and the Croix de guerre, with palm.

Two weeks later Hall was decorated with the second palm to his Croix de guerre. General Gouraud, Commander of the Fourth Army, said in the citation: *"Pilote d'une grande bravoure, qui livre journellement de nombreux combats. A abattu deux avions ennemis."* In less than a month after his assignment, Hall was made a flight commander. On March 25, 1918, he wrote home, telling his sister Marjorie that he had instructed his publishers, Houghton Mifflin, to send her $1,000 so she could go to college after all. Then he told his family about one of his combats:

"Last night three of us chased fourteen Germans about six kilometers into their own lines, and all three of us had jammed machine guns! They must have been green pilots.

"It is quite likely that I brought down another German albatross on the twenty-first. I and another French pilot had a fight with some enemy machines in the same region at the same time. The infantry reported that a German was brought down there, and dove into the ground. It is not quite certain yet which of us was responsible for him, but I'll know tomorrow if I am the lucky man."

The next day came and he learned that the French pilot had been credited with the victory; but on the twenty-sixth, the day after the letter, undaunted and eager as ever, Hall led his flight of three planes over the lines and attacked eight enemy planes—three two-seaters and five fighters. Hall bagged one, sending him down in flames, and forced down two others, which probably were destroyed. The fight had lasted twenty minutes. For this brilliant combat, Hall was one of the first two Americans to be awarded the Distinguished Service Cross.

The U. S. Air Service, knowing that a man like Hall was invaluable with new pilots, assigned him as a flight commander to the 94th, the "Hat-in-the-Ring" Squadron. Hall packed his few belongings and climbed into his Nieuport 28 to fly to Epiez, about thirty miles from the lines, where the 94th was now stationed.

The American pilots at Epiez, like all other U. S. Air Service pilots in France, had heard about the former Lafayette Escadrille aviators and they idolized them. To have one of them in any unit was a great honor. One of the new American pilots, who had been a racing-car driver and had been General Billy Mitchell's chauffeur, particularly looked forward to having a *pilote de chasse* as his flight commander. Lieutenant Eddie Rickenbacker stood by one of the hangars and watched a Nieuport come in. The plane was a stranger, sporting American colors, and it buzzed the field. Motor off, the plane now glided down and skimmed over the ground. It looked as if it was going to be a perfect landing. But suddenly the wheels struck the mud on the far end of the field and the plane quickly somersaulted forward and over on its back. Ricken-backer ran over to the plane to get the pilot out. There, held by his seat belt and unhurt, head down and protruding from the cockpit, hung Captain James Norman Hall.

Despite such an inauspicious assumption of command, Hall in one month had his flight in shape and ready for dogfighting combat. He knew that the 94th had had no luck in knocking down the Hun, and he primed his flight for the first kill. And of all his pilots, Hall noted, Rickenbacker wanted to draw first blood. The opportunity soon came.

It was the twenty-ninth of April, 1918. Hall and Ricken-backer had been ordered on alert. As it had for the last four days, the rain poured, giving little hope for any action. But toward noon the sky began to clear. At last at five o'clock the phone rang. Hall answered. It was the French headquarters at Beaumont reporting that a German two-seater had just crossed the lines and was heading south. The pilots quickly climbed into their waiting planes to take off. Presently one of the me-chanics ran over to Hall's plane. They had to wait, he said, because Major Lufbery, the group commander, wanted to join them; he would be there in a few minutes.

Hall and Rickenbacker did not want to wait. They watched the skies, eager to be off. Over the noise of the idling motors Rickenbacker shouted to Hall and pointed to a small speck against the clouds over the Forêt de la Reine. Rick knew it must be the reported Hun. Hall decided not to wait for Luf-bery, and ordered the wheel chocks to be pulled. The motors roared wide open, and side by side Hall and his wingman sped down the field and into the sky. In a straight line they climbed directly for the Boche, and in a few minutes they were over the observation balloons and headed north toward Pont-à-Mous-son. To his right and slightly behind, Rickenbacker, Hall no-ticed, was behaving strangely. Rick would dip his wings and head off to the right, then stop, come back, and do the same thing again. Hall could not understand these antics. Didn't Rick know that he, Hall, was going straight for the enemy? Suddenly, again, Rick turned and flew off by himself. Amused but uninterested, Hall continued on course.

About five minutes later, as inexplicably as he had departed, Rickenbacker returned. He found Hall twisting, turning, climbing, and diving—he was teasing the German artillery below as they tried to hit him. Now pulling up into a loop and then half-rolling on top, Hall slipped down along Rick, wiggled his wings, and turned toward Pont-à-Mousson. They were well inside the enemy lines and on the way to St. Mihiel. Hall leading, the two planes climbed steeply toward the sun, leveled off, and waited.

Hall pointed ahead and below. Coming toward them from the north was a Hun, flying the new Pfalz. Momentarily, Hall scanned his wings to check the seams of the fabric. In a dive, he knew, the Nieuport had a talent for busting and peeling wing fabric. Hoping for the best, Hall dived for the enemy. Rick quickly followed. They had a thousand feet of advantage on the German. Halfway down, as Hall zoomed for the target, Rick broke off to get around to the other side of the Boche and cut off any possible retreat, but as he did, the German pilot saw Rick leave the rays of the sun. The Pfalz started to climb. But Hall had turned into his side and was firing. The Hun kicked into a right turn, nosed down, and sped for home. But now Rick was on his tail, with Hall following, both with throttles wide open. Rickenbacker quickly closed the gap. He trained his sights along the top of the fuselage toward the pilot, and at 150 yards pressed his triggers. Tracers stitched a fiery seam from tail to cockpit to engine. Rick pulled up. The Pfalz curved off, started to circle lazily down, then in a tightening spin it crashed to the ground.

Hall pulled up alongside Rick, promptly wiggled his wings, then danced his plane through the sky, in a display of loops, Immelmanns, rolls, and spins that Rick had never seen before. On the way back Hall deliberately continued his acrobacy as they went over the Hun artillery. Having enough, Rickenbacker broke away and sped for home; then Hall, at last having sufficiently teased the gunners, soon followed. Back over the field they came in together, landed, and taxied to the hangars.

Climbing out of their planes, Hall and Rick rushed toward

one another, shouting congratulations, whooping, and thumping each other on the back. Now, from every direction on the field, came squadron pilots and mechanics to add their jubilation. Word had just been received from the front confirming the crash of the German. The victory was the first for the 94th, the first for an American squadron, and the first for Rickenbacker, who was to notch twenty-five more victories on his guns and become America's ace of aces.

Major Lufbery, the group commander, came over to join the festivities. He pardoned the two pilots for leaving the field without him. He had missed his chance; if he had gone along and had been the first to spot the Hun, he could have won, perhaps, his seventeenth victory. As they walked to the headquarters building, Captain Hall spoke quietly to Lieutenant Rickenbacker. Where had Rick gone when he broke off on his own? Rick felt suddenly shamed, but he confessed. He thought he had known better than Hall where the Boche was; but when he pulled up from behind to start firing on the enemy plane, he flushed in embarrassed surprise. The "Hun" was in fact a French three-seater!

Two weeks later Eddie Rickenbacker would score another victory, the second for the squadron. But Hall, the flight leader, would be shot down, crash, and be mourned for dead. The mission came on the morning of May 7, 1918, yet another fateful Tuesday in the life of James Norman Hall, the luckiest and unluckiest day of his life. Hall, Rickenbacker, and Eddie Green were on alert duty, waiting for the phone to ring and send them off. At eight o'clock the call came. A flight of four enemy fighters was heading south, last seen near Pont-à-Mousson. Hall and his flight scrambled into the air, and took up the search near Armaville, south of Metz, on the Moselle. They were at twelve thousand feet, and below the river curled and threaded out and around the hills of St. Mihiel westward to Verdun in the distance. Ever on the alert, Rickenbacker spotted a black fast-moving shadow, three miles inside the lines, halfway to St. Mihiel, near Beaumont. Looking more closely, Rick recognized the plane as a Hun two-seater, quickly sped ahead of the formation and in front of Hall, and waggled his wings to indicate his discovery. Hall responded by doing the same, and the three planes of the flight piqued as one and went down for the prey.

As they dived, Rick noticed that the German artillery was sending up shell bursts, not so much to shoot them down as to signal the German plane of the attack and to notify other German planes in the area to come to the rescue of a lone comrade. Hall and his flight leveled off. Rickenbacker looked back toward Pont-à-Mousson to see if there was any answer to the artillery warning. From that direction immediately appeared four Pfalz scouts, cutting a diagonal course to stop any possible retreat of Hall's planes. Again, Rick sped to the front of Hall, signaled, and, convinced that Hall must see as he had seen, turned and dived for the attack. Choosing the Pfalz pulling up the rear, Rick, with true duck-hunting technique, swooped in, closed the gap, and at two hundred yards fired. The Hun lurched up in a tight turn and then fell off in a spin. Rick zoomed up in a climb, checked behind to see if an enemy was on his tail, then looked for Hall.

Hall had followed Rick down at the signal and had picked out a victim of his own. Hall, standing on his rudder pedals in a very steep dive, took careful aim through his sights, and closed for the kill. As he pressed his triggers to fire, he suddenly heard a cracking of wood and a rending of fabric. Pulling up and off the enemy, he saw at once that the leading edge of his upper right wing had broken and was torn, and in the propwash the fabric was tearing further and further back along the width of the wing. Disheartened, Hall at once throttled all the way back. As he tried to glide down, he felt the plane trying to fall off to the left. He slammed the stick to the right. The Nieuport now held in a straight line. To the German artillery below, however, Hall offered a perfect, unswerving target.

Hall knew he was a helpless victim, and now tried to nurse his plane back toward home, back to the lines, which he could see ahead, dimly, in the distance. All of a sudden, he felt a dull thump forward of the cockpit; then, uncontrollably, the Nieuport nosed up and fell off to the left in a spin. Hall looked behind, checking his unprotected tail, then sickened. A German had seen his plight, and firing, started to move in for the kill. Damnably, Hall cursed his luck—it was the same German plane he had just attacked! Hall started to fall faster, now in ever-tightening turns. In desperation, as he saw the ground coming up, he jammed his rudder bar hard right to stop the spin, straightened the wings, and pulled back hard on the stick. Spars cracked and wires screamed, but the plane leveled off. A large piece of fabric flapped crazily on the wing. A few feet below was level ground. The plane fell forward once more; again Hall pulled back hard against the stick. The Nieuport nosed up steeply, the wings stalled. The plane rushed against the earth, the landing gear broke off, and the fuselage, crunching and skidding, shot ahead on its own.

It stopped. Hall's head cracked against the instrument panel, breaking his broken nose; his left ankle, straining against the impact, sprained; and his right ankle, caught in the twisting metal of the rudder bar, broke. Dazed and helpless, Hall sat in his cockpit and looked about him. Fortunately, he had landed in a broad open field and had missed the high trees surrounding it. He listened; after the noise of the crash, the stillness seemed audible. But now, from the wood, as if from nowhere, German soldiers came running and shouting toward him. Two of them pulled Hall from his wrecked plane. As they lowered him to his feet, he screamed and fell to the ground. The soldiers carried him to their dugout in the woods and called for a medical corpsman. In a few minutes the medic came, applied a splint to and bound the broken ankle, dressed the sprained one, and bandaged Hall's again-broken nose. As Hall rested, his captors gave him some water and a cigarette. He sipped and puffed leisurely, then thought suddenly: "My orders!" They were in his pocket, typewritten on a carbon sheet. Looking about him and noting that nobody was watching, Hall slowly reached into his pocket, balled up the orders, then popped them in his mouth. Imperceptibly he chewed and sipped and smoked, until the paper, digested at last, went the way of all food.

Soon afterward an infantry officer came to interrogate him and ask for his papers. Hall showed the officer his wallet and his pilot's identification card, but would not answer any questions about his patrol or the location of his aerodrome. An hour later another officer appeared. It was the German pilot whom Hall had tried to shoot down, and who in turn had tried to shoot Hall down. He told Hall through an interpreter that Hall's flight had defeated two German planes. Hall figured that Rickenbacker and Green, where he had failed, had got theirs. The German pilot invited Hall to lunch at his squadron mess, then left. He wanted, he explained, to go out and examine Hall's plane.

The pilot soon returned, and he brought with him a German artillery officer. The two officers were arguing volubly. The artillery officer wanted credit for shooting Hall down! "How is that?" Hall asked him. "You saw what happened to my plane."

"Yes," the artillery officer answered. "But that isn't what brought you down." Then, with animation, he spoke of an artillery shell, a 37-millimeter, the same, he claimed, that he had fired at Hall's plane from his own battery.

Hall remembered the thump in the nose of his plane and the sudden lurch of the Nieuport directly after. Still incredulous, Hall asked to be taken to his plane to see for himself. His captors complied. When he got back to the scene he examined the plane, and there, firmly lodged in his motor and unexploded, was the shell. It had been, miraculously, a dud.

Meanwhile, back at the 94th squadron at Toul on the St. Mihiel sector, Hall's friends thought he had been killed, and they bitterly mourned his loss. "Captain Hall's disappearance that day," wrote Eddie Rickenbacker, "was known to the whole civilized world within twenty-four hours. Widely known to the public as a most gifted author, he was beloved by all American aviators in France as their most daring air-fighter. Every pilot who had had the privilege of his acquaintance burned with a desire to avenge him."

Leland L. Rounds received a letter from Kenneth Marr of the 94th, written on the very day. The only hope was that Hall was a prisoner. "Sad news today," the letter began. "Jimmy Hall with two others attacked five Boche monoplanes seven or eight kilometers in Boche territory and Jimmy went down in a *vrille* during the fight. He redressed at about six or seven hundred metres and was last seen apparently trying to land, so we have high hopes that he is at least a prisoner. . . . Sad news, though, for old Jimmy was a lot more to all of us than a fellow can express on paper."

Bert Hall, an American in a French squadron, made a quick entry in his diary for May 9: "So, another of us goes by the board. He [Hall] was a great soldier. . . . Now he's finished off." Ted Parsons, once an Escadrille Lafayette pilot with Hall, wrote: "Jim was . . . one of the most lovable men in the world and a bubbling well of energy. . . . Quiet and retiring, almost to the point of shyness, with an even disposition and a sunny smile, brave as a lion, Jimmy made his presence felt in every army on every front. . . . There must be a special Providence that watches over chaps like Jim. . . ." On the ninth of May, Hall won another citation from the Commanding General of the French Eighth Army. It read like a posthumous award: *"Brilliant pilote de chasse, modèle de courage et d'entrain qui a abattu récemment un avion ennemi, a trouvé une mort glorieuse dans un combat contre quatre monoplaces dont un a été descendu en flammes."*

Every pilot who had known Hall, Rickenbacker had said, "burned with a desire to avenge him." But the pilot who burned most with that desire was Major Lufbery, and he rose to the occasion fifteen minutes after Rickenbacker had landed and told him the news about Hall. Lufbery had flown with Hall for France, known and loved him, considered him one of his best and most understanding friends. Without saying a word to anyone, Lufbery walked over to his plane. From the set look on his face, his mechanic could see his intention; he helped Luf into his flying suit, strapped him into his seat, and spun the propeller. After a short run, the plane leaped into the air.

For an hour and a half Luf flew over the enemy lines and found nothing; then, noting that he had yet another hour and a half of gasoline, he flew further into German-held territory. North of St. Mihiel, he found his quarry: three enemy single-seaters. He pounced on them, shot one down in flames, and sent the other two scurrying for home. It was the seventeenth victory for Lufbery, his last before that later time in his career when he would abandon his flaming plane and jump to his death. For the present, however, Hall was avenged.

"Pathetic and depressing as was the disappearance of James Norman Hall to all of us," Rickenbacker said, "I am convinced that the memory of him actually did much to account for the coming extraordinary successes of his squadron. Every pilot in his organization that day swore to revenge the greatest individual loss that the American Air Service had yet suffered."

Oblivious to all these eulogies and chivalric revenges, Hall recuperated in a hospital at Pagny-sur-Moselle. He did not even know that the French government, by direction of the President of the Republic, had conferred upon him a great honor: chevalier de la Légion d'honneur. *"A faire preuve,"* the citation read, *"des plus belles qualités de bravoure et de sang-froid."* Hall did not hear a word for two and a half months.

In Boston, Hall's publishers were waiting for the concluding chapters of his manuscript for *High Adventure*. On the sixteenth of April, Hall had sent them a cable: FINAL TEN THOUSAND WORDS POSTED. HALL. Two days later, Houghton Mifflin received a follow-up letter from him: "I'm an awful liar," he wrote. "This batch of manuscript isn't the final one. I have just a little more to add, to round off the story. . . . However, the last two chapters will be posted to you within a week's time, *without fail. . . .*" Patient, as they must be with their authors, the publishers continued to wait, but in vain. They were shocked later to read in the papers that their author had been shot down, relieved to hear he was alive, saddened to learn he was wounded, discouraged to discover he was a prisoner of war. They fashioned a conclusion to the manuscript with an explanatory epilogue and published the book.

From his bed in the officers' ward of the hospital, Hall wrote home on May 17: "I am being well treated," he said. "Am suffering a great deal, but by the time this card reaches you, will be well on the road to recovery. . . . The doctor tells me

I will not be crippled in any way." One month later his ankle was much better, and he could walk with a cane. In July, now in prison camp, his ankle was still weak and sore, but he could walk fairly well with a stick. The doctor promised that the ankle would be as good as new eventually. Hall asked his family about his Houghton Mifflin book. Was it published? And if so, was it selling well?

It had been published in June. The book had sold over 22,000 copies. And the reviews were good. "Written with charm, imagination and humor," said Cleveland. Springfield liked it: ". . . not only a record of thrilling adventures, but it has the literary charm that will place it among the war books that will be read after the war." New York was full of praise: "No one has described with more lively fancy and more sympathetic interpretation the sensations of an aviator who is not without intelligence and imagination."

Hall would have liked to have had this information. But like all the other Allied prisoners at Karlsruhe, in Baden, all his thoughts now turned first to food. And then to escape.

5
Prisoner of War

The German prison camp at Karlsruhe was terrible. The food was soup, mostly hot water with isolated pieces of meat and vegetables, the boredom was inescapable, and so, Hall quickly discovered, was the camp. Looking out from the window of their wooden barracks, he could see the formidable barriers surrounding them. They were three deep: a tangle of barbed wire in front, followed by a high wooden wall, then an electrically charged wire fence topped by more barbed wire. A prisoner could not walk toward the first without being seen by the guards, and at night the whole area was flooded by lights. Tunnels had been tried, but the diggers were caught by ferrets and punished with solitary confinement. If there were shortages of food and drink, there was none of one commodity—time. Hall had started to call it a *thing*, because "it came to have a sort of material reality," and there was nothing to do with it. It hollowed out and bleached each day with grim monotony.

Disgusted and frustrated, Hall would pace up and down

in the barracks or sit on one of the benches outside. One day as he sat daydreaming, yearning for the active life of combat, he was joined by a young English flier. He was Captain Clark. Hall had known him only slightly, but he liked his cut and manner. For a while neither spoke; then, as if in a rush, Clark said: "I'm going to leave Karlsruhe."

"I'll go with you," Hall said, looking down at his healing ankle, "if we are not too old and feeble to be moved by the time the war is over."

"I mean it," the airman said, smiling. "I've been here quite long enough." He breathed deeply, as if he could smell the air of freedom from outside the walls, from as far off as the Swiss border.

"I can smell it too," Hall said, "even against the wind. It's a tantalizing fragrance. I think it will tantalize us for some time to come."

"Never say that." Clark would not entertain the thought. "The Dutch border is only two hundred miles away, roughly speaking, and the Swiss border about half that distance. Give me two weeks outside these walls and . . ."

Hall tried to be more understanding. "I would willingly concede the condition," he agreed, "if the Germans would. But it looks to me as though they meant to keep us here indefinitely. They've made the place puncture-proof."

Clark had made up his mind. "No place is puncture-proof. No, I'm going. I don't know just how, but I'm going."

A few days later they sat again on the same bench, but another had joined the plans. He was an American aviator, Lieutenant "Toots" Wordell, and he had just heard that thirty of the prisoners were going to be transferred to prison camps near Landshut, in Bavaria. He had examined a map of Germany which one of the prisoners had hidden in his bunk. Landshut, Wordell explained, was forty miles from Munich; but if the transfer train should go through Ulm, the Swiss border and freedom would be only eighty miles away.

"Wordell," Clark said, "you and I are going to leave that train somewhere near Ulm."

"Yes," agreed Wordell, "and poor old Hall with his busted ankle can have the pleasure of watching us bound toward Switzerland."

"I will enjoy that sight when I see it," Hall said, not giving either of them much credence.

"You'll see it," Clark added, "unless they handcuff us for the journey and weight us down with balls and chains."

The next day thirty American and English prisoners—Hall, Wordell, and Clark among them—were ordered to the prison commandant's office. There they had to strip and have their clothes and bodies examined for knives, compasses, and maps. Redressed and lined up in files, they were marched under heavy guard to the train station in Karlsruhe. Just before they boarded, Hall noticed from the platform that there was but one passenger coach; it was undoubtedly for the prisoners, and it came at the end of a string of freight cars. This, Hall reasoned, would slow the train down considerably. The prisoners filed down the narrow corridor along the outside of the coach, and in groups of eight spilled into the individual compartments. The guards took up their stations at intervals along the corridor and before the doorway of each compartment. Hall and Clark sat down, Clark next to the window. Wordell was in the next compartment. Hall looked at the window to the outside. It was easily big enough for one to jump out. But, he wondered, is it locked or nailed shut? The train started to pull out of the station. Along the route and as they picked up speed, Hall judged from the position of the sun that they were moving toward the east and southeast. Later they passed signs indicating the towns of Cannstatt and Esslingen, and Hall guessed, remembering the map, that they were heading for Munich. Ulm would be coming up soon. The guards, who had at first bristled with alertness, now from the lulling effect of the train ride seemed to get sleepy. In the compartment, legs stretched out, bodies awry, heads thrown back, everyone seemed to be sleeping. Except two.

The train came to Ulm, stopped for a few minutes, then pulled out, slowly. Suddenly, Hall and Clark stood up. Hall slammed down the window, and Clark jumped out and to the ground. Hall looked out. Wordell, too, had jumped and was rolling down the embankment. The guard, suddenly awake, stared straight ahead, startled and incredulous, then moved. He stumbled through the tangle of legs in front of him to the window; flustered, he could not release the safety of his rifle. Finally, the German lieutenant came in, took the soldier's rifle from him, and started firing it from the window.

Hall watched, utterly absorbed. Despite the fire, Clark, unbelievably, was walking as nonchalantly across the field to the wood beyond as if he were merely taking the air in Hyde Park. "Run, you idiot!" someone screamed at him, but Clark paid no heed. The train chugged along. The guards leaned way out of the windows and angled their rifles to shoot, but Clark had by now strolled into the woods and disappeared. The train stopped, started to back up; then, when it reached the jump-off place of the two escapees, it stopped.

No one, it seemed, had seen Wordell since he had rolled down the embankment. The lieutenant ordered a search party to go out and look for him. The soldiers spread into a semicircle and searched, probing their rifles into the tall grass. The lieutenant, thinking that they were too late to find anything, ordered them back. At that moment, one of the soldiers in returning came upon a drainage pipe partially hidden in the grass. Out of curiosity, the guard parted the weeds with his bayonet, and looked in. There, snuggled up, was Wordell. The guard pulled out his captive, and beating him with the butt end of his rifle, prodded him back to the train. With Wordell in tow, no further search was made for Clark. No more guards or time, apparently, could be spared.

For the rest of the journey there were no more attempts to escape. At Landshut, the prisoners were separated, American from British, and led off to different prison camps. Wordell was further separated from the American group and, Hall guessed, undoubtedly placed in solitary confinement.

At the station the prisoners were lined up in columns and

marched off through the town, up hundreds of feet to the top of a hill, into an old building, tall, narrow, and turreted, with four wings enclosing a courtyard. It was Trausnitz Castle. To Hall as he trudged, and despite the pain in his ankle, the town in its ancient beauty seemed a perfect setting for a Grimm fairy tale. But as the heavy wood and iron double doors closed behind him and the heavy bolts shot across and were locked, he knew that this indeed was no world of dreams or imagination. Days of boredom, ennui, monotony, unrelieved even by work, for they were officers, would hang heavy on his soul, like a millstone about his neck. "Days," he said, "longer than the longest days of childhood." They were days of stillness and slow time.

Hall often passed the time sitting next to the long narrow barred window, sorting the noises from outside: the creak of wheels, the clump of hooves over the cobbles, the chants of vendors extolling their wares—these were occasionally the audible punctuations of silence; but more regularly, like exclamation marks, was the ringing of the church bells all over town, and nearer to earshot, those of St. Martin's Church, which rang every quarter of every hour, measuring out the eternity of his imprisonment. The sounds took shapes like clouds against the blue sky and floated across the trees and over the wall into the isolated castle.

There were three other captive pilots—Robert Browning of Minneapolis, Henry Lewis of Germantown, Pennsylvania, and Charles Codman of Boston, together comprising four of nineteen Americans at the prison. But there were also airmen from the other Allied nations. They were all young, but many, like Hall, had been hurt. Some could only manage with crutches, others with canes; some were badly burned, face and hands, others were scarred from the crease of bullets. All—day and night bombers, fighters and reconnaissance, artillery pilots and observers—exchanged tales of their exploits.

At first, once and sometimes twice a month, the prison commandant would let them take long afternoon walks in the countryside beyond Landshut. Before they left they had to give their word that they would not try to escape, and they would be escorted by only two old reserve guards. Now and again Dr. Jahn, Professor of Modern Languages at the local university, would join the escort and give lessons in German and French to the prisoners. But by the end of summer this privilege ceased.

For some inexplicable reason, roll calls came at sudden unexpected times during the night, and a closer and more attentive guard had been ordered. Some of the prisoners, despite the fact that the Swiss border was two hundred miles away, still escaped and tried to reach freedom. The more attempts were made, the more severe became the restrictions. The prisoners complained to Herr Pastor, the inspector of prison camps in Bavaria, the next time he called. When he came, it was a cool summer morning, with the nip and promise of autumn.

Pastor was slight and meticulously dressed; though friendly, there was about him an air of haughty deference. "Well, gentlemen," he said as they gathered under the trees in the courtyard, "you all look rather moody this morning. What has happened? Have they cut down your bread ration? Or have they forgotten to put vegetables in your soup?"

"They take away our shoes now at evening roll call," Browning said.

Herr Pastor threw up his hands. "You will insist on trying to leave us," he said, "and we don't want to lose you. Your commandant thinks that you will be less eager to go if you know that you must walk to Switzerland in your stocking feet. And I think he is right."

"*Ja! 'Richtig!*' you say," Henry Lewis said; then he changed the subject. "How much longer do you think the war will last?" he asked.

"Not more than two years at the outside." Pastor sat down on one of the wooden benches and adjusted his cravat. "Probably not later than the autumn of 1919."

"You don't meant that!" Lewis could not entertain the thought. "Another year, or perhaps two, of this life? The

last one of us will be dead on your hands of boredom, before
Christmas."

"Nonsense!" Pastor insisted. "Why not look on the bright
side of things? You ought to be jolly glad you're here rather
than at the front. The aerial battles of the past two months
have been on an unprecedented scale. Enormous formations
engaging each other and planes falling like autumn leaves."

Hall thought he would tease the German. "Have we still
the mastery of the air?" he asked.

"Still?" Pastor would not be taken. "My dear chap, don't
be facetious. The Allies are doing what they can, of course,
and I grant that your men have courage. But so have ours,
and our new Fokkers are vastly superior to anything you
have in the air." Pastor rose from his seat. "But I must be
going. I'm taking the midday train for Munich." He looked
over their faces, for the most part disgruntled. "Any com-
missions for me there?"

Hall responded immediately, "Yes," he said. "Could you
by any chance get us some English books?" For some reason,
no one had thought of the idea before, despite the diurnal
grinding boredom.

Several days later a packing case was delivered from Munich. Hall was the first to start to open it. It contained
nearly two hundred books, all in a pile. Hall began to sort
them, examining the title and author of each, and set them
in two separate piles, English and American. Others came to
help him, and noting his interest, voted to make him the librarian then and there.

Hall took his new job seriously. He picked out a room for
the library, made out catalogue cards, rearranged the titles
according to genre and then according to period. At the
bottom of the crate he found three beautiful leather-bound
volumes. One, as he picked it up, fell open by itself. Hall
looked more closely. It was page 368. Then his eyes sparkled
as he read the lines.

Chaucer! Hall continued to read on, utterly absorbed in
his old favorite, oblivious that boredom was or could be
again. Some of the others came into the room to see if the

books were ready for distribution. Hall, vicariously on horseback with the pilgrims on the way to Canterbury, did not hear his friends enter.

"Look at our librarian, you chaps!" Browning exclaimed.

"Well, I'll be damned!" said Codman, who would rather not.

"See here!" Lewis added. "This isn't what we appointed you for!"

Browning stroked his beard. "He's been sitting here reading all morning."

Hall flushed. Caught red-handed, he didn't bother to apologize. He closed the book and began again to restack the books. He placed *The Canterbury Tales* on the table with the others, hoping that no other prisoner would choose it for himself. As if interested, Codman picked it up and flipped through it quickly. "Good old Chaucer!" he said, but he replaced it on the table and picked up another.

"Don't you want *The Canterbury Tales?*" Hall asked.

"Hell, no!" Codman replied. "I had all the Chaucer I wanted at school."

Hall was sorry for him, but happy for himself. Hall thought: "He must have had some Dry-as-Dust as an instructor in Middle English, who placed all the emphasis on obsolete words and spelling and the unfamiliar grammatical inflections." His own instructor, Professor Payne at Grinnell, had taught the class how to read the language in three days and then had made Chaucer converts out of every one of them, letting Chaucer speak and the pilgrims speak for themselves. Hall remembered that college winter's tour of the fourteenth century as one of the most delightful of his life. If, now at the weekly selection of books, no one picked Chaucer, he would begin that tour again by reading only one tale a week, and stretch out the enjoyment for twenty-five weeks.

The next two months passed quickly. Without complaint Hall submitted to the routine of roll call, meal formation, the walk around the prison yard, the placing of shoes in the hallway, the locking in for the night. Chaucer sustained him the while. In October, a new group of captured airmen was brought into the prison. The fliers told wonderful stories of many victories, about towns which in Hall's time were far into the enemy's lines. Then, at the end of the month, a strange thing happened. The entire detachment of prisoners —except for Browning, Codman, Lewis, and Hall—was transferred to the prison camp at Villingen, in the Black Forest. "The lonely four," they now called themselves. The courtyard was silent and empty; the guards, attentive and watchful as ever, paced a measured step along the high platform; and the library, its many literary voices quiet and unheard, was still and vacant.

Hall, however, impelled by the voice of Chaucer speaking to him over the span of five hundred years, remembered that he too was an author, and decided once more to write. If posterity would not read him as it still did Chaucer, perhaps the Hall grandchildren, if ever he had any, would. Sitting in the waning sunlight of shortened days, he looked at the moss-covered walls of the courtyard, walls undoubtedly built when Chaucer himself sat in a courtyard and wrote, wondering if anyone would read him.

A few days later Hall and his friends were moved from the castle to smaller, adjacent quarters, a small two-story brick building. Hall, having appropriated Chaucer for himself, still continued to read through the *Tales*. By the eighth of November he had almost finished the book. It was a Sunday morning. Outside, the wind blew hard and cold against the bare trees and rattled the window shutters. Inside, at the kitchen stove, Browning was stirring a stew of tinned beef, peas, and carrots; Codman lay on his bunk, reading a novel; Lewis sat on a stool, in his shorts, sewing a patch on the seat of his only pair of pants. Hall sat by the window, reading the "Tale of Melibee"; coming to a passage in the prose that he particularly liked, he started to underline it.

Momentarily, Hall lifted his pencil from the page and looked out the window. The guard was being relieved. Hall looked closer. Something unusual was happening out there. Instead of the customary military precision of the change, the guards, holding their rifles devil-may-care over their shoulders, fairly ambled in and out over the gravel path. Quickly, Hall called to Codman: "Come over here, will you, Charlie? See how they're changing the guard this morning!"

As Codman came over to look, one of the guards threw his cap to the ground and stomped on it. Codman smiled. "I've just had a curious hallucination," he said. "I thought I saw that man throw his cap on the ground and stamp on it."

The German lieutenant now came up to the guards and instead of commanding them to their posts along the walls, he seemed to be pleading with them. Lewis and Browning had now come over to the window to watch the proceedings. Browning stroked his beard; he had sworn not to shave it off until he was a free man. "By God," he said, "companions in misery! There's something rotten in Denmark."

"Bavaria," Lewis corrected.

After more persuasion from the lieutenant the guards reluctantly took up their positions along the walls.

The four prisoners, knowing something important had happened to cause the breakdown in discipline, could not immediately fathom the reason, and began to wonder. Hall stopped reading Chaucer—that day, the next day, and the day after that. The captives, endlessly pacing up and down, inside and out of the building, looked for new signs, omens, portents. Herr Capp, one of the German NCO's, spoke of having seen gunfighting in the streets of Munich, only forty miles away. But what did it mean? the Americans asked him. Capp would not stay to answer.

When Herr Pastor came to visit them a few days later, Hall took a quick look at him and was disappointed in what he saw. Pastor seemed not at all disturbed; in fact, he was as aloofly genial as ever. "Well, gentlemen," Pastor said, slightly solicitous, "I hope you are enjoying your solitude these cool autumn days."

"Herr Pastor!" Browning asked excitedly. "What has happened?"

"Happened?" The German was utterly calm. "What makes you think that anything has happened? Do you mean here in the camp?"

"No, no!" Browning pursued him. "Outside. What is taking place at the front?"

Pastor leisurely filled his pipe, tamped the tobacco in the bowl, lit up, inhaled quickly, then let out a long curl of smoke. "Yes, Browning," he said finally, "you're right. Something has happened. I am sure that you'll all be sorry to learn of it." He took another deep puff from his pipe. "The fact is, the war is over. An armistice was signed at eleven o'clock this morning."

"Whaaaaaaat?" the prisoners screamed as one.

Codman was the first to find his speaking voice. His tone was bantering. "And so you've come to bid us farewell," he said. "We'll often think of you, Herr Pastor. You've been very decent to us, and in some ways we have really enjoyed our stay here." He paused. "Well, good-bye," he continued. "Shall we go out at the main gate or that little one on the other side?"

Lewis was more skeptical. "Herr Pastor," he asked, "you're not joking, are you?"

"If there's any joke about it," Pastor answered, "it's on us, not on you. No, the war is finished."

Browning was impatient to act. "Then let's get ready at once." He was jubilant. "Oh, sweet land of liberty! Think of it! In an hour's time we shall be on our way to Paris!"

"Now, Browning," Pastor cautioned, "don't be in too great a hurry. I said that an armistice had been signed—not that there is to be an immediate release of prisoners. It may be several weeks, or even months, before you see Paris again."

The prisoners now begged the inspector to act in their behalf—simply turn his back and they would be gone. Herr Pastor paced up and down, puffing on his pipe. He was unshaken. "No," he said. "It's quite impossible—out of the question. I'm sorry, but you must stay here until you can be released or exchanged in the usual way."

The Americans were adamant, but to no avail. As Pastor turned to leave, Hall threw a question at him. "Won't you think about it?" he pleaded. The inspector agreed that he would and left.

That night Hall and his friends, embittered and frustrated, talked long and hard about their plight. At last, the subject apparently exhausted, they got ready for bed. Hall took out from his shirt pocket a small calendar, and as he had from the beginning of his captivity, from Tuesday, the seventh of May, through June, July, August, September, October, and almost half of November, he x-ed out another day. It was Monday, the eleventh. He wondered as he lay back to sleep how many more weeks and possibly months would be so marked off before their captivity was over.

Codman broke the stillness. "What rotten luck!" he exclaimed.

Hall rose up on one elbow. "What's on your mind, Codman?" he asked.

"I was thinking of those poor devils who died of the flu."

Only a week before they had attended the funeral of a number of French prisoners who had died of influenza in another prison camp near Landshut.

"Lord!" Lewis said. "I hope none of us come down with the flu at this moment."

Codman would have none of it. "Now, Henry," he said, "no forebodings. Remember, tomorrow we shall be on our way to Paris."

The four fell asleep wishing it would be so.

And so it was. The next morning, Herr Pastor returned. It was close on noon. "You may go," the inspector said. "I think it will be best for you to make for the Swiss border, by the way of Munich, Lindau, and Lake Constance."

The prisoners were momentarily struck dumb. Certainly, they must be still dreaming.

"Once you reach Switzerland, of course," Pastor continued matter-of-factly, "you will have no further trouble. I have wired to a friend, an artillery officer, at Lindau. He will meet you at the station there, so be on the lookout for a well-set-up man of thirty-five, with ruddy cheeks, blue eyes, and a small blond moustache. He wears a captain's uniform."

"And we may go *now*?" Hall asked, seeking reassurance.

"And do you mean that we are to go *by train*?" Browning was still unbelieving.

"You don't want to *walk* to Switzerland, do you?" The inspector smiled. "There is a train for Munich at twelve thirty. You will have to stop there for the night and leave for Lindau in the morning. If you succeed in getting through, you will be at Romanshorn, in Switzerland, before dark tomorrow evening. Remember, this is an escape. . . ."

"Theoretically," Hall commented.

"No, actually." The inspector was serious. "I have no right to let you go and I am doing so on my own authority. The commandant is strongly opposed to the idea, and I have promised to take whatever blame may be attached in the event that you are recaptured. So, whatever you do, don't be so foolish as to let that happen. You might make it very awkward for me. Be circumspect and very self-effacing during the journey. With the revolution on in Bavaria, if you have your wits about you, you should be able to get through. Everything is topsy-turvy just now."

The four could not get ready to leave fast enough. Hall picked up his few belongings, then stopped off at the prison library. "How about taking some books along?" he called to the others.

"Oh, to hell with the books!" said Browning.

"Leave them for Capp," Codman chorused.

As he scanned the stacks Hall felt as if he were leaving behind old friends. All except one. He slipped Chaucer's *The Canterbury Tales* into his coat pocket.

The prisoners said good-bye quickly to Capp, who could not believe what was happening. They walked through the great gate, open at last, to where Pastor waited for them outside. He had already bought their train tickets for them. They shook his hand warmly and marched off down the hill. Exhilarated, they wanted to skip through town, shouting, but they forcefully restrained their enthusiasm and kept their composure—as Pastor had requested—circumspect. At the station they had to wait only ten minutes for the train, then took a second-class compartment. They took their seats as if Americans traveled every day on trains in Bavaria. Browning stroked his beard delightedly, as if off for a holiday; Lewis lowered his head as if in meditation; Codman studied a timetable. Hall opened his

Chaucer and started to read; momentarily, he looked up to watch a military policeman rush by, but he hadn't even noticed them.

At Munich, they debarked and went immediately to a nearby hotel. Walking through the lobby, they decided that Codman, whose German was the best of the four, would speak for all of them.

Codman, as casual as a visiting salesman, asked for a room for four. *"Bitte schön?"* the clerk said; he seemed overcome by the request. Codman repeated. He wanted a room for four, and, he added, dinner served in the room at once. *"Ja wohl, Hauptmann, nur ein en Augenblick,"* the clerk answered. The four were led up to their room, and a few minutes later they were served their food and drink.

Anxious and fearful, the escapees throughout the rest of the day and that night expected a knock on the door that would reveal uniformed guards to march them back to prison. The anxiety, however, was groundless. They slept the night undisturbed, and undisturbed they boarded the train for Lindau the next morning. Late that afternoon they arrived and waited at the station for Pastor's captain friend to appear.

As the crowd broke and swept off through the station, Hall noticed a group of German officers off to one side. One of them left the group and came over to where they waited. Hall gave him a quick once-over. Well-built, with blue eyes, blond moustache, ruddy cheeks, he clearly matched Pastor's description. He came up to them and bowed and spoke in English: "You wish to go to Switzerland, messieurs?" Hall nodded. "In that case," the captain continued, "perhaps I can be of service to you. Will you follow me, please?"

As they followed the officer out of the station, Browning whispered to Hall. "If this is a dream," he said, "let me dream on." They came out to the street to a waterfront. "Look! Lake Constance! Oh, noble sight!" Browning could contain himself no longer.

Hall, less vocal, but intently absorbing the experience, tingled with anxiety. Standing back along the quay, he looked. The expanse of the lake, shimmering and profound, gave on the western side to the thrusting peaks of the Alps, lonely, snow-capped, imperious, and promising freedom. In the fore-front, at one of the piers, a boat was docked. It was taking on passengers.

The voice of the German captain broke the absorption. "There is your boat, gentlemen," he said, "but I can't promise that you will be allowed to cross in her. However, make the attempt. Walk aboard, and, if you are merely turned back, there is still another possibility. You can go by land around the end of the lake. That might be a risky proceeding, but if you have to try it, I will do what I can to help you." He paused, then looked directly at them. "Of course," he added, "if you are arrested here—well, in that case there is nothing more to be done. You will understand that I can hardly be your advo-cate."

They shook hands and quickly parted. The four Americans walked to the landing and up the gangplank. They passed two police officers, who looked them up and down but did not stop them. As they reached the deck, Hall sighed, relieved they were this far, and led the group to a far table in the lounge. Shortly the boat tooted a farewell, backed from the pier, and turned toward Switzerland. Hall looked out a porthole near the table. The German officer was walking toward the town, more, Hall thought, like a relative than a stranger and a recent enemy.

But the pleasant thoughts did not last. At that moment one of the steamer officers entered the lounge and walked directly to their table. He was a short, stout man, and his initial behav-ior upset them. He arched his eyebrows, looking this way and that quickly and abruptly, as if he were a bird dog on the prowl. He looked strange, wearing a long moustache, twisted and angled at the ends, and a small Vandyke beard. But as he spoke, the escapees began to relax. The officer's manner be-came immediately ingratiating and friendly. At first he spoke in German, but when they announced that they were Ameri-cans, he, delighted at the discovery, switched to French and offered them cigars.

"*J'aime les Américains,*" he said. They lit their cigars. "*J'aime aussi les Allemands et les Françaises. J'aime tout le monde!*" He twirled the tips of his moustache and stroked his beard. *"Moustache—Allemande. Barbe—Française."* There was, he suggested, no mistaking his neutrality.

Soon the boat came to the slip on the other side of the lake. It was Romanshorn. Marking the way in were two great stone lions; they sat on the tops of the piers at either side, their heads proud and defiant; like protectors, Hall thought, to those who would escape to their neutral shores. And so it seemed to all four of them—until they were taken by the police soon after they debarked.

After leaving the ship, they had gone directly to a hotel close to the waterfront. Once in the room, Hall came down with a migraine headache so painful he had to go to bed at once. He had known these blinding pains before, and they always came with periods of heightened emotional tension and anxiety. Lewis, Codman, and Browning had gone out to look over the town. When they returned several hours later, Hall was still asleep. Codman shook him awake, and made a dramatic announcement. "We have been placed under arrest by the military authorities," he said.

Hall didn't care. "If going back to Germany will take this terrible headache away," he said, "I would be glad to go." Then he promptly fell back on the bed and went back to sleep.

The next morning Hall's suffering had abated. As Codman had said, they were indeed under arrest. Outside in the hall, a Swiss soldier stood guard before the door to their room. After breakfast an officer appeared. "Why?" they asked him. "Why have we been placed under arrest?"

"You have arrived from Germany in a very irregular manner," he answered. "We received no word about your arrival, either from the Central or Allied Powers. We have no choice but to take you into custody."

"But we've escaped," Browning said. "We made an escape de luxe. We traveled by train instead of walking to the border, and crossed the lake by steamer instead of swimming. Surely you don't object to that, do you?"

The officer was not impressed. The whole affair was completely irregular. None of the regulations covered such a case.

Finally, however, he agreed to call the American authorities at Bern, and walked out the door.

Thirty minutes later he returned. He had been directed, he said, to take them to Bern.

That evening they had dinner at the Hotel Bellevue in Bern. Two days later they were in Paris, looking for old friends at the old haunts. Hall sat in Henry's, a clean, well-lighted place, sipping cognac. It was a crisp November day. Hall had walked about the streets aimlessly, taking in the sights, sounds, smells. German cannons stood at the Place de la Concorde and on either side of the Champs d'Élysées. Children climbed up their long barrels and, squealing, slid down them to the ground. Mothers and fathers laughed and helped the children up the barrels once more. The trees were bare, their multicolored leaves lay on the ground, until, suddenly, a wind would stir and swirl them up and carry them further down the street. As he sat, stroking the stem of his glass between his fingers, Hall watched the faces of the people. Everywhere he looked, they were happy. Despite this flowering gaiety, he somehow felt at the root a strange melancholy penetrating his being. He must get away from it, by himself, completely by himself. He would like, he thought, one more flight over the lines. But how, he asked himself, could such a request be honored? Dr. Gros at his Paris headquarters would undoubtedly recommend that he rejoin the 94th, his old squadron, now on duty in Germany with the Army of Occupation. Hall did not want that. Now that the war was over, he knew he did not want any more operational flying.

As it turned out, Gros had no such plans for Hall. As a matter of fact, he wanted him for a totally different assignment: to write the official history of the Lafayette Flying Corps. To help him in the project, Gros had found another writer, like Hall a published author, and furthermore a contributor like Hall to the *Atlantic Monthly*. Hall had never heard of the other officer before. His name was Nordhoff, Lieutenant Charles B. Nordhoff. Hall agreed to the project but he asked Gros for help in a more immediate and pressing matter. Could the doctor get him an appointment with General Patrick, Chief of the

U. S. Air Service, on a personal matter? Gros picked up his phone and arranged a meeting.

The next day Hall was presented to General Patrick. "Yes? What is it?" the general asked, brusque but not unpleasant.

"General Patrick," Hall started on his rehearsed presentation. "I have a somewhat unusual request to make. I am Captain Hall. I was in the Escadrille Lafayette, I was in the 94th, I was shot down, I was a prisoner for five and a half months."

"Yes? . . . And?" The general was beginning to get impatient.

"Sir, I would like permission to fly over the lines once more."

"Why do you wish to make this flight?"

"Solely for my own pleasure, if it may be called pleasure," Hall replied. "It will satisfy a need I can scarcely define if I may fly over the old front once more, and for the last time."

General Patrick had never heard such a request before. "How long do you expect to be gone?"

"Four or five days. A week at the most, unless I should be held up by bad weather."

The general took a pad of paper, wrote quickly and briefly, tore off the page and handed it to Hall. "Good luck," he said. "Don't get yourself killed now that the war is over."

Hall thanked him, saluted, about-faced, and left. He read the note on the paper. It was an order to the operations officer of the American Aviation Depot at Orly Field in Paris to provide Captain J. N. Hall with a plane for a "special mission."

For two weeks the weather did not clear well enough for Hall to make the flight. Each time he checked in at the depot, rain or snow turned him back from his plan. Christmas passed and New Year's; Hall fearful lest his orders be changed and that he would be sent home with thousands of troops leaving France every day, decided not to wait any longer for a good day. On a cold January morning he went back out to Orly. There was a heavy cloud ceiling, but it was high and looked as if it would clear before noon.

"Same old luck," said the operations officer. "It will be snowing before evening."

Hall was determined. "It doesn't matter," he said. "I'm going to chance it. If it gets too thick I'll land somewhere on the way."

A lieutenant, one of the Orly test pilots, took Hall out to the hangars. They were jammed, wing to wing, and tail to nose, with Spads, brand new and fresh from the factories. "Take your pick," the lieutenant said. "We've got them to burn, now." Hall let the test pilot select one of the planes for him and they wheeled it—it was one of the 180 hp Spads—onto the ramp. Hall climbed in, started the engine, and in three minutes was in the air, circling in climbing turns high over Paris.

Hall was totally alive to every moment of the flight. It was one he wanted to remember for the rest of his life. After taking off, he left Orly and Paris far below in the distance, and headed toward the old front. Following the Marne, he flew over the ruins of the Souain. When he had been stationed on the Champagne front with the Lafayette squadron, he had flown over that village many times; it marked the beginning of the lines. Instinctively and as of old, Hall's senses sharpened for combat. He swung his eyes from right to left, up and down, front to back, looking for enemy planes, waiting for the sudden crack of antiaircraft or machine-gun fire. But stillness was all. The sky was clear, empty, a playground for angels. And below, there appeared the lines of trenches, dark ugly cuts and slashes across the face of the earth, festering quietly. For Hall, it was the abomination of desolation. He listened to the throbbing of his engine, the only sound; it and the plane were the sole reminder of his mortality, which so often during the war had come to its exit only to be turned back again.

Hall looked down at the lines and remembered, his thoughts crowded with ghosts. His British soldier friends—McDonald, Gadd, Harrison, Powell—dead, his American pilot friends—McCudden, Ball, Chapman, Rockwell, McConnell, Lufbery, MacMonagle—dead. Hall felt completely alone, lonely, and abandoned.

At four thousand feet Hall skirted the base of a cloud bank, passed over the remains of the town of Sommepy, and turned west in a wide semicircle over Rheims. Then, turning east again, he flew over the line of trenches toward the Argonne, to Bethoniville, where in the winter of 1917 a crack German anti-aircraft battery could bracket a plane overhead with fearful precision; then he continued to Dontrier, where he had once watched a French three-seater plane in flames, the rear gunner firing all the way down, until, at one thousand feet, the gunner jumped from the plane to his death below. Over the town of Cornay Hall found a hole in the ceiling and climbed through it to the pure sunlight above. With the sun at his back he chased the shadow of his plane up and down the peaks of the clouds, into the deep valleys and up the precipitous walls, de-lighting in every turn and bank, in every plunge and climb, exhilarating to the play of light and shadow. Then the motor sputtered and started to misfire. Hall looked at his gas gauge. It showed empty. He reached over and turned on his auxiliary tank, then headed down to find a place for an emergency land-ing. As of old his luck held, and he found an abandoned air-field. He landed and taxied up to a hangar, where, suprisingly, he found a group of soldiers sitting around a charcoal fire. As Hall climbed out of his plane, one of the soldiers said to the others: *"Voilà le dernier pilote de la guerre!"* Then the soldier added: *"Il n'y en aura plus."*

After refueling and on the way back to Paris, Hall reflected on the words of the French soldier. And after he landed at Orly and thanked the operations officer for having selected a good plane, the words still lingered in his thoughts. The poilu had been prophetic. Hall knew he would indeed be, as far as he was concerned, *"le dernier pilote de la guerre."* He had had enough of civilization and its attendant horrors. He must go somewhere, perhaps somewhere even as far as the South Seas, there to "build a little area of peace, decency and order" around his life.

A few days later Hall reported to the office of Dr. Gros in Paris to start collecting materials for the official history of the Lafayette Flying Corps. Hall had grown curious about his col-laborator, Charles Nordhoff, whom he had not yet met and asked Dr. Gros about him. "He was a little after your time in the aviation schools," Gros said. "When he was breveted he was sent to the French Pursuit Squadron, Spad 99—the Flying Horse Squadron. After you were all transferred to U. S. Aviation, Nordhoff, to his great disgust, was taken from the front and attached to the Historical Section of the Air Service. At my request he has been transferred to work on the L.F.C. History. You two will be the editors of the History. . . ."

They then went into the next room to meet Hall's collaborator. When Gros introduced Nordhoff to Hall, Nordhoff was courteous but aloof and slightly imperious. He stood tall and ramrod-straight, like a Prussian; his blond hair and piercingly blue eyes only added to that impression. When Gros told Nordhoff that Hall was from Iowa, that fact only increased Nordhoff's seeming disdain for what was obviously a midwestern "hayseed."

"California," Nordhoff said to Hall, "is lousy with Iowans."

Hall protested the use of the word "lousy."

"Iowans are rootless people," Nordhoff continued. "They don't belong anywhere."

Hall was incensed. "It's the fault of your so-called 'native sons,'" he replied. "Your Chambers of Commerce spend all their time trying to persuade Middle Westerners to settle in California. You send out special trains filled with exhibits of your products: oranges, lemons, figs, English walnuts, and the like. You boast about your perfect climate. You beg, wheedle, and cajole our people to move to California, and when they do, you resent their coming. If you don't want them, why don't you stop advertising your wonderful Golden State?"

Nordhoff would not be put down. "All Iowans are 'from,'" he said. "You are yourself." He looked directly at Hall, as if he had sniffed a quarry. "All you have to boast about," he continued to turn the screw, "is being 'from' Iowa."

Later Hall, when he had left Nordhoff's decidedly unpleasant company, asked Dr. Gros: "How am I supposed to work with this man?"

Hall would find out, but first it would take a leave back home, and a long spell of work at Martha's Vineyard before a friendship could be started and a partnership begun that would last for twenty-eight years.

6

The Dangerous Element

At the end of February, 1919, Hall returned to the United States. Early in March, he was back in Colfax. But soon after his return to both, he was bitterly disappointed in what he found—in America, in the Middle West, in Iowa, even in Colfax. The changes which had taken place were too fast, too radical, too sudden. He had hoped to return to a life basically unchanged from what he had known as a boy and as a youth; consequently, he was unprepared for what had happened. The war had scarred the beloved countries of Europe; now peace was doing the same at home, not with shells and trenches, but with roads and motorcars. For Hall, the automobile became the symbol of this change, and he grew to hate it with such intensity that he never learned to drive one. To defend such an extreme view he wrote: "I love change only in its aspect of slow and cautious advancement and slow and imperceptible decay. And I dislike change in manners, customs and habits of thought as much as I do in material aspects."

And coupled to the scarring of the land were the men to blame for it, the land developers, the promoters, the speculators. Hall met one of them soon after he came home. "I've made ten thousand dollars today," the man told him happily; "I bought two farms near here and sold them again." The news made Hall sick. Although not a farmer nor a businessman, he did know enough about the land to realize that Iowa farms were not worth five or six hundred dollars an acre. As always at such times, when the world was too much with him, Hall went to his cupboard of memory, there to draw from the past sustenance for the present and nourishment for the future.

Dressed in old tweed pants, a wool pullover sweater, and worn walking shoes, he climbed the hill behind the house, Standpipe Hill, near whose summit the Hall house had stood for forty years. He came to the linden tree at the top of the hill and sat at its base. To the north he looked down to the wooded bottom lands of the Skunk River and beyond to the west to the endless miles of farmland, then back along the river, following its dips and turns, to the railroad track which followed the river and edged its hills; he smelled the damp earth, not yet burgeoning with its promise of spring; he listened for the meadowlark, but presently he heard the whistle of the train, eastbound, echoing among the hills, dropping by quarter tones as the train roared down the five miles of the Middleton grade. Hall pulled thumb and forefinger along the length of his broken nose, then slowly pinched his upper lip, feeling his moustache. His flesh tingled. Trains always did that to him, as far back as he could remember. At night as a boy, alone in his bed, he would hear the whistle of the Rocky Mountain Limited—"The Midnight Flier," and sometimes it would bring him to his knees, his skin prickled with gooseflesh, his heart pounding with excitement. How he had always ached to be on board! And sometimes he would be. Once he had arranged with accomplices to ride late at night the cowcatcher of Old Number Six to Grinnell.

Hall had loved the railroad station, and whenever he played truant from school it was always to go there, to indulge his "worship of trains and everything and everyone connected with them." And like all boys he sometimes got into trouble.

As is often the case with young boys ten years old the young-ster seeks the companionship of older boys, but he is usually rebuffed, unless he can somehow prove himself by deed worthy of that higher society. For Norman Hall and his pal Buller Sharpe, that chance came on the night of Halloween. Cheep Somers was the leader of the older group. He was the best all-round athlete of his age in Colfax and the young boys idol-ized him, sought his approbation quicker than that of their fathers. That night, under Cheep's leadership, the boys had moved a wooden cigar-store Indian to the front porch of the Methodist minister's house, taken the clapper from the bell of the schoolhouse, and hauled a mobile photographic studio to the cemetery. Hall and Buller tagged along with their elders, helping unobtrusively whenever they could. Now the older boys paused to think of what to do next.

"I'll tell you what!" Somers said, after considering various alternatives. "We'll go out to old Go-Quick Smith's farm and run his spring wagon down the hill into Indian Creek."

This suggestion struck a walled opposition of No's. If there was one man feared by all it was Go-Quick Smith, who had a wide reputation for cruelty. Not one of Somers' circle wanted any part of the plan except for the two youngsters on the edge of that circle, Hall and Buller, who thought the idea was bril-liant.

"Come on, Buller," said Somers. "You and Jimmy 'n' I'll go. These babies can run home to their mothers."

It was close to nine o'clock. The moon, skirting along the backs of clouds, shed a half-light down upon them. The three boys moved off. They passed the Wilson farm on the dirt road, then came to a wide stretch of sloping pasture. It was bottom land, planted with cottonwoods and willow trees, and through it looped and curled Indian Creek. Smith's cattle barns, glis-tening in the light, stood on the far edge; the house, command-ing the top of the rise, seemed at least a half mile away. The road grew steeper, and the banks rose higher on either side, offering excellent cover. When they came closer to the Smith house, Hall could see a faint light burning in the kitchen. Off to the side of the house and near the barn stood the spring wagon. They quietly hurried to it.

Somers spoke softly, giving directions. "Buller," he said, "you and Jimmy push from behind; I'll take the tongue." They took their places. "Don't make no noise," Cheep cautioned. "We'll be safe as soon as we get to the road; then we'll dump his old wagon off the bank at the end of the bridge. . . . I guess that'll show him whether we're afraid of him or not!"

The spring wagon pushed easily, but the wheels crunched noisily over the frosted ground. Young Hall winced at the sound, then quickly turned to see if there was any reaction from inside the house. There was not. Down the steep road, Hall and Sharpe had to hold hard against the back of the wagon; then, trying to brake it, they thrust their legs forward and under, letting themselves be dragged.

"Ain't you glad we came, Jimmy?" Sharpe said happily. "Think of all those babies that backed out! I guess we're goin' to pay old Smith back, all right!"

Hall had no chance to answer. Suddenly, against the quiet of the night, a voice cracked, loud and angry. It was Smith, and he was bolting from the kitchen door, shaking his fist. At once, in animal terror, Sharpe and Somers abandoned the wagon and fled; Hall, cold with fright, his loins drained hollow by fear, shot to the front of the wagon and ran for his life. The wagon, on its own, clattered and bounced down the hill. Behind the wagon came the sound of feet quickly pounding in pursuit.

Inscrutably, instead of climbing the banks and heading for the woods, Hall kept to the road. He turned his head to look behind him. The wagon started to careen off the road, then crashed and splintered against the bank. Smith now was not fifty feet away. Hall felt his heart pounding, his mouth dry. He came to the bottom of the hill, ran across the bridge over Indian Creek, turned sharply off the road, and rushed down the meadow toward Smith's cattle barns. He did not look behind him. Presently he came to a barn door opened wide and rushed through it to the darkness inside. Exhausted, he felt along the wall and floor, stumbled, and fell sideways into a pile of grain. From the smell and feel of the grain in his fingers he knew he had fallen into an oats bin, and he burrowed deeply to disappear in it. At last he lay still, deep in the grain, biting his lower lip, breathing hard, feeling hot sharp stabs in his rib cage.

After what seemed to him a long time, Hall slowly poked his head out through the pile of oats. Listening, he could only hear from the other side of the barn the sound of cattle munching hay. More brave, he now sat up straight and started to pick the grain and hay out of his hair. Suddenly, close from the side and against the quiet came a small scratching noise. Hall turned his head and saw the flame from a match. The light revealed only the face and hands, but they were enough. Hall shook with terror. Smith did not say a word; he simply stood there, interminably, it seemed, breathing heavily. At last he reached out, grabbed Hall by the collar, lifted him up, and shook him at arm's length like an old coat.

Smith brought Hall to the house. "The wagon's smashed," he said to his wife as they came into the kitchen. "The wagon's smashed," he repeated. It had turned over on one side and broken some spokes on one wheel, Hall had noted on the way to the house. Mrs. Smith did not answer her husband; she continued with her darning of a sock. Smith sat Hall hard down onto a wooden chair. Terrified, Hall stared straight ahead across the room to a cabinet of shelves and drawers.

Go-Quick Smith walked across the kitchen to the cabinet, opened one of the drawers, and pulled out a long length of rope. He cut the rope into short pieces, then went over to where Hall sat. He yanked Hall up bolt upright in the chair, then with the pieces of cord he tied Hall's feet together and his hands behind his back. Then picking Hall up like a sack of potatoes, he slung him across his shoulder and turned toward the door. As Smith started out, his wife called to him: "Where are you goin'?"

"To drown this little *pfeist* in the water tank—that's where!"

At that announcement Hall fainted dead away. When he came to some time later, Mrs. Smith had propped him up from the floor and was trying to get him to drink from a tin cup. "You're goin' too fur," Mrs. Smith was saying to her husband. "They'll have the law on ye one of these days."

Unshaken by these words, Smith stood nearby with his arms folded and looked down at Hall. "Stand him up!" he commanded his wife.

Mrs. Smith tried to lift Hall up, but his legs would not support him. "Stand up, young-un!" she ordered Hall. "He ain't goin' to drown ye."

Finally believing, Hall found his strength, stood up, and started for the door.

"Now git home!" Mrs. Smith shouted to him. "An' don't you never come snoopin' 'round here agin! An' don't you go blabbin' that he was goin' to drown ye, or like enough he will!"

Smith followed immediately upon his wife's admonition, but did not choose to speak to the boy. "Let me ketch him blabbin'," he said to his wife, "and I'll do worse than drown him! I'll take him across my knee and break his little back!"

The words were like a spur into the side of a colt. Hall bolted from the doorway and ran through the night for home. When at last he reached the bottom of Standpipe Hill he stopped, rested briefly, and climbed slowly up the hill to his house.

On June 15, 1904, when he was seventeen years old, Hall was graduated from Colfax High School, one of twelve members of the graduating class. The class colors were pink and blue; the flower, a pink rose; the motto: "Pluck is luck." And the thirteenth item on the graduation order of events that Wednesday night at the Methodist Church was "The Eighth Wonder," an address to be given by J. Norman Hall.

It was a ten-minute speech on the nineteenth century and Hall had memorized it word for word, for he hated to give speeches. It was an agony for him. As he sat on the platform, banked high on either side with flowers, he nervously ran over in his mind the introductory words, waiting for his turn after Hazel Swihart, who was presently reciting a poem called "Modern Lady with the Lamp." Hall envied Hazel her easeful assurance and aplomb. He looked down over the edge of the stage, trying to locate his younger brother Harvey, who, his mother had assured him, would be far back in the audience where he could not tease him.

Hazel Swihart finished her recitation and took her seat. Mr. Mischler, the principal, introduced the next speaker. "The next oration," he said, adjusting his spectacles, "is by Norman Hall. His subject is, 'The Eighth Wonder of the World: The Nineteenth Century.' "

Hall walked to the podium. He looked out over the audience: the church was full of people. Then he settled his eyes on the first row of pews: there, up front, stiff-backed against the bench with head up and grinning, was Harvey. Norman was shaken with an attack of diffidence. Would he remember his speech? Slowly, tentatively, he began:

> One hundred years ago the morning broke, and in the light of a dawning era, the remnants of once-mighty hosts: Ignorance, Bigotry, and Superstition, were seen scattering in full retreat toward the Night of the Past.

He looked down at Harvey. Still grinning, his younger brother seemed to be asking him a question with his laughing eyes: "Yes? . . . And then?" Hall lifted his eyes and looked for someone else to settle on. He found Mr. Logsten, the church janitor, standing alone in the back, and by talking directly to him he finished the speech.

For his accomplishment, Hall's father rewarded him with a week's visit to the St. Louis Exposition. The gift meant that Harvey would have to take over the graduate's chores, especially the milking of Hattie, the cow. Before he left, Hall could not resist getting back at Harvey, this time with a variation of a woodshed poem that Harvey liked to tease him about. Harvey was sitting on the back porch, black with misery and self-pity over what had befallen him. Hall tossed the quatrain over his shoulder at his brother and ran:

> *Look to the northward, Harvey!*
> *The dear old barn is there.*
> *All next week you can do my chores*
> *While I am at the Fair.*

When he returned from St. Louis, Hall found a full-time job in H. G. Gould's clothing store. During his last two years in high school he had worked there during the evenings, Saturdays, and the summer vacations. Now he was going back to the store for yet another summer, but this time, it seemed, it would be forever. It was his job. He was lucky, everybody told him, "to be in the clothing business." And furthermore, Hall well knew, his father wanted him to be a businessman.

The Gould store was located on Main Street in the Craigin block. Naturally shy, Hall at first could not bring himself to wait on the customers; rather, he would keep his back turned to the door and start to dust the shirt and collar boxes; or, head bent, he would sweep out the store; or, in winter, he would tend the pot-bellied stove in the back of the store. Twice he had screwed up enough courage and had tried to greet a customer, but each time the patron had asked for one of the Davis boys, John or Billy, who managed the store.

Once, when a farmer's wife came in to make a purchase for one of her children, Billy said to Hall: "There's Mrs. Kelly, Jimmie. Go see what she wants."

Hall did and he tried to play the part of a salesman. "Is there something, Mrs. Kelly?" he asked her in his most polite imitation of the Davis boys.

Mrs. Kelly would have none of his salesmanship. She folded her arms across her big bosom and glowered down at him. "I want to see Billy!" she said with finality. Hall slunk back to his duster, nursing an inferiority complex already badly wounded by other customers. From such encounters he was beginning to wonder if he was good for anything.

On yet another day another customer came into the store, and because the Davis boys were busy, Hall had to wait on him. Norman expected the usual rebuff, but instead the man greeted him cordially. He wanted, he said, to see some winter coats. Hall did not know how to react to the man's easy affability. "Well," the customer asked, "what's the matter? Haven't you got any winter coats?"

"Oh, yes, sir!" Hall answered, flustered, but beginning to gain some composure. Hall led the man to the rack holding the overcoats.

The customer tried on one of the coats. Once more Hall

tried to play the part of a salesman. "That will wear like iron," he said to the man.

"It will?" the customer said incredulously. "Iron gets rusty when exposed to the weather. Do you mean this coat will get rusty too?"

"Oh, no! I don't mean that." Hall looked for a way out. "I mean . . ." But he could not find a way out.

"You mean that you don't know what you mean." The man was relentless. "Choose your words more carefully, young man. And don't make such absurd remarks to your customers. But no matter . . ." He began to change his tone, then added, smiling, "I can see that it's a good coat. How much is it?"

"Twenty-two dollars," Hall answered, still not believing he was making a sale.

The man pulled out his wallet and counted out two tens and two one-dollar bills. "Take off the tags," he said. "I'll wear the coat."

After the customer had left the store, the owner, Mr. H. G. Gould, who had come in and had gone to the back of the store to talk with the Davis boys, came forward and offered his hand in congratulations. "That's the way to do business, Jimmie," he said; then he turned to one of the managers and said: "Billy, we'll make a clerk of him yet."

Despite the success of a sale at last, Hall still did not leap at the chance to wait on a customer. As a matter of fact what he enjoyed most in the store was not a sale at all. It was the singing of the Davis boys. Of Welsh extraction, they sang beautifully in harmony together; and Hall, whenever a fourth could be found for bass, loved to join in as second tenor, with John's first tenor and Billy's baritone. But for two years Hall fought his shyness with customers. And finally won the battle.

On a blustery day in the winter of 1906, Hall was alone in the store, the Davis boys having gone to Des Moines for the day. He was opening a crate of fleece-lined underwear, and he had just set down the crowbar when Mr. H. G. Gould, the owner, came in, greeted Hall, and went over to the hot-air register to sit down. Hall watched the big man out of the corner of his eye, as he pulled out a cigar and picked up the Des

Moines newspaper. Hall loved to watch the ritual Mr. Gould followed before he smoked a cigar. It was always the same. Mr. Gould leaned back, squeezed his fat hand into his pants pocket, and pulled out a penknife; then, meticulously, he held the cigar out from his paunch, snipped off the end of the cigar, and replaced the knife in his pocket. Slowly and carefully, he struck a wooden match, held it below and slightly away from the end of the cigar, and puffed. Then he blew out the smoke, holding the cigar out where he could admire it. To Hall, as he looked up from tagging the underwear, it seemed like the ultimate in smoking enjoyment.

Ten minutes later, Mr. Gould put down his paper, then, resettling himself in the chair, he called to Hall. "Norman," he said, "knock off a bit. Want to have a little talk with you. Come over here and sit down."

Hall got up, walked over to the chair on the other side of the register, and sat down. "Been lookin' around up north," Mr. Gould said. "Met a man in Belle Fourche, South Dakota. He's sellin' out his clothing business and goin' to California. Good many Iowa people doin' the same thing. Lot of sissies! Can't stand Iowa winters." Disgustedly, he spat down into the register.

Mr. Gould continued. "What'll they do out in California— sit around in the sun all day, whittlin' sticks? They're no good, that kind of people. Don't belong in Iowa. Didn't belong in the first place. No pioneer blood in *their* veins. Good riddance if they *all* go to California. Get 'em cleared out and we'll have Iowa the way it ought to be."

Hall was disturbed. He could not understand why Mr. Gould was telling him all this, unless it was that the owner just felt like talking, and to anybody. "I bought that clothing store in Belle Fourche." Then Mr. Gould added: "How would you like to run it for me?"

Hall was struck as if by a blow. Breathless, he could only stare. Without doubt, this offer was beyond his most fervent aspirations as a businessman. His father certainly would be proud, Hall thought, if one of his sons became the manager of his own store.

"John and Billy"—Mr. Gould did not wait for an answer—"tell me you're going to be a good clothing salesman. I like to give a young fellow a start in life, and here's yours if you want it."

The job, Mr. Gould said, would start next fall, when the old owner would be leaving for California. Hall would take over the store then, after he had received further training in management from the Davis boys. Hall looked at the steadily increasing ash at the end of Mr. Gould's cigar and wondered when it would fall. The owner resumed his offer. "I'm not as young as I was, Norman," he confessed. "Before long I'll want to take things easier. Not have so many irons in the fire. Well, if you dig in and work hard and save your money, you'll end up being proprietor of that store. I'll sell out to you on terms you'll be able to meet without any trouble. You'll be wanting to get married a few years from now. And there you'll be, settled for life, with a nice thrivin' business in a fine little town. How does that strike you as an end to work toward?"

Hall was too taken aback by the offer to give an immediate reply. He wanted time to think about it. Weeks went by and spring came before he could give his decision. His father, his friends Buller and Preacher, the Davis boys—all recommended that he accept the offer as one in a lifetime. For Hall, the opportunity "as an end to work toward" seemed too much like an end, as something too final, so close was it to the beginning of his life—like the period at the end of one sentence of a story, the book never to be finished.

Unable to decide, Hall climbed to the top of his hill. There, alone, he felt confident, he could make up his mind. The hepaticas were in bloom, and their full deep scent, coupled with the full-throated call of the meadowlark and the full bright view of the grazing meadows and the fields where the oats, wheat, and rye grew, formed a vision, a total vision of the natural life that he wanted to live. These vistas, these "baths of solitude," waited for the man—the writer, not the businessman—who wanted to pay the price for them.

"Life was too precious to be spent in a clothing store," Norman decided. He would go to college, Grinnell, of course, and work his way through. The adventure that was his life could not stop with a period at the end of the first sentence.

At Grinnell, Hall signed up for courses in Mathematics, Political Science, Latin, and English; but, typically, although the reading assignments for the last three courses were considerable, Hall spent most of his time reading what was not assigned, usually from the small dark blue book that he could carry in his coat pocket, *The Oxford Book of English Verse*. He had not yet learned to discipline his time. Luckily for Hall, he met a professor who changed his ways as a student.

Professor Charles E. Payne made an impression on Hall that lasted a lifetime. In the fall of 1906 the professor had come to Grinnell from Terre Haute, Indiana, to be an instructor in history. He had lost both legs from the knees down in a train wreck and had to walk with the help of artificial legs; but, despite his handicap, he was tough and vigorous. He also lived in Chapin House, in the room at the head of the stairs, and Hall would often see him coming and going from class. Because of his diffidence Hall was reluctant to speak to the professor, until one Friday evening.

Hall had been passing Payne's door on his way downstairs. From inside he could hear someone reciting poetry; it sounded like Professor Ryan, who taught the course in Public Speaking, but Hall could not be certain. The voice was deep and resounding as it rendered:

> *Like some young cypress, tall, and dark, and straight,*
> *Which in a queen's secluded garden throws*
> *Its slight dark shadow on the moonlit turf,*
> *By midnight, to a bubbling fountain's sound—*
> *So slender Sohrab seemed, so softly reared.*

Hall liked the sound of the words but he could not place them. By the next day he could only remember the last line, but he felt compelled to find out the name of the poem. On Monday his patience gave in, and as he walked by Professor Payne's room after classes, he risked knocking on his door.

"Come in!" Payne answered.

Hall entered, and to his relief was warmly greeted. With the directness of youth Hall apologized for having eavesdropped on Friday night, but now he had to know who the poet was.

"You're forgiven," Mr. Payne said, "if you promise not to do it any more. We don't always read poetry. Sometimes we talk."

Hall quoted the one line he remembered from the poem.

"It's from Matthew Arnold's 'Sohrab and Rustum,'" the teacher answered. He paused, then asked inquisitively: "I wonder that such a soapy line should have stuck in your mind. You're not familiar with Arnold's poetry?" He pointed to the volume of Arnold's poetry on his bookshelf, and asked Hall to hand it down to him.

Professor Payne riffled the pages. "You may be a bit young to read Arnold just now," he said. "But the time will come when you will read no one else, for some months at least." He ran his eye down one page, then looked up. "I'm going to try to put you off him for the present," he continued, but with a wry tone. "Perhaps I had better say, to prepare you for the Arnold least worth reading, 'Sohrab and Rustum' is a good example of Arnold fulfilling his destiny as a poet. It's the kind of thing he felt that he should write. Later, you will see for yourself the poems he truly wanted to write. You can pick them out without a moment's hesitation."

That evening, History instructor and English student talked about poetry for almost an hour. When Norman looked at his watch, he was surprised that so much time had passed. Mr. Payne rose slowly onto his artificial legs and walked Hall to the door; then he apologized for his overly critical treatment of Arnold. "When I think of the pleasure he has given me . . ." Then he changed his mind again: "Nevertheless, it's a mistake to let your bump of veneration for whatever poet get oversized. Be most wary when one tries to convince you that he is writing at the top of his form."

Arnold and Payne notwithstanding, it was several years before Norman's "bumps of veneration" flattened for his earlier sentimental favorites. But with the tools of critical appreciation acquired in literature classes, Hall's skills in criticism became keen and sharp. As did his tastes in music, thanks to Professor

George L. Pierce. William Cullen Bryant and Henry Wadsworth Longfellow yielded to Matthew Arnold and Francis Thompson, popular music gave before concertoes and symphonies, and Gould's barbershop quartet singing deferred to the four-part harmony of the Grinnell Glee Club. For, as Hall came to appreciate more the music of poetry, so did he come to appreciate more the poetry of music.

Hall had not heard a symphony until he came to Grinnell, and one of the first, which he listened to regularly for the rest of his life, was Anton Dvořák's *New World Symphony*. The introduction of the two, composer and listener, was fortuitous. Hall had been on his way to philosophy class, and passing by the chapel, he heard organ music and went in to listen. Listening he sat, and sitting he became so absorbed in what he heard he forgot all about his class. The Czech composer who had come for one year to Spillville, Iowa, in 1893, to become the organist at St. Wenceslaus Roman Catholic Church, where he was first inspired about the new world to render musically his impressions about it, had literally struck a responsive chord in Norman Hall. Hall thereafter never missed the Sunday vesper services, not for the services, but for the music. He wanted to hear the organ music of Professors Scheve or Matlack. And in the spring he never missed the concerts of the Chicago or Minneapolis Symphony Orchestra in their annual visits to the campus. Slowly, Hall became a sophisticated listener. As for becoming a singer, however, Hall never thought he had a chance, until a friend suggested that they join the Grinnell Glee Club.

Hall's life at Grinnell, however, was not all poetry and music. In the fall of his junior year he was almost expelled from school for a Halloween prank.

With two other friends, Hank Kinser, a freshman, and Roy Gill, a sophomore, Hall and Chester Davis decided to move the Swisher Brothers' streetcar sign. It was a clothing-store advertisement, a large roadside signboard situated off the road about a mile south of Grinnell, built in the shape of a streetcar with passengers painted inside merrily on their way to the store. Hall and his friends never worked harder. They packed the sign into town, and by improvising a system of ropes, pulleys, and derricks, they hoisted it to the top of the YMCA building in the center of town. Then, as Chester Davis nailed the last nail into place, securing the sign for all to see, the town marshal arrived on the scene, caught them, and brought them into custody.

The next day President Main called the offenders into his office. They would return the sign to its place outside of town, he told them; and it would be repainted and replaced to Mr. Swisher's satisfaction. And, he added, they could not return to classes until the job was finished. "The money for the paint job and the dray," Chester said later, "was hard to come by."

Although the money was difficult to raise, Hall discovered, that was easier to do than to find excuses for the next time he was called into the president's office. For three years Hall had not been attending physical training classes, and, he knew, it was not an offense that could be passed off as a college prank, nor could it be paid for and forgotten about. For six semesters of PT Hall had received an "E," which was a failing grade. The instructor, Doc Fisher, tired of never finding Hall, J. Norman, in his class, finally posted a public notification of his delinquency. President Main, kindly and understanding as his reputation was, might not be as readily forgiving this time, Hall had been warned, as last. This offense, after all, was not for a suspension, but for possible dismissal.

Two weeks later Hall was called in to show cause as to why he should be retained at Grinnell. When he reported to the president, Hall had prepared his case carefully. It was true, he admitted, that he had not reported to the great round building for physical training; he could not escape that accusation. What could he say in his defense? Not much. At the appointed hour for physical training he had made it a point to take some exercise. He loved to walk, and he *had* taken an hour's hike every classroom period, regardless of the weather; and, furthermore, he could produce witnesses, like Chet Davis and Bill Ziegler, that he had done so. Moreover, could not President Main *see* for himself that hiking had kept Hall hard and lean, in excellent physical condition? Indeed, was that not exactly the whole point of the physical training program at Grinnell?

Finally, Hall was quick to point out, he had not lost any credits, because PT was a non-credit course. The case rested for two weeks.

Fortunately, Hall was not dismissed. But the fear of that possibility, relieved and put behind him at last, had so filled him with a joy of staying that he translated this joy into the words and music of a college song for his beloved alma mater. At first, beginning with the melody, Hall picked out part of a tune on his mandolin, then tried to find the same notes on the piano; and to the music he tried to fit some lyrics. The first two lines had a lilt to them, like a marching song:

> *Sons of old Grinnell*
> *Let your voices swell*

Then his inspiration failed. Finally, in the spring of 1909, the Glee Club made a two-and-a-half-month trip out west, to Minnesota, Montana, Washington, Oregon, Idaho, and Colorado; and Hall, by achieving a physical distance from the campus, gained the necessary psychical distance to finish the song. He was now far enough away from Grinnell to see what he wanted to look at.

It was the night of April 10, and they had returned to their train after the concert in Colorado Springs. All the others had gone to sleep, even his friends Roy Ray Roberts and Bill Ziegler. Hall was sitting on the observation platform of the train, looking at the moon and stars over the foothills of the Rockies. Then, effortlessly, what had been welling inside of him for more than ten weeks now rose into verbal and musical articulation. To the first two lines he had written before, he added:

> *In a song to the staunch, the true,*
> *In praise of Alma Mater,*
> *As her sons ever love to do.*
> *Thy glory and Thy honor,*
> *Thy fame alone we tell.*

Finally, with steadily rising, then declining inflection, he concluded:

And ever for thee
Our love shall be,
Grinnell—Grinnell—Grinnell.

For the remainder of that night Hall could not go to sleep, so filled was he with the emotional intensity of the experience. The next morning he showed the results to Professor Pierce. The director liked the piece immediately and agreed to work out the harmony for him. When they returned to campus, Hall wrote two more verses. That summer the song was published; and thereafter, to Hall's soaring satisfaction, the Glee Club sang his song in concerts and for reunions. "Sons of Old Grinnell," words and music by J. Norman Hall, class of 1910, became standard musical fare for graduates and undergraduates.

One evening during his senior year Hall walked to the south campus. As he came to the outdoor theater, he felt very tired and lay down by some shrubbery to rest. Stretched out and staring up at the sky, he was surprised that there were no clouds, only the stars which like pinholes of light had been pricked through the dark-blue blanket of night. Against his back and legs the grass was cool, and he watched the moon slide westward. Presently he was startled by the sound of voices. He recognized them as belonging to two of his professors, Dr. John D. Stoops from Philosophy and Dr. Paul F. Peck, Head of the History Department, who were out for a walk also. They stopped walking and sat on the corner of the stage, about twelve feet away from the shrubbery behind which he lay. Apparently they had been talking about their students, and to Norman's surprise, Professor Peck now mentioned his name.

"He's another example of the exasperating type of student," Professor Stoops replied. "They seem to have the ability in the abstract; it can't be defined in any other way. You hope it will crystallize so that you can see what it is composed of, but it remains in solution."

Hall felt embarrassed; he thought of the two classes he had taken with Professor Stoops, in Psychology and Ethics. He had received a B plus from him in Psychology, but an E in Ethics, which at the last minute Stoops had changed to a D, a passing grade.

A moment passed before Dr. Peck answered. "I know," he said. "Their promise is always better than their performance. How do you grade such students at the end of the semester?"

There was another pause. "My tendency," Professor Stoops replied, "is to give them the benefit of the doubt. I've been teaching long enough to know how difficult it is to judge them by classroom performance. I believe that most of them get more out of their work than the record shows."

Norman listened closely. For his part he was happy to be classed with those whose ability was in the abstract; at least, he thought, he had ability, even though it did not always crystallize.

The professors now switched their conversation to education in general and then to the advantages of a liberal arts education in particular. Professor Peck thought that the day was coming when the liberal arts colleges would have served their usefulness; Dr. Stoops, more optimistic, did not agree. "Unless life changes beyond anything we have reason to expect," Professor Stoops said, "liberal arts colleges will never outlive the need for them, provided that they remain true to their long-range purpose." He stopped, then vehemently made his point: "And that is to teach young men and women that the bird in the bush is worth two in the hand."

The two professors stood up and walked away. Norman, puzzled by this last remark, continued to lie on the grass, trying to understand fully what Professor Stoops had meant. Certainly the point was particularly apt for his own yearnings, ever anxious as he was to follow the echoing whistle of a train, the call from the top of the next hill down the road, or even the vocation of social worker.

After graduation in 1910 Hall found a job in Boston with the Massachusetts Society for the Prevention of Cruelty to Children. and soon after his arrival in Boston he found lodgings in Louisburg Square. It was a Saturday. The MSPCC office had closed, and the commuters had returned to the suburbs for the weekend. Hall left the building by the front door and turned right on Mt. Vernon Street; tucking a book under his arm, he started down the long hill toward the Charles River. Halfway down and off to his right, he came to a little square; it was sheltered on all sides by stately brick buildings, and in its center, a square within a square, was a grass plot shaded by trees. "This is the place!" Hall said to himself. "If only I could live here!"

Despite his wish Hall did not think he ever in fact could. The square seemed too aristocratic, too exclusive, too rich. He walked around on the brick sidewalks and on the other side came to Pinckney Street. At house Number 91 he stopped short, not believing what he had just seen. Tucked into the corner of a front window was a small white card; it said simply: LODGINGS. Still incredulous, Hall walked up the steps and rang the front-door bell.

A middle-aged woman came to the door. "Yes?" she said.

"I saw the card in your window," Hall answered. "Have you a room you could rent to a young man?"

"Well . . . yes . . . I might have," the woman answered tentatively; then she asked positively: "Are you single?"

"Oh, yes," Hall said. "I'm an agent for the Society for the Prevention of Cruelty to Children, at 43 Mt. Vernon Street." He pointed up the hill. "I've only just come to Boston."

The reputation of the Society was old and unassailable; the woman, apparently, thought that working for it was recommendation enough. She asked Hall into the front hall. Inside, Hall noticed a small Duncan Phyfe end table against the wall, and above it an oval gold-framed mirror. "I'm not very affluent," he said quickly; "so I'd better ask the price of the room before I see it. I don't want to bother you unnecessarily."

The woman looked the young applicant over, noting his clean suit, his well-scrubbed face, the shock of dark-brown hair that fell across his forehead. "Would four dollars a week be more than you could pay?" she asked.

"No!" Hall blurted out; then he continued more evenly: "That's just what I expected to pay for a room." He paused briefly. "I'll take it," he said.

"Wait till you see it," the woman remonstrated. "You musn't buy a pig in a poke, young man."

Slowly they climbed the stairs to the fourth floor. "I ain't as spry as I used to be," the woman said weakly, puffing as they came to the landing. She opened the door to the room. Hall took it in quickly: it was small, no more than eight by ten, part of a dormer; in the corner stood a small stove, against the far wall on the right were a small couch for a bed and a table with a washbowl and pitcher on it, and against the opposite wall a tall five-drawer dresser. Hall walked in and went to the window; it looked down on Louisburg Square. The room was just what he wanted.

"It's quite a climb," the woman said, panting slightly. "But, then, you're a young man. I guess you won't mind that too much. There's no heat up here, but that little stove will keep you warm as toast in the wintertime, no matter how cold it gets. Coal's included in the rent. That cot bed's real comfortable; my son used to sleep in it. The bathroom's on the floor below; the water never gets good and hot, but it's always warm."

"I'll take it," Hall said. He reached into his pocket, pulled out his wallet and took out four one-dollar bills, which he handed to the woman.

The woman took the money, folded it, and tucked it into her bosom. "You can pay every Saturday," she said, "or once a month." She was, she volunteered as she left, Mrs. Atherton, the landlady.

Alone in his lodgings, Hall walked to the left side of the room, and with the palm of his hand dusted off the top of the dresser. For the moment, the chest of drawers would have to serve as a bookshelf. On the top of the chest he stacked the one book he had been carrying with him. It was *Walden,* by Thoreau. Tomorrow, now that he had found a place to live in Boston, he would go to Concord and to Walden pond, and visit the site of Thoreau's house in town and his hut in the woods.

On Monday morning, Hall stepped up the worn sandstone steps into the vestibule of the MSPCC, and walked left into the large room—once a parlor—which was the office for the special agents. He went to his desk, a small mahogany table that stood close to a high, narrow window looking out on Joy Street. Next to him was Miss O'Rourke, who was already busy on a case.

This morning, it seemed to Hall, she was unduly frustrated. He asked her what the trouble was.

"To change human nature," she answered. "We social workers are supposed to have the training and the ability to correct the error in human conduct that Adam and Eve were responsible for. There are university professors who really believe they can be corrected—men with imposing lists of degrees after their names."

"You mean you're discouraged about your work?" Hall asked.

"No," answered Miss O'Rourke, "I am merely exasperated with Adam and Eve for having made it so difficult."

Hall chuckled. "If it weren't for Adam and Eve I guess we wouldn't have a job. Or priests or policemen either."

Then Miss O'Rourke changed her tone to one more serious. She spoke of the domestic conditions under which her problem girls had to live—no jobs, dirty homes, drunken fathers, slattern mothers. Private social agencies, she thought, could not do much to improve them. She hoped for one great improvement: If only the city of Boston would wipe out the slums! Then she said: "When you have lived here for a while, you will see for yourself how little Boston is concerned about it." Hall soon did.

Several days later Miss Butler, the complaint secretary, handed him a blue sheet of paper. It said:

> Complaint received by telephone from Landlady at ———— Springfield Street. Reports that young mother of two-year-old child (probably illegitimate), leaves him alone all day in her room. Landlady has spoken to mother of her neglect but without result. Requests early investigation.

Miss Butler waited for Hall to finish reading the note. "I judged by her voice over the phone," she said to him, referring to the landlady, "that she's a surly sort of person. That may be something for you to go on at the start."

It was his first case, and Hall employed the professional manner, trying not to reveal his uneasiness. "What do you think of the facts of the case, Miss Butler," he asked, "such as they are?"

"She may be a woman of the streets," Miss Butler said circuitously, "but you mustn't take that for granted. I shouldn't wonder at all if she were a young unmarried mother out of work and trying hard to get a job. This would account for her seeming neglect of the child. If that is the case, we can easily help her by arranging to have the child cared for at one of the day nurseries. But the facts must come first, of course. It is useless speaking of a case until the facts are known."

Hall started to leave, but stopped. He had suddenly realized he did not know where in Boston he was supposed to go or how he was going to get there. "Where is Springfield Street?" he asked.

"It is in the South End," Miss Butler replied. "I suggest that you stroll through that area for an hour or so to get your bearings. You will have plenty of time to get the facts of this case."

Hall set out. He walked down Joy Street, cut across the Boston Common to Tremont Street, to proceed down to Massachusetts Avenue, there to turn left and walk toward South Bay. As he walked down Tremont Street, Hall felt as if he were pushing ghosts aside to get by; in the way were the shades of Longfellow and Lowell, Ben Franklin and Paul Revere, Ralph Waldo Emerson and William Ellery Channing, Cotton Mather and William Bradford; even perhaps, Hall ruminated, Josiah B. Grinnell, late of New Haven, Vermont, before he followed the advice of Horace Greeley, went west, and founded in 1854 a settlement in Iowa that gave his name to Iowa College.

When at last Hall reached his destination on Springfield Street, it was almost three o'clock. He came to the address, climbed the steps, and rang the bell. It was a three-story tenement house. As Miss Butler had warned, a surly woman indeed answered the door. "What d'you want?" the woman asked sourly, wiping her hands on a soiled apron.

Hall explained who he was and why he was there.

The woman scowled. "Why didn't you get here sooner?" she said to him. "I told 'em for you to come right away. Now it's too late. She's cleared out, the little bitch!"

Hall questioned the woman further, but with no immediate results. "Ain't I told you she's cleared out?" the woman squealed. "I don't know her name or her brat's name. I don't know where she's gone or where she came from."

"When did she go?" Hall asked.

"Last night, and owin' me three weeks' rent. But I'll find her! Wait and see if I don't. She'll be sluttin' around the South End somewhere."

With more questioning, Hall learned that the mother was in her late teens, that she would go out about nine in the morning and not return until evening, leaving her child alone in the room with a bottle of milk. "Tryin' to make me believe she was lookin' for work! I know the kind of work she looks for, the bitch! Layin' on her back. But that wouldn't be no business of mine if she'd paid her rent."

"Do . . ." Hall hesitated. "Do," he began again, "women of the streets go out in the daytime? I thought it was only at night."

The woman had a ready answer. "Why shouldn't she go out in the daytime?" she asked. "'Tain't only at night that studs get horny."

Hall was shocked by the woman's language. Recovering, he asked her, "Did you tell the mother of the complaint you made to us?"

"Yes, like a fool!" the landlady answered, angered at herself. "I could see she was fond of the brat and I wanted to scare the livin' daylights out of her. And so I did. She had a big suitcase full of their things. I couldn't see her luggin' that away and the kid too without my knowin' it. But she did, in the night. I might have known some buck would help her."

The woman began to grow impatient with the subject. She started toward the door, showing Hall out. No, she said, she didn't want to answer any more questions. "What is there more to tell?" she said in disgust. "She's gone. Find her for yourself." The woman slammed the door behind him.

Dismayed but undefeated, Hall paused for a moment in the hall to decide on his next move. Noting the closed doors to the other apartments, he went to inquire at them for further particulars about the girl. He certainly could not render a written report on what he had learned so far. Hall knocked at two doors but there was no answer. At the third a small gray old man opened the door and invited him in. The old man was a carpenter and he worked at a lathe by the window making toys for children. He had a German accent. "No, I don't know dot voman," he said. "I don't know nobody in de house, none of de lodgers. I got my vork. Dot keep me busy."

On the second floor Hall did not learn much more. Although as he approached the doors he could hear voices on the other side, his knock brought immediate silence; and after he left, the voices started up again. But he had better luck at another door on the side of the hallway. As he raised his fist to knock, he noticed a card tacked to the door. It said:

MADAME HORTENSE—CARD READER—PALMIST

Hall knocked. Almost immediately the door opened slightly and a voice answered: "Wait just a minute! I'll be right back." After more than a minute, the door opened wide and there stood Mme. Hortense, clutching a blue kimono at her neck. She was short, round, plump and heavy; her hair, bright and yellow, glowed. She seemed to be in her mid-thirties. "Well!" She smiled, delighted to have a visitor. "What a nice surprise! Come in!"

Hall began to explain the reason for his visit. The woman allowed only a few words from him. "We can't talk here," she explained. "I'll catch cold. Come into the studio."

The studio was a large parlor that faced Springfield Street. The woman motioned Hall to a heavy, worn, Victorian sofa. He sat down. Across from him he noticed a small recessed alcove with a brass bed, and in front of it stood a zinc tub of water with soap and towel spread out on newspapers. Hortense quickly pulled the curtains closed across the nook. "I wasn't expecting visitors just now," she said, jerking her head over her shoulder. "Ain't it hot? I've been having a sponge bath. Now I'm all nice and comfy." She went to the front windows and closed the curtains, then sat down on the lounge chair off to the side of the divan, tucking her legs up under herself. "Now we're all cozy," she said, pleased with herself and with her visitor.

Again Hall began his line of questioning. "Oh, yes," Madame Hortense replied. "I know her very well. Her room was on this floor. Poor Edie! She's gone."

"I know," Hall answered. "The landlady told me. Do you know where she's gone?"

The woman smiled broadly; she had inferred an unintended meaning in what Hall had said. "I won't tell *you*," she teased him, "you bad boy! Why didn't you come when she needed you?"

Hall now tried to play the part which Hortense had assigned to him. "I only learned this morning that she was in trouble," he said. "I would like very much to know where she's gone."

"Wouldn't you, though." The woman grinned mischievously. "And you're still just crazy about her?" She rearranged her body in the chair, forgetting about her gown. It had opened at the neck in a deep décolletage. "Listen, honey," she continued familiarly, "she ain't crazy about you, not any more. Oh, I know all about you! Edie told me you'd be coming. And she said: 'When he comes, tell him I hate him and I'll never see him again!' "

Hall flushed in embarrassment. The woman's breasts, large as grapefruit, were burgeoning up and out of her gown. Hortense had not noticed; or, if she had, she was more interested in their effect on the young interviewer. "Honey, let her go," she said. "You'll have to. I ain't going to tell on Edie. But I'll say this: she's left Boston."

"Did . . ." Hall hesitated. "Did," he started again, "you help her go?"

Hortense agreed that she had. "I'm a woman, honey, with a soft heart," she said, "not a bitch like the landlady." She broke into a loud laugh. "Wouldn't she scratch my eyes out if she knew!"

"Was she married?"

"You ask me that, you bad boy! Edie's awful fond of the baby. That's what's made her hate you so. . . . You'll just have to find a new sweetheart."

Hall continued to play his part. "Yes," he said, "I guess I had gone stale for her." Then he wished he had not made that statement.

"Come over here, honey," the woman said. "Let me see your hand. I know just who she's going to be, if you've got two dollars." Slowly, Hall showed his hand. Suddenly, Hortense rose to her feet and dramatically swept open the panels of her dressing gown. Hall gulped. The woman was completely naked. "How do you like my shape?" she asked; then she added: *"You are not stale to me!"*

Disgusted, then thinking he might get sick, Hall turned and ran for the door. "Honey!" Hortense called after him, "Please don't go. I'll make it *one* dollar for *you!*"

Later, when Hall returned to Mt. Vernon Street, he was still shaken by the experience. It was now almost six o'clock and all of the agents had gone home. Except, Hall happily noted, Mr. Critcherson, a former policeman. Hall asked him if he would stay on for a few more minutes so he could talk to him.

"Sure. Why not?" Mr. Critcherson answered. "Won't be the first time I've kept the old lady waitin' supper."

Hall told the older man about his experiences of the afternoon, particularly with Mme. Hortense. "Was she good-lookin'?" Mr. Critcherson asked, smiling.

"She's fat, huge," Hall said. "She must weigh at least two hundred pounds."

The ex-policeman laughed. "I guess you'll be all right," he said, "since it didn't strike you blind and prevent your runnin' away. We see some queer things in this business. Maybe it's just as well you had this kind of start."

Hall was worried about what he could put into his report; then he gave Mr. Critcherson more of the details, none of which seemed worthy of an entry. "You see," the older agent said, "you haven't got much to go on so far. Mme. Hortense's information is not what you would call reliable. She probably does know the mother and that Edie was expecting a young man to call for her. But the message the mother gave for him may have been nothing like the one Mme. Hortense gave you. Maybe what she wanted most was to have the young man know where she's gone. She may have been married to him. Anyway, it seems likely that he is the father of her child. But when Mme. Hortense sees you, thinkin' it's him, she says: 'Oh, oh! Here he is! And he's my meat if he's got two dollars . . . I mean, one dollar if he has to be coaxed.' "

Hall forced a smile. "You think Edie may be a decent girl down on her luck?" he asked. The romantic idealist in him would not be put down.

"Could be. On the other hand, she may be one of the toughest little tarts in the South End. But there's one thing in her favor: She loves her baby. That seems clear because the landlady herself acknowledged it. Plenty of prostitutes have more genuine mother love in 'em than a lot of so-called mothers in respectable homes. I've been in this business long enough to have found that out. Suppose Edie is one of these; then comes the question, in case you find her: Where will the child be better off—with the mother or taken away from her?"

"There can't be any doubt about that, surely?" Hall said. "How could a prostitute be fit to bring up a child?"

Mr. Critcherson took some time before he answered. "Young man," he began slowly, reining in his impatience, "I've never been to college, as I've said. But if I had college degrees yards long danglin' behind me I couldn't answer that question without knowin' the mother. Most of the high authorities in child welfare would say right off she never could be fit. But take this from an ex-policeman who only went through high school: Sometimes they're dead wrong."

Hall was subdued. "What do you think I should do next?" he asked.

"For one thing, I'd see the policeman on the beat. They generally know a lot that goes on in their districts. Then you ought to know something definite about the young man: who he is and whether or not he's married to Edie."

Hall was still frustrated. "But how is it to be *done*?" he asked.

Mr. Critcherson laughed loudly. "I guess," he spoke deliberately, "you'll have to consult some card-reader, or palmist, to find out about that." He got up, closed his desk, and still smiling, left the building.

After the older man had gone, Hall thought more about the

case. He would have to return, talk this time to the lodgers on the first floor, speak to the policeman on the beat, and somehow interview Hortense again. Hall left the building and walked down the street to his lodgings at Louisburg Square.

As he entered the front door, he noticed a letter on the hall table. Picking it up, he saw it was for him. It was from the *Century* magazine. Hall tore open the flap. Inside was a check for fifteen dollars, and there was a note. It said:

> Dear Sir:
> I am enclosing a check for fifteen dollars ($15) in payment for your verses, 'A Foggy Evening.' We shall print them soon and with your permission we will change the title to 'Fifth Avenue in Fog.'

As if bolted to the floor on which he stood, Hall was enthralled. He had sold a poem! Then, while he glowed in his victory, Mrs. Atherton emerged from the side door in the hall. A reminder of reality, she was looking for the rent money. "Well, well," she said. "Friday night again! Land sakes! Don't time fly!"

"It does, Mrs. Atherton," Hall said breezily. "It surely does!" He bent over the table, endorsed the check, and with a flourish handed it to the landlady. "I'll be wanting one of your larger rooms when one is vacant, Mrs. Atherton," Hall said; then he exuberantly rushed up the stairs to the fourth floor.

In his room Hall pulled out from his top dresser drawer a new pocket notebook. He flipped open the blue cover and on the top inside, he wrote:

Three poems per week at $15 = $45.

Exultant, Hall paced the floor. He was a published poet! Why, in years hence, throngs of tourists would undoubtedly seek out 91 Pinckney Street at Louisburg Square, there certainly to read on a brass plaque mounted outside:

IN THIS HOUSE, DURING THE YEARS——
LIVED THE POET——

When he returned to Springfield Street two days later, he first met the policeman on the beat. The policeman readily answered all the questions put to him. He pointed to the tenement with his club. "The place is a dump," he said. "All but that old Austrian toymaker on the top floor. He don't seem to know the kind of neighbors he's got."

The officer had not met the woman and the baby Hall was looking for. "What's her name?" he asked.

"I don't know her last name," Hall answered, "but she's called Edie. That's what a palmist who lives there told me."

"Hortense?" he said. "Ain't she something? She's been livin' in that house for years. We run her in now and again, but she carries right on at the old stand!"

Hall did not enter the building right away; instead, he decided to explore more of the South End, arguing with himself the while about the best way to approach Mme. Hortense. It was not until after noon that he had gained enough courage to try again.

Fortunately, as he came into the entryway, the landlady was nowhere in sight. Softly he climbed the steps to Hortense's floor and tiptoed to her room. He rapped on the panel. The door opened. Hortense sparkled in welcome. "Come in, honey. I knew you'd be back!" she said triumphantly. "You bad boy! Now sit down and let me look at you."

Hall obeyed. He sat on the chair; stiff, dumb, mute, he had completely forgotten the speech he had rehearsed.

Hortense smiled. "You been dreamin' about me, honey," she teased, "and that's gonna cost you two dollars." Thereupon and before Hall could raise even a hand in protest, she whisked off her dressing gown. She was wearing a chemise, but it was very tight and transparent and it only half-contained her huge breasts and immense buttocks.

Hall found his legs and his tongue at the same time. "Wait!" he said, jumping up. "You've made a mistake." He paused, then blurted out, "I am an agent of the Society for the Prevention of Cruelty to Children!"

The woman was astounded. "You are *what?*" she shouted incredulously. Then she started cursing at him, piling profanity upon obscenity on his head, screaming all the time at the top of her voice.

Hall retreated quickly, out the door, down the stairs to the landing, there to be equally reviled by the waiting landlady, and bounded out the front door and down the steps to the street.

Thus did James Norman Hall's social awareness expand and continue to expand for the next few years. He learned "the facts of life" in Boston. But he learned them further and more intimately, not from a Hortense, but discreetly and appropriately, from one of his own kind. She was a Boston social worker.

It was in the spring of 1914. Every Monday evening, Hall had attended the weekly meetings of the Monday Evening Club. Composed exclusively of people in social work, it met nearby, at 3 Joy Street, and the program usually featured an authority on some aspect of the profession. After the talk there was always a round-table discussion about the subject lectured upon. At many of these meetings, Hall observed, was one woman in particular. She was older than most of the others, slender, blond and beautiful, about thirty, poised, very well dressed, and quick to smile whenever Hall chanced to look at her. Hall, shy, slow to seize an opportunity, painfully diffident with girls he did not know, quickly smiled in response, and that was all.

Until one night, not a Monday. It began when Hall reported for work one morning, and as was his custom, checked the complaint sheets impaled on the spindle on top of his desk. He had been made the Roxbury agent, and one of the complaints, a cruelty case, requested help at eight o'clock in the evening on Saturday, in the Back Bay area. The specific time of the request was somewhat unusual, he thought, but otherwise everything was in order.

When he knocked on the door at the appointed hour, he was surprised to be greeted by the pretty willowy blonde. In the center of the living room, a dinner table had been prepared for two. Hall had already eaten his supper, but he was pleased to discover he was the invited guest and readily played the part. The beautiful blonde was the perfect hostess. She put him completely at ease, refusing at this point to discuss any particular cruelty case. After a few tentative conversational castings, she caught the fish of poetry. Jim was hooked. Like him, he was happy to learn, she loved poetry.

After dinner, delicious and meticulously served, she spoke of social workers, particularly the woman agents. "I am not a professional social worker," she said, "only a volunteer for certain kinds of work that interest me. I'm afraid I am what an Associated Charities secretary would call a 'benevolent individual.' Isn't that terrible? You must not give me away to the Monday Night Club." She smiled broadly; her white even teeth glistened. "But my motives are not wholly benevolent."

Then the woman turned to the specific case of cruelty that Hall had been asked to attend to. "Please," she said, "listen and do not speak until I give you leave. . . . I have depended upon my woman's intuition in this particular case of cruelty." She rose from her seat and went to stand behind the easy chair next to the sofa. Hall watched her rise and move, fascinated by her grace and charm. "I am rarely mistaken in such matters," she continued, "although I may be here. It is a case of self-inflicted cruelty, and it concerns not a child but a young man. What makes it so pitiable is the needlessness of his suffering. Any discerning woman could have told him that and have suggested the best possible remedy. But perhaps there are not too many of that kind. I asked him to call here this evening to assure him that, if help is needed, and wanted, I shall be glad to be of service."

She half turned and strode off to the left to a door on the other side of the living room; she turned quickly, her hands holding the doorknob behind her, her body erect, her right leg at a tight right angle to her left, her chin lifted. She smiled softly. "If my intuition has betrayed me," she spoke slowly, "that other door"—she nodded toward the outside door—"is the one to the street." Abruptly, she turned and entered her room.

Much later that evening, Hall walked in the Public Gardens

across from the Boston Common. He breathed deep of the
night air rising from the small ponds, enjoying the blessed
calm, the enchanted release, come at last from a soft and yielding woman, like cool balm on hot flesh.

For any young man like him in the future, in a similar vir-
ginal predicament, Hall wrote:

> My hope is that he may be invited to dinner by a Benevolent
> Individual as discerning, as gracious, and as lovely as the one
> I had the good fortune to be noticed by. And if her motives
> should not be wholly benevolent, so much the better for him.

Such benevolence, of course, was rare, and Hall certainly did
not judge his success as a man or a social worker by it. He did
begin to worry, however, about the direction his life was taking, and he began to feel bitterness because of it. Primarily, it
was an uncertainty of mind about the future. He had not become much of a poet; in the few years he had lived in Boston,
he had sold about fifteen poems and had earned only about a
hundred dollars for the lot of them. Perhaps, he thought, he
should become a teacher; he had applied to Harvard University to study English literature, toward his M.A. in 1915 and
his Ph.D. in 1917. Also he was tempted to go west that summer
to Montana and see Chester Davis, the Grand Canyon of Ne-
vada, and the giant redwoods of California; then, perhaps, he
could continue wandering, like a hobo. Specifically, he was uncertain about his life as a social worker. An old friend from
Grinnell had once asked him in a letter: "Does your work in
social sewerage make of you a philanthropist or a misanthro-
pist?"

In reply Hall said: "A year or more ago I could have answered it easily. I should then have said that I was losing every
illusion that ever I possessed; and that I had no belief in in-
herent *goodness;* and as for ideals and the like o' that—bosh!
Oh, but I was the young cynic a year ago! To me, then, the
only beautiful things in life were those that had not been con-
taminated by contact with men. But gradually there has been
coming to me a new faith that is so much larger than the old,

and a broader and kindlier human sympathy. I think that this change has come very tardily to me. It took me such a great while to learn that no man is perfect and no man inherently and willfully bad. It took me such a great while to discover that nearly everybody is trying to be decent and to live honorably, and that those who don't usually have to struggle against such fearful odds that they are not more than half to blame, oftentimes not so much as half, for their failure. . . .

"The worst of it, in so far as I am concerned, is that while James N. Hall, the ardent social worker, the enthusiast for social betterment, is on his knees praying for the coming of the kingdom [of social righteousness] his arch enemy, [J.] Norman Hall, dreamer, dilettante, idler, who hasn't the social point of view at all, is sacrificing burnt offerings to his pagan gods, in the hope that by so doing he may offset the supplications of the social worker. It is very strange that these two creatures, as opposite as the poles in their likes and dislikes, can live in such proximity, without one or the other ultimately conquering. I have dubbed them the Good Samaritan, and the Little Red Devil of Unrighteousness, and you may well believe that they are leading me a sorry life. Sometimes, for long periods, the Good Samaritan will have the upper hand; and then I go about my work with an enthusiasm and interest that bids fair to move mountains. And then the Little Red Devil, who has been lying in wait, and husbanding his strength, will dart out, have at the G[ood] S[amaritan] and leave him for dead. He will then link his arm familiarly in mine, and together, we 'pass by on the other side.'

"You see, the accursed little rascal attacks me from the unprofessional side. He appeals to my love of the quaint and the picturesque. He tells me that this social betterment business is all very well to theorize about, but that actually and practically nine-tenths of it is folderol. And when I am under his baneful influence, and the Good Old Samaritan is still lying in a state of coma, I can't but agree with him. Perhaps he leads me into a crooked little by-street, edged with rows of unsanitary, ruinous tenements, unsteadily shouldering one another like the tipsy old inebriates who live in them. He will point out a line of many colored clothes, hanging out to dry, between upper windows, and flapping as jauntily and prettily in the breeze. He goes into raptures over it and I, like the sheep that I am—with him. We both swear that we will ever be mortal foes to model tenements with their steam drying rooms and sanitary uninteresting washable apartments. And after we have spent a rollicking night in the North End, peering into dingy little basement shops, stacked high with heaps of Italian delicatessen and have fairly hugged one another for joy at sight of gaily dressed old crones with immense earrings shuffling down narrow streets with great bundles of firewood on their heads, we damn all those who are for making commonplace Americans out of such people. We are seriously considering founding an Anti-Melting Pot Society. We want these new brothers of ours to keep all the curious little twists and kinks that make them so attractive and interesting. The arrogance of *us* Americans! What justification have we in insisting that these people lose their national identity? Do we give them something better? I doubt it very much. . . ."

Apparently in league with the Little Red Devil, his friend Chester Davis, now editor of the Miles City *Daily Star,* made Montana look very attractive. Chet wrote to him: "About a sheepherding job, I have made inquiries and find that there are opportunities. Miles City is the greatest primary wool market in the world. There are great sheepmen left in the country out here; the Yellowstone valley is filled with them. They are in a bitter struggle against the homesteaders who are taking up the lands and the water rights, destroying the free range which is the foundation of the sheep business. . . . The homesteader is bound to win out in the end, for he is constructive and intensive, while the sheepman is extensive and destructive. . . .

"There is no need to warn you about the loneliness of the life. Unless a man has that in his head which eliminates the need for companionship and external amusement, he had better not herd sheep. But I know that, in your case, solitude is an attraction rather than a drawback. There is opportunity for boundless reading; and when, at dusk, you retire to your little wagon for the night, with the wind howling about your ears, there is plenty of time for reflection and meditation."

As there was Chester Davis to pull J. Norman Hall west, so

there were friends to keep him in Boston, the James N. Hall half of him. Roy N. Cushman, a probation officer in Juvenile Court; George C. Greener, a teacher at the North Bennet Industrial School; and Laurance L. Winship, a reporter on *The Boston Globe:* all pulled like tent pegs to secure him to their native New England soil.

In an attempt to change his luck as an author, Hall tried writing prose instead of poetry. It was the winter of 1913, and he first tried the epistolary form, addressing "Dear William . . ." letters to his Grinnell Glee Club friend, William Ziegler, now a Rhodes scholar at Oxford, and titling them "Letters from Louisburg Square." Hall had sent the letters to the editor of *The New England Magazine,* on Columbus Avenue in Boston. The editor liked the prose, wanted to publish the letters, but could offer no money for them. The magazine, he explained to Hall in an interview, was about to expire if he could not solicit more advertising or find a rich patron. Hall decided to hold out for money and wait for a better offer elsewhere.

But the rejection slips continued to come in. Hall had to agree with Henry David Thoreau: he, James Norman Hall, was living a life of quiet desperation. Hall wrote in his notebook:

> The fear of life and the desire to avoid it; to skate over the dark chasms as I had over the 'rubber ice' on the river at home.

He did not know how to resolve the dilemma about his life and his future.

Then, quite by accident on a spring day in 1914, Hall met Joseph Conrad; not in person but through his novel *Lord Jim,* which had been given to him by Jack Winship. The author became his literary father-confessor-counselor. For, like two strangers who have wanted to meet but were prevented by distance, ignorance, or divergence, J. Norman Hall was at last introduced to James N. Hall by Joseph Conrad; in the pages of *Lord Jim* James Norman Hall recognized himself, not as he had imagined himself to be, but as he in fact was. Hall started to read the book one Sunday morning on a park bench in the Boston Common, read it through noon and through dusk, missing lunch and dinner, continued reading into the fading light of evening, ran to his room in Louisburg Square, stayed up all night and read into the dawn of the next morning before he had finished the novel.

In the story Stein had spoken directly to him, he knew; the part of the novel that stuck, like a bone in his craw, was the conversation between Stein and Marlow, when Stein had said:

> A man that is born falls into a dream like a man who falls into the sea. If he tries to climb out into the air as inexperienced people endeavor to do, he drowns—*nicht wahr?* . . . No! I tell you! The way is to the destructive element submit yourself, and with the exertions of your hands and feet in the water make the deep, deep sea keep you up. . . .

That morning by the light of the dawn Hall wrote in his notebook:

> I lack the confidence in my ability to submit myself to the destructive element.

In the past in his life when Hall could not decide on one of several alternatives, he had always turned his back on his problems and taken a long walk in the country. This time, however, he turned to the sea. On May 27, 1914, James Norman Hall sailed steerage on the *Laconia*, for Liverpool and the Continent, there to meet the destructive element again.

James Norman Hall, Class of 1910, Grinnell College, Iowa.

Charles Bernard Nordhoff, Class of 1909, Harvard College, Massachusetts.

Charles Bernard Nordhoff (left) and James Norman Hall at work in Hall's library on one of their early collaborations.

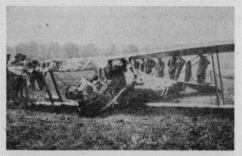

TOP LEFT: Caporal *James Norman Hall*, brevet pilote, *Escadrille Lafayette, French Aviation, World War I.*

CENTER LEFT: *Hall's Nieuport, crash-landed behind the German lines, shot down by an antiaircraft shell that lodged in the engine of the plane and failed to explode.*

BOTTOM LEFT: *Captain James Norman Hall, Flight Leader, U. S. 94th, "Hat-in-the-Ring" Squadron, having miraculously survived from his crashed plane with only a broken nose, is taken to a German prisoner-of-war camp in a staff car.*

ABOVE: *Lieutenant Charles Bernard Nordhoff, U. S. Air Service, after his transfer from Lafayette Flying Corps, World War I.*

Charles Bernard Nordhoff at work on his veranda, Tahiti, French Polynesia, South Seas.

Charles Nordhoff with his Tahitian wife, Vahine Tua Tearae.

Nordhoff taking a siesta on his veranda with his native wife.

James Norman Hall (second from left) with his lifelong friends from Boston: L. L. Winship, Roy N. Cushman, and George C. Greener (left to right).

Hall with his wife, Sarah Winchester Hall, and their son, Conrad Lafcadio.

Hall with his children, Nancy Ella and Conrad.

Nordhoff and Hall in Tahiti, standing in front of Nordhoff's new house; from left, back row, James Norman Hall, Charles Bernard Nordhoff, Nordhoff's wife, and Harrison W. Smith, their early benefactor; front row, native friends and Nordhoff's children.

James Norman Hall and Charles Bernard Nordhoff on Hall's front steps.

James Norman Hall splits coconuts to make copra, at Harrison Smith's plantation and arboretum in Tahiti.

Charles Bernard Nordhoff, shortly before his death in 1947.

James Norman Hall taking a break in his library, 1950.

The riddle of Nordhoff & Hall's collaboration solved by cartoonist John Groth.

CHARLES BERNARD NORDHOFF

1
The Father of the Man

Grandfather Charles Nordhoff, paterfamilias, was a man who had been marked for greatness. Everything he touched turned to success, everywhere he went he found reward, everyone he met was entranced by his presence. "Nordhoff," the distinguished American historian, Allan Nevins, said of him, "was energy personified. For the decade which covered Civil War and Reconstruction he was an editor of the *Post;* for many years he served the House of Harper's; and he was with the *Herald* from 1874 until 1890, when James Gordon Bennett the younger retired him on half-pay for life. The two newspapers and the publishing firm alike have reason to remember his industry, courage, independence, and bluff manliness.

"Nordhoff's early life," Nevins continued, "is an adventure story. His father, a veteran of Blücher's army, was exiled from Germany for his liberalism, and the boy was brought to the Mississippi Valley in 1834, at the age of four. His parents were wealthy and for a time the family lived in anomalous fashion, eating from silver plate and drinking imported mineral water in the Western wilderness. Left an orphan after a few years, young Nordhoff was taken under the protection of Bishop Nast of Cincinnati. In 1844 he ran away to sea, his imagination having been fired by Cooper and Marryat.

"Probably several million American boys in the last half century have read Nordhoff's graphic reminiscences of the sea [among them were *Man-of-War Life, Whaling and Fishing, In Yankee Windjammers*]. The story of how he obtained a berth is an interesting illustration of his pluck and persistency. He had a few dollars and a meager change of clothing when he reached Baltimore. At every ship he met the same rebuff: 'Ship you, you little scamp? Not I; we won't carry runaway boys; clear out!' Undaunted he went on to Philadelphia, found a place on the *Sun* as a printer's devil, and spent his Saturday afternoons besieging ship captains. Finally, hearing that a 74-gun frigate was about to sail to China and Japan, he persuaded the editor of the *Sun*, Congressman Lewis Levin, to introduce him to Commodore Elliott. Levin's note read, 'Please give this boy a talking to,' and this gruff Commodore scolded him roundly; but when Nordhoff came repeatedly to the attack, he finally arranged an enlistment. . . ."

From 1855 until his death in San Francisco in 1901, the grandfather wrote thirteen books, beginning with his experiences in the U. S. Navy, then on merchant ships, a whaler, and Yankee fishing boats, followed by many travel books about the West Coast of the United States and Hawaii, and concluding with social and theological tracts, the last, *God and the Future Life*. In 1855 his only son, Walter Nordhoff, was born, and for his son in 1887 Charles acquired, deeded to him by Porfirio Diaz, through the Mexican International Company, of Hartford, Connecticut, the Todos Santos tract in Baja California—fifty thousand acres of coastal land, between 28 degrees and 32 degrees 42 minutes of latitude, the ranch some fifteen miles south of Ensenada, and including the Punta Banda Cape on the northwest corner. It was a formidable acquisition.

In February, one month after the purchase, Charles Nordhoff, the younger, was born in London. It was on a Tuesday afternoon, the first day of the month. Sarah Cope Whitall had prepared for the event by exposing her yet unborn child to the best of prenatal influences. She hung pictures of beautiful children in her room, listened to concerts of the finest classical music, took art lessons, read the books of the greatest English authors. But, Mrs. Nordhoff complained to her husband, there was no garden to walk in, as advised by all the standard books for expectant mothers. Notwithstanding these preparations, Sarah Nordhoff had not yet heard—and her firstborn would be more than three years old before she discovered it: the greatest single prenatal influence upon her child at the time was the coincidental purchase of the Lower California property. The lure of fish, the scent of game, and the flutter of fowl had already worked their charm on fetal Charles Nordhoff.

Walter Nordhoff, at the time of his first son's birth, had been London correspondent for the New York *Herald,* and later he was transferred to Berlin to head the office there. In Berlin the Nordhoffs took an apartment on the edge of the Tiergarten, where, Sarah Nordhoff noted: "Charlie undoubtedly began his study of water fowl, as his daily outing in a small pram or push cart led him first to the bakeries for a supply of stale buns and back to the lake to feed the ducks."

In the winter of 1889 the young family sailed for Philadelphia, where, while Walter worked in New York and commuted on weekends, Sarah lived with her parents; in the spring they moved to "Overlook," the home of Charles Nordhoff, Sr., on the Hudson River, living in a converted incubator building which they called "The Roost"; then, in September of 1890, they set out for the West Coast, eager to try a new life on the ranch in Mexico. The taxes on their property, Grandfather Charles had assured them, were paid up until 1942; so, he said, they needn't worry themselves about that.

The ranch was a worthy experiment, and Walter Nordhoff never worked harder at anything in his life. "I never forget the arrival in San Diego, after dark," Sarah Nordhoff recalled, "and the luxurious bedroom at Hotel del Coronado recently opened, with the sound of the surf outside. The next night we took the small steamer for Ensenada and arrived at daybreak. . . . How strange and wild that arrival was. The beautiful bay, the Mexicans speaking Spanish, the dusty little town, the point with its very agreeable colony of English people—and the lovely long drive on the mesa and through the river bottom to the ranch house on the flat. . . . I had a very sleepy little boy of three and a half years on my lap during that rough drive, and I wondered how I should manage to make a home there where he might flourish. It was a strange experience for a young woman who only knew housekeeping in London and Berlin; to be put down in our lonely settlement . . . with everything to organize, sources of supply very vague or distant, little knowledge of country life and hardly any knowledge of cookery. Father was wonderful in his sureness and hope—and somehow we made a home and were fed and washed and had a good time, with little Charles the life of the place."

From his first view of it, Walter Nordhoff loved his ranch in Baja California. Austere, serious, dignified, ever concealing a deep sensitivity, he nevertheless had to work his facial muscles and blink his eyes quickly against the beauty—ascetic, classical, rugged—which assaulted him now. He had studied the maps carefully, and from his vantage point on top of the Mesa de Chapultepec he slowly described with his eyes an arc from the deep green purple San Carlos hills on the left to the broad flat pastureland ahead, to beyond the ridge of Punta Banda on the right, out beyond the Bahía de Todos Santos to the horizon on the sea, where the sun, a disc of brilliant red, lingered on the rim of day. Walter breathed deeply against the lively feeling welling up within him, as from the Valle Maneadero which led inland from the bay he could smell the dankness of the bottom land mixed with the salt from the marshes.

He now scanned the length of beach on the estuary, scalloped and sandy, and he heard the restless lapping of waves on the shore and then out beyond on the rocky point, like distant thunder, the crashing of breakers. Overhead, wheeling, the sea fowl cried. From the upland side, down from the Cañon San Carlos, ran Arroyo de Maneadero, lined on either side with cottonwoods which nodded in the onshore breeze, and which now suddenly gathered itself into a wind, swiftly passing, and leaving behind the smell, sweet and lingering, of tarweed and black sage from the distant hills. Here, Walter felt certain, a man could put down roots—here at this settlement which the natives called "Ramajal."

The ranch house sat on the southwest edge of the valley, overlooking the valley and the bay. Old and Spanish, its adobe walls cracked, it nevertheless stood square, solid, massive. The four sides gave on the outside on a covered porch, and on the inside enclosed a courtyard. A heavy, carved mahogany door opened on the entry hall, floored with smoothed flagstones; and on either side, columns and arches framed doorways to large empty rooms. More rooms abounded on the other sides.

At Rancho Ramajal, Charles Nordhoff, the younger, thrived. His life bounded on one side by mountains and canyons and streams, learning soon from his father how to hunt quail and ducks, to shoot deer, to kill rattlesnakes which crawled about the property; and bounded on the other side by the shore, the bay, the sea, where Walter taught him to sail and to fish and to spear the giant turtles. Young Charles grew up close to the soil and the sea, and he learned to love every face of nature and its every name. Early he became independent, self-reliant, living a one-to-one relationship with life, unspoiled by the artificial intrusions of society or the altruistic demands of civilization. He lived in the company of danger and on the edge of violence, and gained the skill and knowledge to enjoy their fascination and mystery.

Mrs. Nordhoff, however, although noting and encouraging her son's love for the land and ocean, also noticed that he was becoming an outcropping of the very outdoor nature—wild, unruly, undisciplined—that he loved. Proper, civilized schooling, she decided, was the only corrective. In 1894, Sarah Cope Whitall prevailed on her husband to move the family from his beloved Ramajal. For four years the Nordhoffs lived at Ellendale Place in Los Angeles, while Charles was broken to civilization at Professor and Mrs. Stephen Cutter Clark's Classical School for Boys in Pasadena. Young Nordhoff hated it, but submitted, making new friends, and waiting for the weekends when he could go with his father back down to the ranch and to the life they both loved above everything else.

By the time he was ten years old, young Nordhoff already knew how to shoot a rifle. One day in spring, with two young friends from Los Angeles he went exploring in the hills of San Francisquito, up from the banks of Arroyo Las Animas. Nordhoff heard a woodpecker stuttering on a tree and set out to follow the sound. Isolating the peck, he looked up; ahead and high on a tall pine tree, he saw the bird. He raised his rifle, took steady aim, and fired. The woodpecker dropped to the ground. Now, Nordhoff insisted with his friends, they must cook and eat the bird. He cupped the woodpecker in his hands and carried him down to the river, found a bank of clay, and set the bird down. He broke some short pine branches into small pieces, gathered up fallen leaves and dry needles and tumbleweed, and with a match he started a fire. He went back to the clay bank, scooped out from the side two thick handfuls, returned to the bird, and packed him in clay; then he placed the mold in the fire. When Nordhoff thought the bird was cooked, he explained to his fascinated friends, he would break off the hard shell, and off with the shell would come the feathers, clean as a whistle, and the meat, tender and tasty, would be ready for eating. He knew it would be so, he said, poking the embers of the fire, because he had read it. His friends, Leslie Gay and Johnny Elliot, skeptical but still curious, had to be shown. When the clay had hardened, Nordhoff rolled the lump out from the fire, then broke the hard shell. The clay came off, but with it—to his unbelieving eyes—came only a few feathers. He poked his finger into a bare spot; the flesh was hard, tough. He bit into the meat, tasted, and quickly spat it out. He took the bird, reached back with his arm, and threw the bird far into the woods. "Well," he said, "it will be better the next time. Tough old bird."

They continued their explorations. Nordhoff led his friends downstream, along the left bank, and came to a point in the river of high flood, where he decided to cross over to the other bank. Gay and Elliot protested; there were no logs or rocks to step over on. "It's simple," Nordhoff calmed them. "We just take off our clothes, tie them in a bundle, carry them on our heads, and wade across." The friends were willing to try. Following Nordhoff's example, they stripped off their clothes, swung up their burdens, and started into the water. Halfway across, the river became too deep for wading; they had to swim or turn back. With one hand gripping the rifle tied to the bundle and pressing down hard, Nordhoff tried to swim upright with one arm. He lost his grip; the bundle slipped off his head and fell into the water. He grabbed the pile before it sank, thrashed out with one arm, kicked with both legs, and pulled his clothes and rifle through the water to the shore.

Gay and Elliot fared no better. Struggling to stay afloat with one hand, they lugged their clothes, hung at arm's length in the other hand, across. Reaching the other bank, they started wringing out their clothes, complaining all the while. Nordhoff apologized, but immediately set about making a fire; without a dry match, he rubbed a stick of wood into a thick branch, and after several frustrating starts, he started a flame. The boys hung their clothes on the low-hanging branches of a pine tree.

As soon as his underwear had dried, young Nordhoff pulled on his shorts, but instead of putting on his undershirt, he set it aside on a bush; then he took his knife, dismantled his rifle, took his undershirt and carefully cleaned dry his box of shells and each part of his gun. He tore the undershirt in half, and from the inside tear stripped two narrow pieces. With a long straight thin twig he pushed first one strip, then the other down through the muzzle to dry the bore of the rifle. The drying finished, he reassembled the gun; then, lifting it up to the light and holding the far end of the bore against his eye, he placed his thumbnail against the other end and sighted. The rifling sparkled clean.

Telling his friends to wait by the fire, Nordhoff set out up the canyon to find some game for lunch. With luck, he had promised them, he could bring in some quail. In thirty minutes he returned, his promise fulfilled, with two birds. But only one of the quail was killed; this one Nordhoff carried by the neck. The other, he quickly explained, had only been grazed; tenderly, with great concern for the quail's life, he bedded the bird down on his khaki shirt in the sun, at the base of a pine tree. The first one he now beheaded, slit, dressed, and plucked. Hastily, he fashioned a spit across the top of the fire, skewered the bird, and set it to roast. While Gay and Elliot watched the fire and the quail cook, Nordhoff returned to the wounded bird. He found it a curious type: of all the quail he knew—the bobwhite, the plumed quail or mountain partridge —this one was strange, different. He must bring it back to the ranch, he decided, nurse it back to health and learn all he could about it. Waiting for lunch, he wondered about the bird, and from the bird about all quail, and from quail about all birds. He would like to be, he thought, a collector of birds; and if this quail lived, he would start his collection with him. Presently, the others announced that the roasted quail was ready for eating. The boys ate hungrily and quickly; and later, after letting the fire go out, they covered it with dirt, and started back for the ranch. Nordhoff carried the wounded quail, gently, solicitously, all the way home.

Such solicitude in young Nordhoff, uncommon in boys, who for the most part torment animals and are often cruel to them, became for him prologue for a lifelong dialogue with nature. Often in his room he would lie in bed far into the night, reading, by the light from the oil lamp on the table, in his many nature books provided by his mother and father who delighted in his interest. His room at the back of the house was tall and square, the walls plastered, the floors tiled. From his double window he could look out on the valley and beyond to the hills in the distance. The bedstead, laced with rawhide, had sideboards and posts of solid mahogany, on the floor, a great bearskin served as a rug. On the far wall across from the bed, his father had hung for him a gun rack for his rifle and shotgun; and on either side of the rack, he had mounted for him the head of his first buck, a bighorn ram, and two antelope. Against these, in three even rows, were hung colored pictures of waterfowl: widgeon, teal, mallard, canvasback, all native to the marshes near Cabo Punta Banda. Along the wall in front of his bed stood his desk and against it his bookcase, filled with primers, books on arithmetic, fairy tales, nursery rhymes, and his books on birds and fishes and animals of all kinds. From these he read closely the volumes on birds. Particularly he studied quail and from his research he learned that his wounded bird now healing rapidly under his constant care, and safe from all intruders in a hastily constructed aviary in the courtyard, was a Gambel's quail, no foreigner, as he had suspected, but actually native to the southwestern deserts of America and to Mexico.

To provide his son with yet another dimension in his study of nature, Walter bought Charles a boat of his own, a 25-footer, with sail, centerboard, and a small cabin. Young Charles promptly christened the boat *Zarapico,* and soon became an expert in sailing, deep-sea fishing and trawling, and in a special kind of sea-hunting—turtle-fishing.

In 1898 the Nordhoffs moved from Los Angeles further inland to Redlands. Before they left, however, Walter Nordhoff, in order to guarantee his family a place near the water, bought a summer place off the Los Angeles coast, on Terminal Island, with a big house, a fine sandy beach, and a dock on the pier for Charles's *Zarapico.* Sarah Nordhoff, one month after their arrival in Redlands, gave birth to another daughter, her fourth child in eleven years, and at their home on Pacific Street for the next sixteen years she raised her family with guiding discipline and loving concern. As the oldest of the children, Charles was the natural leader among them and it was a role he played willingly and with a flourish. He loved to tease his younger brother Franklin (nicknamed "Rudy") and his two sisters, the older Margaret and the baby Mary, and they, for their part, never ceased to wonder and be fascinated by what their big brother was up to. For Charles, ever curious and inquisitive, was never without something to build, some experiment to complete, some concoction to make. His earliest favorite was "Swig."

In one corner of the barn behind the house, eleven-year-old Charles had built a work room for his exclusive use. His sisters, particularly, and their girl friends were absolutely denied admittance. One day Charles emerged from his work room holding a jar of dark-brown liquid. He called to him his sister Peg and her girl friends, who had been playing house in Peg's alcove, putting pieces of lumber in her play wood stove. "What is *that?*" Peg asked, pointing up at the jar. Charles showed each of the girls in turn its contents, then announced: "This is *Swig!*" Then he looked over his shoulder, made sure no one else was about, and added confidentially: "If you don't tell anyone, you can have a taste of it." He unscrewed the cap and offered the lip of the jar. "Drink!" he said. The girls each took their turn. "I like it," Peg said. "It tastes like raisins."

Charles now pulled from his pocket a handful of chocolate bonbons. "I suppose you would like one of these, too?" he said, spreading them out in the palm of his hand. The girls each took one, bit into the chocolate, then quickly spat it out. "Ugh! What's that?" Peg squealed, rubbing the back of her hand across her mouth. Charles had started back toward his work room. "Cayenne pepper," he said over his shoulder, "I made it myself." And he entered his room, and locked the door behind him.

Of special interest to Charles, and a matter about which he never teased, was his aviary, where he kept wild ducks and quail. It had started as a tub that he had sunk level into the ground. Keeping it filled with water, he used it to nurse ducks, wounded from hunting, back to health. This project eventually became a large enclosure built of tall poles, long cross-pieces, and covered with chicken wire. At one end of this aviary Charles provided a brush pile for valley quail, while at the other end he built a long shallow pond for ducks, with a duck house close by under a shade tree. And in its maintenance Charles took a page from Tom Sawyer; like Tom, who made his friends feel privileged in doing his work, so Charles had willing helpers in sister Peg and brother Rudy, who fed the birds, washed and scrubbed the pond, cleaned the duck house, raked the leaves, and swept the ground of droppings. "How's the old mallard? Did the pintail grow new wing feathers? Are there any eggs in the brush pile, do you think?" Charles, home from Clark School for the weekend, wanted a quick accounting from his young helpers.

On February 1, 1905, Charles Nordhoff was eighteen years old, about to be graduated from high school, and getting ready for college in the fall. But first, out before him stretched three glorious months of summer vacation at Punta Banda. One particularly happy outing, which he had arranged as early as spring, was with two school friends, Walter Power and Grosvenor Wotkyns, in August. The boys took a train to San Diego, then a steamboat to Ensenada, and finally they rattled by buckboard over the mesa to the ranch. At Ramajal they spent several days making plans for a long camping trip into the hills, and on the last day before they left, Charles proposed a turtle hunt. His friends readily agreed.

They started out at midafternoon, walking for a quarter of an hour along the road which followed the coastline; then they took a footpath through sand dunes to the triangular beach within the estuary, which is formed by the jutting thumb of Punta Banda and, at right angles to it, the long sandbar that points like an index finger into the bay, and the bay itself; then they continued along the creek, past the marsh, over a huge sand dune, and finally to the cove where Nordhoff's boat lay at anchor. They pulled the dingy from its hiding place under a big sumac bush, and after the other two had climbed into the stern Nordhoff launched the boat from the prow and jumped in. They rowed out to the sailboat and tied up to it. Nordhoff asked Power to take the tiller; he, with Grosvenor's help, unfurled the sail, backed the jib till it filled with wind, and then swung the boat around and pointed it out of the lagoon and toward the bay.

From under one of the thwarts Nordhoff pulled out his turtle spear. It was like a whaling harpoon, he explained, and worked the same way. He fixed a triangular steel-pointed socket to the end of a long pole, then unfouled the line attached to the socket, carefully knotted the end to a ring on the deck, and looped the excess in a neat even circle. The object, he said, was to throw the spear so that it went into the shell straight down, vertically; then, he added, the harpoon would be firmly imbedded, the pole would be pulled loose, and the tug on the line would be at the correct right angle.

The *estero* lay still; overhead a thick layer of fog had spread in over the water, to the shore, and inland to the valley. Nordhoff stood poised with his spear, one foot on the starboard gun-wale, watching intently. The water had become phosphores-cent, and every fish, large and small, outlined its form in fire as it moved. Nordhoff listened. The prow slowly hissed through the water, and from ahead, three points off the starboard bow, came a sound; it was a sigh, almost human, distinct, prolonged —and to Nordhoff, unmistakable. "That's a turtle!" he said. "Be quiet." Again he listened, carefully, then said to Power at the tiller: "He is down again. Turn toward the sound."

The sigh came once more, closer this time. Nordhoff waited for the turtle to submerge again. "He's feeding on eelgrass, and has to come up to breathe," he said. "Then we'll get him."

Suddenly, forty yards away, outlined in phosphorescence, just off the port beam, the turtle surfaced, sending out ever-widening ripples, of which he was the center. Nordhoff shifted his position to the other side, watching carefully, marking the spot as the turtle submerged yet again. Quietly they moved into the area; then, thirty feet away, the turtle resurfaced. Nordhoff was ready. He balanced the pole in his hand, cocked his arm, and shot the spear, up in a clean, smooth arc—and down it came, knifing solidly into the shell. The pole disen-gaged, the turtle started off, pulling the boat, the line angled out hard and taut, the harpoon held firm. Nordhoff now let the line play out, then looped it twice on a peg; again the line tightened, and the turtle, still strong and powerful, pulled the boat. After ten minutes the turtle tired, then played out; Nordhoff called to the others to help draw him in. As the tur-tle came alongside—he looked immense, terrifying, to Walter and Grosvenor—Nordhoff said, "I'll take the back flipper, and you"—to Power—"take the front one, and we'll pull him into the boat."

"But," protested Walter Power, "he will bite hell out of me!"

"No," Nordhoff said. "They never do."

With misgivings Walter reached over the side for the flipper. He and Nordhoff grabbed hold together, front and back, lugged and pulled, and slipped the turtle into the boat. "He must weigh almost two hundred pounds," Nordhoff said proudly as he lodged the turtle helpless on its back against the gunwale, its flippers pawing the air.

"And those jaws," Grosvenor said excitedly, pointing at the massive head, "could snap my hand off as easy as a carrot."

It was dusk before the boys got back to the ranch house. They left the turtle on the beach, feet up in continuing helplessness, for the Mexican ranch hands who would take care of it and turn it over to the cook for turtle soup.

The next morning at table, Mr. Nordhoff heartily welcomed the boys to breakfast, but not to turtle soup. "We have a special treat this morning," he said. "It's a typical Mexican dish."

The cook brought in on a tray the head of a steer. It had been broiled to a black crispness, its thick lips curled away from the teeth, the ears shriveled, the tufts of hair jutting out of the brow. It was the ugliest thing Walter Power had ever seen. The tray was placed in front of the father. "I am going to give you the best part," Mr. Nordhoff said to Walter, whereupon he stabbed a fork into one eye, twisted it out, and placed it on Power's plate.

Walter did not touch it; he blanched, trembled, and swallowed hard. 'A lie,' he thought to himself, 'is a sin and a shame, but an ever-present help in time of trouble.' "I have a very bad headache, Mr. Nordhoff," Walter blurted out, "and I had better not eat meat . . . or eyes either."

Mr. Nordhoff looked over at his son, winked, and smiled. Then he speared the eye on Power's plate, placed it in his mouth, bit down firmly, and pulled his fork away. Walter looked closely; his stomach churned as he watched Mr. Nordhoff slowly close his lips, deliberately chew, and matter-of-factly swallow. "Ah," Mr. Nordhoff said, his eyes twinkling as he looked at Charles, "absolutely delicious. A true delicacy."

Neither Walter Power nor Grosvenor Wotkyns felt like eating again that day until he had ridden far out into the country. They had started out immediately after breakfast—Charles, Grosvenor, Walter Power, and three Mexicans, with five horses, one mule, and six pack-burros. Young Nordhoff led the party out. As point, scout, lookout, seated tall and

straight, his Stetson shading his steady blue eyes, his wide firm
shoulders, lean frame, and narrow hips wedging him into the
saddle, Nordhoff felt at one with sky, animal, earth. He was
doing what he most enjoyed.

All day they traveled south and east, along the Arroyo Las
Animas and into its canyon, where they stopped for the night.
Nordhoff helped the Mexican hands to unpack the burros,
carefully slipping the square and diamond hitches that held
the supplies. In twenty minutes camp was set up. Nordhoff
started the fire, Grosvenor and Walter unrolled the sleeping
gear, the Mexicans laid out utensils, prepared the food, and
cooked. While they ate, the Mexican cook took up his guitar
and sang, sadly, about a *vaquero* who had lost his girl and his
money.

While he was finishing his plate of beans, Power noticed, for
the first time, bushes with shiny green leaves all along the
bank. "Poison ivy," he exclaimed. "I'm not going to sleep here.
I'm going to the top of the mesa." He put down his plate and
started to move his sleeping mat. The Mexicans, noting his
move, started gesturing and speaking hurriedly in Spanish.
"No, no," the Mexican cook tried to explain. *"Tigres!"* Walter
didn't care about the possibility of tigers, and tried to convince
Grosvenor and Nordhoff to join him on the mesa. Wotkyns
agreed, but Nordhoff stood firm. He would stay along the
arroyo and sleep with the Mexicans, he explained. The next
morning, Nordhoff had caught a bad rash on both ankles, but
that was no bother. The important fact, although no tigers had
come prowling on the mesa that night, was that his Mexican
hands had not lost face before the son of the *patrón*.

At the end of the third day, they came to a high promontory.
Far below, to the east and north, stretched the broad plain of
the Colorado River and the head of the Gulf of California.
They stopped to make camp and hunt. Mountain sheep were
plentiful; and the mountain quail—almost twice the size of
valley quail, Nordhoff observed—abounded, and they were so
unfamiliar with man, he walked right up to one without the
bird's moving, and promptly shot the quail's head off. Grosvenor shot two sheep in less than ten minutes, and Walter had
bagged four quail in less than five.

Nordhoff had rarely tasted better lamb and quail. After they had eaten, Walter and Grosvenor went for a short hike; Nordhoff elected to stay, to help the Mexicans clean and cut the rest of the meat. They made jerky, cutting the meat in thin strips, rubbing it in salt, and hanging it up in the sun to dry. As he finished cutting a hind quarter, Nordhoff was approached by one of the hands. One of the burros, the Mexican explained, had a bad sore on his back. Nordhoff went to look. Under one of the heavy tie-straps, the burro had developed a large, ugly ulcer, full of maggots. Nordhoff opened his pocket knife, applied the edge, and started scraping. Meanwhile, Walter had returned from his walk and came over to look. "You'll have to get them all out," he said to Charles, and picked up a stick to help in the cleaning out. Nordhoff was puzzled. "What can we put on it so it'll heal?" he asked. "We don't have any salve or medicine." "Tequila," Walter suggested. "That should be strong enough to kill anything." Nordhoff went to one of the packs and pulled out a bottle of the liquor and poured half of it into the ulcer. Seeing this, the Mexicans loudly complained; they disapproved of such medication at their expense! And furthermore, they added, it wouldn't work!

The Mexicans were right. The next day the maggots were back in force. Nordhoff consulted with Walter, then asked Grosvenor's advice. Again they dug out the worms, but this time applied some potassium permanganate. The next day, after they had turned south toward the San Pedro Martir Mountain Range and had come upon a vast rolling countryside covered with ponderosa pine and juniper, they decided to stop and check the burro's ulcer. Yet again it was full of maggots! Again the young men held a consultation. Power tried to reason out the problem: the maggots came from the flies; so how could they get rid of the flies? "Salt," Nordhoff suggested. "Flies hate salt." Once again they cleaned out the ulcer, and this time packed it with salt. Three days later, by the time they returned to Punta Banda, the ulcer had healed, a complete cure.

In such outings—out to the sea in boats, up to the mountains on horseback—young Nordhoff flourished, as his mother once hoped he would when they first moved to Ramajal. And

IN SEARCH OF PARADISE 144

he grappled to his soul such friends as Gay and Elliot, Power and Wotkyns, their adoption tied "with hoops of steel." But to the north, civilization continued to make its incessant demands upon him—for education, for culture, for refinement, for the social amenities and, most of all, for "making a living."

That same year Charles matriculated into Stanford, at Palo Alto, but only completed the freshman year. The San Francisco earthquake of 1906 had broken the walls of the Beta Theta Pi fraternity house where he was living, and had sent plaster raining down from the ceilings. Charles fled the house unharmed, but strangely attired: in his haste to dress, he had put on one foot a brown shoe, and on the other, a black. Amid the disaster and its aftermath, most of the students returned to their homes as quickly as they could. But not Charles Nordhoff. He prevailed on several of his fraternity brothers to help him set up a soup kitchen for the needy in San Francisco. They bought up as many of the staples as they could find—stew meat, potatoes, carrots, string beans, peas, onions—borrowed a large black scalding kettle, and brought these to the city. They rented a restaurant stove and cooked a great mulligan stew, set up the pot on a downtown street corner, and ladled out the stew for hours, until it was all gone.

Back in Redlands, however, Mrs. Nordhoff, who had thought the worst about what could have happened to her college son, was terrified at his long absence. When Charles finally came home, she was so happily relieved of her anxiety, and so determined that no such disaster would befall him again, she decided then to send Charles as far away from the West Coast and the San Francisco area as possible. She sent him to Harvard.

In Cambridge, Charles was an indifferent student. He studied only those subjects which interested him, and often those subjects were not in courses for which he had enrolled for credit. He was content to be a face in the crowded lecture hall, unknown to his professors, a man of solitude and mystery to most of his classmates, a perfectly proper and respectable gentlemanly C-student. Charles was no hermit, however. One very good friend at Harvard was a classmate, Ed Springer, who, like Charles, was a transfer student, Springer from the University of Iowa. They had both pledged Beta Theta Pi, had both been brought up in Southern California, and both had many mutual friends. Further, they both enjoyed hunting and fishing, which sealed their friendship.

Charles and Springer became roommates, living in Apley Court, attending classes together, endlessly discussing in their room history, literature, hunting, fishing, ranching, and, after taking Dr. Peter's course in mining, prospecting. Charles became so interested in the course Mining 16 that he earned an A, his only one in college, and for good reason: he hired a famous old prospector, Tom Finan, whom he had met at Springer's ranch in New Mexico, to search the Ramajal Ranch for gold, and he wanted to be able to prospect on his own after Tom left. In further relief from the academic atmosphere Charles would often visit his mother's brother, Jack Whitall, in Jamestown, Rhode Island, during the holidays. Here he would sail in Narragansett Bay, fish, shoot birds in the marshes, and swim at the shore.

After Charles had been graduated from Harvard in 1909, he tried the sugar-cane business, taking a job in Vera Cruz, Mexico, and becoming after a short while, because of his fluency in Spanish and his skill in dealing with the natives, the supervisor of the plantation. He fell in love with the dark and beautiful daughter of the owner, who, in love with another, rejected him. This bitter disappointment, coupled with the Madero Revolution in 1911, drove him out of the Mexico he had loved so deeply, never to return.

At that same time in 1911, Walter Nordhoff had become interested in the clay business. He bought a factory site near the railroad in National City, close to San Diego. He asked Charles to help him establish the company; Charles agreed, and father and son formed the California China Products Company. They produced tile of various glazes, yellow bowls, and high-tension insulators, firing the clay in eighteen-foot kilns at 2,700 degrees Fahrenheit by burning oil mixed with compressed air. The clay was pressed under a giant wheel and screw at forty tons to the square inch, producing fine dustlike clay for the firing, with only 10 per cent moisture.

Working at the plant with Charles was a young man his age,

Walter de Steiguer, an expert in glazing, who similarly enjoyed hunting and fishing, boating and riding; they quickly became friends, and with Charles's brother Franklin they rented a house in town and hired an old Nordhoff retainer to be their housekeeper. At the factory the three of them competed in their ability to bring the great circular kilns up to the exact temperature for finishing—never more than five degrees above or below 2,700. The task required constant vigilance for forty hours, and great skill; for, under fire, the kiln developed a momentum and inertia of its own, and, like a heavy freight train, it could run away if the temperature increased too quickly, or fall behind and resist every effort to get it going again. Then came the anxious after-period of waiting for the kiln to cool, of removing the firebrick door, brick by brick, to see the results at last.

At first the Nordhoff company prospered. Up and down the state of California china tiles were used to face fireplaces and hearths, wainscots, the fronts of stores and buildings, the tops of domes, walls, and floors. Most famous was the great dome of the main building in the city park of San Diego, and, in the same city, the walls and floor of the Santa Fe Depot. Charles Nordhoff left his thumbprint—his artist's signature—on many of the tiles. But he never got truly motivated to make a success of himself in the business. And he never got used to the clay dust; it always gave him indigestion.

After work, the two young Nordhoffs and de Steiguer would drop in at the San Diego University Club for a preprandial drink. They would invariably follow the same ritual. At first they talked, of the business of the day, of the affairs of government, of the news and sports results, each trying to outlast the other—thirsty, throats dry from the clay dust, fidgety, glancing at the bar. Finally, one would break and call to the others: "All right, all right! You win! What'll you have?" John, the Negro club steward, would approach chuckling, and take the order from the loser. For Charles, the order was always the same—"the true, the blushful Hippocrene"—his favorite brand of Irish whiskey.

The three young men had little to do with San Diego social

life, not even going to the Saturday night dances at the Hotel del Coronado. At first there had been invitations to social affairs from the best families in town. To such activities Charles's reaction was chilled indifference: these affairs, undoubtedly crowded with pretentious mediocrities, loud and uncouth drunks, and twittering, brainless women, could only bore him to death. Rather, on the weekends, Charles, Walter, and Franklin would quickly escape from the city, to surf-fish and swim on lonely beaches, to troll for barracuda, albacore, and yellowtail around the Coronado Islands, to hunt quail on mesas and ducks in the lakes, sloughs and bay shallows, to catch trout in the high mountain streams, to explore abandoned gold mines around Julian.

Of the experience Walter de Steiguer wrote: "It is difficult to describe, exactly, the quality of that happiness we experienced on these expeditions into regions not yet befouled and desecrated by trampling human herds. The mere hunting and fishing, as such, had little to do with it—they were the excuse rather than the purpose, and often neglected. We were angered by the destruction of natural beauty anywhere, and were perhaps subconsciously hostile toward the world of men because of it. In effect, we escaped from that world, into a world of nature with which we felt in harmonious accord. I believe that, unspoken, there existed in us an almost awed realization of how wonderful and beautiful the Earth is—of how grateful we should all be that we can live on it and see it."

Despite the initial successes of the company, over the next few years two factors contributed to an insurmountable problem: the tile factory could not continue in business without clay and without labor. Walter Nordhoff had been offered the Corona clay pits at a favorable price, but because he already owned the kaolin mine on top of Mount El Cajon, he declined. The kaolin mine, three thousand feet up the mountain, produced a fine white clay which was packed twice a day, carried down a looping three-mile trail on thirteen burros, each carrying 150 pounds, then hauled by truck to National City. Supposedly good in the manufacturing of porcelain, the kaolin proved unsatisfactory; the clay from the Corona pits, however, turned out to be worth a fortune. Then, with the beginning of the war in 1914, skilled workers became more and more difficult to hire and to retain. Disgusted, Walter Nordhoff early in 1916 sold his company to the Bauer Tile Company.

Charles, for his part, was not saddened. He did not particularly like the tile business; as a matter of fact, he did not like any industry. His outlook in commerce had never thought much of fame or fortune. And making money in trade was, somehow, vulgar.

In the fall of 1916 Charles Nordhoff sailed for Europe. He would rather, he thought, seek his destiny among soldiers fighting a war.

2

An Ambulance Driver

When the United States declared war on Germany on April 7, 1917, Charles Nordhoff had already been serving France as an ambulance driver since the previous December. He had been at the front in Alsace on the Vosges sector since the first of the new year and had not yet heard the news about America. That afternoon, a Saturday, the commanding general of the division had ordered Nordhoff and the other Americans to report to headquarters at four o'clock. As the drivers polished shoes, pressed trousers, and cleaned puttees, Nordhoff speculated about the order.

At the appointed hour the Americans appeared at head-quarters, a fine old château, and were met by an English-speaking French officer, who greeted them warmly, took their names, and led them inside. The general and his staff had formed a reception line, and as each man's name was called by the adjutant, the American marched forward, saluted, and shook hands. When Nordhoff, as last man, had been presented and introduced, orderlies started to bring in glasses and bottles of champagne. Glasses were filled.

The general glowed with friendliness. He raised his glass in toast, and gestured toward Nordhoff, who stood tall, erect, blond like a Prussian. "Your country, gentlemen," he said, his black eyes sparkling, his back straight as a rod, "has done France the honor of setting aside this day for her. It is fitting that I should ask you here, in order to tell you how much we appreciate America's friendship, which you and your comrades have been demonstrating by actions rather than words. I am an old man, but I tell you my heart beat like a boy's when the news came today that the great sister republic—united of old by ideals of human liberty—had thrown in her lot with ours. I ask you to drink with me to the future of France and America —the sure future. You have seen France: our brave women, ready to make sacrifices for the motherland; our little soldiers, invincible in their determination. Let us drink then to France, to America, and to the day of ultimate victory, which is coming as surely as the sun will rise tomorrow."

The general stopped and went from man to man, touching glasses; then, as they started to drink, a band standing ready outside now started to play "The Star-Spangled Banner." Nordhoff and his group quickly drank the champagne and came to attention, through the American national anthem, and then through the "Marseillaise."

Later as they stood outside in a group on the lawn, the general, who had been raising his head each time he talked to Nordhoff and the other drivers, had to comment on the stature of the Americans. "Mais vous êtes des gaillards," he said, brusquely but in good sport. "See, I am five or six centimeters shorter than any of you. But wait, we have a giant or two." He stepped over to a tall French captain, brought him back to where Nordhoff stood, and placed the captain and Nordhoff back to back. The French officer topped Nordhoff, who was just six feet tall, by an inch. The general laughed.

"But, mon général," the captain said in good humor, "it is not good to be so tall—too much of one sticks out of a trench."

The time came for the American guests to take their leave, but before he departed Nordhoff was introduced to the owner of the château. A small and frail woman in her late fifties, she carried herself tall and proud. Nordhoff had been told by one of the French officers that her husband was dead, and that her two sons had been killed in action, one, the older, in the Battle of the Marne, and the younger most recently and nearby, with whom had gone the hope of continuing the family name. Nordhoff offered her his sympathy. Erect, head held high, the woman smiled. She looked straight into Nordhoff's blue eyes. "Why should I weep?" she said. "There is nothing finer my boys could have done if they had lived out their lives."

Nordhoff had become very fond of the French, and constantly marveled at their courage. This admiration from him had been earned from the very beginning of his ambulance service. One of his first days at the front was typical.

He had been on the road all day and well into the evening. That morning he had taken out a few wounded, one on a stretcher and two with smashed legs who had refused stretchers and struggled up to the ambulance on crutches. As one climbed into the back, he hit his wounded leg against the side and cried out. Nordhoff was starting the engine, stopped, and called back to help. "*Ça pique, mon vieux,*" the soldier said, "*mais ça ne fait rien.*" He waved Nordhoff on. "*Allez!*"

The hospital was several miles behind the lines. When they arrived, there was the usual wait for identification papers. Nordhoff tried to explain the cause for the delay to his passengers. "The bookkeeping is tiresome"—he shrugged—"but necessary. I'm sorry." The soldier on the stretcher moved; the blanket covering him was heavily stained with blood. The soldier looked up, wondering. "*Oh, là là!*" he said, resigned, "*c'est une guerre de papier. Donnez-moi une cigarette, s'il vous plaît.*"

That afternoon Nordhoff made the same trip again, bringing back four stretcher cases. One of the wounded, offhanded and almost flippant, explained their plight. "*Il faut faire attention aux mouches.*" The flies—the bullets, shells, and shrapnel—could not always be brushed off.

Again that evening, just before he turned in, Nordhoff had another call. It was from a dressing station at the front. He dressed hurriedly and stepped outside. The night was ink black. He shrugged. He did not like the three kilometers he had to drive without lights over a narrow twisting road. He had no sooner started down the road when he had to stop. He could not see. He rolled down the window and put out his head. It had started to snow; large, thick flakes fell on the side of his face. He reached for his flashlight, pointed it forward, and flicked it on, then quickly off. He could see a few feet of straight road followed by a curve to the left. He started the ambulance again and drove it as slowly as it would move, by the inch, by the foot, by the yard. After one kilometer, he heard from far off on the right the sound of guns. He looked toward the sound and saw flames on the horizon. Then, closer, another battery opened up. Shortly after it had fired a few rounds, the German guns answered. Nordhoff strained his eyes looking forward on the road. Suddenly, a shell exploded a few yards to the right and ahead, slamming dirt and debris against the cab and along the right back panel, knocking the ambulance into a jackknifing skid. Nordhoff corrected, turning into the skid, and straightened out. Slowly, he continued on.

It took more than three hours to get to the front. The snow had stopped. The dressing station, Nordhoff discovered, had been converted into an emergency hospital because of the number of casualties. It was a dugout, heavily reinforced with extra beams, and crowded with wounded soldiers. When Nordhoff reported in to pick up his patients there was a great noise of complaint going on inside. But it didn't come from the patients. The stretcher-bearers, bearded and grimy, had just been told they would have to be vaccinated against typhoid. *"Sacré espèce de typhoïde,"* said one, spitting the words out through the spaces between his yellow and blackening teeth; and the other stretcher-bearers agreed with him.

Leading the stretcher-bearers out of the trench to his ambulance, Nordhoff noticed as he came up an ugly silhouette of what had been: fractured willow trees; broken walls and blasted windows of houses; the shattered steeple of a church. And as he picked his way carefully along he noted that the ground underfoot, almost as far as he could see, was pocked, slashed, and cut with trenches and shell holes.

The three kilometers back to the hospital proved better than the trip out, now that the weather had cleared, and Nordhoff, remembering the road, drove quickly and with confidence. As his patients were being unloaded, he heard from one of the orderlies that one of the wounded brought in by another ambulance was a German prisoner. Never having seen one of the enemy, he went into the hospital for a close-up look. A crowd of curious visitors had encircled the German, and Nordhoff had to work his way through to see him. The prisoner lay on a stretcher on the floor, covered by a gray overcoat; the man's eyes stared fearfully from a thin bearded face; his chin and mouth shook from shock and exposure.

Someone in the group reached out, grabbed the German by the foot, and started shaking his leg; as he did, he spoke a profanity, short, vile, abusive. A French soldier who lay on a cot nearby lifted up his bandaged head and reprimanded first the culprit, then the crowd. "Enough," the soldier commanded. "He is a Boche, I grant you, but first of all remember he is a soldier, wounded and in your power!"

Nordhoff felt guilty and ashamed. He should have been, he knew, the first to come to the prisoner's aid. His attention now turned to the poilu who had spoken out. The soldier, Nordhoff discovered in talking with him, had been on a raid into enemy lines in order to get a few prisoners; he called it a *"coup de main."* Noting the late hour and despite the soldier's willingness to talk, Nordhoff waited for two days to get the full story.

When he made his visit he found the soldier sitting up; glad to have company, the soldier was bright and talkative, and seemed happily progressing to full recuperation. He was full of enthusiasm about the coup. "Our battalion commander called for one platoon of volunteers to make the attack," he began, "each volunteer to have eight days' special leave afterward. It was hard to choose, as everyone wanted to go—for the 'permission,' and to have a little fun with the Boches."

Nordhoff offered the soldier a cigarette, then lit it for him and another for himself. "At noon we were ordered to the first line," the soldier said. "Our rifles and equipment were left behind, each man carrying only a little food, a canteen of wine, a long knife, and a sack of grenades. Our orders were to advance the moment the bombardment ceased, take as many prisoners as possible, and return before the enemy had recovered from his surprise. At the point of attack the German trench is only twenty yards from ours—several nights before, they had rolled out a line of portable wire entanglements. At four thirty in the afternoon our 75's began to plow up the Boche trench and rip their wire to shreds. It was wonderful. Along the line in front of us hundreds of our shells, bursting only twenty meters off, sent earth and wire and timbers high up into the air, while not one of us, watching so close by, was hurt.

"At five-fifteen the guns ceased firing, and the next instant we were over the parapet, armed with knives, grenades, and a few automatic pistols. After the racking noise of the bombardment a strange quiet, a breathless tranquillity seemed to oppress us as we ran through the torn wire and jumped into the smoking ruins of the enemy trench. In front of me there was no one—only a couple of bodies—but to the right and left I could hear grenades going, so it was evident that a few Germans had not retreated to the dugouts. Straight ahead I saw a *boyau* leading to their second lines, and as I ran into this with my squad, we came upon a German at the turn. His hands were up and he was yelling, '*Kamerad, Kamerad!*' as fast as he knew how. Next minute, down went his hand and he tossed a grenade into our midst. By luck it struck mud, and the time fuse gave us a moment's start. The corporal was killed and my pal, Frétard"—he paused to point out his friend several beds down the line with his leg bandaged and hanging in traction—"got an *éclat* through the leg. We did not make a prisoner of that Boche.

"The *abris* of the second line were full of Germans, but all but one were barricaded. A few grenades persuaded the survivors to come out of this, with no fight left in them. But how to get into the others? In vain we invited them to come out for a little visit—till someone shouted, 'The stovepipes!' Our barrage fire was now making such a fuss that the Boches farther back could not use their machine guns, so we jumped on top of the dugouts and popped a half-dozen *citrons* into each chimney. That made them squeal, *mon vieux—oh, là là!* But it was time to go back—our sergeant was shouting to us; so, herding our prisoners ahead, we made a sprint back to our friends."

It was during this sprint, the wounded soldier explained, that the German machine-gun fire opened up, winged him in the left arm, and grazed the left side of his head. Nordhoff felt envious. He too, he knew, would like this life of action; if he was going to take chances as an ambulance driver, why not as a full-fledged combatant? He walked back to his quarters slowly, thinking.

Although the idea of combat had taken root, two other incidents would have to nourish it before it could flourish into action. One was Nordhoff's association with an infantry sergeant named Jean. The other was the time he watched his first aerial dogfight.

The soldier Jean had been in Spain when the war started, but soon rushed home and volunteered for service. He had had only two weeks of basic training when he was ordered to the front. Jean saw action, distinguished himself immediately, and was promoted to corporal in a few days. In one big attack, he led a squad of soldiers into a German trench and captured a new German machine gun and many boxes of ammunition to go with it. Jean promptly had his men hide the equipment in some bushes nearby.

Often during the ensuing days, the lines on both sides would be captured, lost, and recaptured, only to be lost again. Patrols had to be made day and night to locate the latest movement of the enemy. Here Jean shone. Swearing his squad to secrecy about the location of the weapon, he had drilled each man for a quick and efficient assembly and disassembly of the machine gun, and looked for his opportunity to strike. It came one morning at dawn when Jean moved his squad in close to the German lines, set up the gun on the top edge of a dry riverbed, and waited. As light broke, Jean looked down, watched, and counted—first thirty, then forty German soldiers some seventy yards away, come above ground to work on a new trench. Jean's companions became excited, anxious to fire at once, but he held them off, forced them to wait—one hour, two hours, three. Then the Germans, having grown tired from their digging, put down their picks and shovels, lay down on the ground, and rested. Jean was ready. He pointed the machine gun and opened fire, pouring a full belt of two hundred rounds into his helpless victims; then, quickly, his men dismantled the gun, each man took his piece, clutched his ammunition belt, and they scurried back to their own lines.

Nordhoff, who that day had been driving the division commander on an inspection tour of dressing stations, had seen most of the action from an advanced observation post, had watched through binoculars from a platform high up and hidden in a thick pine tree. That evening he met the squad leader. Jean's commanding officer had brought him to the command post at the colonel's request.

"Ah," the colonel said, his face breaking into a quick smile, "so this is the type who was on patrol this morning—hm. I was in the advanced observation post on the hill above you and saw the whole affair with my glasses. And how many of those poor Germans did you kill?"

"I did not wait to count, *mon colonel*," Jean said, his face flushing. His gray eyes sparkled proudly; he brushed back a shock of thick black hair with a quick sweep of his hand.

"I will tell you then," the colonel continued. "Six escaped out of thirty-eight. Most remarkable rifle fire I remember seeing. It sounded like a *mitrailleuse* at work. How many in your patrol? Five? Remarkable! Remarkable! *Eh bien,* good day, *sergent.*" Jean had thereupon been promoted.

Several days later Jean invited Nordhoff to come along on a raid, promising him a leave, for they would certainly capture a German. Even Jean's lieutenant thought the idea superb. "Better come with us," the officer said. "I want to run down to Paris next week, and if the sergeant here and I don't get a prisoner or two, it will be because there are none left in the first line. Come on—you'll see some fun!"

Nordhoff was forced to decline. According to the regulations of the Geneva Convention, he could not be a combatant as an ambulance driver. "But," Nordhoff said, "what is there in it for me? Just this: I'm ruined if I'm caught in any such escapade. And," he added half smiling, "in any case, I get no permission."

"Oh, we'll fix that," Jean said. "Maybe you'd get a nice little wound . . . and if not, I'm an expert with grenades. I think I could toss one so you would just get an *éclat* or two in the legs—good for a week in Paris."

"No thank you!" Nordhoff said quickly. He certainly did not elect that alternative; and although he would have liked to join in a *coup de main,* he simply could not.

The next morning as he lay in his bunk, rereading a letter from home, an orderly broke into Nordhoff's dugout, excitedly explaining that a fight between three aeroplanes was going on in the sky just outside. Nordhoff immediately joined the spectators.

Nordhoff looked up and squinted his eyes. A large two-seater French reconnaissance plane, fairly low and swerving right and left, was being chased by a German one-seater fighting plane—it looked to Nordhoff like a Fokker because of its neat circular tail—which in turn was being plunged upon from on high by a French Nieuport fighter, "like a falcon on its quarry." The Nieuport held its burst, started down on a loop up and around the Fokker, straightened out, came in broadside, and fired. The German, decidedly hurt, started to drop, first gently to one side then to the other, "like a leaf falling in still air," then more quickly and steeply, and finally crashed behind a distant hill. The French plane, despite his kill, was now having trouble of his own. The German artillery had opened up on him and some of the bursts were coming close to the tiny plane. Defiant, the Frenchman danced among them, up and down, left and right—exultant, proud, full of scorn, passed over the lines, and, safe for another day, sped home.

Watching the spectacle, Nordhoff had been delighted and amazed. To fly—what a wonderful way to fight in the war and be away from the muddy trenches! To be clean and free as a bird and still do the dirty work of war, detached, objective, cool, impersonal like a surgeon, cutting out a cancer in the body of civilization.

It was April. Soon after America's entry into the war, Nordhoff submitted his resignation from the Ambulance Service and left the front. On May 25, in Paris, he made out his application for the French Foreign Legion. After passing the physical examination, he was enlisted. It was Sunday, June 3, 1917. That night he wrote home: "I have passed the French examination and am to leave for the school in a day or two. I have been lucky!

"It was interesting at the Paris recruiting office. I stood in line with dozens of other recruits for the Foreign Legion—all of us naked as so many fish—in the dirty corridor, waiting our turns. Each man had a number: mine was seven—lucky, I think! Finally the orderly shouted, '*Numéro sept,*' and I separated myself from my jolly polyglot neighbors, marched to the door, did a *demi-tour à gauche,* and came to attention before a colonel, two captains, and a sergeant.

" 'Name, Nordhoff, Charles Bernard—born at London, 1887 —American citizen—unmarried—no children—desires to enlist in Foreign Legion for duration of war—to be detached to the navigating personnel of the Aviation,' read the sergeant monotonously. In two minutes I had been weighed, measured, stethoscoped, ears and eyes tested, and passed."

The colonel looked at Nordhoff "coldly and turned to the captain. 'Not so bad this one, hein? He has not the head of a beast.' "

Nordhoff "bowed with all the dignity a naked man can muster, and said respectfully: '*Merci, mon colonel.*'

" 'Ah, you speak French,' the colonel rejoined with a smile. 'Good luck, then, my American.' "

3

A Fledgling Birdman

The École Militaire d'Aviation at Avord was larger than Nord-hoff had expected. Located in the plains of central France, it was eighteen kilometers from the town of Bourges, and only a few kilometers from Avord itself. There were, he had been told, more than 2,000 élève-pilotes in training, 150 of them Americans. As he entered the main gate in a taxi, Nordhoff was impressed by the neat arrangement of the roads and buildings, the great number of barracks, row upon row, the red tile roofs, the crushed-rock and gravel paths. He paid the driver and walked over to the aviation field and stopped; it was immense, flat, covered with green grass, more than three and a half miles wide, and down one side stretched groups of hangars, busy with hundreds of aeroplanes. Overhead dozens of planes were flying, it seemed in every direction. Nordhoff turned down the road and walked to headquarters. The adjutant assigned him a barracks number, issued slips to take to the quartermaster for flying gear, and told him where he could mess.

When Nordhoff checked in at his barracks, it seemed empty.

He went to his cot, one of twenty he counted from the door, dropped his gear on the bed, and was about to leave when he heard a voice coming from the far corner of the room: "Come on, 'leven—little seven, be good to me! Fifty days—little Phoebe—fever in the South! Read 'em and weep! Ten francs—let 'er ride. I'll fade you!"

Nordhoff walked over to where the voice and found two men shooting crap on the floor behind a bed. One of them was a Negro, the one apparently who had been coaxing the dice to performance. Nordhoff introduced himself. The Negro rose and shook his hand warmly; the other dice player smiled and gave a friendly salute, got up, and limped over to the bed. The Negro was Eugene Bullard; from Columbus, Georgia, he said proudly. His appearance, Nordhoff observed, was brilliant: from his jolly, smiling black face to his breeches of bright scarlet, to his gleaming tan aviator boots, he glowed. The other gave his name as Harrison, from San Francisco. He was a young, freckle-faced redhead; not yet, Nordhoff guessed, twenty-one years old. Nordhoff was full of questions about the program at Avord, but first he had to know about Harrison's leg, what had happened to it.

"I made a bum landing yesterday," the young pilot explained. "Turned the cuckoo over and twisted the old game knee."

"Were you flying a Bleriot?" Nordhoff asked.

"He'll never finish his *tour de piste*," Bullard said jovially, "unless he learns to keep his nose high on landing." The Negro laughed and started to leave, explaining he had to get back to the flight line. He pointed to the pair of enormous gold wings which decorated his black tunic. "You have to be able to land to win these," he said, and left.

"You'll start on Penguins tomorrow," Harrison explained. "They are tricky little cusses to run in a straight line. When you can run 'em straight at full speed with the tail up, they'll put you on the 'rollers'; they can fly, but you're not supposed to let 'em do it. After that you'll try your hand in the *décoller* class. That's where you're first allowed to get into the air—just a few yards up and in a straight line." He chuckled at what he had just said. *"Décoller*—pretty good, huh? You 'unglue' yourself from the ground in that class. And after that, you'll be where I am now—*in tour de piste."*

"Tour de piste? That's one I haven't heard before," Nordhoff confessed.

"That means you fly around the field about two hundred meters up. After that you do a few spirals and an altitude flight, and then they send you off cross-country for your brevet flights. When you've done those you can stick a couple of wings on your collar and call yourself an aviator." He shifted his weight on the cot and puffed the pillow for his head. "Then," he continued as he lay down, "if they think you're any good, they'll make a pursuit pilot out of you and send you down to Pau to do acrobatics; and if you get through without pushing up daisies or smashing too many machines, you'll be ready to try it out on the Boche."

"I'm going to end up in a pursuit ship or bust," Nordhoff exclaimed.

"That's the stuff," the redhead said approvingly. "That's the way we all feel."

That night after an undistinguished meal of bread and soup and lentils at the mess—the *ordinaire,* they called it—Nordhoff turned in early, thinking that as long as he had francs to spare he would have to find another place to eat. For the ordinaire was certainly very ordinary, in every respect.

At 3:00 A.M. he felt a hand shaking his shoulder. It was one of the orderlies, an Annamite Chinese who, smiling a betel-black smile, told him it was time to get up. The Annamite carried a large heavy pot and offered to pour Charles a cup of coffee from it. Nordhoff got up and reached for his tin cup. On the top of his forearm he noticed a red welt. "Damn bedbug!" he cursed as he held out his cup while the orderly poured. *"Beaucoup bon! Beaucoup bon!"* the Chinese repeated as he tipped the pot. Nordhoff took a sip, almost spat it out, but held it in his mouth without swallowing. The coffee was boiling hot, its taste bitter. Nordhoff set down the cup, thinking he might try another sip later. He lighted a cigarette and started to dress. He had never worn so many clothes all at once: breeches, golf-stockings, high leather boots, khaki shirt, wool sweater, and leather coat. He carried his flying helmet, a ridiculous thing, he thought, made of leather and cork-lined and shaped like a beehive.

Sleepily the men dragged themselves out of the barracks for the morning roll call in front of the Bureau de Pilotage. Names were answered to; then the students checked the wind gauges, read the barometers, and noted the great red balls for indicating that day's passing side as right or left. The various flying units formed and were led off by their adjutants. Nordhoff was left with a small unclaimed group; obviously, he reasoned, they were all of them beginners.

A short stocky French officer with a thick moustache came over and stood at attention in front of them. *"Rassemblement!"* he commanded. *"Mettez-vous sur quatre!"* They formed fours, clumsily but reasonably in line, and the officer marched them off down a long road. By the time the adjutant had halted them before a hangar, the mechanics had already rolled out the planes for their use. The planes were the famous Penguins—Bleriots incapable of flying because the wings had been cut off short, and the three-cylinder Anzani engines, he was told, provided a frightening amount of power for beginning taxiing.

The instructor was tough and obstreperous. He called out the names, giving the order for the morning's practice. Nordhoff watched those ahead of him most attentively. *"Allez! Roulez!"* the sergeant shouted. The student had to open the throttle, keep the plane in a straight line, lift the tail up, and run several hundred yards across the field; there he stopped, idled the motor, had the tail turned around by an attending Annamite, and returned to where he had started. The requirement, Nordhoff thought, seemed simple and easy enough. The sergeant started to call, in turn, the names of the rank beginners.

Four of the new students climbed into the little planes. The blasts of air from the propellers, combined with the simultaneous handling of the throttles, joy sticks, and rudders, were too much for most. The planes dashed in every direction, missing by feet and inches head-on collisions and crashes into the sides of fuselages; it was only the steel tusks that protruded from in front of the planes that saved them from nosing over. The instructor ran up and down the side of the field, waving his hands in the air, shaking his head to the right and left. *"Oh, là là là!"* he screamed in staccato. *"Les cochons! Ils veulent tout casser! Oh, là là là!"* The beginners returned at last, stopped their motors, and climbed down, flushed and embarrassed.

Nordhoff's name was called. He walked over to the plane slowly, and climbed in. Seated, safety belt fastened, head down in the plane and trying to ignore the blast from the prop, he appraised the inside of the cockpit. At his left hand he worked two short-stemmed levers, one the fuel mixture, the other the throttle. Between his legs he gripped the stick—the *manche à balai*, or *cloche;* he pushed it forward and watched the tail lift up; he leaned it first to the right, then to the left and saw the wings warp up and down in response. He rested his feet on a horizontal bar ahead and just off the floor; he pivoted the bar down and up, and watched the rudder at the tail fan back and forth. It was as easy as working the tiller on *Zarapico* and swinging her out into the bay, Nordhoff thought, his confidence secure.

Nordhoff opened the throttle, first cautiously, then wide open; the propeller clattered loud in answer. He started down the field. Gently he nudged the stick forward and brought up the tail; he kept the rudder bar even, firmly but lightly under the balls of his feet, steering the plane straight, even, smooth, like his boat with a full sail. He came to the Annamite waiting on the edge of the field, stopped, and was turned around. He rushed back to the hangar as arrow-straight as he had set out. He brought the mixture and throttle levers back to idle, and at the same time pulled back the stick to drop the tail skid. The plane stopped. Nordhoff jumped out.

The instructor was full of congratulations. "If you can run her out and back a second time as well as you did this," he said, clapping Nordhoff on the back, *"mon vieux,* I'll send you to the rollers this afternoon."

Less than twenty minutes later Nordhoff was walking back to the barracks, a graduate of the Penguin Class.

At Avord Nordhoff quickly grew accustomed to the regimen.

But some of the conditions were intolerable. The fleas and bugs, particularly, were impossible, and he had to take frequent baths and many chrysanthemum powderings to keep them at bay. And with a ground and flying schedule that started at 3:00 A.M., ended at 11:00 P.M., and allowed few breaks, he had to readjust his sleeping habits by taking frequent naps. And after the one meal he had eaten at the ordinaire, he quickly learned where and what to eat elsewhere. He went to Farges for breakfast, and to Avord for lunch and dinner. In the morning he ordered fried eggs, hot chocolate, thick slices of hard-crusted homemade bread spread with rich butter, then confiture, and cheese. In the evening, at the Café des Aviateurs in Avord, he dined substantially: soup or omelette, roast veal, peas, fried potatoes or string beans, salad, cheese or confiture, and coffee.

Often, Nordhoff would take his meals in the company of Tom Buffum, another American, from New York, who became a good friend; but if they were joined by two or three of their colleagues, Nordhoff would invariably get up and find another table, for one. He simply could not abide a crowd, especially at table.

At the flying field, the roller class had become overcrowded, and it was announced that Nordhoff's group would have to wait; meanwhile, however, they could all have permission to take leave for a few days. Some of the Americans had decided to go to Nice, and asked Nordhoff to join them. Reluctantly, he agreed. Of Nordhoff's aloofness, one of the group reported:

"He took his fun in public with the rest of us with a puckered nose, but his private fun was private, very private indeed. For the rest of us, fun in all its categories, like the work we had to do, was strictly a communal affair. But not Charlie! . . .

"One of us had learned that a wonderful Madame Elaine's was just the place to spend a noisy week with Madame's lovely charges. So we left Paris one day by train for Nice. Charlie was one of us. All the way down, the conversation was nothing but of Elaine's, of course, and Charlie was not approving at all. We were just a lot of guttersnipes out to waste our beautiful young lives. So we laughed at him and tried to smooth his feathers. His frown only deepened.

"The train made a short stop at a suburb of Nice and by that time Charlie had decided that we were no fit company and that he was going to get off the train. No amount of arguing could stop him. So we got to Nice without Charlie. But on the way to Elaine's we somehow discovered another Madame's . . . which, it seemed, was much better than Elaine's. So there we went instead. . . .

"After dinner that night things began to get noisy and Madame warned us that the police called at intervals and that we should quiet down and try to deport ourselves as respected burghers should when they did call. All the shades were drawn. At about ten there was a rap on the front door at the bottom of a long flight of stairs. We were all up the stairs. Madame came flying, stage-whispering, '*Les flics, les flics.*' So we hid behind drapes and furniture, but not where any of us would miss watching how Madame handled '*les flics.*' Everything arranged, she went sedately down the long flight of stairs and opened the door. And who should walk in but Charlie? We let him get to the stop of the stairs before we pounced on him! Needless to say, Charlie spent the rest of the week with us. His nose was still puckered, we still laughed at him, and he had just as good a time as did the rest of us."

Back at Avord after the *congé*, Nordhoff rededicated himself to the art of flying. Days of intensive training passed. With as much ease as he had enjoyed with the Penguin, he hoped for the same luck with the Bleriot. He had studied its performance carefully, watching the successes and failures of the other élève-pilotes with it. The plane had to be pointed down the straight-away, lifted a few feet off the ground, and quickly returned to earth. It seemed as easy as the Penguin itself; but because his name began with "N" and was far down the list, and because his classmates before him had a number of crashes, Charles began to get anxious about himself, his anxiety sharpening with every crack of wing, snap of spar, and scrape of an engine in a nosing-over. Two hours passed before his name was called.

Nordhoff described the event in a letter to his mother: "At last the monitor called me and I was strapped in behind the whirling stick. The monitor waved his arm, the men holding the tail jumped away, and I opened the throttle wide, with the *manche à balai* pushed all the way forward. Up came the tail: I eased back the control bit by bit, until I had her in *ligne de vol*, tearing down the field at top speed. Now came the big moment, mentally rehearsed a hundred times. With a final gulp I gingerly pulled back the control, half an inch, an inch, an inch and a half. From a buoyant bounding rush the machine seemed to steady to a glide, swaying ever so little from side to side. A second later, the rushing green of grass seemed to cease, and I was horrified to find myself looking down at the landscape from a vast height whence one could see distant fields and hangars as if on a map. A gentle push forward on the manche brought her to ligne de vol again; a little forward, a reduction of gas, a pull back at the last moment, and I had made my first landing—a beauty, without a bounce. Tonight I may crash, but I have always the memory of my beginner's luck—landing faultlessly from fully twelve feet!" The décoller that followed was easy.

A few days later Nordhoff made his tour de piste—a flight at three hundred feet around the flying field. On takeoff, the Bleriot flew itself into the air. But Nordhoff, worried about landing later, because he knew the plane to be heavy for its supporting wing area, could, at low speed, fall off on one wing, or worse, pancake in a stall. Nordhoff made his turns around the field, shallow with the wind, steeply into the wind, keeping his required distance, then headed down for a landing. Gently he eased forward on the stick, throttled back, and nosed in. The ground rushed up at him. He started to redress, "precisely as a plunging duck levels before settling among the decoys," skimmed close to the ground, brought the nose up slowly, stalled the wings, and smoothly settled back on the field.

Nordhoff's good luck, firmly abetted by skill and daring, continued to hold until a routine flight one week later. It was the last flight of the morning. He had leveled off for a landing too high above the ground, quickly stalled, and pancaked from ten feet up. Fortunately he escaped unhurt, and the plane was only slightly damaged.

"I was not sorry for the experience," Nordhoff confessed later. "[It] blew up a lot of false confidence and substituted therefore a new respect for my job and a renewed keenness to succeed."

On October 30, 1917, Nordhoff was breveted. He had hoped to use a sixty-horsepower Bleriot for the trials, but only a Caudron was available, a small single-seater biplane. In it he had to fly for one hour at an altitude of more than seven thousand feet, do a number of vertical spirals from three thousand feet, and finally on other days make five cross-country flights—two round trips fifty miles out and back, and three triangular flights, one hundred and fifty miles to a side.

On a chill, damp Tuesday morning the trials began. Against the cold Nordhoff dressed in heavy fur pants and jacket, fur-lined boots and mittens. He felt clumsy walking out to the plane and had to be helped by the mechanic to get into the cockpit. He put on his leather helmet and adjusted his goggles.

"*Coupe, plein gaz,*" the mechanic shouted as he pulled the propeller through. Then he added: "*Contact?*"

"*Contact!*" Nordhoff answered, his head poked over the side.

The motor spurted to life. Nordhoff carefully fed it throttle, nursing it with enough mixture, listening for the even fire in the cylinders.

"*Contact réduit,*" the mechanic yelled back at him.

Nordhoff agreed. "*Contact réduit,*" he shouted in response, then listened again. All ten cylinders were hitting with precision. Nordhoff signaled for the removal of the chocks.

The plane turned and headed into the wind. Nordhoff advanced throttle, held his feet steady on the rudder bar and pointed the plane straight down the field. Slowly he inched the stick forward, raised the tail, then eased back on the stick and lifted the plane off. He looked down over the side. The wheels were still spinning, the ground rushing by, and the engine, snarling, clattered at full power.

He raised the nose slightly, leaned stick and rudder gently to the right, and started to ascend in wide shallow spirals. He climbed for eight minutes, then checked his altimeter: six thousand feet. He looked up. Thick clouds were rushing by just a few feet overhead; he had to find a way up. He found a hole, blue and clear, started up through, adding throttle, climbing in tightening circles, and broke out on top. Above the clouds, he felt suddenly different, like an escaped soul, gathered into the artifice of eternity:

"I began to float about in a world of utter celestial loneliness," he said of the flight, "dazzlingly pure sun, air like the water of a coral atoll, and beneath me a billowy sea of clouds, stretching far away to infinity. Here and there, from the cloudy prairies, great fantastic mountain ranges reared themselves; foothills and long divides, vast snowy peaks, impalpable sisters of Orizaba and Chimborazo, and deep gorges, ever narrowing, widening, or deepening, across whose shadowy depths drove ribbons of thin gray mist."

The hour was soon over. Nordhoff nosed back down in broad easy spirals, sunk into the tops of the clouds, looked out, then suddenly began to feel very strange, unsure of himself and the plane, completely out of balance, totally without a sense of direction. The clouds had enveloped him, and in them he could tell neither up nor down, right nor left. He pulled his head into the cockpit and glued his eyes to the instrument panel. He would have to trust to the numbers and dials, working throttle, stick, and rudder according to their readings, all the way down and through the clouds.

When at last he broke out below, Nordhoff was relieved. He brushed the back of his mitten across his perspiring brow and smiled to see the ground, clear, lined and quilted below and, in the distance and off to the right, the unmistakable hangars of Avord.

After he had landed and parked the plane, he walked back to the barracks slowly. After such an experience, anything to follow in the trials, he felt, would be mundane, pedestrian. For the spirals he would simply climb a few thousand feet, stall the wings and kick rudder, count three turns to the right as he fell, straighten out, and pull up. For the cross-country flights, he would simply follow the roads and railroads, rivers and canals, counting the towns as he went, watching altimeter, tachometer, and compass, straight out to Châteauroux and back for the first two flights; then for the last three he would go triangularly to Châteauroux, Romorantin, and back to Avord.

These trials were for Nordhoff as easy as he had expected. After he had finished the last cross-country flight, one of the new beginning students approached him as he climbed out of his airplane. "How were the tests?" the beginner asked anxiously. Nordhoff was deliberately casual, almost imperial. "I was lucky," he said, "and had no trouble at all." Taking off his helmet and goggles, removing his mittens, unwinding his long white silk scarf, Nordhoff knew: He was ready now for the school for combat at Pau.

Before reporting to the new assignment in the south of France, Nordhoff was granted a delay en route in Paris. He stayed at the Chatham. Checking into his room, he quickly washed and changed into a fresh uniform. Carefully, he pinned small gold wings on either collar of his uniform, and over the right breast pocket of his tunic the wreath and wings of an *aviateur*. Then he went to the Folies-Bergère, the favorite rendezvous for Lafayette men in the city.

He sat at the bar and ordered champagne. During the first two glasses he was bright and affable; then, suddenly, with the third, his disposition soured, and dourly he held forth on any subject raised—"a tirade of gloom," Bradley Fairchild, one of his American friends from the Lafayette Flying Corps reported. "But," Fairchild added, "his lectures were beautifully spoken masterpieces."

Nordhoff ranted: "Russia is through for good and may sign a separate peace. Italy's army is permanently crippled probably. The French are scrapping terribly in politics . . . and America—good Lord! the amount of rot we read in the papers! Her 'latest' airplane specifications were six months out of date seven months ago . . . the Liberty motor is useless for a Front machine . . ."

Bradley Fairchild sat and listened, enraptured at Nordhoff's sardonic eloquence. "He damned our civilization," Fairchild said, "our mores, our general inanities, and the small cramped minds, in particular, of idiots like us who joined other peoples' wars . . ." Then Nordhoff ended on the note of costs and taxes: "It costs the government from thirty thousand to forty thousand dollars to turn out a fighting pilot. Three, six, ten

machines—costly, delicate things—are smashed daily. . . .
We will be paying for this war for generations to come. The
taxes on the yet unborn will be awesome and tremendous."
Glumly he finished his bottle of champagne, left the bar, and
returned to his hotel.

After this bitter siege of melancholy, Pau proved for Nordhoff a palliative. He loved the school and could not say enough
in praise of it and its location. Pau, situated in the Gave Valley
at the foot of the Pyrenees, was to him "like the foothill climate of California: cool nights, delicious days, wonderful
dawns and sunsets." And of the school he said, ". . . the hundreds of splendid machines, the perfect discipline and effi-
ciency, the food, the barracks, the courteous treatment by officers and instructors . . ." He looked forward to the month of
intensive training in the Nieuports—the fastest and most difficult planes in France. The students, all breveted pilots and
treated accordingly, started by flying twelve training flights a
day. They had to master acrobacy, formation flying, and gunnery; only then would they be ready for the front and for combat.

Nordhoff was eager to start. He began on an eighteen-meter
Nieuport and started by doing vertical spins to the left and
right from 3,000 feet. As opposed to the other *vrilles* done at
Avord, this time he had to shut off the motor, pull the stick all
the way back until the wings were absolutely vertical, and kick
the rudder a hard right; down he was supposed to plunge for
five tight turns, losing about 300 feet for each turn. But Nordhoff, too anxious to do well the first time he tried, neglected to
pull the stick all the way back, lost 2,100 feet in three-fourths
of one turn, went into a long glissade and, almost crashing into
the tops of the trees edging a forest, finally turned into the slip,
recovered, and straightened out in time. Not wishing to land
after such a bad performance, he now climbed again to a thousand meters, stalled and kicked to the left, and this time did
five turns in a thousand feet; then he climbed back up again
and did the same to the right. It was a splendid, redeeming
performance.

"*Oh, là là là!*" the moniteur greeted him after he landed.

"Go to the next class!" he ordered. "I won't have you killed in mine! What's more, I'm sick of buying flowers to put on the graves of suicides. Your two spirals were not bad. But I do not teach wing slips into forests on this field. I ought to give you ten days in the guardhouse—you didn't pay attention to what I said about pulling back on the stick! But I'll promote you instead!"

The next class was a joy, for it offered many opportunities for pleasure flying. On his first day of formation flying, this time in a small, fast and powerful fifteen-meter Nieuport, Nordhoff climbed to the designated altitude for rendezvous and found none of the other planes there. They were all, he decided, joy-riding; Nordhoff, happily noting he had fuel for three hours, decided he would do the same: "I rose to about four thousand feet, and headed at a hundred miles an hour for the coast. In thirty minutes I was over Biarritz, where my eyes fairly feasted on the salt water, sparkling blue, and foam-crested. I do not see how men can live long away from the sea and the mountains. My motor was running like a clock and as I was beginning to have perfect confidence in its performance, I came down in a long coast to the ground, and went rushing across country toward the mountains, skimming a yard up, across pastures, leaping vertically over high hedges of poplar trees, booming over the main streets of the villages, and behaving like an idiot generally, from sheer intoxication of limitless speed and power.

"In a few minutes I was at the entrance of one of the huge gorges that pierce the Pyrenees—the sort of place up which the hosts of Charlemagne were guided by the White Stag; deep and black and winding, with an icy stream rushing down its depths. Why not? I gave her full gas and whizzed up between black walls of rock that magnified enormously the motor's snarl, up and up until there was snow beneath me and ahead I could see the sun gleaming on the gorgeous ragged peaks. Up and up, nine, ten, eleven thousand feet, and I was skimming the highest ridges that separate France and Spain. Imagine rising from a field in Los Angeles, and twenty minutes later flying over the two-mile ridges of Baldy and Sheep Mountain, swooping down to graze the snow, or bounding in the air with more speed and ease than any bird."

Nordhoff checked his time: the hour was almost over. He turned back toward Pau and when he saw the hangars in the distance, started down. Suddenly the engine clattered, and with one loud blast, stopped; a broad tongue of flame, bright and fierce, licked back over the motor; several hunks of metal, broken and loose, lashed back against the nacelle and fuselage. Nordhoff closed the throttle and nosed down, trying to maintain flying speed. Smoke, thick and black, squirted out and enveloped the cockpit. "Holy mackerel!" he thought, "this is the end of me! Let's see—in case of fire, shut off the petrol, open throttle, and leave the spark on. Then go into a nose dive."

Dutifully, automatically—and surprisingly, he thought—he obeyed his commands to himself. He piqued, leveled off at five thousand feet, and shut off the motor. The fire and smoke stopped. He went into a shallow glide and started to look out over the cockpit, from one side to the other, hoping to find soon an emergency landing place. Poplars, tall and lovely, but decidedly in the way, edged all the fields he could see. He would have to come in high, he decided, to get over them. He found one field, long and in the direction of the wind, and decided to try for it. He glided down, shallow, just over stalling speed, made one wide S turn, then, disgustedly, saw that he had fallen too low to make it over the trees. He would have to take a chance. He pulled up, sailed over the poplars, stalled, and pancaked into the field. Luckily, he was unharmed; his plane, however, was crumpled. The wheels had come to a stop when they hit a ditch, and the wings, hitting the bank, had badly splintered.

For this caper, however enjoyable before the crash, Nordhoff was punished. The monitor sentenced him to ten days in the school jail. Nordhoff was crushed by the verdict. The only consolation in the sentence was that his friend Tom Buffum was in the same cell with him, but for another offense. Tom had run out of gas and landed in an apple orchard. For his part, Buffum was not at all unhappy at being in jail. "Actually," he said, "we were more comfortable than in the barracks and we went out to fly every day. Charlie [however] was sunk in gloom at the humiliation of it all and suffered acutely during his whole sentence, especially as he did not think he deserved it."

Despite his jail sentence Nordhoff finished formation flying in ten days and was ready for the final stage of training, the *Haute École du Ciel*—acrobatics. All the pilots were apprehensive about this final test, since only the most skillful, with cool minds and strong stomachs, could survive. Many who didn't lay under white crosses in the little cemetery at Pau. The instructor of this class, a lieutenant, was a personality of great reputation. Nothing and no one could impress him. Impeccably uniformed, he would lie in his steamer chair, monocle firmly in place, calmly watching his charges. The officer's most complimentary remark, and that only for the finest possible performance, was a laconic, *"Pas mal, celui-là."*

One day one of the Russian fliers had killed himself doing a spinning nose dive, and the class was sad, depressed, and fearful. The lieutenant knew the only remedy for this kind of malaise. Slowly he rose from his steamer chair, handed his riding crop and gloves to an assistant, and climbed into the cockpit of his own thirteen-meter Nieuport, the "Black Cat." What followed was an exhibition of flying that left Nordhoff and his classmates dumbfounded. The lieutenant was quickly off the ground; then, at breakneck speed and close to the ground, he looped, rolled, spun, pulled up in a long climb and then over and right side up in an Immelmann; then around and back again, now with his motor throttled back, he skimmed over the hangar, stalled into a smooth and effortless landing, and stopped, not ten feet away from where Nordhoff stood with the others. The lieutenant, Nordhoff had to admit, was the most *gonflé* pilot he had ever seen.

It took two weeks before Nordhoff learned all the intricacies of acrobacy, but with the lieutenant as model of courage and skill he finally began to master the spirited thirteen-meter Nieuport. "Think of it," Nordhoff said of the plane, "only thirteen square yards of supporting surface." And like the other pilots, he dreaded having to do a *vrille* in it. Finally the order came.

"Nordhoff, Nordhoff!" the moniteur called one day.

"Present!" came the reply.

"You will take the checkerboard," he ordered, "rise to twelve hundred meters, and do one vrille and two upside-down turns."

"Yes, sir, *mon lieutenant,*" Nordhoff answered and walked out to the plane.

Nordhoff never forgot the experience. "Two turns of the field gave me thirty-six hundred feet," he said of it. "This was no time to hesitate, so, as I reached the required spot, away from the sun, I shut off the motor, took a long breath, and pulled back a bit on the stick. Slower and slower she went, until I felt the rather sickening swaying that comes with a dangerous loss of speed. The moment had come. Gritting my teeth, I gave her all the left rudder and left stick, at the same moment pulling the stick all the way back. For an instant she seemed to hang motionless—then with unbelievable swiftness plunged whirling downward. 'Remember, keep your eyes inside—don't look out, whatever happens,' I thought, while a great wind tore at my clothing and whistled through the wires. In a wink of time I had dropped six hundred feet, so I carefully put the rudder in the exact center, centered the stick, and pushed it gently forward. At once the motion grew steadier, the wind seemed to abate, and the next moment I dared to look out. It was over. . . ."

And, now, sure of himself and to show the lieutenant that he was as *gonflé* as his master, Nordhoff climbed back up twice and did two more vrilles. It was one of his great days, and when he heard the lieutenant say to the adjutant, *"Pas mal, celui là,"* about him, he knew with certainty that he wanted to become a *pilote de chasse.*

For this reason he worked extra hard at his gunnery, practicing every day at the Vickers and Hotchkiss machine guns. He preferred the Vickers because it could fire an unlimited number of cartridges from a belt feed; but finally he had to admit with the other pilots that the best shot in the air was mostly a

matter of good piloting and of good luck with a gun that did
not jam.

On November 26, 1917, Nordhoff, now fully fledged, was ordered to Plessis-Belleville for G. D. E. Groupe des Divisions
d'Entraînement, he knew, meant only one thing: Reassign-
ment to the front. Happily and at last, he was ready to fight in
the war.

4

The Escadrille N. 99

Plessis-Belleville in December was bitter cold. Nordhoff had arrived and was waiting on the platform at eight in the morning after a long sleepless night sitting crowded with others in the dining car of the train from Paris. The trip to the little village in the north of France was only thirty-five miles, but there had been interminable and unaccountable delays; and Nordhoff, who had not yet had a cup of coffee, stomped restlessly back and forth, waiting for the camp truck, the snow squeaking underfoot as he turned in his pacing. Thirty minutes later the truck came.

Nordhoff swung his gear up and boarded. The truck traveled one kilometer and broke down. Nordhoff unloaded, paced and waited in the snow another half hour until relief transportation came—a tractor pulling a flat-bed truck. Wearily, stiffly, he climbed up. Two hours later he was unloaded at his barracks, his face frozen, his hands numb, his toes immovable in his boots. Another hour passed checking in, presenting credentials, signing papers, before he found the mess hall. It was,

Charles noted readily, the converted hay loft of an old barn; it was unheated, the floor boards creaked from the cold, and through the slits in the front wall behind the serving trays an icy wind whined. The food—scrambled eggs, fried bacon, and broiled kidneys—was cold; Charles ate hungrily and quickly, drinking frequently from his coffee, which was hot. He returned to his barracks and found the billet assigned to him. It was a cot, with a shelf overhead, one of seventy in a great bay, vast, formidable, and cold. Needing no further encouragement, Nordhoff had himself transferred back to town and took a room at the only hotel there, the Hôtel de la Bonne Rencontre. Although it was old and run down, dirty and dusty, and *la patronne* had no help, a cheery fire burned in the fireplace, his bed was comfortable, and at last, he was warm. Even the yellow, flowered wallpaper, stained and streaked, took on, after some scrutiny and reservation, a homelike quality.

For flying the next morning Nordhoff dressed as warmly as possible. He pulled on thick flannel underwear and heavy woolen socks, a flannel shirt, and a sleeveless woolen sweater; then he climbed into breeches and tunic, boots and puttees; and finally, over all, he struggled into great fur-lined, waterproofed, canvas-covered jacket and trousers, squeezed into knee-high fur-lined flying boots, fur-lined tight-fitting leather flying helmet, and fur-lined leather gloves; upon his forehead he adjusted triplex Meyrowitz goggles. With a flourish he gave three turns about his neck to his long gray muffler, and left the room.

He wanted to spend at least half of his time at the field, flying. The average training period at Plessis, he had learned, was only three weeks, and he wanted all he could get of acrobatics, simulated combat, formation flying, and machine-gun practice before he received his combat orders. And so, he quickly discovered, did three hundred other pilots at Plessis, and they were flying anything that could get off the ground— Voisins, Bréguets, Sopwiths, Caudrons, Letords, even Morane Parasols. Nordhoff hoped for a Nieuport or a Spad. When, only two days later, the Bureau de Pilotage assigned him a Nieuport and prescribed his flying schedule, he was delighted:

he might manage now to get his orders even sooner than he had expected. Absurdly, Nordhoff had the fear—one common to every young man who had gone through flight training—that the war would be over before he could take part in it. And with even greater luck, he hoped—along with every other French-trained American pilot—to be assigned to Escadrille N. 124, the famous Escadrille Lafayette, and fly with the great aces Thaw and Lufbery.

Nordhoff practiced his flying assiduously, but not without diversion. One day after an afternoon session of combat tactics with five other planes, diving and tangling with six "enemy" fighters, he broke off from his group, climbed to twelve thousand feet, and headed for Paris. Regulations forbade such a flight, but all the pilots tried it at least once, because after all, it was against standing orders and it was a thrill not to be missed by any flier. And the altitude, a wise precaution, was one high enough that in the event of motor trouble it would allow him to glide over and out of the city into an emergency landing field in the suburbs.

Twenty minutes out, Nordhoff looked over the side of the cockpit. Ahead and below was an unmistakable Parisian landmark: the great airport of Le Bourget. Nordhoff throttled back to cruising speed, then in great wide arcs he slowly circled the city. With ease he picked out the Tour Eiffel, Nôtre Dame, the Bois de Boulogne; the Seine, a silver ribbon unspooled, lay across the city, elliptically looped the Île de la Cité, spun out, curled, and played out through the woods and parks into the outskirts, into the suburbs, stretching and thinning out, and disappeared at last into the east. It was not a dream, he assured himself, and a shiver of delight accented his view.

It was dusk when he returned to Plessis and landed. As he waited for transportation, he decided to check the bulletin board at the Bureau de Pilotage for the latest assignment orders. He ran his eye down the lists. To his surprise, his name was there:

Caporal Nordhoff, Charles B.
Escadrille N. 99
Groupe de Combat 31

He was overjoyed. It had only taken two weeks for his orders to come through, and they meant he would be flying a Nieuport, out of Lunéville, in Lorraine; for that was the location of the squadron on the front. One other American was on the same list for the same squadron: Clifton B. Thompson, who also lived at the Hôtel de la Bonne Rencontre.

One hour later Nordhoff was at the station at Plessis. On the way to Paris he slept, having no intention to waste any time sleeping in bed in the city. The Gare de l'Est was jammed with soldiers returned from the front. Many of them were still covered with mud, but the mothers and sisters, the wives and sweethearts hugged them in their splattered overcoats and kissed their dirty unshaven faces. Nordhoff took a room at the Chatham, changed, then walked to the Cercle des Alliés, formerly the Rothschild palace, where he dined. Indulging his gourmet taste, he treated himself to a thick slice of rare roast beef with a rich wine gravy, browned potatoes, and creamed asparagus, sipping with the entrée a light Burgundy of marvelous bouquet, and with the dessert, which was a light *gâteau* with chocolate frosting, a bottle of champagne. After dinner he went to the Olympia to see the show. The tables were crowded with aviators, and the gossip was loud. Charles caught snips and snatches of conversation: "Luf has bagged another Boche"; ". . . is a prisoner, badly wounded"; "poor chap, shot down two days ago."

The few hours of permission had soon passed. At eleven Nordhoff returned to his hotel, picked up his luggage, hailed a taxi, and went to the railroad station. The train, predictably, was filled with officers and men returning to the front. "Not," Nordhoff readily noticed about his peers, "the *embusqué* type of officers . . . clerkish disciplinarians, insistent upon all the small points of military observance; but real fighting men and leaders; grizzled veterans of the Champagne and the Somme, hawk-nosed, keen-eyed, covered with decorations."

Toward noon he arrived at Lunéville. At the station a welcoming committee from the escadrille waited for Nordhoff and Tommy Thompson, who promptly joined them on the platform. They were brought by touring car to the base and directly to the mess hall, where lunch awaited them. That af-

ternoon Nordhoff met his commanding officer, Captain Rougevin, whom he found charming, poised, and affable. The captain showed Nordhoff and Thompson their billets, first-class
arrangements obviously for officers, with stove, dresser, easy
chair, and bathtub. Then they were taken to the hangar and
shown their planes. Nordhoff marveled at his. It was a brand-
new Nieuport, fresh from the factory, and the *mécanicien* was
installing a Vickers machine gun on it. Other parts and instruments lay on a workbench.

Later that afternoon Nordhoff returned to the hangar and
helped his mechanic with the plane; together they installed
altimeter, tachometer; timed the clock; and sighted the machine gun. Nordhoff sat in the cockpit and adjusted the seat
belt. *"Voudriez vous le voler?"* the mechanic asked. Impulsively, Nordhoff decided to test-flight his plane then and there.
"Oui!" he answered.

On first pull-through, the engine sprang to life. Nordhoff
taxied out and turned into the wind. On takeoff he forced the
nose to stay on the ground, then eased back on the stick; the
motor snarled, the plane leaped off the field and started to
climb, steeply. He banked slightly to the right, and the plane
rose in a spiral, up, up, hundreds of feet in seconds. He
checked the altimeter: three thousand feet; then, straightening
out momentarily, he pulled back on the stick, all the way; the
plane, hanging by the prop, quivered; he kicked hard right
rudder, the plane fell off in a *vrille,* once around, twice, three
times it plunged headlong; then he applied opposite rudder,
brought the stick forward, eased back, and pulled the plane
out, skimming the tops of the trees edging the west side of the
field.

Now to test the machine gun!! He turned toward the river.
There, anchored in the water, was a practice target. He came
in low, lining up with the banks on either side, nosed down,
aimed the cross hairs of the sight on the bull's eye of the target,
and fired. A stitch of little geysers seamed the water. He was off
the target, to the top and right. He turned up steeply and
came around for another pass. This time he nosed further
down, aimed, and fired again. The target shuddered and shook

as the shots grouped in the center. He pulled up and off the target; he was exultant; for that would be good enough to bring down any Hun. Then, before turning for home, and to make sure the last pass was not luck, he tried three more times with equal success.

At dinner that evening as guest at the commanding officer's table, Nordhoff learned that more than his mechanic had watched his performance that afternoon. *"Il marche pas mal, celui-là, cet Américain Nordhoff,"* he overheard Captain Rougevin say to the squadron adjutant. Nordhoff, realizing that the remark was made deliberately in a stage whisper for his ears too, bowed his head politely and said: *"Merci, mon capitaine!"*

If his first day, Nordhoff thought, was any indication of how his assignment to the squadron would go, he could not ask for a better start. Before returning to his billet, he watched an orderly post a notice on the escadrille bulletin board. It was the next day's schedule. "Patrouille Haute," he read, "5,000 metres, 8:45-10:45." He read down the list of pilots posted for the sortie; then he saw: "Caporal-Pilote Nordhoff, Charles B." Immediately, Nordhoff was delighted; then, upon reflection, he started to worry: What would he do if a Boche got on his tail?

Before he turned in that night, Nordhoff was visited by the flight leader of his morning mission, who explained the standard operating procedures. Nordhoff, he said, would be the last man on the right side of the V formation, about three hundred feet behind the man in front of him. He was cautioned: Watch the movements of leader's plane. If he moved his rudder back and forth, that meant: "Open your throttle, we're off!" If he wriggled his wings: "I'm going to attack, so stand by!" or, "Easy, I see a Boche."

Long after the flight leader left his room, Nordhoff lay in bed, wide awake, trying to remember everything he had been taught, but remembering most the last injunction of the leader: "You'll have to watch your step, Nordhoff," he had said, "and limber up your neck so that you can keep a lookout in three directions at once when you're in the air. You have the-sun right in your eyes, and often you won't see the Boches till they're right on top of you. Remember," he had added over his shoulder as he walked out, "keep your head on a swivel!" It was Monday, January 10, 1918.

The next morning Nordhoff was awake before he was shaken by the orderly. He washed and dressed quickly and went to the mess for *café au lait*. At eight o'clock he was at the hangar to pre-flight his plane; at eight thirty he took off, climbed to the designated altitude, and waited for the patrol to join up. As each plane took its place in the formation, Nordhoff, the last to take his turn, fell in at the rear of the flight. Alive with excitement, he looked about: to either side, up and down, front and back. He checked his instruments. He looked ahead. The flight leader fanned his rudder, opened throttle, and started to climb. Eagerly, Nordhoff followed.

Ten minutes out, he was surprised by a strange, yet somehow familiar, sound. His plane rocked to the concussion. It was the archies, throwing up thick black balls with red centers, and they thumped as they exploded just below. For the first time Nordhoff was hearing them from above, rather than below on the ground as he had from the trenches. The flight leader started to thread his way through the bursts, banking hard, first to the left, then to the right, twisting, turning, climbing, diving in evasive action. Nordhoff tried to keep up, but in his anxiety to follow close on, he was not flying his plane as well as he knew how.

Try as he would, he kept falling further behind the others. In his steep turns to the left and right, although he was applying enough rudder, he was not using enough back pressure on the stick to keep his nose level. As a result, he was sideslipping each time he turned, and now, to his frightened concern, he looked out and saw there was no one to follow. He had been left behind, alone. Quickly, he looked about him, scanning the sky, from wing tip to wing tip, from nose to tail, below, up. . . . *Up?* The sharklike bodies and the pointed noses were almost unmistakable. They looked like Albatrosses. Hoping they weren't, Nordhoff's heart sank.

When five of the planes broke from the patrol and started

down, Nordhoff was now certain they were the enemy. And they had drifted in on him before he could decide what to do if they did. He was surrounded. The Boches opened fire from behind, below, above; the rattle of machine guns, faint at first, then loud and distinct; the acrid smell of smoke; the stab of tracers into his fuselage. It seemed eerie, untrue, a dream; then the slow realization: he was being hit, the enemy was trying to kill him, he must do something, fast. The Albatrosses had lifted off, but had started around again to make another pass at him. Nordhoff drove the throttle forward, pulled back on the stick, and started climbing, steeply in zigs and zags. He leaned over in a hard right turn and headed back for his lines. He looked back: he had shaken off all but one of the Albatrosses. This one, Nordhoff figured, was either a beginner anxious for his first kill, or a grizzled veteran seeking yet another laurel. Either way, he decided, he must tangle with him.

Nordhoff checked his altimeter: twelve thousand feet. Below and behind him, the Hun was maneuvering in to get off another burst at him. Nordhoff moved fast. He slammed his controls to the left, turning sharply, circled back, dove, and then climbed back up from behind and slightly to the left. The tables had now turned. Nordhoff kicked right rudder, sighted the cross hairs of his Vickers on the iron cross, and fired. The burst was wide and to the right. Disgusted, Nordhoff pulled up and veered off left and away; as he did, he turned his head and saw the Boche dive, turn, and run for home.

If, Nordhoff mused as he flew back to base, he had been victorious, he would have had to treat the squadron to champagne; perhaps it was just as well, he tried to convince himself, but with little success. Especially was this true when, after he had landed, he heard that Henri, the young Frenchman in his same patrol, had scored his second victory in as many sorties. That night Nordhoff reported to his mother by letter, giving her most of the particulars: "He [Henri] ran across a very fast German two-seater ten miles behind our lines, fought him until they were twenty miles inside the Boche lines, followed him down to his own aerodrome, circled at fifty feet in a perfect hail of bullets, killed the Hun pilot as he walked (or ran) from machine to hangars, riddled the hangars, rose up, and flew home. He shot away over four hundred rounds," Nordhoff concluded, incredulous at the performance, "a remarkable amount from a single-seater bus, as the average burst is only five or six shots before one is forced to maneuver for another aim."

Mrs. Walter Nordhoff in Pasadena, California, read the account, and for her part was impressed once more by her son's report, as she had been by all his adventures at the front and in the air. Thinking that her son Charles had the same kind of literary talent as his grandfather and namesake Charles Nordhoff—who, like his contemporary, Herman Melville, had been a seaman and an author—she sent a sample of Charles's letters to Ellery Sedgwick, editor of the *Atlantic Monthly*, in Boston. She had read in that magazine the stories of another young American, James Norman Hall, first from the trenches at the front with the British, then about air battles with the Lafayette Escadrille, and she thought her son's reports were as good.

Ellery Sedgwick agreed with her. "We have had many and many a journal," the *Atlantic* editor wrote to her, "and were quite ready to give your son's letters a rather casual reading. We had not read a paragraph or two, however, before we saw readily that here is a genuine record of things as they are, full of life and fire and color. The vignettes are vividly done, and the whole diary certainly worth preserving . . . with the privilege of cutting, we shall be most glad to accept it." The letter was simply signed, "The Editor."

Sarah Whitall Nordhoff quoted Sedgwick in her next letter to her son. ". . . a genuine record of things as they are, full of life and fire and color." Nordhoff read the words, hardly believing this was the reaction of such a distinguished editor. Nordhoff had not thought when he was writing letters home that he had been serving an apprenticeship to the craft of writing, but now with such a favorable reception, and that by the *Atlantic,* he gave more thought and care to his compositions. The accounts of his days as an ambulance driver started appearing in the January issue; then, for later publication, Sedgwick accepted some letters about the air war. "This last letter of your boy," he said to Mrs. Nordhoff, "is so fresh and delightful that I cannot help but print the series you have been so good as to send me."

Because Sedgwick was now getting separate stories from Nordhoff and from Hall, who were total strangers to one another, about similar activities, the editor, growing perplexed about which to accept, accepted both. "These letters of your boy are extraordinarily vivid and refreshing," he wrote to Nordhoff's mother. "I wish I had known him, but happier days may yet bring us together." Then he went to the heart of the problem: "I have hesitated about writing to you to accept this new article on account of the existence of the same old complication regarding Mr. Hall's papers, discussing many of the same things, but I think I cannot forego the pleasure of giving these last letters to our public."

Charles Nordhoff now lived and flew to write. At first he became self-conscious of his style, too aware of word choice, sentence structure, and paragraph arrangement; then, being enough of a self-critic to see that he was getting stiff and formal and losing his easy and natural manner, he corrected his own bad habits. Occasionally, however, an ironic tone crept in, and perhaps too many adjectives: "On a raw foggy day," he wrote, "in the cozy living room of our apartment, with a delicious fire glowing in the stove, and four of the fellows having a lively game of bridge, one is certainly comfortable—absurdly so. Talk about the hardships of life on the front!"

On February 19, 1918, Nordhoff was transferred to the American Army, commissioned as a second lieutenant, assigned to the Aviation Section, Signal Corps, and on the same day reassigned to his same outfit, Escadrille N. 99. Without ever having changed place, and in less than twenty-four hours, he had been elevated from the enlisted ranks to the officer corps, promoted from corporal to lieutenant, and greatly improved in his economic welfare.

Nordhoff's basic life, nevertheless, remained unaltered; his activities continued in the present as they had in the past, flying missions and recording his impressions. "For myself," he wrote to his mother, "there is nowhere and nobody I would rather be at present than here and a pilot. No man in his senses could say he enjoyed the war; but as it must be fought out, I would rather be in aviation than any other branch. A pleasant life, good food, good sleep, and two to four hours a day in the air. After four hours (in two spells) over the lines, constantly alert and craning to dodge scandalously accurate shells and suddenly appearing Boches, panting in the thin air at twenty thousand feet, the boys are, I think, justified in calling it a day. I have noticed that the coolest men are a good bit let down after a dogged machine-gun fight far up in the rarefied air. It may seem soft to an infantryman—twenty hours of sleep, eating, and loafing; but in reality the airman should be given an easy time outside of flying."

After one such two-hour patrol at three thousand feet, Nordhoff was called into the captain's office. It was Sunday, March 10. Nordhoff could not guess the reason for the call, for he did not know of anything he had done wrong. Even last week when he had a *panne de moteur,* had to make a forced landing in a ditch, and had smashed up his new Nieuport, Captain Rougevin had been unruffled, without complaint. The captain smiled as Nordhoff entered, relieving his anxiety. "Charlot, I am very happy to announce," he said, extending his hand in congratulations, "that you are the new *popotier* of the escadrille!" Nordhoff was surprised, and flattered. He, an American in a French squadron, was to be the mess officer, a tremendous gastronomic responsibility among a nation of gourmets.

Nordhoff enjoyed his additional duty. Almost every day he went to town in the supply truck, bought the fish, meats and vegetables, and the wines. He prepared the menus for a week at a time; he kept the accounts, collected the fees, balanced the books; he supervised the cooking and sampled the offerings, adding spices here, tasting a special sauce there. He soon was an acclaimed success, and the word quickly traveled up and down to the other escadrilles, and to higher echelons, that there was an excellent cuisine at the 99th.

One day the captain notified Nordhoff that an inspection team from *groupe de combat* headquarters would be arriving in two days, a Saturday, and to please work up something special. Nordhoff surpassed himself. For an appetizer he offered the visitors hors d'oeuvres of sardines and caviar, an entrée of grilled salmon steaks followed by roast veal, asparagus, crisp lettuce salad with a tangy oil-and-vinegar dressing, and scalloped potatoes. To go with the fish, he served a dry Chablis, and with the veal a Burgundy. During and after the dinner, the compliments were profuse and extravagant.

Nordhoff had indeed become the gastronome, wanting the best whenever possible, and often preparing it himself. And this attitude started to carry over to other things as well. About his aeroplane he began to show the same preoccupation: he wanted to know everything about the technical and mechanical aspects of the plane, and having acquired the knowledge, insisted on doing most of the work himself. "The only way to get work done well," he said, almost in desperation, "is to know about it yourself."

He soon had a tremendous interest in the workings of his motor, in the intricacies of his instruments, in the operation of his machine gun, in the manipulation of wires connected to rudder and elevator and ailerons. To insure against a possible "jam" in a dogfight, he spent hours on the ground inspecting the long belt of cartridges that fed into the Vickers, checking each bullet, making sure it fit tightly in its shell, tapping up and down the belt until all the cartridges were exactly even. "There is an unwholesome fascination about it," he had to admit; "hundreds of delicate and fragile parts, all synchronized as it were and working together, any one of which, by its defection, can upset or even wreck the whole fabric. A simple motor failure, even in our own lines and at a good altitude, is no joke in the case of the modern single-seater. Small and enormously heavy for its wing surface, it first touches ground at too high a speed for anything but the smoothest and longest fields. In *pannes* of this sort, the pilot usually steps out of the most frightful-looking wreck smiling and quite unhurt; but you can scarcely imagine the chagrin and depression one feels at breaking a fine machine."

For Nordhoff, although the fascination might have for him

become unwholesome, the anxiety and concern kept him constantly alert, and the alertness kept him alive. Particularly in
the months ahead. During the last week of March, Escadrille
N. 99 was transferred to Manoncourt, near Nancy, to help
form a new unit, Groupe de Combat 20. Its mission was to
patrol the Lorraine Front. For Nordhoff it was the first opportunity in the many months since the early days of flying school
to meet other Americans. For, in addition to Thompson, only
one other Yank, Clarence Shoninger, from New York, had
joined the 99th, and he less than a month before. In the other
escadrilles in the new group were three others: Reginald Sinclair, from Corning, New York, in Spad 68; Bradley Fairchild,
an old friend, in Spad 159; and Gay Bullen, from Chicago, in
Nieuport 162. For the entire group, the initial period of the
assignment to this sector of the front was charmed, easeful.
Nordhoff called it a "dreamy life"; one of many safe patrols,
few casualties, and no fatalities. But the dreamy life soon
changed: the German spring offensive began with an all-out
attack on the Champagne Front.

The first sign that life had decidedly changed in the 99th
came casually for Nordhoff. One afternoon in May, after
lunch, instead of returning to his billet, he went to the group
lounge to visit with the pilots from the other squadrons and to
read some of the back newspapers and magazines. As he entered, he bumped into a former colleague, a French officer he
had not seen since Avord.

"See you in two hours," the Frenchman said quickly, rushing out the door. "Let's have a poker game. I've got a patrol
right now."

"All right," Nordhoff replied. "I'll be right here." He waited
outside until the planes, five of chem, had taxied out and
taken off. The he went into the lounge and picked up the *New
York Herald,* Paris edition.

Two hours later the planes started to return. Nordhoff had
dozed at his newspaper; the sound of motors and the rush of
wings woke him up. He went to the doorway and counted the
planes as they landed. There were only four. When they had
parked, he went over to the flight commander's plane and

waited for him to cut his engine. What, he asked of him, had happened to his friend, the lieutenant?

"Brought down, I'm afraid," the captain answered. "We chased some two-seaters twenty-five miles into the Boche lines, and nine Albatrosses dropped on us. Got two of them, I think. But after the first mix-up I lost track of your friend, and he didn't come back with us."

The three pilots of the patrol and the captain walked to the lounge and went into the bar. As they ordered their drinks, Nordhoff asked them for further particulars. Before they could answer, the telephone started to ring.

Nordhoff answered. The lieutenant had been found just inside their own lines, the voice at the other end explained. "He was shot through the chest, but managed to regain our lines before he died. He was on the point of landing in a field when he lost consciousness. The machine is not badly smashed."

Nordhoff resettled the phone in its cradle and retold the report to the others at the bar. He finished his drink and walked away. He reoccupied the chair he had been sitting in and started again to read the paper, but gave up. He wandered over to a dice game in progress, tried to follow the play, couldn't, and left. He returned to his room, undressed, and went to bed, but could not sleep. Outside his window a nightingale sang.

The next morning a bright sun shone warmly into the room. Nordhoff went to the window. A few feet away a quail—it looked like the mountain partridge from the San Pedro Martir range in Baja California—skittered back and forth on the grass. Nordhoff wished for his rifle and horse and for a hunting trip back into the hills from the family ranch at Punta Banda. Just the sight of the bird filled him with nostalgia. And spring's burgeoning, the budding of flower and leafing of tree made him yearn for peace.

But with the change to good weather came many and frequent changes in location for the squadron. The 99th was quickly ordered, in turn, to Villesneux, Lormaison, and Villiers Saint-Georges. Often the orders would come at dawn; the pilots would have breakfast, and in an hour and a half be relocated at their new station, ready to engage the Boche. Nordhoff became expert in what to put into his musette bag; quickly he would pack a change of underwear and a pair of socks, toothpaste and toothbrush, tobacco, sponge and soap, razor and mirror, first-aid kit, and a bottle of cologne; put the bag in his plane, and be on his way.

During the initial period at Villiers Saint-Georges, Nordhoff enjoyed his greatest success as a *pilote de chasse*. But his fellow American, Clarence Shoninger, suffered a defeat; and, most alarmingly, a visiting French ace was reported killed. All three actions occurred in the first two days. For the first mission Charles and Shoninger were ordered on the same patrol with five others. None of them had ever flown over that section of the front before, and for Shoninger, because he was so new to the squadron, it was only his second flight over the enemy lines. On May 28, a Tuesday, the third day of a strong German offensive driving south from the Chemin des Dames, a request had come from the front to the 99th to determine the extent of the advance, and to attack any Germans doing *réglage* between Rheims and La Fère-en-Tardenois.

Nordhoff and Shoninger climbed into their planes, started their motors, and waited for the signal to take off. Nordhoff pulled out the maps of the sector and studied them, memorizing the landmarks; then he cleaned the new telescopic sight of his machine gun, and with a pull of the lever, he engaged the cartridge belt. The *mécanicien* climbed up the side of the fuselage, reached into the cockpit and adjusted the safety belt holding Nordhoff in his seat. Meanwhile, from the east, foul weather had started to move in, low thick cumulus clouds heavy with rain, which presently started to fall, light and soft, badly reducing visibility for takeoff. But the flight commander ignored it. *"En l'air, mes enfants!"* he called back to them and waved them forward. Nordhoff taxied into line behind the others; then, looking back, saw that Shoninger was having trouble starting his engine.

After takeoff the planes circled under the base of the low-hanging clouds as each man in the flight took his place in the formation. They waited for Shoninger to join up. Finally, all in a place, "bunched like a flock of teal," they headed for the lines. Nordhoff looked down. They were skimming the roofs of houses and the tops of trees, which gave on black, walled cavities and blasted trunks. They were at the front. The weather had begun to clear, and they started to climb. Nordhoff scanned the area below. To the west and south, the entire countryside to Rheims and beyond was shattered. The Boche had started to attack, and he could see wave after wave of soldiers sweeping forward. They were moving to the Marne. Nordhoff made mental notes for future use:

"A great battle was raging below us—columns of smoke rose from the towns and the air was rocked and torn by the passage of projectiles. Far and near the woods were alive with the blinding flash of batteries. Soon we were far into the German lines: deep coughs came from the air about us as patches of black sprang out. But we were still too low and our speed was too great to be bothered by the Boche gunners. Suddenly the clouds broke for an instant, and across the blue hole I saw a dozen Albatrosses driving toward us—German single-seaters, dark ugly brutes with broad short wings and pointed snouts. Our leader saw them, too, and we bounded upward three hundred feet, turning to meet them. . . . Out of the tail of my eye I saw our leader dive on an Albatross, which plunged spinning to the ground. At the same instant I bounded upward to the clouds and dropped on a Boche who was attacking a comrade. I could see my gun spitting streams of luminous bullets into the German's fuselage. But suddenly swift incandescent sparks began to pour past me, and a glance backward showed three Albatrosses on my tail. I turned upside down, pulled back, and did a hairpin turn, rising to get behind them. Not a German machine was in sight—they had melted away as suddenly as they came.

"Far off to the south four of our machines were heading back toward the lines. Feeling very lonely and somewhat *de trop,* I opened the throttle wide and headed after them. Just as I caught up, the leader signaled that he was done for, and glided off, with his propeller stopped. Praying that he might get safely across to our side, I fell in behind the second in command.

Only four now—who and where was the other? Anxiously I ranged alongside of each machine for a look at its number. As I had feared, it was the American—a . . . fearless boy, full of courage and confidence. . . . Did he lose the patrol in a sharp turn and get brought down by a prowling gang of Albatrosses, or did he have motor trouble that forced him to land in the enemy lines?"

Nordhoff had to wait until he returned to base before he could find out what had happened to the flight commander and to Shoninger. The lieutenant had landed inside the lines, and Nordhoff and two soldiers were sent in a staff car to fetch him. "The machine is in plain view on a hill," Captain Rougevin said. "I am giving you two mechanics, so do your best to save the instruments and machine gun. The Boche artillery will probably drop shells on the machine before nightfall."

Fortunately, the flight leader had survived his crash landing unhurt and he was waiting to be picked up when Nordhoff arrived. But getting to the plane was difficult. They had to crawl over open ground under enemy fire to the crash; on either side of them French infantrymen were hiding in wheat fields, shaking their heads in disbelief and wonder while the pilots and mechanics dismantled the plane of its machine gun and instruments, and crawled back to the valley where they had hidden the car.

Concerning Shoninger, an enemy plane flew over the field and dropped a note. The young pilot had become separated from the patrol somewhere between Rheims and Fismes, and had been attacked by a flight of Albatrosses. His plane was hit and his controls cut, and he crashed into a German antiaircraft battery near Crugny.

When Nordhoff checked the bulletin board that night, he saw that he had been posted for another patrol on the following day. He went to bed early, and at dawn the next morning he went to the mess hall for breakfast. At the *popote* and already eating when he arrived were some of the other pilots, and a French captain whom he did not recognize, undoubtedly a visitor. Nordhoff was introduced. The captain, to Nordhoff's marvelous surprise, was Nungesser, the famous French ace, second only to Guynemer in his number of victories. Nungesser, Charles learned happily, was going to lead their patrol that morning. As he finished his coffee, the French ace was particularly ebullient, regaling his eager listeners with tales of some of his conquests in the air. He was a close friend of Lufbery and a frequent visitor to the Escadrille Lafayette. Nordhoff delighted in his company. The captain had a brilliant smile, flashing two solid rows of gold teeth, and accented his remarks by tapping his cane on the floor. Blond, blue-eyed, with a squarely chiseled face, he brushed his small sandy moustache with a forefinger as he spoke. "None of us dreamed," Nordhoff said later, "as he laughed and joked with us at the breakfast table, that [he would crash that same day]."

Nordhoff remembered every detail of the flight. There had been only three of them on the patrol, with Nordhoff on the captain's right, and they flew the mission at six thousand feet, over a solid mass of clouds. Then Nordhoff saw the enemy, high and coming from behind, "like migrating fowl." He signaled to the others. Then, surprisingly, for he seemed to Nordhoff like a porpoise leaping out of the sea, a Boche two-seater rose up through the clouds and plunged right back down again, in one clean movement. Immediately, Nungesser started to climb, then turned and backed his flight into the sun, and weaving back and forth, waited for the Hun to reappear. He did, "like a timid fish rising from a bed of seaweed," and he was heading for his own lines. Nungesser banked hard to the right and dived. Nordhoff followed to the right and behind. Nungesser pulled up from below and behind the Boche and squirted a round into the underbelly; Charles zeroed in on the pilot, fired, and pulled up and off, turning over and back in a chandelle. Looking behind him, he saw the German machine-gunner in the rear seat swing his gun around and start to fire, first at the captain, then at him. Nordhoff turned steeply to the left, dived, pulled up under the Hun's tail, and fired again.

Veering off, Nordhoff pulled back on the stick and started to add throttle; but the engine sputtered in response, caught briefly, sputtered again, then quit completely. Quickly, Nordhoff dived, hoping to keep the prop turning. Then, guessing that the long steep dive had reduced his fuel pressure, he reached up under the instrument panel and turned on the gravity tank. But it, too, would not work. Nordhoff now reached down to the hand pump and started working it. He stole a glance over the side of his cockpit and looked below. He was in enemy territory and falling rapidly. One thousand feet. Five hundred. He could see a blasted village, clearly outlined. He pumped harder. Three hundred feet. The motor sputtered, caught, and at last roared back to life. Nordhoff turned, added full throttle, and unable to see any signs of any of the others in his flight, sped for home.

Nordhoff learned about Nungesser from the other pilot after he had landed. After the initial attack on the first Hun, the captain had climbed again through the clouds to look for the flight of Albatrosses. When he found them, below him and floating on a sea of clouds, they were eleven strong. Nungesser pounced on the last man, fired, and sent him down in a flaming spin. Surprised, but now alerted, the other Boches climbed and dispersed in all directions. Three of them turned back into the fight and bore in on Nungesser. Badly outnumbered, he was hit, caught fire, and went down. Luckily, he managed to get to friendly lines before he crashed. But when the infantrymen of that sector found him, they thought he was dead. (Actually, he survived several more air battles.)

Nordhoff felt sick over the news that one of the greatest pilots of France had been killed, as he thought, on a flight with him. Fortunately for Nordhoff, the demands made upon him daily—the two, sometimes three, flights a day, the tangles with the enemy, even the responsibilities required of him as mess officer—these kept him occupied, alert, and sane. But, once having served as psychic restorative, they soon ended.

Nordhoff's fame as an author, serially and recently published in the *Atlantic Monthly*, had spread to higher headquarters. In July orders came down assigning him to the Executive Staff, U. S. Air Service, in Paris. Here, Nordhoff spent the remainder of the war, in disgust, "removing split infinitives from military reports—a task for which the training of *pilote de chasse* fitted him perfectly," he said bitterly to anyone of his old friends who asked him what he was doing in Paris.

Even the citation that accompanied the Croix de guerre, presented to him in a formal ceremony in Major General Harbord's office, did not help his bad humor. *"A fait preuve de courage et de décision en livrant nombreux combats,"* the adjutant read from the orders, but Nordhoff was unimpressed. Throughout the ceremony his light-blue eyes shone hard and passively.

For it was only at night, alone and in his dreams, when he relived the ordeal of combat, could he expiate the guilt he felt for living in peace far behind the lines, when the one part of his nature, conservative and sedentary, would argue with the other, combative and aggressive, part:

"You're all alone," the conservative one would say. "No one will ever know it if you sail calmly on, pretending not to see the Boche."

"See that Boche?" said the other. "You're here to get Germans—go after him."

"See here," said the conservative, a master of rationalization, "time's nearly up, petrol's low, and there are nine Hun scouts who will drop on you if you dive on the two-seater."

"Forget it!" rejoined the combative half. "Dive on that Hun," he ordered, "and be quick about it!"

Nordhoff obeyed the order, dived, got the rear-gunner in his sights, fired, swept below him, pulled up and over in an Immelmann, banked, straightened out, and fired again; the German gunner returned the fire, and suddenly a splash of hot oil struck Nordhoff full in the face. Nordhoff woke up from his dream, shaking, his hands over his face. This nightmare recurred often—the actual event so vivid, his face felt hot to the touch. But by autumn the images of the dream began to blur and to lose focus, until by November they had dissolved altogether.

Soon after the Armistice on the eleventh, the 99th had a party for all members of the squadron, past and present, in the escadrille *popote*. Nordhoff attended. It was one of the few times in his young life when he became thoroughly drunk. The champagne was abundant, and Nordhoff stopped counting after his fourth glassful. The highlight of the evening was a foot race, pitting Clifton B. "Tommy" Thompson against all comers. It began as a game, with Captain Rougevin the squadron commander, bragging about his young lieutenant who had been an intercollegiate cross-country champion. *"Allons, mon vieux Thompson, ça gaze?"* teased the captain, and dared anyone to try and defeat his young harrier. The challenge started an argument which ended with a wager from an officer from another squadron, who bet that Thompson could not run some incredible number of kilometers—Nordhoff could not remember the number—in an hour. Thompson's friends rushed him outside and asked him if he could win the bet; he said he thought he could, and every officer of the 99th scurried for every sou he could find to cover the bet.

Outside the night was flooded in moonlight. Thompson began his race, followed by every available bicycle, motor scooter, and automobile in the squadron area. One hour later, Thompson fell exhausted into the arms of his comrades; but he had won the bet, giving large amounts of money to his friends, who promptly bought more bottles of champagne to celebrate his victory.

When Nordhoff reported to work the next morning, he was in no mood for removing split infinitives, and even less for the news that actually greeted him. He had been reassigned, he was told, to work on a history of the Lafayette Flying Corps; his coworker would be Captain James Norman Hall, a recently returned prisoner of war.

Charles Nordhoff did not look forward to the undertaking; but he was anxious to meet Hall, whose accounts he had read in the *Atlantic,* and of whom everyone spoke in the highest praise.

5

The Neural Itch

The first meeting of Nordhoff and Hall began in suspicion and ended in argument. Hall, who had spent a great deal of time in prison camp thinking *about* himself, thought little *of* himself; Nordhoff, who spent little time thinking *about* himself, thought a greal deal *of* himself. The initial conversation between them reflected these attitudes. Nordhoff had been told that Hall was from Iowa. "California," he said in an opening gambit, "is lousy with Iowans." Hall protested. Nordhoff continued: "Iowans are rootless people," he said. "They don't belong anywhere." Hall countered, blaming Iowan emigration on California advertising, which begged, wheedled, and cajoled his people into leaving. Nordhoff parried, then thrust: "All Iowans are *from*. You are yourself. All you have to boast about is being *from* Iowa." Decidedly, it was not a good beginning, not to a partnership, and certainly not to a friendship. Yet it became one of the best of both.

On February 20, 1919, Embarkation Order No. 51 was posted ordering Captain James N. Hall and 1st Lt. Charles B.

Nordhoff, "whose services [were] no longer required in the A.E.F. [to] proceed from Paris, France, to Headquarters Base Section No. 5 [Brest] reporting upon arrival to the Commanding General for return to the United States." It was the first time the two names had appeared together on official correspondence, and the order was the happiest one either of them had ever read. On the twenty-eighth they sailed for home on the S.S. *Mauretania*. With them they carried crates of original materials for compiling the history of the Lafayette Flying Corps.

After the first head-on collision between them, Nordhoff and Hall backed off, turned, and started on parallel courses pointed in the same direction. Now proceeding cautiously, each discovered after much discussion that there were a few small areas of agreement. A tentative relationship developed in a distant attraction of opposites. Intellectually, each learned, they were not compatible: Hall was a romantic; Nordhoff, a realist. Nor were they temperamentally suited: Hall was an optimist; Nordhoff, a pessimist. Nor were they socially: Hall, though shy, liked people, and the company of women; Nordhoff, though charming in company, hated crowds, preferred privacy, and although greatly attractive to women, was uneasy in their presence. But both liked travel and adventure: Hall preferred to hike and climb mountains; Nordhoff, to hunt birds and to sail and fish. Both agreed that the winning of the war had not won much in the betterment of mankind, that the peacemakers were again sowing dragon's teeth to every corner of the globe. All the way home Nordhoff and Hall paced the decks of the *Mauretania* or sat at table, talking, laying plans for the future. For each wanted desperately one thing in common: to become writers.

"How soon," Hall asked grimly of Nordhoff, "will the world come a cropper again?"

"Hall," Nordhoff said, preferring last names to first, "our best course is to retire as far as possible from the mess and muddle to come."

"But where?" Hall asked, innocently. Anywhere on the other side of the world seemed far enough away to him, but he had no particular place in mind.

"What better than some remote island in the South Seas?" Nordhoff suggested matter-of-factly, as if he had thought of it for a long time.

"Are you serious?" Hall inquired, looking with wonder at Nordhoff.

Whereupon, to Hall's surprise and incredulous fascination, Nordhoff started upon a dissertation about the South Seas, the ocean seas of Conrad and Melville, the entire island world south of the equator, about Polynesia and the Society Islands, and spoke for thirty minutes without pause.

In total agreement, the subject of the South Seas now occupied them for the rest of the trip home. They would leave the Army immediately, write their history of the Flying Corps, and start looking for a publisher-sponsor. The lines had been drawn between them and around them, defining beginnings and ends.

On March 10, 1919, Nordhoff and Hall were ordered to report to Garden City, Long Island, for discharge. Hall looked forward to becoming a civilian again. An Air Service major, however, who signed the discharges and made them official, had other plans for Hall.

"Do you want your discharge?" the major asked.

"Why, yes, of course," Hall answered.

"Have you thought of staying in the service?" the officer inquired. "Making a career of it?"

"No, sir," Hall admitted.

"It is a matter well worth considering," the major continued. "I believe you would be able to keep your captain's commission. The Air Service is just in its infancy and you would be in on the ground floor. There will be enormous developments from now on."

"I will take my discharge, please," Hall said.

"Very well," the major said. "But I think you will live to regret it." He gave Hall his papers and paid him his $60 in bonus money.

As Hall was not interested in a service career, so neither was Nordhoff, who silenced the sales pitch with cold refusal. The new civilians, almost as soon as they had changed into mufti, turned their attention to the Lafayette history, and immedi-

ately had to find a place to work. Hall tentatively suggested a
New York hotel room, but Nordhoff dismissed that proposal,
thinking he could find something much better—and did.
Through a friend from Boston, Nordhoff arranged the loan of
a small beach cottage on Martha's Vineyard, off Cape Cod, at
Gay Head. Here they happily labored on the project all summer long. From their crates of files and notes and photographs
they compiled a history in two large volumes. The first told the
history of the Lafayette Escadrille and its brilliant record at
the front, the story of all other Americans who also served with
other French squadrons and their triumphant performances,
followed by biographical sketches of all the Americans who
served in all French escadrilles. The second volume gave personal reminiscences and quoted letters which had originally
been sent home to families; they explained enlistment and
flight training, combat experiences, life at aerodromes at the
front, and prisoner of war camps and escapes; these were followed by appendixes full of statistical data.

As editors, Nordhoff and Hall early established finely de-
marcated work habits. They wrote only in the morning, broke
for a light lunch; then, after setting aside papers and letters
and photographs and deciding what they would do the next
day, they quit at 3:00 P.M. for the day to pursue their separate
interests. Invariably, Nordhoff walked to Squibnocket Pond,
there to watch the wild and domestic ducks, sometimes numbering in the thousands during their migrations. Nordhoff was
enchanted, for he could sit by the hour studying and classify-
ing them: the mallard, with his head and neck of glistening
green, the neck ringed in white, the chestnut breast; the canvasback, with black bill, chestnut head and neck, whitish behind and underbelly; the merganser, with slender serrated
bill; the sea ducks, unlike the river or fresh-water types, with
webbed hind toes that dived under water to feed. Nordhoff
most liked the eider, one of the sea ducks, for it was a swift
flier, and an expert swimmer and diver.

Hall would climb to the top of the cliff and look far out to
the distant reaches of the sea and then nearer to No-Man's-
Land Island, daydreaming, letting his mind lie fallow and
receptive; then he would climb down to the shore, take off his

sneakers, and walk the lengthy stretches of lonely beach, feeling the cool mud underfoot and smelling the salt air. These were good days, Hall thought as he walked, and they paid, thanks to the sponsorship of William K. Vanderbilt, $200 a month. But they would soon end.

In midsummer Hall received a letter from the Pond Lyceum Bureau in New York, which proposed a lecture series on his wartime experiences. At first, Hall was appalled by the offer. He hated to make speeches, but decided to accept the proposal because of the changing family fortunes at home in Colfax. His father's savings had been wiped out by his long illness, and now his mother was asking for help. Hall could not refuse, even if it meant doing what he detested most. He signed the contract with Pond, arranged for a sizable advance, which he promptly sent home, and started preparing his lectures by pacing up and down the beach and practicing on the sea gulls wheeling overhead.

When the history was finished in early September, the manuscript filled two large suitcases. Nordhoff and Hall lugged these off to Boston and dropped them on the desk of their editor at Houghton Mifflin. Then they went to see Ellery Sedgwick on Mount Vernon Street; they had made up their minds about a joint adventure in the South Seas and wanted to give the *Atlantic* first refusal rights on the project. Ellery Sedgwick was not enthusiastic, at least for his magazine, because the *Atlantic* no longer ran travel pieces; but, the editor brightened, his good friend Thomas Wells, the new editor of *Harper's* magazine, might indeed be interested. Sedgwick gave them a letter of introduction.

When they arrived in New York they went directly to the *Harper's* offices. Wells liked the whole idea, liked the seriousness of Nordhoff and the enthusiasm of Hall, liked even more the solid reputation that each author had separately earned writing for the *Atlantic*. He readily broached the terms of the contract. "How are you fixed for money?" Mr. Wells then asked. "I suppose you will need an advance, for expenses?"

"Yes, sir!" Hall blurted out, admitting more to his own need than to Nordhoff's.

Mr. Wells drew up the conditions of the agreement, then

decided on the amount of the advance. Hall was delighted with its generous provisions: *Harper's* would pay $7,000 now—$1,500 against the magazine articles, and $5,500 against later book royalties. "All I ask," the editor added, "is that one of you insure his life for $7,000, and make Harper and Brothers the beneficiary on the policy. This is merely a precaution in case you should both be drowned at sea or killed by the savages in the South Pacific."

After they left the building they walked downtown to the New York Mutual Life Insurance Company, and Hall took out the policy for the required amount.

With such security about their future plans, Nordhoff and Hall now parted company for the remainder of the year. Nordhoff saw his friend off at Grand Central Station, the first fearful step of Hall's lecture tour.

Hall delivered his first speech before an audience of several hundred young girls, at the Monticello Seminary in Godfrey, Illinois. He began his talk uneasily, then promptly forgot his introductory paragraph. For an attention-getter he had memorized the words of Lloyd George about Allied pilots at the front—had solidly memorized them on the dunes of Gay Head—and now they had left him forever. Or so it seemed, for an eternal thirty seconds. Then, blessedly, they returned in a rush: "Far above the squalor and the mud, so high in the firmament as to be invisible from earth . . ."

When he had finished, the girls applauded, most appreciatively. They liked this shy veteran with the broken nose, and the moustache, and—when they saw him up close—the deep warm brown eyes. The men liked him for his sincerity and combat experience; so did many more audiences, from New Hampshire to Virginia to Iowa. But Hall could not truly warm up to his public role and did not like it. Nor in his travels did he like what he saw happening to his beloved America—the rape of the land by real-estate speculators and road builders. Nor did he like a letter he had received from *McClure's* magazine, offering him a sizable fee for an article about his experiences as a German prisoner: the editor wanted Norman to reveal the Germans for the brutal and sadistic monsters they undoubtedly were. Hall was incensed. "I was marvelously treated," he wrote to the editor, "considering the wartime conditions; and my captors were by no means cruel and inhuman." The editor withdrew his offer. Hall fumed in silence. It was this kind of world, he had decided, that he had to leave—and soon.

Nordhoff, meanwhile, was similarly unsettled, but for different reasons. In New York before his return to his home in California, he had visited two wartime friends out on Long Island—Bradley Fairchild, who had been in Groupe de Combat 20 with him, and Tom Buffum, with whom he had been in flight training at Avord—and they both had noted Nordhoff's uneasiness. "We often had him out to Massapequa," Bradley Fairchild said. "He was quiet, pleasant, and my two sisters were very fond of him. He was interesting and pleasant to talk to. He fitted much better here than amongst a lot of brawling youngsters on vacation.

"He was not at all the religious type, but . . . the occult impressed him. At that time . . . the Ouija board was all the rage. We had one out one weekend and Charlie asked what had happened to Sid Drew. Sid had not returned from a flight that had had a fight (on May 19, 1918, near Arvilliers, Drew had been attacked by five Albatrosses), but from what we had learned at the time, no one had seen him go down. The Ouija said that he had not been shot down, had not been taken prisoner, but that he was drowned.

"A few days later Charlie told us he had heard that news had come in that Sid had landed behind the lines, and in trying to escape had drowned in the Rhine. The fact that the Ouija had apparently been in touch with Sid affected Charlie much more, we thought, than it should have. He was really shaken. Much later we learned that Sid had not drowned but was outnumbered in a flight with German Albatrosses. . . ."

Nordhoff was delighted to run into Buffum again. It happened as a complete surprise for both, at the Harvard Club in New York City. Buffum had just returned from Haiti, where he had been recuperating from his prisoner-of-war experiences. He spotted Nordhoff sitting at the bar. They exchanged greetings. Buffum was effervescent, brimming with life; Nordhoff, drinking by himself, had grown morose. Buffum asked him what he had been doing since his return from France.

Nordhoff explained about the Lafayette history, and then about his and Hall's plans. "We are leaving this unbearable rat race as soon as we can," he said. "We are bound for Tahiti in the South Sea Islands." He paused and rattled the ice in his glass, finished the drink, and ordered another for himself and one for Tom. "Everybody here"—Nordhoff waved toward the windows and outside—"seems to have gone crazy. The automobile traffic is the worst part of it all. I just can't take it."

Buffum became concerned. "Nordy," he suggested, "why don't you come down and stay with me for a few days, if you have time before leaving for Tahiti. I can guarantee you peace and serenity. My sister and I with her family have rented a house at Wainscott, Long Island, for the summer. It is a small colony on the south shore near the eastern end of the island where we were brought up as children. There is no social life. We have the best surf bathing on the East Coast, lovely stretches of beach and high dunes, and no automobile traffic. I think you would like it."

Nordhoff agreed. Quickly they finished their drinks, went outside, and climbed into Tom's car. In the city traffic Nordhoff tensed, as another car would get too close, as they came to an intersection, as a car would pass them. Finally across the Brooklyn Bridge, and at last shaking loose from the congestion, Nordhoff leaned back, crossed his legs, breathed deeply, and started to relax. Three hours later, they turned off the highway, drove down an unpaved road between the high sand dunes, and stopped the car before the open sea. Nordhoff got out and looked up and down to the sweep of beach on either side, then climbed to a high dune and saw, a half mile to the east, a large fresh-water duck pond. Here, he thought, as at Martha's Vineyard, he could be at peace, backed against a dune and facing the eternal mystery of the sea. Buffum called him down from his revery; they would be late for dinner, he said, if they did not hurry.

The next morning they slept late, awoke, and decided on a swim in the ocean. A bright warm sun sparkled on the sands of the beach, and the surf gently rolled in on long even swells. They dived into a wave, swam out a few yards, and pounded back in on a breaker. Lying on the sand, warming their bodies under the high sun, they talked. Nordhoff turned on his side and looked toward the small group of bathing houses facing the beach. "No wonder you love this spot," he said to Tom. "It is associated with your childhood memories, and it is also unspoiled by what they now call the Law of Diminishing Returns." He turned over again on his back and closed his eyes to the sun. "I think you ought to enjoy it as much as you can, because it will not last."

Later they walked along the beach. They came to an unusually high dune, one that towered over the others. Nordhoff looked closely. The wind, he noticed, had neatly eroded the dune in half, and in the space between the mounds, an old dirt road, rutted from wagon wheels and pitted from oxen hooves, still ran through. Nordhoff was greatly interested. "I wonder," he said, pointing to the tracks, "how old those really are? I suppose it would take a professional scientist to find out." He shook his head, wondering.

For that afternoon Tom's sister had invited her brother and Nordhoff to a picnic lunch on the beach. Her husband had come down from the city for the weekend and her four-year-old daughter was being treated to a cookout. Nordhoff and Tom gathered driftwood and built the fire. They ate and drank heartily. Toward dusk, after the others had gone into the house, Nordhoff and Buffum sat on the beach, talking. Tom pulled his knees up under his chin and watched the ships out along the coast turn on their navigation lights. "Isn't it wonderful," he said, "to have the lights on again all over the world? The sight of those ships going by to unknown destinations has always thrilled me."

"Why don't you come down to Tahiti," Nordhoff suggested, "after Hall and I get settled there?"

"Maybe I will, Nordy," Tom said. After a pause, he asked: "Nordy, what are you and Jimmy going to do in Tahiti?"

"Write," Nordhoff quickly answered, "and write what we want to write, which is what we won't be able to do here."

Nordhoff then explained about a letter he had recently received from Hall, telling him about Hall's difficulties with *Mc-Clure's* and how the editor there wanted to give his readers what they wanted to hear, rather than the truth. "When I get home," Nordhoff said, "I want to make a trip south and do a piece on Mexico. I hope I can find an editor who will buy it." Nordhoff did not discuss the matter further, but he chafed under a tentative rejection of the Mexican project from Ellery Sedgwick. The *Atlantic* would run the article, the editor explained, "if only our attention is sufficiently turned toward Mexico to make it worthwhile to print a picture of life there."

Nordhoff did not get home to California until the middle of fall. Happily he visited with family and friends, but not for long. One day, out of fun, he shocked the young girl friends of his sister Mary. They had come to the Nordhoff house to admire the hero of the flying war; the girls giggled, wondering what the big brother would say or do. Suddenly, a bright idea occurred to Nordhoff, and he smiled wryly as he thought of it. From his coat pocket he slowly pulled a leather cigarette case, deliberately opened it, ceremoniously took out a Lucky Strike, and casually tapped it against the case. The ritual, so ostentatious as to call attention to itself, produced the desired results. The girls were full of questions about the cigarette case. "That," Nordhoff explained, holding the case out at arm's length before them, "is the tanned hide from my best friend's amputated leg!" The girls screamed as if struck with horror and retreated. Nordhoff laughed, gloriously.

A few days later he traveled down to Ensenada in Lower California, to visit the family ranch at Punta Banda. It was one of the few places in the world that he truly loved, and he always sorrowed that his father, after investing thousands of dollars into the ranch and property and an equal amount of hard-working hours, could not make them pay. For the Mexicans who worked for his father, Nordhoff had deep regard and great respect, and from them he easily generalized this affection to include all Mexicans. And in the piece he planned to write about them, he wanted to emphasize their great human qualities. After three days of hunting and fishing in the Santo Tomas hills and out on the Bahía de Todos Santos, he swung inland to get the bulk of his local color.

He readily dismissed the charge of laziness about the Mexican, explaining, "The chief incentive which drives the European races on to struggle and progress is the desire for material gain, but in the life of the Mexican this motive plays only a secondary part." He cited the example of the Vera Cruz sugar planter who, when he doubled the wage to double the number of workers he needed, did so, "but they worked only half time!"

In further illustration, he told of the old woman in the marketplace of Córdoba from whom he regularly used to buy fruit. On this particular day she had only Manila mangoes in her basket. Nordhoff asked the price. For her friends, she said, one penny each.

"How many are there, Doña Ignacia?" Nordhoff asked.

The woman counted them, twice, to thirty. Nordhoff reached into his pocket, produced thirty cents in change, and presented them to the woman.

"But no, señor," she said. "If you take them all, I must charge forty cents."

"Why so?" Nordhoff could not understand; perhaps, he reasoned, he was not her friend. "You can get no more if you sell them one by one," he explained, "and by selling them all to me you will have the rest of the day to yourself."

The woman shook her head in disagreement. "No, no," she said. "You don't understand. Take half a dozen, if you like, at a penny each, but I cannot let you have all at that price. If I sell them all at once, I lose the pleasure of a day's market."

Nordhoff wrote: "This attitude of mind is difficult for us to comprehend. Mexico is a wonderfully fertile land, where crops seem to grow almost without attention. . . . Long ago the country Mexican discovered that he could live with a minimum of effort. There is food in the house, the sun is warm overhead, there are amusing neighbors with whom to gossip— why overdo the business of work? It is a pleasant philosophy, fit for a pleasant land."

Mexicans were a kind and gentle people, Nordhoff observed, whose gift for hospitality and consideration for others was tremendous, and for which compensation was out of the question. "A few years ago, in southern Mexico," he recalled, "I set out on a forty-mile ride to get money for the plantation payroll. The east was brightening as I passed the quarters; lights were appearing in one hut after another as women began to work at their charcoal braziers and I heard the patting of tortillas and a sleepy hum of talk. Drowsy chickens were waking, to flutter down from the trees. Beyond the pasture the trail led straight into the blank wall of the jungle, above which the morning mist was rising in slow wreaths.

"Hour after hour I penetrated deeper into this tropical forest—the trail a tunnel, with soft decaying vegetation underfoot, and a dim roof of green. The enormous trunks of trees, shrouded in creepers and pale orchids, stood like columns seen by twilight in some ruined temple. My horse's feet made no sound. Strange little animals—sloths, anteaters, and coatis—walked slowly and noiselessly along the branches; small gray birds flitted silently from tree to tree, always just ahead. There was a sense of veiled watching, oppressive and unreal as the atmosphere of a dream—one felt that it would be dangerous to whistle, even to speak above a whisper.

"At last, as I reached the edge of a forgotten clearing, I realized that something more than imagination was at fault, for my head was throbbing painfully and I felt the cold touch of a malarial chill.

"I got off my horse and spent a bad thirty minutes beside the trail, shivering and half delirious, until an old woman came hobbling up in great concern. There were no men at her hut, but she would lead the horse if I could walk. . . . Come, it was only five minutes away.

"My chill developed into a brisk attack of pernicious fever; for two weeks I lay on a mat under kind old María's grass-thatched roof. There was no quinine, but she took delight in compounding certain doubtful brews which I was too weak to refuse. She was poor; there was not even a dog about the place, for dogs must eat. Her one possession was a pig, the very apple of her eye, christened Narciso after a departed son. Had he looked in a pool, Narciso would scarcely have fallen in love with his own image, but in the eyes of his mistress he was perfect. His mate, she informed me, had been killed by a jaguar.

"As I grew stronger, I began to think of my departure. Knowing that she would take no pay for what was a common duty, I cast about for a way to save her face and yet make fair recompense for all that she had done. The idea came one morning as I lay on my mat, watching Narciso trot pensively from the jungle in answer to María's shrill summons.

" 'I have a favor to ask of you,' I said, when the day of parting came. 'It is evident, to one in sympathy with pigs, that Narciso feels the absence of his companion. It would relieve my mind to know that he was not lonely, so please take these twenty pesos and provide him with a fitting mate.' "

When Nordhoff finished writing the article, he then typed it, rewriting as he went. He sent it—he called it "The Human Side of Mexico"—to Ellery Sedgwick, with little hope for its acceptance. Because Nordhoff had not left a return address so he could be reached in Mexico, Sedgwick wrote a reply to Mrs. Nordhoff. "Quite good enough to run in the *Atlantic*," the editor commented upon the piece, and ran it in the October issue.

Meanwhile, James Norman Hall was finishing his lecture tour. He took a train to San Francisco, then started down the coast to Los Angeles to meet Nordhoff there at his parents' home in Pasadena. More than he expected—for after his argument with Nordhoff about Iowans in California, Hall was prepared to dislike the West Coast—he found California a beautiful place, the coastline particularly. But his good impression became severely compromised by the presence of oil derricks; and he joined his bad feeling to a couplet:

> *They must be vermin, surely, who defile*
> *Their very Homeland coasts, mile after mile.*

Nordhoff took immediate exception to the lines. When Hall quoted them to him, Nordhoff became angry. "So you think Californians are vermin?" he snapped. "I wonder that you are willing to associate with one of them."

Hall recoiled; he did not mean his couplet as bitingly as taken. "I was only getting a little of my own back," Hall hurried to explain, "for what you once said about California being *lousy* with Iowans."

Nordhoff was not assuaged. "If you owned some of that coastal land with great reservoirs of oil beneath it," he replied, "you would be one of the vermin yourself."

Hall did not want to pursue the matter further. It was not worthy of his energy; moreover, he really had not been that serious about it.

December and the holidays quickly passed, and just after the beginning of the new year of 1920, Nordhoff and Hall had completed plans for their trip to Tahiti. Tickets had been purchased, steamer trunks packed, immunizations taken.

Shortly before he left, Nordhoff visited some old friends in Pasadena, Tod and Anne Ford. Tod, like Nordhoff, had volunteered for French aviation, but had been removed from training for ill health. The Fords discussed with Nordhoff his commitment to Harper's, and his plans thereafter. Tod wanted his friend to live in California, where they could visit together frequently. Anne, knowing her husband's feelings, turned to Nordhoff and asked: "Do you intend to remain in the South Seas after the articles are finished?"

Nordhoff answered almost at length, as if he had rehearsed the reply for a long time, "After being in France for these past few years and seeing what civilization has done to mankind, I want to get as far away from it as possible; so, if the South Seas are as I hope they are, that is where I want to spend the rest of my life."

At the end of January, Nordhoff and Hall sailed for Tahiti, the Pacific stretching out before them—challenging, uncertain, and mysterious, like the possibilities in their future.

NORDHOFF
& HALL

1
Wanderings in the South Seas

No traveler over the vast and endless stretches of the Pacific has not been enthralled by his first landfall in the South Seas. It strikes a virginity of sense, Stevenson had said. To Nordhoff and Hall, standing on the schooner deck, feeling the salt spray in their faces, and alerted for this singular experience, Tahiti touched them with breathtaking awe. There before them, dead ahead, what had first been a blur, faint and purplish against an interminable sea, now began to take on shape and form. Hall climbed the mainmast for a better view. As he shaded his eyes against the morning sun, he saw unfolding a scalloped sky of dark silhouette suddenly thrusted upward from a blue sea. And as the island came into closer view, he caught in a panoramic sweep the great twin mountain peaks, the bright ridges and dark gorges, the spume-topped waves against the reef-enclosed lagoons.

Strong now was the smell of the island, a siren scent, heavy, fragrant, and seductive. Nordhoff asked what the flowers were that sent their reputations out to sea before them to greet visitors. The captain explained the fragrance as the combined perfume of the frangipani, *tiare* Tahiti, and *hinano*.

They came through a pass in the reef. Strange sounds struck the air, a diapasoned mixture. Hall tried to sort them. On either side he heard the roar of the waves, like claps of thunder, as they crashed on the barrier reef. High overhead the cries of sea fowl seemed to protest their arrival. Forward and off to the left, against the black volcanic sands of the shore, the waves from the lagoon gently lapped.

Edging closer into the harbor they watched the village of Papeete come into full view. In a broad arc, palm fronds and the sweeping tops of coconut trees, a green mass of lush growth, backed the red and green rooftops of the stores, warehouses, and public buildings. Moored along the sea wall were ships, schooners, and all kinds of small craft. Horse-drawn carts and buggies and natives in brightly colored *pareus* crowded the narrow tree-lined dirt streets.

A crumb of land in the middle of the Pacific, it was totally different from anything they had known before. As Nordhoff and Hall debarked at the quay, where the schooner had tied up to an old cannon cemented into the wall, it looked to them as if the whole population of the island had turned out to greet them. The crowd at the landing platform opened to let them pass. Broadly smiling natives came forward and circled their necks with leis made from native shells. Here and there stood whites and Chinese, curious but aloof.

Nordhoff and Hall started for the hotel, the Aina Paré in Papeete. After thousands of miles of bracing their legs against the pitch and roll of the ship, the ground felt strangely solid and level. Hall stopped to light a cigarette, and swung his canvas sea bag over his shoulder. Two hundred years after Cook and Bougainville, he could see that, outwardly at least, little had happened to change the island. Away from the harbor front the streets were empty. In Papeete proper the Chinese storekeepers sat in front of their shops, waiting for customers. Clusters of native women floated by carrying on their heads baskets filled with fruit and fish.

For Hall, the stillness of the island was almost eerie; against it, as they came to the steps of the hotel, a ripe fruit swished through the foliage and thumped to the ground. If, thought Hall, this silence were any indication of what they would find elsewhere in the South Seas, then they could not have picked a better departure point than Tahiti for their year of wanderings. Here were a few thousand natives, half-castes, Chinese, and whites, living in charmed placidity. He looked back at the harbor. There, fronting the vast Pacific, were many ships ready to set sail in all directions—north to the Marquesas, south to the Australs, east to the Tuamotus, and west to the Cooks.

The Aina Paré was just as they expected in the South Seas. It belonged to another time. Upstairs and down, wide verandas ran the length of the building. They were the only guests, the landlord said, as they signed the register. Having their choice of rooms, they picked one which opened on the veranda. It commanded a splendid view across the lagoon and west of it, in the distance, the island of Mooréa. Nordhoff bounced on one of the two lumpy double beds. Hall went to the marble-topped washstand and poured water from the pitcher into the bowl. Nordhoff propped a pillow behind his head and stretched out on the bed. "Hall," he said, "look at the walls. They're riddled with termites."

Hall dried his hands. "Don't lean against one," he said. "It might topple over." He kicked off his shoes, undressed to his shorts, and plopped on the other bed. Nordhoff rose and stripped, wrapped a towel around his waist, and went down the back stairway to the bath. He found a shower, a great tin enclosure with sides knee high all around. When he came back up, he warned Hall as he started down. "Be careful going down those stairs, Hall. I'll find you in a heap of sawdust if you take more than one at a time."

"If you can find me at all," Hall said. "I think out here it might be better to live in a native hut. The white man's ways soon end up in dust."

"Maybe they do anyway," Nordhoff answered.

When they had dressed they went out to find a restaurant. The hotel, they discovered, served only breakfast. Off the perimeter road they found a little café. It was a frame house built on stilts over the lagoon. A few of the diners still remained, lingering over coffee. Nordhoff chose a table with a wide view of the harbor. Hall, his hands thrust deep into his trouser pockets, stood entranced at an open window. He was watching the afterglow of the sun behind Mooréa; although it had set a half hour before, it still splashed a brilliant fan of pink, blue, and white. When he had sat down, Nordhoff passed him the menu. The fare was thoroughly native, but they decided to try something of everything.

The food was served. In turn they tasted, then ate heartily because they found each course surprisingly delicious—fresh water shrimps with French dressing, roast pork, baked bananas, breadfruit to dip in the pork gravy, and heart of palm salad. Hall decided on a mango for a dessert, and liked it so much he asked for another. Nordhoff settled for black coffee. As Hall sliced the fruit from either side of the fat oblong seed, he announced his travel plans. He would like to go east, to the Low Archipelago, and wander among the Tuamotus.

"Did you notice, Nordy," he asked, "the name of one of the ships at the dock when we came in? It was like a friendly greeting from Gloucester, or Portland, Maine."

"Do you mean the *Caleb S. Winship?*" Nordhoff pushed back his chair from the table. "If you look closely you can still see *Boston* painted on the stern."

"That's the one," Hall said. "It reminds me of the Yankee hospitality of my friend from *The Boston Globe,* Larry Winship. And furthermore, the butterfat made from the coconut oil in the Tuamotus is the creamiest in the South Seas. The *Winship,* I understand, leaves tomorrow."

"It sounds sort of silly to me. That isn't where I want to go. You go. I don't want to wander among clouds of butter-fat islands. I'll go west, I think, and follow in the wake of Captain Cook."

The next morning each made his own ship arrangements, set plans for an indefinite reunion in Tahiti some time later, and went his individual way. It was agreed between them, as they had informally decided in Boston before setting out on the assignment, that Nordhoff would take photographs, and send

Hall letters about his travels. Hall would set down his impressions and write the book, somehow incorporating Nordhoff's accounts into the narrative.

An hour before departure time Hall had his sea chest brought down to his cabin in the *Winship;* then he walked over to the front of the post office, sat down on one of the benches, and waited. The activity along the wharf intrigued him. Boats had arrived from Mooréa and Bora Bora, their decks swarming with bare-legged natives; others had docked from more distant points, sails stained, decks warped, sides blistered, and stinking with the smell of copra. Hall liked the musical names of some of the ships—the *Curieuse,* the *Avarua,* the *Potii Ravarava,* the *Kaeo,* the *Liane,* and Nordhoff's three-master, the *Faaite.*

Hall slouched on his spine and crossed his legs in a tight double lock. He opened his copy of Findlay's *South Pacific Directory* and flipped to the section on the Tuamotu Islands. There was little to attract the romantic traveler. No accounts of peaceful lagoons, swaying palm trees, and naked smiling maidens. "They are all of similar character," he read in Findlay; "they exhibit a very great sameness in their features," it redundantly continued. "Some have good passes with anchorages inside the lagoon; others . . ." Hall closed the book. The report echoed what he had heard earlier this morning from one of the old captains. "By and large," the skipper said, "they are as much alike as the reef points on a sail."

There was a commotion at the dock. Hall looked up to find the cause and beheld a strange sight. A white man, an old native woman, and two native boys were standing in front of the *Winship;* the white man was arguing with Tino, the supercargo. On the wharf and off to the side of the loading ramp was a wheelbarrow stacked high with four crates of live chickens, cultivation tools, and fishing tackle; and beside it, one on top of the other, were an old black sea chest and a great roll of bedding. Someone standing close to where Hall sat asked who the white man was.

No one seemed to know. "No, sir," one of the agents said, "I never laid eyes on him before. I've been living in Papeete for years and I don't know him. Where has he been hiding himself?"

Hall walked to the ship to meet the stranger. As Tino stepped off the gangplank, he turned to Hall and said: "He wants to go to Taioro. Why, I don't know. There's no copra or pearl shell there. Not enough to make it worthwhile anyway."

Hall introduced himself. The man's name was Cridland, Arthur Cridland, an Englishman. "I simply want to book passage," he said, "for myself and this woman. I'm not interested in copra or pearl shell. I want to live there." His accent slid over vowels and slurred consonants, as if he had not spoken English for a long time and had spoken Polynesian instead.

"I know Taioro from the sea," Tino said. "Passed it once coming down from the Marquesas. We were blown out of our course by a hurricane. Didn't land. There's no one on the Godforsaken place. Now here you are," he nodded toward Cridland, "asking to be set down there with four crates of chickens and an old Kanaka woman for company."

Cridland noticed a softening in Tino's attitude. "I will pay you well," he said. "And it's only a short way off your course to the other islands."

When Cridland had gone back to the dock to direct the loading of his gear, Tino threw up his hands. "Well," he said with resignation, "you meet some mighty queer people down in this part of the world. I don't believe in asking them their business, but it beats me sometimes, trying to figure out what their business is."

Hall talked with the native woman and learned a bit more from her, but only enough to quicken his curiosity. The Englishman had not told her very much. She, he discovered, owned Taioro, a tiny atoll about a hundred and fifty miles away from the routes of the trading ships. No more than twenty natives had ever lived on it, and now there were none. Cridland, she explained, had taken a long lease on it, and she was going to live there with him as his housekeeper and only companion.

An hour later the schooner weighed anchor. A light land breeze carried them out, but only a few hours later, the sails emptied of wind and flapped against the mast. Hall was not in the least discouraged. Amid the calm of sea and sky, he felt a contrary feeling flood over him like a wave. After months of longing for something remote and beautiful, this sudden stillness struck him as a dream fulfilled. He was peacefully one with nature. In a flash of understanding, he knew it and it made him inexplicably happy. But the feeling left as quickly as it came, just as it always had whenever it happened in the past. He walked the length of the ship, taking stock of cargo and passengers.

The schooner was crowded. In addition to the Tuamotu captain, the crew, and the supercargo, there were thirty native and three white passengers; a horse, a monkey, five pigs, and four crates of chickens; and tied down in various stacks, lumber, corrugated iron, flour, rice, sugar, canned food, and dry goods. There was enough, Hall thought, to establish a colony.

Forward on the cabin deck Cridland sat, his freckled hands cupped over his knees, looking out across the solitude of the ocean into the distant horizon, where still visible were the peaks of Tahiti and Mooréa. To Hall, they seemed like islands of sheer fancy. Then, rapidly, dusk began to fall, and abruptly the wind rose, bringing with it a light cool shower, like fallen mist, and when it passed, the night was dark and deep.

Walking along the companionway to go down, Hall stumbled over a figure stretched out across the deck. In the darkness he had not noticed it. It was the old woman who had come on board with Cridland. She asked him to sit down and pushed over to make room for him. Hall, still wanting to know more about her and about the strange silent Englishman who wanted to live so far away from the white man's world, plopped down beside her. The woman reached into a fold in her pareu and pulled out a leaf of tobacco and a strip of pandanus. She rolled them tightly into a cigarette, placed it between her lips, and lit it. As she puffed deeply and slowly exhaled, Hall asked her carefully phrased questions. Not only could she not tell him about Cridland, but, ironically, she expected Hall, because he was white man too, to tell her all about the Englishman. After all, she asked, were they not both from the same island of the white world? Cridland was young, like Hall. He must have people somewhere. She could not understand why Cridland wanted to go to Taioro. No, he had never said a word to her, only that he wanted to go to her island—"to write and to think—alone!" She called him "Pupure" because of his fair skin and blond hair.

But she did tell Hall all he wanted to know about herself. She was Ruau, the last of her family. The original population of Taioro had been so reduced through death and emigration that in the end only she was left on the island. She could not endure the loneliness and abandonment any longer, and for months on end she had set out signal fires, hoping to attract a passing ship. Finally a schooner saw her signal, picked her up, and took her to Tahiti. But in Tahiti she became even more unhappy than she had been in Taioro and yearned to return home. Then she met Cridland.

He had been living in Tahiti for more than a year. For the last ten years, since he had been eighteen, he had wandered eastward across the Pacific, from Borneo to Celebes, from New Guinea to Samoa to the Society Islands, ever seeking the solitude he craved. Despairing of realizing his dream, he found Ruau and heard her story about Taioro. She agreed to give him a renewable ten years' lease, if he agreed in turn to take care of her until she died. The papers were drawn up and signed, ready against the day when a ship would sail to their part of the world.

For more than three weeks on board the *Winship,* Hall and Cridland exchanged no more than a few words of greeting. Each kept jealously to his reserve. Until one day, when the ship put in at an atoll for copra, and they both went ashore. Cridland was the first to break the silence between them. "I wish," he said as they walked the beach together, "I had come out here years ago. They appeal to the imagination, don't you think, all these islands?"

Hall, stunned by this sudden loquacity, could only say in reply: "Yes, very much." They went back to the ship without exchanging another word. The spell of the loneliest ocean in the world had gripped them both. Like a pair of hermit crabs each retreated to his own shell. Not embarrassed by silence, neither felt the need for talk.

Nevertheless, after a few more weeks at sea, as the schooner made its landfalls, exchanged lumber and corrugated iron, or rice and flour and tinned beef, for copra, and as days succeeded days when there was no sight of land, Hall would look toward the solitary figure of Cridland gazing out to sea, and wonder what his story was.

Cridland, Hall thought, was like a medieval anchorite, chained to a rock of solitude, but apparently without a need to pray. The Englishman's experiences in the world of men must have been most disillusioning for him. People obviously held no interest for him, not even the natives. Whenever the ship tied up on shore, Cridland quickly walked away from the villages along the lagoons, struck out across the island to the ocean side, there to sit in silence and watch the tide. Occasionally, Hall would join him, to wade the shallows at low tide, or when the wind was onshore and the surf heavy, to sit on the beach and watch the seas gather force way out, build in walls higher than the island itself, and crash like steaming caldrons on the reef.

Months passed. One day the *Winship* came to a small atoll, rounded a point of land, and encountered two ships anchored in the lagoon. Exchanging greetings, Hall learned that one had just recently left Tahiti. Hall asked for the news and in answer the skipper gave him a pile of newspapers. That night Hall spent several hours glancing through them. When he had set them aside, he took out his notebook and started to write.

". . . I heard as in a dream the far-off clamor of the outside world—the shrieking of whistles, the roar of trains, the strident warnings of motors; but there was no reality, no allurement in the sound. I saw men carrying trivial burdens with an air of immense effort, of grotesque self-importance; scurrying in breathless haste on useless errands, gorging food without relish; sleeping without refreshment; taking their leisure without enjoyment; living without the knowledge of content; dying without ever having lived. . . ."

Hall had to admit to himself that this picture was distorted, even untrue. He had become attracted to the lonely life of the islands almost as much as had Cridland. But he knew one thing with certainty: The old feeling of restlessness had gone.

And in its place had come a gift of happiness, a sense of contentment. He had not known anything like it since boyhood.

The cause, Hall felt, lay for the most part among the natives. The Polynesians were the happiest people he had ever met. Here were the true successors of Adam and Eve in innocence, for here was Eden before the Fall, before man sought wisdom and found despair. And the more distant the island from civilization, the happier he found the people. Among the Tuamotuans, as stripped of artificiality as they were of clothes, there was no deceit, no cunning, no grasping acquisitiveness. Like children who had never matured, they were gentle, generous, and trustworthy.

On island after island he found no sickness or doctors, no crime or insanity, no jails or asylums. Because everyone loved children and cherished them, there were no orphanages; and because all necessary skills for survival were passed from father to son, from mother to daughter, there were no schools. Where nature was bountiful, there was no need for mutiny.

Hall loved the native children. He played with them as often as possible, fishing, shell-collecting, joining in their games, singing their songs. In the afternoons when occasion offered, he would swim with them in the lagoons. Here the children were at their happiest. Most of the boys had goggles and spears and would go far from shore to fish. One day Hall swam with them to the barrier reef. He soon discovered he was not their equal in their element. The boys lay face down, barely moving on the surface; then, as they saw a school, they would upend and dive, spearing the fish far below with one sure thrust. They asked Hall to try, laughing with him as he tread water with pumping arms and legs. They placed a spear in his hand and put goggles on his head. Hall did not want to disappoint them. He took a deep breath and dived, saw a swarm of brightly colored fish, and took aim. The spear shot out. He missed. He had misjudged the distance by at least a foot. When Hall surfaced he laughed at his lack of skill. The children loved him for it. At least he had tried.

Such, however, was not the case on shore, when Hall played for them in an element not their own. After changing into dry clothes, he went back to the ship. He entered his cabin, pulled out his sea chest, and unlocked it. He reached in under his clothes and took out his mandolin. Inexplicably, he had not played it before on any of the island stops.

The natives had never seen anything like it. Hall settled against the base of a coconut tree, and after tuning the strings and running through a few chords, he strummed and hummed a tune, then raised his clear tenor voice to his own accompaniment. The natives heard, stopped their work, poured out of their huts, and came to join the children already gathered about him. Instinctively fond of music, their joy over the new instrument was immediate and continuing. They smiled and clapped and begged him to play another and yet another tune. Although Hall's repertory was limited, they cared not at all and asked him to repeat, and until the last fire began to die out that night, he sang for them the songs he had learned in the Grinnell Glee Club, and even the hymns he had sung as a boy in his church at Colfax.

Hall hated to leave that friendly island. Even if he were an amateur who could not play in all the keys, the natives made him feel like a professional. The *Caleb S. Winship* worked her way slowly through the islands of the archipelago, until at last they sighted at the outmost reach of it, the small coral atoll of Taioro. It was dawn. The sky, overcast to great height, veiled the sun. The island, a flat black finger of land, lay in a circle of unbroken reef that sprouted seven separate tiny islands. Because there was no pass, the captain announced that they would have to put to shore by whaleboat—through the crashing waves and over the ledge of the reef. It was an operation, Hall knew, that only a native crew, with great skill, could manage. Cridland, his old native woman, and their supplies were loaded into the whaleboat. Hall, never having made such a landing before, decided to go in with them.

Hall held fast to a thwart and braced himself as the boat settled in the troughs of the giant waves. Looking forward over the gunwales, he saw the sea break, then pour back, baring a sheer deep and jagged wall of rock. The crew backed on the oars, waiting the command from the boat steerer, who stood with his head half-turned to the oncoming seas, the tiller firmly grasped with his arms and hands. Suddenly he shouted his order. The oarsmen reacted in unison. A great wall of water, crested to the point of breaking, caught the aft end of the boat. The sailors pulled, bending their long oars against the contrary sea, staying with the crest. Then the wave passed under, carrying the whaleboat over the reef, into the peaceful shallows of the lagoon. Hall wiped the sweat from his face and neck. The skill of the boat crew had struck him with wonderment and awe.

Hall debarked and followed Cridland and Ruau to her house on the beach. The hut had badly weathered the elements. The thatched roof had broken through at the peak, and the bamboo sides had splintered and broken. About the house fallen coconuts and dead palm fronds lay everywhere on the ground. Wild pigs grunted and fed on sprouting nuts. Out of sight, but somewhere close in one of the trees, a bird sang. It reminded Hall of a hermit thrush. As he listened, Cridland suddenly stepped up from behind him and took Hall by the arm. Hall turned, but Cridland said nothing, and quickly withdrew his hand. Strange, Hall thought; if this, somehow, were a bid for closer affability, then it was accompanied by nothing more. The man was inscrutable. If this aloofness on his part, impenetrable and mysterious, sprang from some deep-seated defect in his character, then perhaps it best explained why Cridland's search for solitude now stopped at Taioro, thousands of miles from anyone. Try as he would, with tentative probes that quickly recoiled, Cridland would not, or could not, establish a bridge to another human being.

Hall walked back to the beach. The crew of the whaleboat had gone to the ship to bring in another load of supplies, Cridland's only provisions until another ship at some distant and other time would call. Hall watched the boat as it tried once more to shoot the pass. This time it swerved and caught the breaker at the wrong angle; it swung broadside, then crashed against the reef and overturned. The backwash swept the supplies into the sea. The natives dived into the water, hoping to rescue something, but all had been lost. Cridland had come down to the beach; he looked on at his loss, unperturbed, calm as any stoic. The old woman, resigned that there would be no tinned beef to supplement the diet, went out into the lagoon to catch some fish for dinner.

The next afternoon a strong wind started to blow. Tino, the supercargo, decided that they would push off immediately. There was, he said, no time for farewells. Hall looked for Cridland and Ruau, but they had gone to the other side of the island. As the schooner got under sail, Hall went aft and looked back to the shore. Deep from the shadows Cridland emerged and stood on the beach, staring out across the water. Hall waved. There was no answer.

2

Nordhoff in the Cooks

Nordhoff had set sail in the *Faaite* as the sun began to disappear behind Mooréa. He was going to the Cook Islands, some six hundred miles south and west of Tahiti, to what the natives called the Land of the Bright Heavens. The season of the trades had not yet begun, and all the sails could pick up was a lazy northeast breeze. It made the heat unbearable on board. Nordhoff could not force himself to go below. He would not meet the calls to mess; the dining room sweltered, and the stink of copra lingered over the food. He spent most of his time on deck, even to sleep, and when he became hungry he would send below for a banana or a mango.

After a few days out, one day toward dusk Nordhoff perched himself in the shrouds. It was somewhat cooler there, the air slightly more fresh and clean, and it was the best possible vantage point for making a landfall. As the ship rose on the crest of a wave, he spotted a blue scribble on the horizon. Before he could call attention to it, a native boy, higher in the rigging than he, shouted: *"Ahu Ahu—Ahu Ahu!"* The native passengers stirred from their somnolence. Men started to climb the masts for a better look at the island, mothers held up their babies so that watchers on shore could see them, grandmothers shuffled to the bulwarks and peered across the water hoping to see a familiar face.

Despite the native excitement at their imminent homecoming, it was not until midnight that the schooner finally drew close to the land. Leeward of the island it was calm. The ship rose and fell gently on the long swells. The air carried the soft fragrance of frangipani, but soon it mixed with smoke and the smell of damp earth. Natives on shore started to light torches to mark the way through the pass. On the forward hatch of the ship four native girls started to sing, a melancholy, even piteous, chant, which was answered in turn by the men standing nearby. To Nordhoff, the music seemed to echo the long low moan, rhythmic and insistent, of wave on reef.

Nordhoff moved forward to the mainmast and lay down on a mat. The chanting recalled a line from Wordsworth, "the still, sad music of humanity." Next to Nordhoff sat Tari, the supercargo, who was talking in whispers with his native wife. The music ended abruptly. Tari turned to Nordhoff. "They sing well, these Ahu Ahu people," the supercargo said. "I like to listen to them. That is a hymn, but a stranger would never suspect it. The music is pure heathen." He pulled himself over close to Nordhoff. "With that singing in one's ears, it is not difficult to fancy oneself in a long canoe, at the end of an old-time voyage, chanting a song of thanksgiving to the gods who have brought us safely home."

Since they had left Tahiti, Nordhoff had become intrigued by the white supercargo and had spent many hours wondering about his background and why he had decided to live in the South Seas. Tari reached over toward his wife for a bottle of rum he had been drinking with her; then he tipped it up and drained it. He brushed the back of his hand across his mouth. Warmed by the rum, he began to talk, freely and cheerfully.

He was an Englishman and had been educated in public schools. As a young man he had gone to New Zealand; bored and seeking adventure, he enlisted in the army, served in Gallipoli, was wounded, and earned the Distinguished Service

Medal. After his discharge in England, as a captain, he found that he could not stand civilization. Two weeks were more than he could bear. He came to the islands and had been a trader for twenty years. He would never return to that other island.

"Home is all very well for a week or two," he said, warming to the subject he would not discuss before, "but for a steady thing I seem to fit in better down here." He paused. "What is it that makes a chap stop in the islands? You must have felt it yourself, and yet it is hard to put it into words." He lifted his arm and with his hand described a wide arc. "This sort of thing, perhaps—the beauty, the sense of remoteness, the vague and agreeable melancholy of these places. Then I like the way the years slip past, the pleasant monotony of life. My friends at home put up with a kind of dullness which would drive me mad. But here, where there is even less to distinguish one day from another, one seems never to grow fretful or impatient of time. One's horizon narrows, of course. I scarcely look at the newspaper any more."

Tari now became more serious. "If you stop here," he said, "you will find yourself unconsciously drifting into the native state of mind, readjusting your sense of values until the great events of the world seem far off and unreal, and your interests are limited to your own business, the vital statistics of your island, and the odd kinks of human nature about you. Perhaps this is the way we are meant to live. At any rate, it brings serenity."

The supercargo stretched his arms in a deep, tired sigh. It had grown late while he talked. He now lit a match to find his mat, blew it out quickly, and lay down beside his wife. Nordhoff returned forward and lay down to sleep under the stars. As he dozed off, he knew there was one story left he would have to hear from Tari. How he had met, fallen in love, and married his native woman. Nordhoff knew that permanent alliances between white and brown in the South Seas rarely occurred. Incredibly, Tari and his wife seemed deeply in love forever.

The next day, Nordhoff heard the complete account. Tari

had known Apakura from the time she was a little girl. He would visit Ahu Ahu two or three times a year, and each time he came ashore the little one would always be there to meet him. She would follow him wherever he went on the island. By the time he went off to war, she was eleven years old. But when he came back, five years later, she was a fully developed, mature woman, and beautiful to behold. Tari, nevertheless, still looked upon her as a child. One day, Apakura's mother called him to her house and proposed marriage. Tari was dumbfounded. He was forty, he protested, and the child was only sixteen!

"Young wives are best, if they are faithful," the mother persisted. "Apakura will never look at another man."

"I will think it over," Tari answered. "Let us leave it so. Not this year, at any rate. She is too young."

Tari got up and started to leave the house. "Bear one thing in mind," the woman said. "It will help you to decide. Consider, now and then, the thought of my daughter married to another man."

The next day, Tari recounted, he did not board his schooner until the last moment. As the ship moved off from the shore, he went to a quiet corner and studied his accounts. He stood up to light his pipe, looked over the side, and noticed that they were now far out at sea. As he bent down to pick up his papers, Tari noticed one of the native crew members standing by the binnacle; mysteriously, the boy's face broke into a wide gleaming smile. At that moment, Tari felt a soft hand slip into his own. A voice behind him spoke, "I am here." Tari turned and Apakura reached her arms about his neck and smiled. "I will not leave you," she said. Two weeks later they were married in Tahiti.

When Tari finished talking, the men had started unloading. The sun slanted across the deck, but the morning air was still fresh and cool, and the sky clean and blue behind white scattered clouds. Six large native canoes shot through the pass, paddled over to the ship, and tied alongside. Nordhoff went to the side to look at the island. It shone brilliantly in the sun, the gray cliffs and green peaks grandly thrusting upward from the sapphire-blue lagoon and a foaming reef. Tari came over to where Nordhoff stood.

"There is to be a feast in my honor," he said. "Apakura and I want you to join us as our guest." Nordhoff readily accepted. They crawled over the side, climbed down the rope ladder, and dropped into one of the canoes. When they docked on the shore, the natives circled Tari and his wife, shouting cries of welcome, embracing, and shaking hands. Nordhoff knew now why the Englishman could never go back to British civilization. Tari was home.

The festivities on the island lasted for several days. When at last the schooner made ready to set out again, Nordhoff was most reluctant to leave. The hospitality of the people had captivated him, and when alone in his cottage at night, the serenity had enthralled him. But now they had to move on to other islands and pick up copra. The next stop was Mauke. The day began mild, with a faint breeze blowing from off the shore. But toward noon a strong wind, abaft of the beam, drove the ship, heavy with many tons of copra, headlong into each passing sea. Gray clouds began to scud low, and black squall lines laced the horizon, north-northeast, directly on the course line. They had hoped, by going west of Mauke, one of a group of three low islands, not to miss any of them. Certainly not the first, which was their destination.

But now a squall, heavy with rain, broke over the ship, dumping water over them, onto the decks, and out the scuppers. They lost their line of sight; but just as suddenly as the rain poured, it stopped, and the sky began to clear. Several hours later, close by and off to starboard, Mauke rose from the sea, as if Maui of old had fished it up from the deep. The schooner came alongside the reef, looking for a pass; then it turned, its back to the wind, and waited. The skipper had chosen a narrow passage, one meant only for boats, but he fully intended to take his ship through. Nordhoff watched the angry surf pour into the breach and shook his head. Although an experienced sailor himself with smaller craft, he would not have attempted it.

Riley, an American planter on board, sidled up to Nordhoff and winked. He wanted to ruffle the skipper, an old friend, who stood behind them at the wheel. "If this old hooker was mine," Riley said, not turning his head, "I'd start the engine every time I came about. She can't sail fast enough to keep steerageway!"

"If this damn fine schooner was yours," the captain retorted in the same good humor, "she'd have been piled up long ago. Like as not in broad daylight, and on an island a thousand feet high." He then brought the ship through the pass with nerveless ease.

Riley laughed. He took Nordhoff by the arm. "Let's go below and have a drink," he said. As they drank, Nordhoff uncovered Riley's story. It was one of adventure and romance from a South Boston Irishman who, at thirty-five, still lived such a life and fully intended to continue it in the same way.

From boyhood on, Riley had wandered for fifteen years from Cape Cod to Cape Horn to Cape Town. He had been, at one time or another, cabin boy, millhand, cowboy, fisherman, and seaman. Once in his travels he had found himself in San Francisco and had shipped out for a trip to the Marquesas and Society Islands. When he returned to the mainland, an unpredictable change had come over him. The wanderlust of old no longer gripped him. As he lay on his bed in a rooming house, fretful and sleepless, one vision recurred and persisted. A dark-eyed, brown-skinned maiden, as gentle as the night wind and as graceful as a palm tree before it, stood on the beach, hands outstretched, and cried for his return.

Riley took a berth on the next southbound schooner to Tahiti. There he found his Polynesian girl, still waiting for him, and they were married. He learned the native tongue quickly. And because of his ingratiating ways with the natives, he was soon offered a job as a superintendent of a copra plantation in the Cook Islands. He had been there ever since.

"It makes me laugh to think of when I first came down here," Riley said. He set his glass down among the wet rings on the table. "I was working in Tahiti, and when I came home in the evening my girl would look up from her sewing and sing out, 'O Riley.'"

"'For the love of Mike,' I'd tell her, 'don't you know my name yet? It's Riley, not O'Riley.'"

He took a quick short swallow of whiskey. "Finally, I caught on. I had been fooled in the same way as Cook and Bligh. You remember they called the island 'Otahiti.' That 'O' is simply a special form of the verb used before personal pronouns and proper nouns. The old navigators, when the canoes came out to meet them, pointed to the land and asked its name. 'O Tahiti,' the natives said, meaning 'It is Tahiti.' My girl didn't mean to call me O'Riley at all," he said, chuckling to himself. "She was simply saying, 'It's Riley.' "

Riley was in great demand among the islands because of his ability to manage the natives. On this particular voyage he was on a recruiting trip for laborers on his atoll. The natives of Mauke had a reputation for being lazy, unwilling to work for anyone at any price. Riley, because they liked him, never had any trouble hiring them. They always worked very well together. Except for two occasions.

Like many Boston Irishmen, Riley perhaps believed that his body was a temple for the Holy Ghost. In any case, he was in perfect physical condition, deeply bronzed, his stomach a washboard of muscle. The Kanakas, proud of their strength, undoubtedly looked upon Riley as a test of it. One day, inevitably, one of the native boys tried to kill him with a spear. Riley acted quickly. He called all the workers in from the field, made a referee of the foreman, and decided to fight it out with the native, a towering six-foot two-hundred-pounder. They squared off. Coldly and methodically, his Irish temper under control, Riley proceeded to beat the black man to a whimpering mass of bleeding flesh.

The second time, Riley was taken unexpectedly. He had been sleeping in the shade of his cottage when one of his workers stole up behind him and cracked him over the head with a club; then, as Riley lay unconscious on the ground, the Kanaka kicked him again and again in the ribs, rolling him in the dirt like a log. Riley had been left for dead. That night his wife Tetua, noting that his time for return had long passed, went out to look for him. She found him on the ground against the house, bleeding and scarcely breathing. Somehow she dragged him into their cottage.

When Riley revived, he groaned in pain from his broken ribs. He struggled to his knees, then pulled himself slowly to his feet. Gripping his wife's shoulder, he dragged himself to the table and sat down. He poured out half a glass of whiskey and drank it in one gulp. Then he sent for his manager.

The native boy had disappeared; but after a long search they found him hiding on a small island in the lagoon. At first afraid at what his punishment would be, the boy relaxed and then smiled when he learned that Riley only wanted to meet him in a man-to-man contest of strength. Fresh and unharmed, the boy became arrogant with defiance; Riley, his ribs taped and hurting, felt weak and unsure of his legs. When they first came at one another, Riley had the worst of it. He took a blow to the chest that knifed him with pain and sent him reeling into the dust. But now he raged with anger and revenge. He got up and moved in on the Kanaka, pounding him with swinging lefts and rights to the face, body, and arms, until the boy fell to the ground; then Riley jumped on the prostrate body, his legs astride and holding him down, and struck at the boy's face and head, determined to kill him. The manager, seeing what was happening, called three others to his aid, and went in and pulled Riley off the boy.

But these were the exceptions. For the most part, life was as peaceful for Riley as the islands themselves. The islands themselves, Nordhoff thought, not the reefs with no passes through. The crashing waves on the reefs could in minutes tear men and boats to shreds. The landing they would have to make now on Mauke was a case in point. The island was the peak of a once-submerged volcanic mountain, ringed with a terrible jagged ledge of coral.

A whaleboat had been sent out from the island to the ship. It had made it over the reef to the sea with success but only because twenty men from shore had pushed it through the breakers. To get back to the shore, however, the steersman argued, would be a far more difficult operation. But he was willing to try it. Nordhoff lowered into the whaleboat with the supercargo and Riley.

The oarsmen rowed to a point outside the reef about a quarter of a mile beyond the schooner. As the boat rose on a crest, Nordhoff looked forward over the side and watched the back-wash run off the coral. The oarsmen backed into a towering wave. The steersman, his head quickly swinging backward and forward, waited for the exact moment to shout his command. The order came, short, loud, and direct. The six crewmen pulled their oars against the sea. A great wave rose and drove the boat headlong, the bow pitched down, but the wave passed under the keel and away. Now the boat caught the backwash, heaved to one side, and steeply rolled over to starboard. Nord-hoff fell out onto the reef. Gulping the sea water, he fought through the foam for a footing and reached out to grab the gunwale. The boat, stern high, tilted on the ledge. Nordhoff jumped back in just as they caught another breaking sea. Bow and keel scraped on the coral, but kept straight and even, and the force of the wave carried the boat safely into the lagoon. Nordhoff rubbed a sleeve across his brow and sighed with deep relief. Riley, sitting behind him, was equally relieved. "I think I'll get a job diving for shell," he said. "I'll swear I haven't breathed for a good three minutes." "Nor I," Nordhoff quickly added.

Riley's native friends crowded about him when he came to shore. They called him "Rairi" because of their inability to pronounce *l*'s; and Nordhoff became for them "Teari." Nord-hoff liked that name much better than others he heard the na-tives later use for two white men on the island they did not care for, one a fat imperious snob, and the other a hated Brit-ish colonial. The natives called them "Salt Pork" and "Pig Dung."

After lunch with a trader friend of Riley's, as they sat smok-ing and drinking rum punches, a native boy came in and whis-pered into Riley's ear. Riley asked to be excused, then turned to Nordhoff. "There's a beer tub going full blast out in the bush," he said. "I think I'll drop in on them and see if I can pick up a man or two. You'd better come along."

They walked for twenty minutes along a narrow path deep into the center of the island. Shouts of joy went up for Riley as they came to a clearing. It was a stag affair and it must have been going on for some time. The men stood in a circle, happily singing, dancing, and drinking. In the center were two five-gallon cans, their tops cut off, bubbling with a colored brew. It was orange beer, Riley explained, made from orange juice, sugar, and yeast. And it was very potent.

Following custom, Riley and Nordhoff in turn had to finish in one long pull a hollowed-out coconut full of the beer. They drained them off. Now, in accordance with the ritual, they expected Riley to dance for them. He did not hesitate. He stripped to the waist and started doing the *tamure,* now taking the woman's part, then the man's response. The men clapped their hands in a fast rhythm; Riley still held his legs and upper body perfectly still, and gyrated his pelvis in every direction. When he finished, the natives roared in appreciation.

Then they asked Nordhoff to follow suit; for, having drunk from the cup, he must dance, too, like the others. Nordhoff protested, but in vain. Unable to wiggle in the native fashion, he offered them a dance he had learned in New York after the Armistice. The natives had never seen a Charleston danced; and as Nordhoff kicked his legs out, then swapped his hands from one bent knee to the other, the men shouted with joy. The American "Popaa" was a fine man, they said to Riley, just as he was.

That evening, full with orange beer, Nordhoff and Riley took leave of the island. The whaleboat lay in the lagoon waiting for them. In the west the sun had started to set, and from behind great white clouds it stitched their edges in a hem of golden light. As they set out through the pass, from the shore came shouts of "Rairi" and "Teari."

Charles Bernard Nordhoff was becoming one of them.

3

Hall in the Tuamotus

Before Hall had left Papeete, he happened to stop in front of a Chinese stall along the quay and, to his incredulous surprise, noticed for sale a box of marbles. He promptly bought them. He had no way of knowing at the time, but later the marbles would be the cause of a long experiment in solitude for him.

The *Caleb S. Winship,* having dropped Cridland at Taioro, was on the way home. Tons of copra had been picked up at islands on the way out and in along the route, but there was still room for more. The captain decided to put in at Rutiaro, a lonely atoll, less than ten miles long and thinly populated, but with a large copra plantation. Tino, the supercargo, stood next to Hall on deck. They had just spotted abeam in the distance a thin blue line, faintly visible on the horizon, which marked the island.

"Look here," Tino said. "What is it that interests you in these islands?" I've never known anyone to visit them for pleasure before. Is it women, or what?"

"No, it's not the women," Hall replied. "Not the Tuamotuan women, anyway. I find the Tahitian girls far more attractive."

"You're right," continued Tino. "The women here are healthy enough, of course, but they don't set your heart beating a hundred to the minute. They have fine hands and white teeth, and you won't find such black hair in all the world as you find in these atolls. But that's the size of it. You can't praise them any further for looks."

"That's true. And their feet and ankles are too big, and all scarred from the coral." Hall reached into his shirt pocket for a cigarette.

"Well, if it isn't the women, what else is there to be interested in? Not the islands themselves? Lord! When you've seen one, you've seen the lot. Living on one of them is like living aboard ship. No room to stretch your legs. And in a hurricane, these people on Rutiaro would drown like rats."

Hall did not want to continue the discussion any further. Although it was the islands, and the people on them, that did in fact interest him, he saw no point in trying to justify himself before anyone who understood only a sexual or a profit motive. "I think I'll climb the mainmast for a better look," he said, finally.

From the crosstrees Hall looked through his binoculars to windward. The land was broad and flat, but narrowed at one end to a ledge, and just off the end, beyond a small lagoon, was an islet. Together they looked like a ship with a small boat in tow. Great green waves broke on the reef, then changed in color from light blue to dark blue from inside the reef to the shoals of the lagoon. The shore was a wide white beach edged with leaning palm trees. "It is true," Hall thought; "the islands are like so many reef points on a sail, just as the skipper in Tahiti told me. But what about their desolate beauty and their romantic loveliness? They might be as monotonous as the sea itself, but they are also as fresh as the sea with its varying interest."

A French flag waving in the wind marked a pass in the reef for small boats. The schooner turned and dropped anchor outside the reef. A voice shouted up from the deck. It was Tino.

"Hello, up there!" he said. "Kai-kai's ready." The whaleboat was being lowered over the side. "All right! I'm coming!" Hall shouted back.

As he climbed into the boat, Hall could not resist befuddling the supercargo about his motives. "You know," he said to him, "there isn't probably one in a million who has even seen this island or ever will see it. What a piece of luck for me!"

Tino did not seem to be listening. "I wonder how much copra they have," he said vacantly. "Not much, I bet. They're a lazy lot on this island."

When they landed Hall learned that there had been no boat to visit Rutiaro in over four months. As a result, the natives were overjoyed to have company. The entire village came to the shore to welcome them. The chief, a large, heavy man; his wife, slight and short; and an old retainer, with only two eye-teeth in his mouth, shook their hands as they debarked. But the center of attention quickly changed from the visitors to a Chinese, the only storekeeper on the island. As supplies were unloaded from the boat for him, the natives began to crowd about him as if he were a Polynesian Santa Claus. One of them kept patting him on the shoulder, saying: *"Maitai! Maitai!"* as if to say—judging from the inscrutable smile of the Oriental— "You know me, Moy Ling. You know me!"

Tino paced up and down on the beach, throwing up his hands in disgust. "I told you they were a lazy lot," he complained. "They've seen us making in for three hours, and what have they been doing? Loafing on the beach, waiting for us instead of getting their copra together. Moy Ling is the only one in the village who is ready to do business. Five tons all sacked for weighing. He's worth a dozen Kanakas." He stopped and thought for a moment. "Well, I'll set them to work in quick time now. You watch me! I'm going to be loaded and out of here by six o'clock." Lamentations to the contrary, Tino did not know that Hall carried in his pocket a box of marbles.

In a clearing under a coconut tree, Hall noticed a group of boys and girls playing hide and seek together. He walked over to them, got down on his knees, and spilled out his marbles. The children were wide-eyed with curiosity. Hall picked up a marble, placed it between his bent thumb and forefinger, and shot it hard and straight into the others. The pile of marbles scattered in every direction. The children begged to try it too. Hall showed them how to hold the marble and shoot; then he taught them how to play two of his favorite games when he was a boy, "Bullring" and "Tom's dead." Getting up, he passed among the children, handing out equal lots of marbles, explaining the while the idea of playing "for keeps." Then he watched them play, making sure they followed the rules. Satisfied with their degree of skill, and thinking of Tino's statement about a short stay, he left them to make a quick trip about the island.

Hall walked up a small hill toward the middle of the island and noticed an old grave marker stuck in a mound of earth. There was only one word on it: "Repose." He walked quickly by it and down the other side of the hill toward the ocean side of the island. He came to the beach and sat down. Although he had seen more than his share of death in the trenches and in the sky of France, and although he had come close to it himself three times and narrowly escaped each time, he did not like to think about it. But he took out his small pocket notebook and a pencil. "To most men, I believe," he wrote quickly, "with the best of life before them, there is something terrible, infamous, in the thought of unrelieved blackness of an endless, dreamless sleep."

Suddenly, he felt a hand upon his shoulder. It startled him. "*Haere i te pai!*"—"Come down to the boat!" a voice said. It was one of the native boys, and he began to run, waving his arm to follow quickly. When Hall got back to the village, he stopped at the shore, huffing and trying to find his breath. He looked out beyond the reef to the ship. Anchor weighed, sail set, it was slowly moving out to sea.

Hall cupped his hands to his mouth. "Wait, Tino!" he shouted. "Wait a minute! You're not going to leave me behind, are you?"

An answer came back, slow and carefully pronounced. "You can stay where you are and play marbles till hell freezes over! I'm through with you!" The schooner turned and sailed into the darkening horizon. Hall was stranded.

Then the natives told him what had happened. The older

people had become as interested in playing marbles as the children. Forsaking all intentions of collecting and sacking copra, young and old, mothers and fathers, joined in, until families pitted their skill against one another. Puarei, the chief, became one of the great competitors. He had won nearly half of all the marbles. The supercargo finally despaired of getting any work done, cursed the name of Hall, and went back to the schooner to get drunk on a bottle of rum. The only copra loaded on board was that of Moy Ling and that had to be done by the crew.

The natives had gathered about Hall to commiserate with him over his plight. *"Aue!"* Puarei said, patting him on the back, "We are sorry for you!" Huirai, the man of two teeth and the constable of the island, enlarged the native sympathies in fractured English. "I been Frisco," he said. "You go to hell, me!" Puarei waved the others aside and put his arm around Hall and led him away. The white man would be his guest.

They went to Moy Ling's store, where the chief, in a grand display of hospitality, ordered the finest of feasts from the Chinese. Large palm fronds were spread on the ground. The two men sat, crossed their legs, and waited to be served. The meal began with smoked herring, followed by soup, curried chicken with rice, and crab meat, all served with white bread. Hall could not keep up with the chief, who had set to with his fingers, quickly scooping large handfuls into his mouth. Hall started to eat with a small tin fork and spoon, but soon gave up to follow in the native fashion—to the delight of the islanders, who thought his implements for eating were ridiculous when nature had already provided man with two excellent ones.

When at last the chief asked that the remnants be cleared away, Hall asked to be excused to take a walk. Puarei waved him off graciously and he promptly went to lie down and sleep for a while. Hall wandered about the village. Families were themselves eating, dipping raw fish into a coconut-milk sauce, putting it in their mouths, and sucking their fingers clean. In the lagoon, three dogs dived among the shallows, trying to catch fish; one of them soon did and then ran to the beach, the prey wriggling between his jaws. Back at Moy Ling's store, a group of natives had gathered, and one of them played on his accordion while the others danced and sang. Farther away, near a crackling fire, a number of children had started playing marbles again. Puarei, as eager as any of them, came to join the circle. One of the girls, Hall was surprised to see, was beating anyone she met. She soon had all the marbles of the other children. Puarei decided that he and the girl must play it out in a grand contest, to see who was the champion of the island.

A new wide circle was drawn in the sand. The word spread about the match, and soon the whole village came to watch and cheer. Puarei was an excellent shot; but the girl, slight, fierce, and determined, with big black sparkling eyes, was a brilliant strategist. The game continued far into the night. Moy Ling, never one to miss a sale, passed among the spectators selling loaves of freshly baked bread. Some of the younger children had fallen asleep, their heads resting on the laps of older brothers and sisters. Two old men dozed, their heads fallen between their knees. By eleven o'clock the chief had lost almost all his winnings. The girl, calm and self-confident, moved in for his last few. Puarei's wife teased him about losing to such a small adversary. The chief shrugged her off, trying to make excuses. At last the chief had one marble left. The girl, thumb and forefinger ready, was poised for the final kill. Firing, she knocked the chief's marble out of the ring and into the lap of one of the spectators. A roar of cheers and applause went up. The chief's wife shook with laughter. Puarei, soundly defeated, head bent, slowly dragged his way home.

As the crowd dispersed and everyone returned to his cottage, Hall went to the lagoon and sat aganist the base of a coconut tree. It was now past midnight. The golden light of a full moon brightened the ripples of the water. In sequent file the waves lapped the shore. A light breeze tipped the palm fronds and cat-pawed the shallows. Hall thought of Cridland, the solitary figure of a lonely atoll, and of Tino, the man of business. Upon reflection, Hall had to admit that Tino was better for the world: his death would be a loss; but Cridland and he, living out their dreams, contributed nothing to life: they would never, should never, be missed.

The next morning, awakened by the crowing of a cock, Hall

turned his thoughts to the practical matters of daily life. He had left all his money in his sea chest on board the *Winship*. All he had was what he wore—khaki shirt and trousers, under-wear, a pair of tennis shoes—and an ocarina in his back pocket. At first, he thought he might borrow some money from the chief, but the natives thought that all white men were rich. To seek a loan would be unseemly. He decided to act as if indeed he were rich. He would go to Moy Ling's store—and charge everything he needed.

The Chinese was singularly impressed and readily agreed. Hall was lavish in his wants. He ordered quantity and variety and quality, giving no thought to price. The shop began to fill up with curious natives, astounded at the incredible wealth of the white man, who, it seemed, was buying everything in the store. Moy Ling kept running back and forth, filling the order. He brought back a bolt of white drill cloth, for suits; cotton cloth, for underwear and shirts; the entire supply of notebooks and a package of pencils; a dozen silk handkerchiefs; a flash-light; twelve pairs of earrings; four lockets and chains; ten kilos of flour, two of coffee; three bottles of perfume; four large bolts of colored ribbon, and one of mosquito netting. The pile of goods grew on the counter and began to spill to either side.

Hall felt reckless, like a sailor on leave with a year's pay in his pockets. He kept making selections. Moy Ling grew tired, but smiled at the thought of his profits mounting with every purchase. He kept trotting back and forth, now bringing a monkey wrench, two lanterns, a box of black combs for women, a pandanus mat, a bow tie. Hall enjoyed the stir he was making and continued to order anything that fell to his eye. Moy Ling piled on two bolts of pareu cloth, for women's dresses; four pocketknives; two cans of green paint, one of white; twenty packages of chewing gum—the entire supply. The Chinese's shelves were almost bare. There remained on one but a single package of tobacco. Hall ordered that too, for a clean sweep.

Then Hall, swelling with new-found affluence and wanting to repay the natives for their kindness to him, now gave to them from his abundance. First to the children he passed out the chewing gum, then to the women the dress goods and combs, necklaces and bottles of perfume, and finally to the men the pocketknives. To the chief and his wife, Hall brought the flour, the monkey wrench, and the bolt of mosquito netting, and for Puarei's ten-ton cutter, blistered and peeling on shore, the three buckets of paint. *"Aue,"* the chief said— "Thank you," grateful but utterly bewildered by the white man's munificence. Hall, now sobering from his buying spree, looked toward Moy Ling's store, and prayed that some day soon the *Winship* would return with his money.

On a day several weeks later Hall went for a long and leisurely walk to gather shells on the other side of the island. When he returned about midafternoon he found the village silent and empty of people. Coming to the shore, he stopped. Across the lagoon he could hear the shouts of the natives on the *motu,* the islet near the entering pass at the barrier reef. He took one of the smaller outrigger canoes from its drying rack, dragged it to the water's edge, climbed in, and paddled the four miles across the lagoon. As he arrived at the motu he noticed that all the natives of the island were at work building a thatched hut. The bamboo sides were up, and workers were at the moment completing the roof of pandanus thatch.

Puarei and his wife, smiling broadly, greeted Hall effusively. "How do you like *your* house?" the chief said.

"My house?" Hall, taken by surprise, could not understand.

"And your island, for as long as you remain," the chief added.

Still unbelieving and bewildered, Hall walked about the cottage, looking and touching. He stepped inside the doorway. Native women were spreading mats on a floor of crushed shell, and two of them were tacking to the walls old magazine advertisements.

"Aue, aue," Hall said. "Thank you, thank you. Gosh, it's just wonderful. My own house, and my own island. *Aue."*

"The place where the souls are eaten," Puarei said.

"The *what?"* Hall asked.

Then the chief explained. Many years before a family came to the motu to fish, but before they could make their catch, they all died mysteriously. Their bodies were eaten by vengeful spirits in the form of sea birds.

Hall felt suddenly disquieted but presently shook it off. Puarei asked him if he would not be lonely living by himself on the islet, if he would not, on second thought, rather come back to the main island and live with them?

As he was about to give a long explanation about the pleasures of solitude, Hall remembered that he still carried a postcard from New York in his shirt pocket. It would help give an answer much quicker than his poor mixture of French and Tuamotu. It was a picture of the Woolworth Building. He showed it to the chief. Wasn't it terrible to have to live in such a crowded place? Hall asked. He had done so for many years. To get away from such a life, he had come a very long distance to the islands to find peace and room to breathe. Puarei now understood, completely.

The work on the house had been finished, and Hall stood on the beach to wave farewell to the natives as they paddled back to the island. He went to the cottage. It was dark inside and he lit one of the lanterns that hung from a crossbeam in the ceiling. The natives had built for him a small table and a chair, and on the far wall they had put up some shelves and stored his provisions on them. From pegs in one of the posts hung his extra clothing, and on one of the mats on the floor his bedding was rolled out. Hall blew out the light. He wanted to get a good night's sleep and be up at dawn to explore his island.

His rest was a short one. At first Hall thought he was dreaming. He felt the brush of a hand on his face and heard the sound of hushed laughter. Frightened, he awoke, looked about the room but saw nothing, and got up to look out the window. The natives had returned. They stood outside his house, the women giggling, the men chuckling. Hall went outside to discover what was going on.

The sky was bright with a full moon. Natives were everywhere on the motu. Children had climbed the palm trees and were dropping coconuts to the ground. From one tree, its trunk curving far out over the water, boys and girls took turns climbing up to the top, crawling out on a branch, and jumping into the lagoon. Canoes were paddled to the shore, unloading more people. One young man, who had brought his accordion, started to play. Couples began dancing, and everybody clapped hands and sang to the music. Hall found Puarei sitting in a chair under a coconut tree, directing proceedings. His wife, Poura, lay on a mat beside him, offering her advice for the proceedings. "We didn't want you to be lonely," the chief said to Hall. "And we wanted to celebrate your new house."

Hall smiled. Even natives believed in housewarmings. *"Aue!"* he said. Then he thought: Was this the way to begin an adventure in solitude? He would simply have to postpone it another day. Down on the beach the boys were piling up green drinking nuts in one place and ripe nuts in another; the girls took the ripe ones, split them, and grated the meat for coconut milk. The women spread palm fronds on the ground, set out large shells for serving, slit and cleaned fish. The men were digging a deep hole in the ground and bringing in rocks to make an oven. Hall walked along the shore, delighting in the scene. It was to him so real and yet so unreal. In the moonlight, on such a faraway island, at such an hour, children everywhere laughing and playing, and the parents preparing a feast: It was something of a South Seas Mother Goose Land.

Hall noticed a group of five- and six-year-olds standing by the coconut tree where the older children climbed and dived into the water. When he came to them, they looked up at him sadly. They were too small to climb the tree. Hall shook his head. He couldn't climb the tree either! Then, one of the men, seeing the difficulty, came over, threw one of the girls on his back, climbed the tree, and dropped her in with the others. Then he jumped in himself. The man kept this up until all the little ones had had their plunge.

From out across the lagoon came a big canoe which was loaded with fluttering chickens and squealing pigs. Shouts greeted the paddlers as they made for the beach. Here at last was the main part of the feast. But no one had noticed that on the way across some of the chickens had worked themselves loose, and now, wild, and as capable as any bird, they beat their strong wings against the air and rose in flight. The natives scrambled to catch them, but in vain; the chickens flew one by one to another islet, across the pass, more than a mile away, and protected by an impassable sea.

To make up for the loss, Hall went to his hut and brought from his shelves four cans of beef and salmon. But these were not enough. The natives grabbed their spears, climbed into their canoes, and paddled out to sea to catch some fish. Hall went along with them. Watching through the clear water, he marveled at their quick and accurate skill. In less than an hour the canoe he was in was almost filled with fish. Dawn was breaking as they came back in, but along with the success of the other canoes, there was more than enough fish caught to make up for the escaped chickens.

When Hall took his place next to the chief, the women started to bring the food—large piles of baked and raw fish; roast pork and chicken; bread the size and shape of cannon-balls, which had been boiled instead of baked. Like the others, Hall dipped the fish and meat into the coconut sauce and ate with his fingers. He relished every morsel. Puarei thumped the side of roast pork. *"E mea maitai,"* he said—"A good thing, that."

"E, e mea maitai roa, tera," Hall replied, nodding his head —"A very good thing that."

Puarei went from food to food, dipped it into the sauce, and without losing a drop, whipped it into his mouth. *"Katinga ahurua katinga,"* he added—"Food and yet more food."

Huirai, the toothless constable who had been to San Francisco, was anxious to impress his chief by speaking English. "What's the matter? Oh, yes! Never mind," he said rapidly together, obviously not knowing what the phrases meant.

Hall decided to tease him. "Huirai," he said, "you are the worst old fourflusher in all these islands, aren't you?" Hall looked straight into his eyes.

"You go to hell, me!" Huirai answered, as if he did know what he was saying.

At last Puarei pushed back from his place, patted himself on the stomach, and groaned. *"Aue! Paia 'huru paia to tatou,"* he said—"We are all of us full up to the neck."

Hall agreed that they were indeed, at least the men. Now it was the time for the women to sit down and eat what remnants the men had left. There was plenty of food left for everybody, and before all had had their fill it was the middle of the morning. Hall got up, lit a cigarette, put his hands in his pockets, and walked along the beach. He was content. Not even in the white man's world, he reflected, had he ever been so spontaneously, and so royally, entertained.

Alone on his island, James Norman Hall let the weeks slip by, one after the other, paying no heed to the days of the week. He was in, yet out of, time, barely mindful of one day's following another. It had been his intention, if he could abide by it, "to loaf and invite his soul" as much as possible. In his notebook he had written soon after he settled in his hut: "I was to delve deeply, for the first time, into my own resources against loneliness. I had known the solitude of cities, but there one has the comfortable sense of nearness to others; the refuge of books, pictures, and music—all the distractions which prevent any very searching examination of one's capacity for a life of retirement. At Soul-Eaters' Island I would have no books, no pictures, excepting a colored postcard of the Woolworth Building which had won me this opportunity; and for music I was limited to what I could make for myself with my ocarina, my sweet-potato whistle which had a range of one octave. Thus scantily provided with diversions, I was to learn how far my own thoughts would serve to make a solitary life not only endurable, but pleasant."

Hall had kept so close to his announced purpose, he discovered later, that these were the only lines he had written in his notebook, and under the title, "Rutiaro: Observations on Life and Character in the Low Archipelago," he had written nothing at all, except for a few reminders that led nowhere. He had, like the hermit crab on the beach, retired into his own shell; and like Thoreau of Concord, whose Walden Pond he had visited during his very first week in Boston, he had learned what he could live without.

But again like Thoreau, who found comfort in making occasional visits to town, Hall would sometimes paddle the four miles across the lagoon to the village. One day, after putting up his outrigger on the beach, Hall walked along a path, playing his ocarina. A woman whom he had not noticed as he came ashore ran up alongside him, and took him by the arm. Her name was Takiero, she explained, and she wanted to learn how to play his ocarina. Hall obliged. They stopped at her hut and went inside. In the corner a young girl sat on a chair breast-feeding a baby. Takiero said that the baby was hers but that she had given it to the girl nursing it because the girl had wanted it. Hall had noticed this phenomenon before in Polynesia, but never understood the reason for it.

Takiero tried to blow a note on the sweet potato. Hall showed her how to cover the holes with her fingers, and soon taught her the simple octave scale. Then, because she mastered the instrument so quickly, he demonstrated the playing of a melody. It was "Conquer the North," a song he had learned while marching to battle with the British Army. Takiero soon played the song to perfection. Because she seemed so happy in her new ability, Hall decided to seek the answer to the question which had perplexed him for such a long time.

"Why have you given your baby to the girl?" he asked.

Takiero seemed stunned at the need for such a question. "Because she asked for it!" she replied.

"But, see here, Takiero," Hall continued, "I should think that you and your husband would want to keep your own baby. It is none of my business, of course. I ask only because I would like to get some information on this feeding-parent custom. Can't you feed it yourself? Is that the reason you gave it away?"

Takiero was stabbed with insult, both as a woman and as a mother. She ripped open her pareu and bared two full firm breasts. "Does that answer your question?" she countered, defiantly. Thereupon she rushed to where the girl sat with the baby and snatched the child up into her own arms. She hugged the baby firmly to her bosom, kissing it passionately about the head and face.

Meanwhile the deprived girl began to understand what was happening. She now asserted her rights with the child. She rushed to Takiero and tried to pull the baby from her. Takiero would not yield. The child started to cry, then scream, as the two women fought. Neither would relent. Then, pulling and fighting to no avail, they stood apart from one another and started spitting insults at each other. Neighbors began to crowd into the house, and to take sides. At last Puarei, the chief, came and settled the matter. He gave the baby back to the girl. "Don't be upset," he said to Hall who seemed most upset. "You know how women are." Hall wanted to console the mother. But Takiero needed none. Acting as if there had been no argument at all about anything, she strolled out of the house, playing "Conquer the North" on Hall's ocarina.

Hall, remembering some of the disastrous calls he had made in tenement houses in Boston as a social worker, now added another mistake he would avoid in the future. He would never ask about child adoption in Polynesia again. He went back to the beach, climbed into his canoe, and paddled back to his motu, determined to try once more his solitary venture.

But as Hall felt the need on occasion to visit the natives, so they on their part had to come to see him. Many visitors came; some to spend the day, others to stay the night. Although alone, he was never lonesome. But the natives, naturally gregarious and bound by disaster to common survival, would not let Hall endure by himself. One day, several canoes had come to the islet across the pass from Hall, to collect coconuts and make copra. After working for a few hours, the natives paddled across to Hall's island. As was his custom, Hall went to his shelves to get some canned goods. He wanted to treat his guests to a meal of tinned beef and salmon. As he reached up, he noticed that his provisions were almost all gone. And he knew, after many sorties to Moy Ling's to resupply his stock, that his charges must be incredibly high. He could see the Chinese at his abacus, gleefully clicking the beads, adding up the bill. When Hall had finished serving lunch to his visitors, he went down to the beach with them to see them off. As they worked across the pass to the other islet, he looked across the barrier reef and beyond to the open sea. Against the horizon in bare outline he could see the tops of some sails. He blinked his eyes in disbelief. It would have to be the *Caleb S. Winship*, returning at last to pick him up!

When the ship was just a few miles away, Hall could see that it was not the *Winship*. His hopes sank. It was a smaller schooner, coming in to pick up copra. The only chance would be that it might be going to Tahiti. The village, knowing that the ship would anchor near Hall's motu, came out to welcome the visitor through the pass. It was the *Potii Ravarava*, with a native skipper and crew. The ship dropped anchor just inside the reef and furled her sails. Hall went aboard to visit. On deck, cargo was being set aside for offloading. Huira, the constable, had joined the crew to help. Suddenly, he rushed over to where Hall stood talking to one of the men. He pulled at Hall's sleeve, and pointed to one of the piles. "You like?" he asked. "You like?" Hall went over to look. There was his sea chest, and nailed to the top, a letter addressed to him. It was from Tino, the supercargo of the *Winship*.

Hall tore open the letter. Tino explained that he was sorry, after he had sobered up, for having left him behind. He had met the *Potii Ravarava* and, knowing she was going to Ruti-aro, had put his sea chest on board for him. The native ship was going to Papeete, but he urged Hall to take with him a demijohn of water in case of long calms at sea, and, he added, because the skipper wasn't a very good navigator. "Give my regards to all the marble players," he said, ending the letter.

Hall knelt down and opened his chest. There at the bottom, under his camera and binoculars, was his wallet, fat with hundred- and thousand-franc notes. Moy Ling would have his reckoning at last. When he returned to the main island, Hall waited till the Chinese was busy with customers. He walked in slowly, caught Moy Ling's eye, pulled out his wallet with an elaborate gesture, and dealt out on the counter several large bills. Moy Ling broke into a golden smile and quickly made the final tally and counted out the change.

The schooner left Rutiaro the following day. Hall took his leave as quickly as possible. He had gone on board, crawled into the cabin, and huddled with a book against a stack of filled copra sacks. There he remained as the ship moved through the pass and out to sea, unable to go on deck and wave farewell to an island and its people that he loved. He had never been able to say good-bye to friends.

4
Return to Tahiti

Nordhoff had continued westward in the Cook Islands, putting in now and again to unload supplies and pick up copra. After the stop at Mauke, there was never much time for a lengthy stay, until the *Faaite* came to Rarotonga, the final call before making for the Society group and home. During the many lay-overs Nordhoff had especially enjoyed, however briefly, watching the natives fish. As he had for many years during his youth and young manhood before the war, setting out in his yawl from Punta Banda below Ensenada in Baja California to fish from sunup to sundown, so now in Rarotonga, he decided, now that there was time, he would learn the Polynesian way to catch fish.

Nordhoff, Tari the supercargo, and Apakura his native wife, were staying in separate cottages on the beach at Avarua, the central village of the island. Nordhoff sat on his veranda drinking a rum punch, looking out over the peaceful lagoon. Down on the beach a group of native boys were probing with long sticks into deep holes in the sand and overturning fallen coconut fronds. They were looking for hermit crabs, the bait for the big fish near the reef. Nordhoff quickly finished his drink and went down to help them fill their buckets.

For two hours he joined in the search, having little luck, until, toward nightfall, the *kakara*—a big red crab—started to come out from his hiding place in the bush. The native boys explained that the kakara were making their nightly trip to the shore, for an evening bath before returning to the beach to find their dinner—of dead fish, fallen mango, or opened coconut. The tracks were easy to follow in the wet sand. Nordhoff watched one crab with deep curiosity. The crab protruded from his shell, the tail anchored inside, and with his big claws out front, his antennae scanning the air, he crawled on his tiny legs. It reminded Nordhoff of the small New England chicken lobster. Soon the crab was followed by many others. In twenty minutes Nordhoff had filled his pail. The native boys were greatly pleased with the help of the *Popaa,* and invited him to come fishing with them the next morning on the reef. They would leave very early, they said, two hours before daylight.

Nordhoff was awakened at three. He dressed quickly, putting on an undershirt, a pareu which he hitched up into swimming trunks, and a pair of high-quarter thick-soled shoes. Six of the boys waited for him on the beach, holding torches. They sat in their outriggers, ready to push off. Nordhoff held the torch for one and sat in the back of the canoe as the boy paddled them across the lagoon. The water was calm and at low tide. They came to a shallow point on the reef, and the boy shipped his paddle, jumped out, and tied the canoe to a jut of coral.

Nordhoff climbed out, trying to keep his balance as he carried in one hand the torch and in the other a spear. The water came to his knees. He waded carefully, following behind the boy, watching his footing at every step. Under the soles of his shoes he could feel the sharp honeycomb of coral, and he could see the dark spots which marked deep holes into which he could slip and fall to the waist. A ripple broke the water. It was a big bluefish close to the surface. Nordhoff poised his spear, but before he could take aim, the boy in front of him had thrust his spear and impaled the fish. The boy pulled off the fish, and tied it through gill and mouth to a cord about his waist. It was his first of many.

Nordhoff watched another fish swim in close to him. It was an ugly thing, with big fins and long wavy feelers sticking out all over it. The native boy speared it quickly. It was a scorpion, he said, with a venomous bite. Nordhoff hoped he would see no more of them, or of another he had heard about from the natives—the *noo,* which had a stiff ridged spine that could inject a deadly poison.

Nordhoff held his torch high, looking for more bluefish, and held his spear at the ready. About six feet away one swam by, a foot under the water. Nordhoff shot out his spear, but missed by at least six inches. He could not readjust his depth perception to the refraction of the water. Up and down the reef the boys had almost filled their buckets, and the cords about their waists hung heavy with the morning catch. But Nordhoff was determined to learn. For another hour he lunged and stabbed, but pulled in the spear and line with no success. Finally, noticing that the boys were ready to go in, he gave up with the spear. He did want to stay on, however, this time to try with the hook and line out in the deeper waters. It was more like fishing at home.

A gray line of light appeared against banks of cloud in the east. Nordhoff put out his torch. He waded over to the canoe, climbed in, and paddled toward the pass. He dropped anchor, playing the line out deep. Here he would try for the *titiara.* The morning sun broke through the clouds. Nordhoff adjusted his goggles and climbed over the side. He had always had his best luck at dawn.

Head down, swimming an easy breaststroke, he could see different schools of fish at various depths. Many of them flitted in and out of holes in the coral and skirted along the steep walls of the reef, which looked at least fifty feet deep. Against the pink and white of the coral face, the fish formed a multicolored and ever-changing kaleidoscope. Beyond the edge of the reef and at the entrance of the pass, he watched swimming in from the sea the fish he wanted. He recognized the *titiara* at once. It looked like the mackerel or the pompano, and the natives said it was fast and ravenous. These were the big ones, and when fully grown they could run to a hundred pounds. Nordhoff climbed back into his outrigger and quickly prepared his line.

He picked up a rock and crushed the shell of one of the crabs, tore out some of the meat, balled it with sea water into bait, and slipped it onto the hook. Taking a pebble, he hitched it with a bowknot to the line for a sinker. Slowly he lowered the line over the side to attract the fish and keep them near. The sinker carried the hook to the middle of the school, and Nordhoff snapped the line quickly, freeing the pebble. One of the fish nibbled at the bait, then took the hook. Nordhoff jerked up, and the line started to run out. The fish, frisky and strong, fought well, but Nordhoff had him. He pulled in the line. It was a twenty-pounder, two feet long.

Nordhoff dropped his line and caught another, a young one, ten inches long, about three pounds. Then he lowered the line again and jerked free the sinker. Suddenly, from the deep, a big one struck, swallowing the hook, and sped off, down and away and fast. The line whistled through Nordhoff's hands, burning his fingers; but he let it go, giving the fish his head, until he saw that there were only a few feet of line left in the canoe. Nordhoff jerked up hard. The line snapped. The fish was free and gone. Nordhoff pulled in and rolled up the slack line. He stashed his tackle in the box and picked up the paddle. As he made in for shore, the paddle smarted in his raw cut hands. The next time, he had made up his mind: with a heavier line and a stronger hook, he would bring in the big one.

That afternoon Nordhoff cut up his two fish into thin filets and let them marinate in lime juice for six hours. Having been invited by Apakura for dinner, he presented them to her as a gift. She served them as hors d'oeuvres with the drinks. And Tino, never one to exaggerate, pronounced them excellent.

For several days afterward Nordhoff did not fish again. He wanted to give his hands a chance to heal completely, and he needed to get some pictures of the island for the book. He had promised Hall, he reminded himself, that they would have a good number of photographs to choose from for illustrations. For Nordhoff, photography, like fishing, had proved a worthwhile hobby, but during one afternoon, it conflicted with yet another hobby. He had decided to photograph the outline of the island against the sky. He put his camera and tripod into an outrigger and paddled out into the lagoon, looking for the best view. The sun had started to go down behind the mountains, and the light was beginning to fade. He wanted to take a time exposure, but he needed a firm base to set up his tripod. As the shadows lengthened, he paddled out to the reef to shoot from there. Opening his lens as wide as he could and holding the shutter speed, he took ten exposures, hoping that peaks, ridges, valleys, and shallows had still enough light among the shadows.

Satisfied at last, he dismounted the camera, folded the tripod, and stowed them in the bow of the canoe. Paddling back to shore, he heard overhead the sound of wings in flight. It was a duck. To have a better look, Nordhoff twisted suddenly in his seat. The movement was too much for the outrigger. It capsized, and out fell Nordhoff, the anchor, tripod and camera. Nordhoff caught the camera just as it began to sink out of sight, but the rest of the gear went to the bottom. He righted the canoe and placed the camera inside, then he dived for the tripod. He found it lying on the bottom in the sand. As he came up for air, streaming water from his hair and clothes, squeals of laughter greeted him on the shore. It was Apakura and some of her friends. Nordhoff pulled the canoe onto the beach. "Ah, you have come to bathe in the sea," Apakura said, but she could not continue. The humor of a dripping Nordhoff, holding a wet camera and tripod, was too much for her. Again overcome with laughter, she fell to the beach and rolled in the sand. She called to her husband, *"E Tari! E Tari! Aere mai iknei!"*

Tari came out of the bush, rubbing sleep from his eyes. He had been taking his siesta. Still half asleep, he offered his hand in greeting; then he brought Nordhoff to his house. While Nordhoff changed out of his wet clothes, dried off, and put on one of Tari's suits of white drill, Tari made him a Scotch and

water. Nordhoff came into the living room, but stopped to admire a native paddle hanging from the wall. He took it down
to examine it. It was smoothly carved, the blade narrow, the
handle long, and along the entire length were imbedded little
diamonds of mother-of-pearl.

Tari came in with the drinks. "A pretty paddle, isn't it?" he
said. "You won't find a more curious one in the Pacific. Notice
the way the reinforcing ridge runs down the blade from the
haft? Everything has a meaning in primitive stuff of this sort.
The original pattern from which this has descended probably,
came from a land of little trees, where the paddles had to be
made in two pieces—blade lashed to handle. Look at the shape
of it—more like a Zulu piece than anything else. It is a weapon
primarily. A thrust of it would kill a naked man." He paused
to take a long swallow from his drink.

"The natives of course spend a lot of their time in canoes,"
he continued. "They go out to the open sea, after the bonito
by day and the flying fish by night. And those waters swarm
with sharks. The natives, in self-defense, have developed their
paddles into a weapon."

"What about those sharks?" Nordhoff asked. He took a cigarette from some on the table between them. "When I fell out
of my canoe, I was afraid one might swim in from the pass and
snip off my leg. Are they a real menace or not?"

"I've heard a lot of loose talk," Tari replied. "How learned
societies have offered rewards for a genuine instance of a shark
attacking a man, but I have seen enough to know that there is
no room for argument. Some idiot goes swimming off a vessel
in shark-infested waters, and talks all the rest of his life, perhaps, of the silly fears of others—never realizing that he owes
his life to the fact that none of the sharks about him chanced
to be more than usually hungry. I have seen a hungry shark
tear the paddle from the hand of a man beside me and sink its
teeth, over and over again in a frenzy, in the bottom of a heavy
canoe. How long do you suppose a swimmer would have
lived?"

Apakura came in and announced that dinner was ready.
"Kaikai," she said. "Aere mai korua!" They sat at a table set

for two. Nordhoff immediately noticed that there was no place set for Tari's wife. As a matter of fact, she would not be eating with them at all, for she sat nearby on a mat, her legs crossed, weaving a hat from pandanus strips.

Sensing Nordhoff's awareness, Tari offered an explanation. "It probably strikes you as odd that she doesn't sit with us. I tried to get her into the way of it at first, but it's no good. For generations the women of her family have been forbidden to eat in the presence of men, and the old taboo dies hard. Then, she hates chairs. When she sits with me she is wretchedly uncomfortable, and bolts her food in a scared kind of way that puts me off my feed." He paused to look at his wife, lovingly. She did not understand his Popaa talk. "It is best to let them follow their own customs."

After dinner Nordhoff begged to be excused. He had letters to write to his friend Hall, and he best get to them now, before the next ship left for Tahiti. Tari readily agreed. On his way along the path to his own cottage, Nordhoff thought about Tari, how he seemed to fit in so easily to the native life. He went into his bedroom and lit a small lamp on the table.

"Everywhere in the islands, of course, the color line exists," he wrote to Hall. "It is a subtle barrier between the races, not to be crossed with impunity. But the better sort of white man is ready to admit that God, who presumably made him, also made of the Polynesian a rather fine piece of work. Tari had stepped across with eyes open, counting the cost, realizing all that he must relinquish. He is not a man to make such a decision lightly. In his case the step meant severing the last material tie with home, giving up forever the Englishman's dreams of white children and an old age in the pleasant English countryside. His children—if children came to him—would have skins tinted by a hundred generations of hot sunlight, and look at him with strange, dark eyes, liquid and shy—the eyes of an elder race, begotten when the world was young. His old age would be spent on this remote and forgotten bit of land, immensely isolated from the ancestral background to which most men return at last. As the shadows gathered in the evening of his life there would be long days of reading and reflection—

stretched in a steamer chair on this same veranda, while the trade hummed through the palm tops, and the sea rumbled softly on the reef.

"At night, lying wakeful as old men do, in a hush broken only by the murmur of the lonely sea, his thoughts would wander back—a little sadly, as the thoughts of an old man must—along a hundred winding paths of memory, through scenes wild and lovely, savage, stern, and gay. Dimly out of the past would appear the faces of men and women—long since dead and already only vaguely remembered—the companions of his youth, once individually vibrant with the current of life, now moldering alike in forgotten graves. They would be strangely assorted company, Tari's ghosts: men of all the races, scholars, soldiers, sportsmen, skippers of trading vessels, pearl divers of the atolls, nurses of the Red Cross, Englishwomen of his own station in life, dark-eyed daughters of the islands, with shining hair and the beauty of sleek, wild creatures—bewitching and soulless, half bold and half afraid. Whether for good or ill, wisely or unwisely, as the case might be, no one could say that Tari had not lived. I wonder what the verdict will be when, in the days to come, he casts up the balance of his life."

Nordhoff spoke of Tari, his friend, with understanding, insight, and compassion. Perhaps he knew that he also spoke of himself in the days to come. He folded the letter, put it in an envelope, and addressed it to Hall.

On board the *Potii Ravarava* Hall was homeward bound to Tahiti, after a fashion. As Tino from the *Winship* had warned, the skipper was indeed a poor navigator, and only a fair sailor. Three days out from Rutiaro, the wind fell off and the schooner lay in a dead calm. Fortunately, however, according to the charts, a short distance away was a small atoll, called Whitsunday Island. The ship rode with the current, slowly, until at last they came along, north and west, to the side of the island.

Under the blazing sun the heat was intense. Miti, the skipper, ordered one of the crewmen to wash down the deck. As he did, the water steamed on the blistering boards, sluiced off and out the scuppers, and soon left the deck as hot as before. Another crewman joined Hall at the gunwale and pointed to the beach. "You see him?" he asked. "What he do there?"

Hall raised his binoculars and looked to the shore. There stood a white man, his arms folded, leaning against a coconut tree. He wore no shirt or shoes, and his pants were ripped off at the knee. Hall wondered if this Popaa were not another Cridland. But this island was even more bare and desolate than Cridland's Taioro. This man looked more like a stranded mariner; but there were no signal fires, no anxious wavings of arms or ready-made flags. To the contrary, the stranger seemed perfectly content simply to stand under the shade of a tree. The schooner anchored along the reef.

Hall went to shore with the two sailors, who went off to gather some drinking coconuts. Hall walked over to the stranger, who was bent over a small fire, frying some fish. Hall apologized for breaking in on him. "I haven't seen a white man in three months," he said. "And our skipper speaks very little English."

The man got up and offered his hand. He was strongly built, but seemed friendly. His eyes were piercingly blue, like Arctic ice. "I saw your ship coming in," he said. "I was about to look you up."

"I haven't seen any natives on the island. Are you alone here?" Hall pulled a thumb and forefinger along the length of his nose.

"Alone, yes," he said. "But I can't say that I'm lonely here. I manage to get along without much companionship." He tapped an empty pipe against the palm of his hand. "But to be frank, I'm hungry for tobacco. You haven't a fill, by any chance? I've been sucking empty air through this pipe since last November."

Hall took out his pouch and offered it. The stranger filled his pipe, lit it, and inhaled quickly. He let the smoke out slowly, relishing every puff. "I imagine you are in for several days," he said. "Have you noticed the sky? Not a sign of wind. I can't offer you much in the way of food. But the fishing is good, and if you care to, you are welcome to stay."

Hall accepted the invitation. He went back to the ship for a few things, and for more tobacco. When he returned, the stranger had prepared dinner. While they ate, Hall told him about his recent experiences on Rutiaro. How his attempted experiment in solitude had for the most part failed. The natives were too friendly, he explained.

"Yes," the stranger said, "they are rather too sociable, these natives. They are the same way here in the neighboring islands. When I first came to this island they used to bother me a good deal. I thought nine miles of open sea would keep them away. But they often came over in sailing canoes—a dozen or two at a time when the wind favored. And they would stay until it shifted back into the southeast. I didn't encourage them. In fact, I made it quite plain that I preferred to be alone. The island is theirs, of course, and I can't prevent them coming during the copra-making season. But they no longer come at other times. Nine months out of the year I have the place to myself. But they are damnably inquisitive. I don't like Kanakas on the whole, although I do have one or two good friends among them."

They talked for three hours. And when the fire died out, all that Hall had discovered about the stranger's life was that he liked to fish. As with Cridland, it would take some time before he could learn the white man's story, if at all. They went into his little hut. It was bare. In one corner the stranger lay down on a mat and soon fell asleep. Hall looked about him. Except for a few clothes, old and worn, which hung from nails in the wall, there were few things other than fishing tackle and a sea chest that gave any clues about the man's solitary life on the atoll. Except for some picks and shovels. Hall lay awake for another hour, wondering about them.

It was not until the morning of his third day on the island that Hall finally got the full account. He rose at sunrise to find his host gone from the hut. Outside were two fish, cleaned and ready for cooking. Hall fried them, and after eating, went for a walk around the island. He found the stranger on the other side of the lagoon, ready to dive off a ledge of the reef. The stranger waved. Hall came over to where the man had been standing.

The man broke through the surface and climbed out of the water onto the ledge. He held a spear in his hand. "Tiresome work," he said, sitting down. "I need a rest. Have you seen the digging I've been doing?" He waved his arm behind him.

Hall turned and was amazed at what he saw. Into the side of the high land, the man had dug deep long trenches, one on top of the other, and they extended for a quarter of a mile, with other trenches cutting down into them. Doing the work himself, the stranger must have been at it for many years, digging day after day, month after month.

"I suppose you know what I'm doing here?" the stranger offered at last. "If you have been in Papeete you must have heard. There is no secret about it. At least not any longer."

"No, I have not heard," Hall replied. "I was not in Tahiti for more than a few days. I did not meet many people, and left on my trip soon after I arrived."

"So much the better," he said. "Yes, seven years is a long time, and I'm not keen about feeding gossip. But when I first came down here there was a clacking of tongues from one end of the islands to the other. I believe I have since earned the reputation of being rather queer. I thought you must know. The fact is I'm looking for treasure. Would you care to hear the story?"

"Very much," Hall answered. "If it won't bore you to tell it."

"On the contrary, it will be something of a relief. Seven years of digging, with nothing to show for it, must strike an outsider as a mad business. Sometimes I'm half persuaded that I am a complete fool to go on with the search. But you can't possibly know the fascination of it. It seems only yesterday that I came here. As you see for yourself, it's not much of an island. And to know that there is a treasure of more than three million pounds buried somewhere in this tiny circle of scrub and palm."

"But do you know it for certain?" Hall asked.

"I'm as sure of it as I am of smoking your tobacco. That is, I am sure that it was buried here. Whether it has been removed since, I can't say, of course. The natives remember a white man who came here about twenty years ago and stayed for more than a month. One of the four men who stole the gold, Luke Barrett, he, I think, was the one who brought it here." He rose to his feet. "Let's take a walk," he suggested. "I want to show you something very interesting."

They went down the beach, started across the island, then stopped before a huge piece of broken coral. Carved upon it was a design, from left to right, of an arrow, a carpenter's T square, and a dot in a circle over a straight line. Hall was thoroughly puzzled by it. "What does it mean?" he asked.

"If I knew that, I think I would have left here a long time ago with the treasure. I think it's the key. But I can't master it!" He shook his head.

They sat down on the ground. The stranger now told the whole story. Hall listened, enrapt, for more than an hour. Four renegade adventurers had joined the Peruvian army and fought in the war against Chile in 1859-60. They heard about some gold buried in a church and, upon investigation, found it and stole it—seven chests filled with large sixty-pound ingots, worth nearly three and a half million pounds. They buried the cache elsewhere, then found a vessel to carry it away. Traveling in the Tuamotus, they discovered Whitsunday, abandoned and desolate, and hid most of it there. Then they went to Australia to spend some of it. After fights, murders, penal sentences, and deaths in jail, only one of the four survived, an Irishman named Killorian.

Because of a favor rendered to him by Hall's host—the gift of a cheap coat against the cold, Killorian, now old, poor, sick, and near death, told him in a deathbed confession where he could find the remainder of the treasure. "It's there," Killorian had said. "And it will always be there if you're bloody fool enough to think I'm queer. It ain't likely I'd lie to you on my deathbed."

"I tried to forget the incident," the stranger said to Hall. "But it was one of those things that refuse to be forgotten. It was always in the back of my head. Finally I could stand it no longer. I booked passage for Tahiti and then came out here. I've been here, digging, ever since."

They got up and walked back toward the beach. Presently

one of the crewmen ran up to them. He spoke excitedly. There was enough wind beginning to blow to fill up the sails. The skipper wanted to leave as soon as possible.

Hall shook hands in farewell with his host. "When shall you come to Tahiti?" Hall asked.

"Not until I have found what I'm looking for."

"Well," Hall said, departing, "I hope that will be soon."

Charles Nordhoff sat on the veranda of the Aina Paré hotel in Papeete, leisurely sipping a Scotch and soda. He had returned to Tahiti four weeks before, and now he waited for Hall's return. More than a week of calms, during which the lagoon lay unruffled, followed by three days of violent storms that brought the sea right into the harbor, had undoubtedly held up his friend. There had been some worry about the *Potii Ravarava* among the traders and skippers because she had no motor. As had been his custom every morning and evening, Nordhoff walked down to the quay to see if there was any news. Night was beginning to fall, and a strong wind blew in from the sea.

"There she is now!" one of the skippers shouted, and pointed to the little ship rounding the point of land beyond the harbor and coming in through the channel. The hull peeled, the sails patched and torn, the schooner looked tired. She anchored out in the lagoon and lowered a boat.

Nordhoff waited for Hall at the dock. When Hall stepped out of the boat, Nordhoff was shocked by what he saw. Hall was tanned as black as a Kanaka, and he had grown very thin; his clothes, worn and ragged, hung loosely from his waist and shoulders. His dark-brown eyes, usually smiling and sparkling, had a wild look in them. "My God, I'm hungry," Hall said. "I feel as if I could eat a shark—raw!"

They walked to the hotel and into the dining room. Without stopping to talk, Hall ate two complete dinners. He lit a cigarette and sipped his coffee. "It was a damnable experience," he said finally. "We drifted for seven full days, not a breeze in sight. Even my demijohn, which I had filled with three gallons of water, didn't last long. And the ship, jammed with copra, stunk to high heaven. On the third day the sharks began to circle the ship. They made us feel like doomed men." Hall leaned back in his chair. "I tried to kill one of the big brutes, but my spear just bounced off his hide. Soon the drinking nuts were finished off, one by one. Things were getting truly desperate. We spread an awning to catch water, if it ever came. At one point I thought of chewing copra, but the smell of it turned me away. It was too much. At last a squall hit us, giving us water; and later, a breeze began to fill our sails. Thank God. Another couple of days would have been absolutely unendurable. Then the wind grew stronger, almost to hurricane force, but it carried us, fast. Point Venus looked mighty good."

It was dark when Hall finished. He had told Nordhoff about the white man on Whitsunday Island, the man in search of gold.

"I wonder," Nordhoff asked, "if he will ever find what he is looking for?"

"I don't know about him," Hall said. "But I do know about me."

"What are your plans?" Nordhoff had grown curious about the future. "Our year in the South Seas is just about up. Where are you going now?"

"I have no plans," Hall said, "except that I doubt if I will ever go north again. I may be wrong, but I believe I've had enough of civilization to last me a lifetime. I'm happy here."

"Even with calms at sea, and the stink of copra?"

"Even with calms at sea and the stink of copra! As I said, 'I'm happy here!' "

"So am I," Nordhoff added quickly. "Why should we leave the islands?"

5

Their Island Home

It was June, 1920. One evening, after dinner, Nordhoff and
Hall took a walk down the perimeter road toward the outskirts
of Papeete. As they stepped out in easy gait, they discussed the
final revisions on the manuscript of their travel book, *Faery
Lands of the South Seas,* before sending it off to Harper's. Suddenly they were interrupted by a greeting, spoken in English,
from off the side of the road. It was a man calling from the
porch of a large white house, asking them to stop and visit
awhile. Hall and Nordhoff walked up the path to the house.
The man introduced himself; Bunkley, he said, was his name,
and he had heard how they had both come to the South Seas
to write some travel pieces, and how they hoped to settle in
Tahiti. He asked his visitors to sit down and offered them a
liqueur. Although his advice was unsolicited, he continued, he
was going to give it to them anyway.

"Let me tell you what my own experience has been," he said.
"I came to this place forty years ago, and at first I thought I
could never be thankful enough for the chance which had

brought me. I am sure that I was, and am still, as much a lover of the islands as either of you. There is scarcely a fragment of land in all this part of the Pacific that I have not explored from one end to the other. I had a little money—not a great deal, but a small sum went farther in those days than it does now, and I invested it carefully, here and elsewhere, but chiefly among the Low Islands. I now own two atolls of that group, both of them well planted to coconuts. . . ."

Hall interrupted. "You own *two* islands?" he asked, surprised. "Would you, by any chance, consider selling *one* of them?"

"Willingly," Roland answered. "I will sell tomorrow, tonight, this minute. If you are in the market for an island, you have come to the right place."

Nordhoff asked the man how much such an island would cost. "Well," he said, "there are thousands of coconut trees on both. One of them would sell for forty thousand dollars."

Hall gulped. He knew that between them, he and Nordhoff had no more than two thousand dollars.

"In any case," Roland said, "I'm afraid I can't sell this evening. But to return to what I was saying a moment ago. I have long since realized that I made a mistake in coming here. I have done well enough. I live pleasantly and comfortably, but I have entirely dropped out of the lives of my old friends at home, and I've largely lost contact with what is taking place in the outside world. I thought I could keep in touch by means of newspapers, books, reviews, but believe me, they offer a very poor substitute for personal contacts. The years have slipped by, and now I am well into my sixties. When I look back over my life, what have I to remember? You may be surprised when I tell you that it is largely only such evenings as this—pleasant chats with strangers from outside, who bring with them, whether they realize it or not, a breath of cold, invigorating air from the higher latitudes. I mean no disparagement to you or the others when I say that a man's memories of forty years should have higher lights than these."

There were many disadvantages, he explained, even on the emerald isle of Tahiti; monotony, loneliness, boredom could grind away at a man's sensibility, primarily because of the lack of stimulating company. He got up and walked down the path with them to the gate. He seemed resigned. "What a pity it is," he said, "that one man's experience can never be of the slightest use to other men! I am sure you are making a great mistake —one you will both live to regret, and yet I'm powerless to prevent it. Well, good night. If I can be of service at any time, you have only to let me know."

As they walked back to the hotel in the moonlight, Nordhoff and Hall could not guess at the cause of the man's disenchantment; because as enchanted as they were, they could not see through the film of their own desires, nor did they want to.

The next morning they set out on an ambitious hike; packing haversacks, they wanted to walk around the island, but not the entire perimeter; for, although Tahiti, shaped like a skillet with a fat handle, was thirty miles long and twenty miles wide, they intended only to skirt the four-hundred-square-mile area of the main island of Tahiti-Nui, saving for another time the isthmus of Taravao and the peninsula of Taiarapu. They had a hundred-mile walk before them, but they were in no hurry, having agreed to stop and stay whenever they found something of interest, and maybe even test it as a possible site for a future home.

During the first few hours they followed the road along the lagoon beach, delighting in the neat plantations of the Chinese and the Europeans, the truck gardens backed to the steep ridges, the rice swamps in the lush valleys; then they came to cart tracks which gave on either side to the thatched houses of the Tahitian natives, to the great yards of coconut trees with long graceful trunks reaching to their nut-clustered, green-palmed tops, to the fat trunks of the treelike banana plants with their thick bunches of yellow-handed banana-fingers, and, hanging obscenely at their base, the long pendant stem with the male flower at its tip.

At noon they came to a wide river rushing out of the forest and spilling out in a broad delta into the sea. They followed a path long its bank into the interior, passing under the branches of lime and orange trees, their fruit round and fat.

Hall picked an orange and started to peel it. As if to a great rotunda they came to a wide still pool, walled around by lean tall trees and vaulted on top by long overhanging and intertwining branches. Through the green dome filtered shafts of green and golden light. They stopped to take a swim. As they undressed to their shorts, suddenly they noticed on the other side of the pool a number of native children run for cover behind large green ferns. As they hid, the children would peep out, then laugh and giggle. Holding his nose, Hall jumped in.

Nordhoff dived into the pool, swam to the farther side where the children were, and pulled himself up on the bank. As he sat, he heard a giggle; it sounded to him like a little girl. Nordhoff walked to the sound, held out his hands, and encouraged the child to come out. A fern was pushed aside by a little hand, and a brown-skinned, black-eyed four-year-old emerged, with long black, glistening hair. Nordhoff took her hand and led her back into the pool with him. He let the girl hang from his neck and swam with her across the water, then released her. When the other children saw that their visitors meant no harm, they too came out from their hiding places and jumped back into the water. Then the older boys climbed a big tree on the bank and crawled out on a long branch that drooped over the water, hung from the lowest branches until some of the others shook them loose, and splashed into the water. The others took their places with the same results. Hall and Nordhoff climbed out of the pool, dried off, and dressed, leaving the children to their play.

Later that evening as dusk fell and the stars pinholed the sky with light, they decided to stop for the night. Hall had plucked a bunch of bananas and Nordhoff pulled out from his haversack a can of biscuits and a bar of chocolate. They started to eat. "I have eaten better appetizers, entrées, and desserts," Nordhoff said wryly, "but never, I think, as hungrily."

Hall lay on the fine, soft, black volcanic sands of the lagoon beach, his head propped on his haversack. "I don't care what I eat," he said, "just so long as I eat, and I guess I have eaten almost everything."

"You have an undeveloped palate, Hall," Nordhoff said. "Probably just like those kids this afternoon. The curse on Iowans and Polynesians."

Hall would not take the bait of argument. "Nordy," he asked, "what about this native upbringing? Kids free of schooling and restraint? Would a white child, do you think, brought up under the same conditions, develop the same easygoing ways? Or is our restless, aggressive spirit too ingrained to lose?"

"Interesting," Nordhoff said, "because that recalls an experiment I used to dream of making. My idea was to seek out an uninhabited island in this part of the world, a small, fertile place where living would be easy. I would need a dozen children for my experiment—baby boys and girls young enough to know no word of speech. I would want white children, brown children, and Chinese—young civilization, no civilization, and the oldest civilization of them all. I would put a comfortable shelter for them, stocked with what is necessary, and a place for myself at the other end of the island. In the beginning my children would need a certain amount of attention, of course, and as they grew up I would teach them the rudiments of fishing, and how to gather yams, breadfruit, plantains, and the like. Beyond that I would teach them nothing, and in all my intercourse with them I would be careful never to use my voice. You see what I am driving at—to let them bring themselves up in a state of nature, without handicaps other than those of race and birth."

Hall pulled up his long legs. "Did you ever seriously think of making this experiment?" he asked.

Nordhoff drew squares in the sand with a stick. "I said I used to dream of it," he replied. "But what an enormously interesting one it would be! What, for example, might one expect my isolated children to develop in the way of speech? And in a primitive environment, with conditions equal for all of them, which race would excel?"

"The Chinese," a voice boomed from behind them.

Nordhoff and Hall jumped up, frightened, and looked around. There, leaning against a tree, was a white man. "I'm sorry," the man said in a friendly tone, "I didn't mean to eavesdrop, but you took it into your heads to camp right at my doorstep, so I couldn't avoid hearing what you were saying. I was dozing in my chair, and your voices wakened me." He invited them into his house.

"I was much interested in what you were discussing," he continued after he had seated Hall and Nordhoff. "But it would interest me more," he said, turning to Nordhoff, "to drop in on you during the early days of your experiment while you were playing nursemaid to a dozen American, Polynesian, and Chinese babies. As I said, I think the Chinese would come out on top, but don't let me get started on Chinese civilization. I'm an enthusiast on that subject, and enthusiasts are always bores. Come out on the veranda—it's cooler there, and we'll talk of something else."

Hall marveled at the house and its location. By the faint light of the moon and stars he could see that the house had been built on stilts, up from the lagoon, so that the veranda jutted out over the water with steps that led down from it to a small pier. From the left he could look across a broad inlet to the hills in the distance, and back to the land side on a deep valley and into the mountains. He could feel the *hupé*—the night wind, cool and refreshing, gentle as a woman's touch. The man lit a lamp on the table. In its light Hall could see neatly stacked rows of magazines and learned journals—English, German, and French; and against the wall, shelves of books. From the wall above the bookcases hung knives, necklaces, capes, and embroidery.

"Sir, if I may ask," Nordhoff said, "what brought you to Tahiti?"

"You may," the man replied affably. "I had been living in China, in Hong Kong, and met a traveler who had just come from here. That was the first time I had heard of the place. This man told me something of the native language, how beautiful it is, and how rich in many respects. I asked him for specimens of it, and among others he gave me the following. They may seem sheer gibberish to you, but they haunted me like the thought of buried treasure.

Nordhoff and Hall listened with wonder as the man spoke the language. The vowels rolled from his tongue, mellifluously, articulately, incredibly, for he pronounced each vowel separately in each word, translating as he spoke:

"*Aaoaraa-moa:* the hour of the crowing of the cock.

"*Hui hui mania:* a great calm without wind.

"*Ahiahirumaruma:* cloudy evening.

"*Moana faréré:* the unfathomable sea."

"Wonderful," Hall said. Nordhoff agreed. "Marvelous," he added.

The man continued. "You will admit, I think, the beauty of the meanings, but you may think I'm a little mad when I tell you that these words, and some others like them, decided me to leave China for Polynesia. I wanted to know all there is to be known of this language, and to make the story short, I've been studying it on the spot ever since. I can't tell you what an absorbing task it has been! For it *is* treasure of the richest sort, buried treasure, too, a great deal of it. In these days the natives are forgetting the stately speech of their forefathers, coining all sorts of hybrid words out of English and French and Chinese, which have nothing to commend them but the fact that they're useful."

The man, they learned, was Frank Stimson, an American, from Plainfield, New Jersey. He had studied at Yale and at the Beaux Arts in Paris, and had been a successful architect, in New York and San Francisco, before he first came to Tahiti in 1912, on vacation. He returned to Tahiti in 1917, and was now a research associate in linguistics for the Bishop Museum in Hawaii. He was compiling, he explained, a Tahitian grammar, and a Tahitian-French-English dictionary.

Stimson opened his notebooks and showed them to his guests. They represented, he said, years of research. Hall was spellbound. Many of the words seemed to him like short poems —about stars, the moods of the sea, the colors of the mountains and valleys, the shades and shadows of clouds and trees. And the man fascinated Hall, for Stimson seemed totally absorbed in his undertaking. Hall, remembering what Bunkley had told them about island living in the South Seas, asked Stimson: "Do you think the islands are suitable places for white men to settle down in?"

"Suitable?" he said. "I should think they are! But wait—I

must qualify that, of course. Most men have gifts which could find no outlet here, and to me the greatest unfaithfulness is unfaithfulness to one's self. In each of us there is, perhaps, the gleam of an ability, a power, a gift, to do *something*"—Stimson emphasized the last word—"a little better than someone else has done or could do it. Or it may be only the faculty for feeling some emotion a little more keenly than another may feel it. I have found among these islands the best uses for my small talents, and it seems to me that I haven't the right to consider them as nothing. As for you, for another, who can say? There is an old island saying: *O te puoé te muhu na ta taata anaé'iho o te ité i te faaroo,* which means, 'The seashell murmurs for him alone who knows how to listen.' If you know or can learn how to listen, I think you might be very happy here. If you can't—well—the world is wide. . . ." He lit his pipe and smoked silently for a few minutes. Then Stimson asked them to stay the night, and Hall and Nordhoff readily accepted the invitation. Beds, they admitted, would be better than the beach.

The next morning Stimson served them some bread and butter and *café au lait* for breakfast, and, their knaversacks packed, he saw them off down the road, wishing them well, reminding Nordhoff that anytime he wanted to start his experiment with children, he, Stimson, stood ready to help, and telling Hall to listen closely for the murmur of seashells.

For ten more days Nordhoff and Hall leisurely hiked around the island, through the fourteen districts, each with its native settlement, church, and Chinese store. And, despite their good intentions, when they had returned to Papeete they still had not settled where on the island they would like to live. They had seen many places they liked, particularly in Punaauia, Papeari, and Arué, but could not decide on one. Undecided about where else to live, they continued to rent a room at the Aina Paré.

One day later in the summer of that year, after a fishing trip to nearby Mooréa with John Russell, another writer, Russell asked Nordhoff to join him in a visit to the Richmond family in Tahiti. Russell had fallen in love with Ahuura, one of the

Richmond girls, and wanted Nordhoff to meet the family. At the house Nordhoff met a beautiful Tahitian native girl who was being raised by the Richmond family; she was Vahine Tua Tearae Smidt, nineteen years old, and Nordhoff, charmed by the way she sang and played the guitar and by her dark sensuous loveliness, promptly fell in love with her. Thereafter, Nordhoff was a frequent visitor to the Richmond home.

But it was not until several weeks had passed, when he came down with ptomaine poisoning, that Nordhoff fully discovered Vahine's worth as a woman. Learning of Nordhoff's condition, that he lay in bed helpless at the hotel, Mrs. Richmond sent her adopted daughter to care for him. Vahine nursed Nordhoff back to health expertly. Grateful and in love, Nordhoff took Vahine to dinner at the Aina Paré or the Hotel Tiare almost every evening thereafter. One night after they had eaten, they were sitting on a bench on the quay, looking out over the harbor. "I want to ask you a question," Nordhoff said to Vahine.

Vahine, who knew what most white men thought of Tahitian girls, thought that he was going to ask her to live with him. She looked up at the blond and golden man beside her, looked into his piercing blue eyes, and watched his slow smile. "If he asks me to live with him," she said to herself, "I will push him into the water."

"All I want," Nordhoff said, "is a simple Yes or No. Will you marry me?"

"No," Vahine said. "We must ask Mamma Richmond first."

That night they asked Mrs. Richmond for her permission. She agreed, with reservation. Nordhoff, because he was a white man, would first have to get approval from the French government in Papeete.

To gain his ends, Nordhoff enlisted the aid of the American consul in Tahiti, Thomas B. L. Layton, who agreed to help him in every way he could, with Paris, and with the local governor. Nordhoff first applied for the permit in June and waited for five months, until November 11, 1920, before it was approved.

Nordhoff and Vahine were married in a civil ceremony on December 4, 1920. Hall was the best man, and at the reception almost every white man on the island was present. Among them were Thomas Layton, the American consul; Frank Stimson, the linguist; John Russell, the writer; Harrison Smith, a former Harvard physics professor; Carl Beecher, the former head of the Northwestern University School of Music; and Dr. Cassiau, a French surgeon, who provided his open touring car for the wedding party.

By his marriage, Nordhoff, in less than a year, had committed himself to Tahiti. With the completion of the *Faery Lands* manuscript, however, his commitment to the Nordhoff-and-Hall partnership was over. Nordhoff for his part wanted to try his hand at writing books for boys. He was already at work on the manuscript of his first juvenile, *The Pearl Lagoon,* was satisfied with its progress, and on the basis of the first two chapters, Harper's had sent him a contract and a sizable advance. Hall, less sure of himself, with no advance or contract to buoy him up, and trying to stay afloat by writing poems and sketches, foundered. Hall, despite his Thoreau-like decision to discover what he could live without, almost did not survive.

As he had done with the money from his lecture tour in America, so Hall had sent home to his family most of the $3,500 earned from the serialization and against the publication of *Faery Lands.* And although he could live well in Tahiti for less than $100 a month, what little money he had left would be gone soon. If he did not sell some manuscripts during the next few months he would have to find another way to make a living. Grimly, without a sale, Hall held on through the summer of 1921. But he had to move out of the Aina Paré and find a less expensive place to live. After much inquiry among the Chinese shopkeepers along the waterfront, he learned of a house thirty-five miles down the perimeter road to the southern side of the island. Hall decided to take it because of the rent—three dollars a month.

The house, one room with a veranda, overlooked the lagoon and sea at Papeari. Close by ran a fresh-water mountain stream that emptied into the lagoon. Out behind the house, he happily discovered, was a yard big enough for a garden. With river, sea, and garden he had defined the limits for his sustenance; together they would have to provide for his physical well-being.

Several months passed. Hall had never been a very good fisherman, and his luck had not improved, despite his assiduity with hook and line, waist deep in the lagoon fishing for sardines, or with multipronged spear in the river trying to spike shrimp. Nor was he very successful with the garden, although he had spent more than fifteen dollars on seed and gardening equipment. He had no sooner planted his seed than immediately unknown enemy armies of ants and land crabs and rats that had lain in wait struck; in the forefront of battle, the ants attacked the seed, carrying it off; the crabs, following in isolated penetrations, cleaned off any tender green shoots that had dared to raise their heads above ground; and pulling up the rear came the rats, gnawing off the kernels of the corn which somehow had sprouted from grown stalks. After several months the only vegetables that Hall could claim were the miraculous survivals of three small tomatoes and one squash. Hall was discouraged. Obviously, he could not provide for himself either as a gardener or as a fisherman. He would have to go back to the only way he knew how to make a living—to his writing.

Hall pulled his typewriter out of its case and oiled it. He rolled in a piece of yellow paper and started to type, testing all the keys, then he pulled out the paper and rolled in a clean white sheet. As he started to type he heard the sound of a truck down the road outside. He went out to look. It was his neighbor, and landlord, Hop Sing, driving up to his place further down on the lagoon beach. Hall shouted and waved him to a stop. He had a surprise for him, he said to the Chinese, and presented him with packets of seed he no longer needed—for peas, Golden Bantam sweet corn, squash, pumpkin, lettuce, and tomatoes. He wished Sing better luck than he had enjoyed with them. "How much?" the Chinese asked. "Oh, nothing at all," Hall replied. "It's a little present for you." Hop Sing thanked Hall politely, his black eyes glittering, and drove off down the road. Hall reentered the house, reached into his pocket, and emptied it of its contents. He counted: one hundred and eighty francs and five American dollars—all he had left. Even if he did sell a story in America, he quickly figured, he would have to wait three months to receive the check from so many thousands of miles away.

Many bananas, coconuts, and other fruit abounded on the property, there for the picking, but the Chinese landlord had insisted on his rights to these. Hall felt like Adam in the garden of Eden faced with the forbidden fruit. Hop Sing, however, did not allow temptation to be too provocative: he scooped up the fallen coconuts, put them into large copra sacks, and hauled them off; and he picked the bananas before they ripened. Hall reconsidered his 180 francs and how he would best invest them. He decided to spend twenty-five on tobacco, seventy-five on canned goods, and keep the remainder against an uncertain future. Then he reapplied himself to his typewriter, readdressing himself to his work—a humorous sketch about a native who had announced his imminent departure from this world, who attended, with family, friends, and relatives, his own funeral, then, to the disappointment of all, refused to die. Hall worked through the week, into the weekend.

One Sunday he had visitors. Hop Sing, his wife and three children, and his wife's old father came to the house and knocked. Hall, happy to have company, invited them in. His guests entered, bowed, and smiled. "My fadda-law," Sing said, introducing the old man; then, abruptly turning to Hall, he asked: "What name, you?"

"James Norman Hall." He distinctly pronounced each syllable.

Sing produced a seed package Hall had given him some months before. "What name this?" he asked.

"That? Sweet corn, Golden Bantam! Very good. Tahiti corn no good—too tough. This corn fine."

"Where you get?"

"From America."

Hop Sing pulled out from his pocket the other seed packages. "All this Melican seed?"

"Yes," Hall said. "The best that money can buy."

Sing now explained to his father-in-law in Chinese what they had been discussing about the seeds; then he said a few words to his wife. Man and wife excused themselves, went outside, and presently returned to the house with their arms full. Hop Sing cradled three small watermelons in his arms, and his wife brought in a bottle of wine and a basketful of eggs. Sing went out again and returned with a live chicken. "Little plesant, you," he said to Hall, putting the fowl on the table with the other gifts.

Hall was overcome, and thanked them profusely for their kindness to him. After they had left, he cooked six of the eggs into an omelet and ate heartily. He found some string, tied it to the chicken's leg, and hoping she would lay eggs, staked her outside to the ground. Refreshed, Hall returned to his type-writer and wrote as if inspired for the rest of the afternoon. By six that evening he had finished the manuscript, and paused to think. Again considering the frugal allocation of his remaining twenty-eight francs, he decided, rather than spend twenty-four francs for bus fare, he would carry the manuscript by foot to the post office in Papeete, for, he figured again, he would need at least ten francs for mailing. Before he left, he fortified him-self with another six-egg omelet and finished the wine.

Jauntily he marched off up the road to town. The night was lovely for walking. A full moon was rising behind the palm trees of the Taravao Isthmus, behind him; to his left, the white-topped breakers crashed against the barrier reef of the lagoon; and to the right, he admired the deep green and purple-enshrouded valleys, ridges, and mountains. "How pleasant it would be," he thought, "really to settle down in this remote tropical paradise, to remain here for the rest of my life." From the native houses on either side of the road came the sound of music, native songs to the accompaniment of guitars. "Where else," he mused, "could I find kindlier people, or a life more suited to one of my indolent habits?"

Toward midnight he craved food again, thinking only of breakfast the next morning, and hoping he would have enough money to afford to buy one. Presently, attracted by a fire up the road and off to the side, he came to a native hut on the lagoon beach where an elderly couple were cooking some food. Hall stopped to inhale the delicious smell. *"Haere mai ta maa!"* the man called out to him—"Come and eat!" *"Paia vau,"* Hall lied—"I'm not hungry." The couple, obviously guessing his hunger, and undeterred by his polite refusal, asked him again. "Come!" the old woman said, "try this. It is very good." She ladled out a generous portion into half a coconut shell and offered it to him.

Thankfully, Hall accepted. The food was delicious; it tasted like lobster meat, and mixed with it were some nuts, unknown to him, but very sweet. "Eat! Eat!" the old man said to him. "We have plenty, enough for a dozen people." He pointed to a bucketful of the food, yet uncooked.

"What kind of shellfish are these?" Hall asked. "Did you catch them on the reef?"

The native laughed. "Shellfish! These are not shellfish! They're *tupas!*"

"What?" Hall did not understand.

Then the native explained. *Tupas* were land crabs, the same kind that had ravaged Hall's garden out behind the house. The nut was a *mapé*, like a chestnut, and the tree from which it profusely fell grew in abundance everywhere about the island, especially along river banks. Having noted in his garden how quickly the land crabs, at his slightest and most noiseless appearance, would scurry into their holes, Hall wondered how the little devils could be caught. The old man showed him. He took a bamboo pole with a line and attached to it not a hook, but a bunch of hibiscus leaves. They walked to the other side of the hut, and in the moonlight they could see numerous land-crab holes. The old man cast his line. Several crabs came out of their holes and grabbed hold of the leaves with their claws. The native snatched the pole back, quickly pulled them off with both hands, and plunked them into his bucket. Hall now tried and, to his surprise, succeeded on his first try.

Hall thanked the old couple deeply. They had not only fed him when he was hungry, but they had also taught him how in Tahiti he would not have to go hungry again.

The next morning he was the first in line at the post office when it opened. The manuscript, fortunately, required only four francs for postage. With a prayer Hall dropped the envelope into the slot. Outside, Papeete was coming to life as the Chinese shops opened for business, dock hands started unloading boats tied up at the quay, and the native women hurried to market for the day's provisions. Hall ambled down the street fronting the harbor, looking in at the shop windows, and stopped to have breakfast—fried eggs, bread and butter, and coffee—for four francs. As he ate, someone tapped him on the shoulder. Hall turned; it was a short, fat, balding Chinese, who spoke quickly in an incomprehensible South Sea argot. Hall shook his head, but the Chinaman continued talking nevertheless. Finally, Hall caught only two words, but they were enough: *Hop Sing*.

"Hop Sing?" Hall said, smiling.

"*É! É!*" the Chinese answered, delighted. "You know Hop Sing? Hop Sing *flen*, you?"

"Yes," Hall replied. "Hop Sing live close me, Papeari."

The Chinese's face lit up. "*Maitai! Maitai!*" he sang. "Hop Sing send me letta! I know name, you! You give seed, put in *gloun*, make garden. *Maitai! Maitai!* Hop Sing glad! Me glad! Hop Sing brudda-law me."

"What name, you?" Hall asked.

"Lee Fat. Keep store, over there." He pointed down the street. "When do you go back Papeari?"

"Go this morning on motorbus," Hall answered.

"Goo-bye," Lee Fat said, and promptly left.

Despite the conversation, Hall felt as mysteriously uninformed after the exchange as before, and could not fathom the reason for the talk in the first place. He walked back to the post office and sat on the bench out front, waiting for the bus. At the scheduled hour it arrived, an open truck, full of people inside, hanging on the sides, and riding on top on the roof, carrying fresh fish, newly slaughtered meat, net bags full of fruit and vegetables, and squeezed in beside them live chickens and squealing pigs. Hall found a place next to the driver, and the bus moved off.

At noon they arrived at Papeari. Hall debarked and as he

paid the driver, a box was dropped at his feet by a boy who was the driver's helper. Hall, seeing that the box was intended for him, spoke to the boy. "You've made a mistake," he said. "That isn't mine."

"Yes, it is," the boy answered.

"No, no. I didn't have a box and I've ordered nothing from town."

The driver insisted that the boy was right. A Chinese had brought it to the bus, the driver said, just before the bus left the market, and he had paid for its delivery. Hall asked the driver to hold up the bus for a moment longer, pried off a board from the top of the box, and found a card inside. "Lee Fat, No. 118," the card had printed on it, and beneath the name, written in pencil: "Mr. Hall, for you."

Hall waved the bus off and carried the box inside to his house and opened it. He pulled out a two-pound box of chocolates, a large bag of lichi nuts, one quart of champagne, and, from the bottom, a lacquered box with a gold dragon painted on the front. He opened the box and found inside two silk handkerchiefs and a pair of silk pajamas.

Hall was now even more filled with wonder and incredulity than he had been before. This sudden and inexplicable munificence from the Hop Sing family and now from Sing's brother-in-law was totally beyond him. Unwilling any longer to challenge a generous fate, he went outside to find his chicken. It was gone, broken away from its stake. Hall thought at first that it had been stolen, or had flown away. Then he heard it clucking from under the front stairs. Hall looked in. The chicken had built a nest; Hall reached in and pulled out an egg.

Several months passed before Hall could understand fully the kindness of the Chinese toward him. He had by that time heard from America about the fate of his manuscript; it had sold, he was delighted to learn, to the *Woman's Home Companion*, for $500. And in that time he had become totally proficient in snaring land crabs with pole, line, and the bait of hibiscus leaves, and at finding *mapé* nuts along the nearby banks of the Vaihiria river. Even the chicken was laying enough eggs to provide a change from a diet of canned meat and crab.

Of all the presents Lee Fat had given him, Hall had saved the champagne, waiting for an occasion to serve it. No occasion ever came, so Hall one day, having cooled the wine in the river and seeing Hop Sing and his family walk by, invited them in. Hall opened the bottle and poured out three glasses. After his first glass, Hop Sing became affable and talkative. His last tenant, he explained, was an Australian, a white man of the worst kind. That scoundrel had eaten Sing's bananas and coconuts without permission, and one night had disappeared without having paid his rent, three months of which were still due. Hall poured out more champagne and commiserated with his landlord until the bottle was empty. From that day forward, Hall could not have prayed for better, or kinder, or more understanding neighbors.

The very next morning, a bunch of bananas and sackfuls of oranges and mangoes were left on his back porch. That evening at dinner time, Mrs. Sing sent over, by one of her children, some freshly baked fish, breadfruit, plantain, and six gorgeous steaming ears of Golden Bantam corn; and with the compliments of her husband, who in addition to being a gardener was also a baker, a fresh loaf of French bread and a half dozen pineapple tarts.

And so the Sing generosity continued for as long as Hall lived in Papeari. From the gift of a few packages of seed which he himself could not plant with success, had grown a rich and satisfying friendship, both to the spirit and to the body.

6
Hall in Iceland

Hall sat at the mess table of a trading schooner as it plied the southern waters of the Low Archipelago. He was writing to Marjorie Sutherland, his former coeditor on the Grinnell *Tanager:* "No, I have no intention of becoming an island king, but I confess that the attraction these lonely places have for me is almost as strong as ever. But if you believe me, Marjorie, that these islands are to be desired as places to live—always, you are greatly mistaken. I mean, of course, for people of our race. The loneliness of them can be appalling at times. I have always thought that I was a lover of solitude, and I believe so still. That is, I am sure that I have more than my share of the love of it. But I have learned that complete isolation from one's own kind is a terrible thing. It does very well for a few weeks or months but there are very few men who have within themselves such resources as to make a life of it endurable, to say nothing of pleasant.

"Do you remember, in *Lord Jim*—which is still, for me, the book of books—where Marlowe, writing of Lord Jim to his friend, says, speaking of Jim's choice of his lonely life and his determination to stay always at Patusan: 'You prophesied for him the disaster of weariness and disgust,—you said you knew so well "that kind of thing," its illusory satisfaction, its unavoidable deception. You said also—I call to mind—that giving your life up to them (*them* meaning all of mankind with skins brown, yellow or black in color) was like selling your soul to a brute. You contended that "that kind of thing" was only endurable and enduring when based on a firm conviction in the truth of ideas racially our own, in whose name are established the order, the morality of an ethical progress. "We want its strength at our backs," you had said. "We want a belief in its necessity and its justice to make a worthy and conscious sacrifice of our lives. Without it the sacrifice is only forgetfulness, the way of offering is no better than the way to perdition." In other words, you maintained that we must fight in the ranks or our lives don't count.'

"There's a heap of truth in this," Hall said to Marjorie, "as I have learned during the past two years of wandering in this midmost ocean. Yes, we must fight in the ranks not only to save ourselves but to keep what we have gained through all the centuries of struggle upward. This may sound dubious to you, living a gregarious life, daily aware of all its unpleasantness. In that case, all I can say is come for three or four years or even two to some stagnant back water of the world. You will learn soon enough that one can be happy though civilized. . . . In speaking of civilization I don't of course mean living next door to a moving picture theatre and owning a Rolls Royce.

"You ask me what I think by this time. Well, that is something too curious to tell. At any rate I couldn't sum it up briefly. I've learned a good many things since I left Grinnell, some of them too late to be of service. I've learned among others my limitations, although ostrich-like I still refuse to look at them."

Concerning his future, Hall had said: "My immediate plans for the future are still fragmentary; but I think I shall be going back to France shortly." The letter was dated February 15, 1922. With Nordhoff married and already the father of a daughter, Hall had no idea particularly what to do. France was a possibility, and so were India, China, and Japan. The rest-lessness of old had returned. Hall noted in his commonplace book:

> G-Note:
> The conflict between the part that wants to remain in the world of here and now and everyday, and the part that can't abide this world. Then having been driven to desperation by evidence of greed, selfishness, indifference to the rights of others, the escape to the Road.

Although he did not specify instances of the covetous, selfish, or indifferent, nor was he particularly at the point of despera-tion, Hall turned his eyes once more to the sea and to the dis-tant horizon. Unable to settle down in Polynesia, he wanted to move but he knew not exactly where.

Casually, abstractly leafing through a book, aboard ship one day, only sometimes noting its contents, Hall's attention was caught by one paragraph:

> "I read," Macaulay says in his journal, "Henderson's *Iceland* at breakfast—a favorite breakfast book with me. Why? How oddly we are made! Some books which I never should dream of opening at dinner please me at breakfast and vice-versa."

It was from Trevelyan's *Life and Letters of Lord Macaulay*.

"How rarely in these days," Hall thought, "does one hear even the name of Iceland! Yet it has been a nation for more than a thousand years. From there had come the actual discov-erers of America five centuries before Columbus crossed the Atlantic. There, too, poetry had flourished and a splendid prose literature at a time when most of Europe was without either, and America still a wilderness. What would it be like today, and what of the descendants of those ancient poets, sag-aners, warriors, explorers?" Hall pulled out his pocket atlas and read:

> Iceland. Capital, Reykjavik. (Population 14,000)
> Exports: fish, mutton, wool, and dairy products.

Impulsively Hall pointed north, some seven hundred miles in the opposite direction, decided he wanted to go, not to the Orient, but to Iceland.

Hall got up and stepped over a native. *"Haeré oé hia?"* the native asked—"Where are you going?"

"Hacré, oé haeré," Hall answered—"For a walk." But he wanted to say, "To Iceland."

That night Hall wrote a long letter to Harper's, outlining his plans for a travel book on Iceland, and when they docked back in Tahiti, he mailed it. Three weeks later, Wells, his editor, wired back, approving the idea.

When Hall announced his plans to Nordhoff, his friend told him he was insane. "Only a genius or a fool," Nordhoff said, would undertake to write, alone, in a year's time, a one-hundred-thousand-word book of travel."

Several days later Hall booked a passage and left, his ultimate goal ten thousand glorious miles away. From the South Pacific to the North Atlantic his destination lay almost in a perfect line northeast from Tahiti, but to reach it he would have to travel north 4,000 miles to San Francisco, 3,000 miles east to New York, 3,000 miles northeast to Iceland. Restlessly he paced the decks of the steamer; then tensely he fidgeted in his seat on the train. The overcoming of horizons and the rise and fall of ocean waves gave way to the rise and fall of telegraph wires and receding horizons. At night and during the day ensuing Hall stared out the window from the train and watched the mountains yield to foothills, the hills to the plains, the plains to the rolling prairie lands of the Middle West. Invariably, "on the station platform at every lonely town," he wrote, "there seemed to be one boy of ten or twelve gazing wistfully as the train flashed past. 'Don't be impatient, sonny,' he wanted to say to him, 'your time is coming. I used to stand just as you are now, looking at the trains. Look at me now. The day after tomorrow I will be in Iceland.' "

When the train stopped in Iowa, Hall got out to stretch his legs. Home again, if only to pause in his travels, he was overcome with emotion. "What lagoon-fringed islands set in the bluest of tropic seas," he wrote, "could compare with this in loveliness? The smell of the meadowlands, of the warm, rich earth; the damp odors of tracts of woodland along the river bottoms was like a fragrance in the blood, something nearer than breathing. . . . I fancied I could hear the song of the meadowlarks, and the old, cheery 'Bob White! Wheat's ripe!' of the quail."

In Chicago, between trains, Hall searched the secondhand bookstores for books on Iceland: luckily, he found three in one store. He told the clerk he was going to Iceland. "I don't see why anyone goes to Iceland," she said. "I didn't suppose anyone ever did. It must be a dreary sort of place. It's right under the Arctic Circle, isn't it?" Hall didn't feel like answering her, and fortunately before he could she was called away by another customer.

He read the books, alternately sampling among sagas, letters, and horseback tours, all the way to New York. In the city, Hall decided he would try to learn more about Iceland, at firsthand if possible, from someone who had lived there. In his search, he first came upon the American-Scandinavian Foundation and went to its office for information. The man at the desk could tell him little, except that some fifty thousand Icelanders lived in America. As Hall turned to leave, the man called to him: "Wait a moment! It seems to me that I remember seeing something about Iceland in the new telephone directory." He fanned the pages. "Yes, here it is: 'Iceland Information Desk.' This is probably just what you want."

Hall found the place easily, an old brownstone just west of Broadway; there was a sign in the window: ICELAND: INFORMATION. Inside, two men in shirtsleeves sat at a table in a gray, austere room, playing cards. Hall addressed himself to the nearer one, a big, heavily built man, with blond hair and blue eyes—a typical Icelander, Hall thought. "I suppose you speak English?" Hall said to him.

"Well, I suppose so," the man answered. "What can I do for you?"

"I plan to visit Iceland shortly," Hall said, "and I would like some firsthand information about it. I'd like to know about boats."

"Boats?" the man said, unbelieving. "What do you mean—

seagoing hacks? They don't have 'em any more. Take a taxi, or you might walk."

Hall was getting exasperated at the man's manner. "Yes," Hall answered, "I suppose I might if I had on my seven-league boots. But seriously, I do want some information. I have made many inquiries, to no purpose whatever. It is really surprising how few people in America have any knowledge of Iceland. They all think you belong to some tribe of Eskimos, and live in igloos, and eat whale blubber."

The two men were dumfounded. The other man, short, bald, and red-faced, turned on Hall. "See here!" he shouted. "What are you talking about?"

"About Iceland," Hall replied, keeping his patience.

"Well, what Iceland?" the bald man asked.

"Why, there's only one," Hall said.

"I know it," the man answered, his red face getting redder. "Anyway, there's only one that amounts to much. That's right here in New York." The man gave him a card. On it was advertised a skating rink.

Hall laughed. Unwittingly, he had played a merry joke on himself. The New York Iceland, he learned, had just moved to a new location, and until its opening, it had temporarily established an information desk to answer questions from curious customers.

"Well," the big man said, "live and learn. I guess you've learned something about Iceland that you couldn't find in the geographies."

Two days later Hall sailed aboard a Danish ship, via Scotland, Norway, and Denmark. Before he left, he had called on Wells at the Harper's office, giving him further particulars of his proposed travel book on Iceland, and working out the terms of the contract. The agreement, Hall thought, was most encouraging to him; it provided, for a ninety-thousand-word book which would be serialized in the magazine before trade publication, and an advance payment of $5,000. This sum was singularly generous, Hall thought; he would have to produce a superb book, one in keeping with the faith his publishers had in him.

He reached Iceland in August and fell in love with it immediately, he said. At first Hall stayed at a hotel in Reykjavik, but soon he rented a room with the Havsteen family, to get closer to the people and to an understanding of their language.

The land he found, like its people, to be grave, austere, and melancholy. "There is an element in the landscape here," he wrote, "which satisfies more than the demand of the senses for beauty—a spiritual element, for lack of a better word. Perhaps I imagine this. It may be merely the clear cold outlines, the economy of Nature in her effects, the lack of trees and dense vegetation in such contrast to the overwhelming luxuriance of the vegetation on the high islands of the South Seas which I have left so recently. It may be that I was weary, without having realized it, of tropical color, and light and shade, and of man's never-ending struggle with tropical Nature. Here, too, there is a struggle, but against frugality, not prodigality—the sort of contest that will always appeal most to men of Northern blood."

Hall wrote to Nordhoff regularly and frequently. "This is going to be rather a lonely year for me, Nordie," he said to his friend, "so I shall write often to you; and I hope that you will write when you can. I shall be awfully glad to hear from you." He solicited his friend's advice: "Do, please, let me have your criticism, just as soon as you receive the installments of my story, for you are to receive them all! That is, unless you make too violent an objection. I don't ask you to criticize them in detail, or at great length. Heavens no! Only send me a paragraph or so, with a few of those brief, illuminating judgements which are always such a help."

He reported on a trip to the eastward in September: ". . . we—that is, my guide and I—covered about 350 kilometres of some of the wildest, loveliest country in Iceland, and some of the most desolate too. By Jove, Nordie, but this is a weird land! Sometimes we traveled for miles upon miles without seeing a single human habitation. In many places and particularly in the interior of the country, the volcanoes have poured lava over the vast areas. Here, often there is not a sprig of green; nothing moves but the clouds overhead, and nothing is to be heard but the wind, and the sound of the ponies' hoofs clip-clopping over the rock. There is a majesty in such desolation, but something awful in it too. One feels too keenly that the world was not made for man; that he is only an accident here, too trivial an accident perhaps to be worthy of notice. I saw majesty of another sort, the glaciers, and hills smoking and steaming, pouring out hot water and a villainous ill-smelling liquid, and mud springs bubbling and brumbling, and great moorlands alive with wild ducks and geese. We crossed several ranges of mountains, half covered with snow even in August, where the wind blows pitilessly cold, and descended by long zigzag trails to green valleys dotted with farms where everyone was at work in the fields making hay. It is a country of infinite variety, and the love of it grows upon you the more you see of it. What a fitting land for the mighty race of men and women who once flourished here, who harried far and wide, as the old saying goes in the sagas. . . .

"I hope to get a good deal of work done this winter, despite the curse under which I seem doomed to labor: the too-keen awareness of my feeble talents. Oh! that I had a great gift, or not the faintest glimmer of one! But how foolish and weak it is to complain! I must try and be content and make the most of one-tenth of a talent.

"With respect to my work for Harper's, one thing gives me, or is beginning to give me concern: I am afraid that life in Iceland is pretty much the same the country over, and so I am wondering how I am to tell, in ninety thousand words, what might, it seems to me now, be told a deal better in fifty thousand. My contract says, all too clearly, 'At least ninety thousand words' and that appalling number haunts my dreams, and the noughts dance and whirl around me like moons around some bewildered planet. Sometimes I imagine that I have 90 000 000 words to write, and sometimes, that I must say all there is to be said about Iceland in one-ninety-thousandth of one word. In the end very likely I shall go insane, and imagine I am to be paid $90,000 for saying nothing at all. . . ."

Hall did not talk about it much in his letters to Nordhoff, but giving him at least as much trouble as the ninety thousand

words for Harper's were the far fewer words of the Icelandic
tongue which he was trying to learn how to speak. He remembered the words from Bacon's essay "Of Travel": "He that
travelleth into a country before he hath some entrance into the
language, goeth to school and not to travel." Wanting to
travel, he nevertheless went to a bookstore and bought an Icelandic grammar and an Icelandic-English dictionary. About
the dictionary, noting that it was of old Icelandic, he asked the
clerk: "Will it serve my purpose?"

"Very well," she replied. "Icelandic has changed very little
from what it was in the Saga period."

"Is the grammar so very difficult?"

"Not at all. If you have any talent for languages, you will be
speaking Icelandic fluently in a year's time. I have known Germans master it in less than a year, but they, of course, are more
patient and industrious than most people."

"Could you give me a few hints about the grammar?" Hall
asked. "Merely something to show me what I have in store?"

She thought for a minute. "Yes, I think I can. Perhaps it
would be best to speak of the nouns; they seem to offer the
chief difficulty to foreigners, although I don't understand why.
There are two classes of nouns, the strong and the weak, and of
the strong nouns there are three groups. Each noun, whether
strong or weak, has, of course, the same number of cases: the
nominative, accusative, dative, and genitive. If you know the
ending of the accusative plural, you can usually tell to which
class a noun belongs. Shall I give you an example?"

"I wish you would," Hall answered.

"Very well," she began. "Consider the word *skip*—in English, 'ship.'" She declined the noun; her performance was brilliant.

Hall was amazed, almost devastated. He interrupted the lesson: "I'm afraid I'm not quite following. Isn't a ship, in Iceland, always a ship, as it is with us? And must I learn the
declension of every noun before I can hope to speak the language?"

"Of course," she answered. "But you will not find it difficult
once you are fairly started. Now let me tell you of the prepo-
sitions and the cases they govern."

Hall was discouraged, but not yet defeated. He returned to his quarters determined, although he had always been weak in the study of language, not to be defeated by a strong noun. Fortified by a good supper, he went up to his room and prepared his battle plan. In the past the best way for him to memorize anything had been to put it into a jingle. He took out his grammar and a piece of paper, and tried writing rhymes, but with no success toward memorization.

On October 3, Hall received from Nordhoff letters of July 17 and 18, containing reports of Bastille Day—*La Fête* in Tahiti. He read them twice over, and answered Nordhoff immediately: "Your account of the July celebrations at Papeete delighted me beyond measure. How I should have enjoyed being there. Nordie, I am so homesick for that island of islands that I have actually been within an ace of throwing up my work here, and hurrying back to you as fast as steamers, trains and Harper's money could carry me. Only the thought of this last has prevented me; and in this connection, let me give you a piece of advice. Never, never, under any circumstances, Nordie, take on a piece of work for which you must have the money in advance! Keep your independence although you have nothing but bananas and raw fish to sustain you in it. To follow any other course is to lose your peace of mind, and to be deprived of the power to do good work. How bitterly I regret my own folly now that it is too late! There is nothing for it now but to see the thing through, but to be deprived of Tahiti and your companionship—forgive me for speaking thus frankly—is almost too great a price to pay for even the most asinine folly. . . . When I have finished my work here, I shall return at once to Tahiti, never, I hope and believe, to leave the islands again."

In order to get his work done, Hall put himself on a daily regimen. He awoke at seven thirty, studied Icelandic in bed until the young Havsteen daughter brought him coffee and sandwiches. Then he lit a fire and wrote until lunch time at twelve. Lunch was the main meal: soup, roast beef or mutton, potatoes and other vegetables, and all kinds of smoked and dried meats and fish, and coffee. In the afternoon, he would take a walk until coffee and cakes at three thirty, followed by more study of Icelandic. Then supper at seven, more reading in bed until nine thirty, when coffee was served again.

By October Hall had moved to Akureyri in the north, hoping that the change in location would inspire him to greater effort. He took a room at a hotel, a two-story wooden building standing on a peninsula jutting into a fjord, where he could look south to the upper fjord yielding to a broad valley backed by mountains already peaked with snow. On the fifteenth he wrote to Nordhoff: "I couldn't help laughing at your marvelous description of Iceland: 'A rugged, barren, treeless, slagheap, under semi-arctic skies, where life flows along with a singular monotony.' The worst of it is that it comes so nearly to being the truth.

"It is not a slag-heap, however. On the contrary, the mountains are beautiful beyond description. But I am beginning to see—in fact, I see already—that it will be next to impossible to write a 90,000 word book about Iceland. I have now traveled some 400 miles on horseback, both inland and along the coast, and I am forced to confess that life varies very little in different parts of the country. I have been very much worried about this, and finally decided that the only thing to do was to write Mr. Wells telling him frankly what my opinion of the prospects is. I made three suggestions: first, that he let me change my plans entirely, and write a travel book under some such title as 'A Wanderer at Large.' In that case I would begin with Iceland, go on to the Faroes, the Shetlands, through Scotland and England, France, Spain, Africa, and on eastward and southward, ending up at Tahiti sometime next spring. As a second suggestion, I proposed that he let me write a 50,000 word book on Iceland, the Faroes and Shetlands, I to return $1,000 of my letter of credit, and to forego any royalties on the sale of the book. Third, I suggested returning $2,000 of my letter of credit, and writing a series of six articles of from six to seven thousand words in length. . . . Well, I'll let you know as soon as I can what Mr. Wells has to say. . . . I rather hope he accepts the second plan. If he does, I shall be with you again before a great while, and with such a bellyful of travel that I think I shall never thereafter go farther afield than Mooréa or the Low Archipelago. . . ."

By December Hall had reached the point of despair. On the second he wrote to Nordhoff: "I have at last decided that Iceland—keen as I am about the country—does not offer a sufficient variety of material for a 90,000 word book; at least not such a book as I can write. I am not willing to re-hash old stuff, or to drag in the flora and fauna twins. I know, however, that I can write a really good narrative of from sixty to seventy thousand words, and this I shall do. Meanwhile I am writing to Mr. Wells, suggesting that Harper's take back whatever sum seems to them fair for the short rations I mean to give them. I am willing to return as much as $1,500, should they ask it. Twenty or thirty thousand words of my deathless prose, is of course worth that sum, but I hardly think they will demand so much. If they should, they may have it; in which case I will arrive at Tahiti with about $500 or $600 to keep me going until I can earn some more. By living economically, I can make that amount last me for seven or eight months. I can surely do it at the Skipper's; and oh Nordie! if you were to have your little house on the river completed by the spring! I am looking forward, with what buckets of joy, to working with you again as of old. You and I pounding our Coronas on the Skipper's verandah with Roget [Roget's *Thesaurus*] between us; and the long talks at night, and the discussions of our work, and all the rest of it. If there is one thing in this world of uncertainties I am sure of, it is that I want to live with you and the Skipper henceforth forevermore. And I shall if you two are willing."

On Christmas day, Hall wrote to his mother: "What a pity it is that I must earn a living by writing! I do get so eternally sick of having to be eternally garrulous. My heaven is one where I may travel forever without ever being under the necessity of writing of my experiences."

In Tahiti, Nordhoff, for his part, had been doing very well, artistically if not financially. He had had a short story, "Savagery," published in *Harper's* in April, cited by Edward J. O'Brien for the "Roll of Honor" in *The Best Short Stories of 1922;* and, most recently, Ellery Sedgwick had sent him a contract and a $500 advance for a proposed boys' book, yet another after *Pearl Lagoon*. Hall, hearing the good news in an October letter from Nordhoff which he received on January 1,

1923, was full of exultation for his friend: "So you have broken into O'Brien's Annual! Hooray! If you are "3*" grade with the second short story you have ever published, you will be at the head of the list with the fifth or sixth. And while I think of it, Nordie, I have just been re-reading portions of that book of books, *Faery Lands*. . . . Let me tell you this, Nordie: your share in that book is very fine indeed. I am more impressed than ever with the beauty of your prose, and with the way in which you catch the very spirit of the islands in your stories. It makes one lonely and sad to read some of them, just as the islands do to see them; but it is the kind of loneliness that one hugs to one's self, so to speak, and the sadness which is in all beautiful things. My share in the book is simply trash beside yours. I have always known it, but I feel that too, more strongly than before."

Nordhoff, in his latest letter to Hall, would not accept Hall's defeatism; he urged his friend to knuckle under and finish the book, according to the terms of the original contract.

For the next nine months, Hall did his best, but to no avail. He returned to New York and to Boston, where he reestablished residence on Pinckney Street, the street he had lived on in the city when he first arrived, a young graduate from Grinnell and a beginning social worker of the Massachusetts Society for the Prevention of Cruelty to Children. Hall, deep in melancholy, paralyzed into complete literary inactivity by his diffidence, was at the lowest period of his life. On November 15, 1923, he wrote to Nordhoff:

Dear Nordie:
I wrote to you a long letter last month and then destroyed it. Silence seemed better than a tale of woe, and my story was lugubrious to say the least. Your own letter came duly and did me good as your letters always do. You are right Nordie; I have been going through a "hellish crisis" and the end is not quite in sight. However, I think I shall win through eventually and gain the peace of mind which is necessary if one is to work to any purpose. As you know it has been almost impossible for me to write this long while. This has been horrible. To sit at one's desk day after day without being able to set down one

decent paragraph—Lord! I hope that I shall never have to go through such a period again. It has been precisely as though a man, who had lost both of his legs, were under the absolute necessity of reaching a certain destination at a given time. . . .

Now let me tell you what the Skipper [Harrison Smith, the former Harvard professor] has done for me, and entirely upon his own suggestion. But this is for your ears alone of course. He loaned me the money to repay Houghton Mifflin, and in addition placed to my credit here an additional sum sufficient to repay Harper's in case I should not be able to fulfill my contract with them. . . . The Skipper wanted this money to be a gift, Nordie! Think of that. But if I don't repay every penny of it I am no true man.

When I return, Nordie, I am going to take over the Skipper's vanilla [plantation]. I am sure that I can make something of it for both of us. This time I return to the islands for an indefinite period. . . . Although my own troubles have bulked large this past month I have thought of you many many times. I was most awfully sorry to learn of the old glandular trouble, and I hope that it is over and done with by now. . . .

Had lunch with Mr. Sedgwick a few weeks ago, and dinner with him last night. He thinks you have a fine future ahead of you if you stick at the business and let nothing prevent your succeeding. But he thinks that the tropics may "get" us both. He said, "It would be a splendid thing if you two could succeed where so many have failed and rise superior to a climate which is notoriously hostile to men doing creative work." I asked him the precise situation, now, with regard to your boys' book. He could not tell me just what it is, but said that he wanted to do whatever you suggested. . . . He said that Mr. Howe had the matter in hand and could tell me definitely about the developments in so far as The American Boy is concerned. Perhaps you know all about this by now. Thinking that you might not know, I have tried twice to get Mr. Howe on the telephone. He was out both times. I shall try again this afternoon, and send another note to you about the business. . . .

Pratt of the H-M [Houghton-Mifflin] syndicate asked me to lunch with him the other day. He says there is always a market for South Seas stories and feels sure he could dispose of another series in case we want to prepare it. I have some ideas on this which I will talk over with you when I see you. But I think we might make more money by doing magazine articles in case we have time for this scattering sort of work.

I have been thinking Nordie that you and I ought to publish another book together: something in the nature of a series of South Seas sketches and stories. *Faery Lands* has undoubtedly given us a public, and we ought to keep it. My idea would be that the book should be about 75,000 words in length, and contain from six to ten things—depending upon the length— by each of us. I am sure that this book would have a sale, and that we could finish it in three months' time if we set definitely about it. Not "high brow" stuff, necessarily: something light and readable. In fact we already have material which could very well go into such a book. Think this over, will you? I am ready to go into it if you are.

No more for this time. Give my love to Vahine and the youngsters. I am coming back this time prepared to work as I have never worked before. We are certain to make good, Nordie, if we keep hard at it.

Yours,
[signed] Hall

Hall, although he had told Nordhoff that he could not tell Wells or anyone else what he had been going through for the last six months, did finally tell Wells. On November 29, 1923, he returned to his editor at Harper's the $5,000 advance for the Iceland articles and added to that sum another $300 which represented 6 per cent of the $5,000—a return which Hall considered fair if Wells had invested the sum for the year Hall had the money. In his letter to Wells Hall said, "I have lost the *joie d'écrire* and don't know where to find it." Then he used again the same metaphor he had used in the letter to Nordhoff: ". . . a man who had lost both legs could not be expected to walk and one who has lost his *joie d'écrire* cannot write, however hard he may try. He can only put words on paper."

At Christmas, 1923, Hall, sad and depressed, left Boston by train for New York, Chicago, Des Moines, Omaha, Denver, and points west, then by boat for Tahiti, there to rebuild his shattered fortunes, and there to find again, he hoped with all his heart, his lost joy in living and in writing.

7

Writers Alone

"Hall, you old rascal," Nordhoff welcomed his friend back to Tahiti, "it's good to see you!"

Hall reached out and gripped Nordhoff's outstretched hand as he stepped off the gangplank. "Gosh!" he said, excited, "I've never been so happy to return to one place in my whole life. It's wonderful."

Vahine, Nordhoff's wife, placed frangipani leis about Hall's neck, and kissed him on both cheeks. Then Hall noticed Nordhoff's two little girls, the one-year-old Rita whom Vahine had taken up into her arms, and the three-year-old Sarah, who clutched at her mother's leg. Hall hugged and kissed them both. "What beautiful children, Nordy!" he exclaimed. Then, noting their beautiful brown complexions and bright eyes, he said: "If I were you, I would have a dozen of them!"

Nordhoff ordered some native boys to get Hall's bags and had them brought to a chauffeured car he had hired. "Come, Hall, you have to stay with us at Taunoa for a few days," Nordhoff insisted. "Then you can go to Papeari to visit the

Skipper; he's waiting to see you." At Nordhoff's Vahine had prepared a marvelous feast. First she served several rum punches, then roast suckling pig, raw shrimp marinated in lime juice and coconut milk, baked bonita, yams, and bread-fruit, and fried bananas and plantain; then she retired from the room, leaving the men alone.

Nordhoff told Hall about his recent good luck and his plans for the immediate future. His first novel, *Picaro*, was now in production at Harper's and would be out in a few months. He had created a hero modeled after himself when he lived at the family ranch in Ensenada, and made him into a successful aer-onautical engineer who designed a new kind of airplane motor during the war.

"And I am well along on the new one," Nordhoff said, "a juvenile. I have a boy hero, Charles Selden, who leaves his fa-ther's ranch in California to sail to the South Seas with his Uncle Harry. They search for gold-lipped oysters for the mak-ing of mother-of-pearl, and in their adventures they meet man-eating sharks and modern-day pirates."

Hall was charmed. "I hope it keeps thousands of kids up beyond their bedtime," he said.

Nordhoff smiled slowly. He refilled their glasses from his pinched bottle of Scotch. "It's funny," he said, holding up the bottle, "I can drink a quart of this a day and it doesn't bother me." Then he told how Wells wanted him to write a travel book for Harper's, not so much on South America as Nordhoff had proposed, because Wells felt that that part of the world was overdone, but rather on New Zealand, especially if it car-ried the same suggestion of romance as the other islands did in the South Seas. And, Nordhoff added, Pratt at the Houghton-Mifflin syndicate and the editor of *The London Mercury* in England had told him they could use any sketch he wrote.

Hall was sadly impressed. Nordhoff was succeeding, he thought, in everything he tried—in short stories, juvenile nov-els for boys, and travel pieces. Where he had failed to disci-pline himself and his talent, Nordhoff had succeeded. Nord-hoff followed a tightly controlled schedule, rarely deviating from it. He would write in the morning, fish at the reef in the afternoon, and read and sometimes make notes in the evenings. Nordhoff had shown him a letter from Wells. "I have no doubt that as you go ahead and acquire the knack," the Harper's editor had said, "you will produce things that are really big."

After his visit with Nordhoff and his family, Hall moved for a time to the Aina Paré, occupying again the room he and Nordhoff had stayed in when they had first come to Tahiti. Then Hall went to see Harrison Smith, hoping that the Skipper would have some words of sound counsel for him.

Harrison Smith, originally from Boston, where he was born in 1872, had been graduated from Harvard in 1895 and after taking a graduate degree had become an instructor, then a professor there in physics. He, too, like Nordhoff, had been an ambulance driver during the war, but had been coming to Tahiti, first as a vacationer, since 1903. Returning to his office from teaching a class one day in 1919, he had found a letter on his desk; opening it, he read, dumfounded, that he was the sole heir of a fortune left by an aunt in Maine. Leaving everything in his desk as it was, he slammed shut the rolltop and promptly left for Tahiti, where he settled. On either side of the perimeter road, in the district of Papeari, south of Papeete, he gave his time and fortune not to physics, but to the raising of a botanical garden. To plant it, he traveled the world collecting flowers, plants, and trees. Before he was satisfied with his arboretum he had introduced 250 new botanical species to the island.

A tall, husky man, balding and graying, with a goatee and steel-rimmed glasses, Smith was a gentle, kind, and patient man; but he worried continually about his health, constantly checking the state of it. Though rich, he was curiously penurious, using the backs of letters he had received for writing his own letters, and readdressing used envelopes to his correspondents. Toward Nordhoff and Hall, however, the Skipper was charity itself, though sometimes deviously by sending money to them anonymously through Sedgwick. For both seemed to him like adopted sons, with excellent credentials for adoption: Nordhoff was a Harvard man, Hall had worked in

Boston, and both wrote well enough to be published in the *Atlantic Monthly*.

Unknown to Hall, Harrison Smith had been in correspondence with Sedgwick, and both of them had tried to decide what to do with Hall. "We are dealing with a complicated version of human nature," the *Atlantic* editor had written to the Skipper; but he added: "I am terribly interested in Hall, and shall keep in touch with you."

"Indeed he is a complicated version of human nature," Smith replied to Sedgwick. "I have noticed that when his work is going hard, Hall's idea seems to be to find some adjustment of his environment, some expedient that will make it easy. . . . I have for a long time wished to do for our friend any service that would really help him and I have given him— or loaned him—considerable sums of money; but I doubt whether the results have always been beneficial.

"He was with me while doing the best piece of work he has done ['Sing: A Song of Sixpence,' in which the seeds were from Smith and the Chinese neighbor across the street], and he seemed to have a curious resentment against having to work hard for good results. He would have dropped that piece of work when half done and gone for a cruise to the islands if I hadn't interfered. I think his chief difficulty is that he doesn't know how to concentrate on something that interests him."

When Hall arrived at Smith's place, the Skipper was ready for him, lectured him on personal discipline, artistic responsibility, being true to one's commitments to others. Referring to the Iceland debacle, Smith told him: "You don't know how to work. You have a curious resentment against working when the mood is not right. It is worthwhile to work," he added, "even when it is a grind to do so." Then, softening and smiling, indulgent for Hall's health and welfare, he asked him to stay for dinner.

Harrison Smith would have none of Hall's proposal to work for him in order to repay his loan. "Your responsibility is to your talent," Smith said. "Go back to the Aina Paré and to your work as a writer." Then he added as Hall left: "You make me mad; but I am always happy to help you when you need it. Don't hesitate to ask."

Despite Smith's preachments and Hall's resolve to heed them, Hall did not. He did not feel like working, and there was no way he could overcome the feeling. He sought relief from his ennui, from his acedia, but not at the typewriter; rather he would go canoeing in the lagoon, letting his mind lie fallow; he would go to Nordhoff's or Frank Stimson's and he would saw and split wood for them for hours, thinking of plans and projects; he would hike the paths into the valleys and climb the hills and mountains, daydreaming the while, *tête-au-ciel;* often, he would seek companions in misery, not in real life, but in literature and music—in the Russian novelists, and in Chopin, Tchaikovsky, the blues of American jazz; more often, he would sit down on the beach and look out to sea, musing. He felt lonely, alone—and, by his own choosing, abandoned; and he thought of the loneliest man in the world, his friend Cridland in Taioro, and decided he would like to see him again. He reached into his pocket and pulled out a slip of paper which he had retrieved from an old white drill suit he had left in his hotel room at the Aina Paré four years before. On it he had made some notes about Cridland:

> He is one of those lonely spirits—without friends or any of the ties which make life pleasant to most of us—who wander the unpeopled places of the earth, interested in a detached way at what they see from afar or faintly hear; but looking quietly on, taking no part, being blessed—or cursed—by Nature with a love of silence, of the unchanging peace of great solitudes. Now and then one reads of such men in fiction, and if they live in fiction it is because of individuals like Cridland, their prototypes in reality, seen for a moment as they slip apprehensively across some by-path leading from the outside world.

Several weeks went by before Hall could find a trader to take him to Cridland's island. He was turned down by the *Caleb Winship,* which had taken him the first time, and had almost given up the idea when he ran into Chan Lee, owner of the schooner *Toafa,* who agreed to take him. The trip took thirty-eight days. Hall, on the lookout with his glasses, sighted the southwestern tip of the island at three in the afternoon. At four they were skirting the coral reef of the atoll. At five they had scraped by whaleboat over the barrier reef into the shallows of the lagoon and onto the beach. Cridland was waiting for them with his old grandmother-housekeeper. His was the largest of seven small islands, spaced almost equidistant around the lagoon. Hall guessed that Cridland's piece of coral atoll measured no more than a mile in length and three hundred yards in width.

"*O vai tera? Chan?*" Cridland called when they debarked on the shore—"Who is it? Chan?"

"Yes, yes!" the old woman answered him. "Don't you believe me? It is Chan and the white man who first came here with you." Then she turned to the visitors: "*Ia ora na orua!*" —"Health to you!" She put her hands on Jim's shoulders, holding him to confirm her empirical belief that he was present. "*Ua tae mai oé?*"—"You have come?" "*Ua tae mai oé?*" she repeated.

Cridland, still tall, straight, barrel-chested, and youthfully handsome, looked out at them from behind smoked glasses. "You will forgive me for not recognizing you," he apologized. "Until recently I've never taken any precaution against the glare of the sun. It was very unwise, and the result is—well, I'm nearly blind."

The old grandmother interrupted. "Don't encourage him to talk about it," she urged Hall.

"Rather a nuisance," Cridland continued. "I may get over it, of course; but in six months' time I can't say there has been any change for the better. Well, enough of that. Shall we go to the house? Luckily, I know my way about after four years. I could go anywhere, blindfolded."

As they walked to the house, Hall noticed how much the island had improved in appearance in four years—the wild brush cleaned out, the pandanus and coconut trees spaced out, a road leading from ocean beach across the islet to the lagoon. "You've not been idle here," he said, looking up to Cridland.

"No, there's been enough to do. I found that I needed some help at first. I had Chan bring me a dozen natives from another island. They stayed three months, clearing the land. They helped build my house, too."

Hall liked the house. It was very large, with a high, steep roof of pandanus thatch that also enclosed a wide veranda: three feet off the ground, it faced the lagoon beach. When they came to the steps, Cridland begged to be excused. "I think I must be rather excited. I've some instructions to give Chan about my copra, and he never stops ashore unless his schooner is at anchor. Will you make yourself comfortable? You might look over the house if you care to."

It was the last Hall saw of his host. At first unaware, then concerned, and then disturbed, and finally angered, Hall at last realized that Cridland had no intention of joining him. Hall sat on the top stair of the veranda, waiting, listening for an hour to the pounding surf on the reef; then he went into the library waiting, leafing through a few of the hundreds of books which Cridland owned; then he went in to dinner, waiting, barely tasting the food which Cridland's man put before him. Hall wished with all his heart that he had not come. But there was nothing for him to do: the schooner had left; he would have to wait for its return the next day. It was nine o'clock. Hall went back into the library and started again pulling books from the shelves for idle examination, settled on a volume of Shelley's poems, and sat in a chair to read.

For fifteen minutes Hall pored over "Alastor," appropriately subtitled "The Spirit of Solitude," when from the other side of the wall behind his head came, nervous and sudden, the drumming of fingers. Hall was frightened almost out of his chair. Quickly, he got up, blew out the light, and stole back to his room. The drumming fingers were undoubtedly Cridland's. Why had he done it? Hall got into bed, but he could not go to sleep for wondering. He heard the ticking of the clock from the library; it was eerie, almost ominous, punctuating the lugubrious silence of the night. At last Hall fell off to sleep, but was immediately startled awake by the crowing of a cock. But this chicken was hailing, not the rising of the sun, but of the moon. Unable to go to sleep, Hall climbed out of his window, and in the shadows of the trees and the overhanging palms he walked down to the lagoon and along the length of beach. While on his way back twenty minutes later, the cock crowed again, stopping Hall in his walk, not a hundred and fifty feet from the house. Then Cridland appeared on the veranda, came down the stairs, went to the bushes where the cock crowed, and pulled out the bird. As Cridland started down to the shore with the chicken tucked under his arm, Hall slid behind a tree so he wouldn't be seen. Cridland passed by, and then a few feet away he stopped. He was talking to the chicken: his voice was scolding, apologetic, like a father to a naughty child. "You shouldn't have made such an infernal racket," he said. "And just under my window, too! It isn't the first time either, and you know you have been warned. Now I'm going to punish you—a quite serious little punishment. You won't like it in the least."

Cridland, his face passive in the moonlight, his eyes without glasses staring vacantly, now took the bird, one leg in each hand, and slowly tore it in half. The cock gave only one screech. Cridland, his hands and arms and chest splattered with blood, took the two pieces in one hand, slammed them against the trunk of a tree, forehand and backhand, then threw the bloody mess into the lagoon. He stepped a few paces down the shore and started to wash himself off, then pulled up the front panel of his pareu and wiped himself dry. Now he sat on the beach, staring out over the waters of the lagoon, and presently started talking to himself. For one agonizing moment Hall thought that Cridland had seen him, for Cridland spoke as if he were speaking directly to Hall. "Why did you come?" he asked, plaintively. "Did you think I was lonely?" He was totally absorbed in his own thoughts, undoubtedly unaware that he was speaking them aloud. "Ah, my friend!" he continued, "you are too kind! Too considerate by far! Your companionship—your conversation—oh, charming! No doubt! No doubt! But you will forgive a solitary man if he deprives himself—"

Hall held his breath through the soliloquy, happy when it was over and Cridland had returned to the house. Hall did not go back to sleep that night. The next morning he left his room and the house at dawn, climbed in with the first boatload of copra being brought out to the schooner, went below to his bunk, and promptly fell asleep. When he awoke it was after noon and the ship was well out to sea. Obviously, Hall thought as he peeled an orange for his breakfast, Cridland not only wanted solitude, but seclusion as well; and as far as Hall was concerned, Cridland could have both until he died without any further interruption from a visitor named Hall.

Although Hall, like Cridland, liked solitude, he was no hermit and certainly had no intention of being a celibate. A frequent visitor to Nordhoff's house, he envied Nordhoff his family and hoped one day to have one of his own. As early as April 1924 Hall was giving thought to the hopes of marriage, but with qualifications. He wrote to his friend Larry Winship in Boston: "I received the Christmas greeting, the one with the picture of the youngsters sitting by the fire-place. Wish I had two like that. The older I become the more I wish it, and the more I wish it the older I become. And that is as far as I get with my family. You don't know of a good peripatetic wife for me, do you, Jack? One who can raise babies en route, so to speak?"

Sooner than he thought, in the spring of 1925, Hall got his answer to that question, but not from Boston; and although he was not granted the kind of peripatetic wife he wanted, he did win the young and beautiful daughter of a Tahitian mother and a peripatetic English sea captain father. Sarah Teraivéia Winchester was dark, fair-skinned, exquisitely well shaped, a vivacious sixteen-year-old when Hall, now thirty-eight years old, met her; and when he met her, he wanted to marry her. But his diffidence of old stalked him at every turn, and he tried to make light of a heavy matter. He wrote again to Winship in Boston:

Sir:
Knowing the sympathetic and intelligent interest you take in the afairs of your friends—particularly in their approaches, or near approaches to the state, or sea, of matrimony—it has occurred to me that you might be able to advise me in a matter which has, of late, been giving me a good deal of concern.
Some time ago, in an unguarded moment, I expressed a certain amount of enthusiasm for a young lady of these parts, and I was so foolish as to express this enthusiasm in her presence. I

suppose it could be called enthusiasm, for I said to this young lady, "I wonder whether you would be willing to marry me?" Of course I thought she would say, "Of course not! What put so curious a notion into your head?" Unfortunately she replied that she was not only willing but even eager to marry me, and that the *summum bonum* which life could offer her would be to be called, with truth, Mrs. James Norman Hall.

It goes without saying, of course, that the moment she made this reply, I regretted my rashness in putting my question. "Well," I thought, "there is still a chance. Perhaps her mother will object." Alas! Her mother was even more willing, and, to be brief, within a day or two I learned, from various sources, and to my complete consternation, that I was engaged.

However I did not entirely abandon the hope that I might yet escape. In Tahiti it is extremely difficult for a foreigner to enter upon a contract of marriage. As a preliminary he must produce both a birth certificate, and secondly, seven witnesses who will swear that either he has never been married before, or, if married, that his wife is dead or divorced. . . . [For Hall, because he had been a war hero serving with the French during the war, the governor waved these two requirements.]

Now, sir, what I would like to know is this: Are my fears that I am about to be married well founded? Has this young lady the right to assume that she is my affianced bride, and is her mother justified in believing that she is about to become a mother-in-law? If you could give me reason to hope that my fears are groundless and their assumptions, merely assumptions, without basis, I would be eternally your debtor. Meanwhile I pshaw and pooh-pooh to no avail. I cannot convince myself that I am not a doomed man. When I look at the *mairie* bulletin-board, where the marriage notices are posted, I have the gravest fears that the James Norman Hall mentioned in one of these notices is no other than myself.

Here is another complication: Granted that I am about to be married, how am I to do this on $35? That is the extent of my capital at the present moment. . . . Of course, my prospective mother-in-law has no inkling of this state of affairs. Recently she said to me, "Hall (she always addresses me by my last name), Hall, please forgive me for speaking of this, but since you are engaged to my daughter and the banns published, don't you think it would be a good thing if you were to buy her a ring? I don't know how it is with you in America, but here it is customary to give your fiancée a ring of sorts so that people may know that she is really engaged."

"Well, well! Mrs. Winchester," I replied. "I forgot all about that! A ring! Of course I must buy a ring! I'll get it at once."

So I rushed away, but as soon as I was out of sight I slowed down, in order that I might go over ways and means to buy a ring, and still have enough left of my $35 to provide for a wedding feast and furnish a house. I have not yet been able to devise these ways and means, and in this state of doubt and uncertainty I remain at the present moment. What I think I shall do, in this juncture, is to fall sick. I shall eat some laundry soap or a box of talcum powder and thus gain time until the arrival of the next steamer from San Francisco. Hope springs eternal in the human breast, and I am human—all too human. Perhaps I shall find that some editor has accepted some of my deathless prose. In that case, I fear that I shall *have* to be married soon, for it is only too clear that my prospective mother-in-law is eager to enter upon her new duties.

Au Revoir Sir. A horse! a horse! My kingdom for a horse to carry me away from this doom.

Hall had sent the same letter to Ellery Sedgwick, but his *Atlantic* editor did not by any means take it in a spirit of fun. The letter was, he wrote to Harrison Smith, "one of the strangest communications of my experience." He sought the Skipper's advice on what they both could do to prevent the marriage. "How strange it is," Sedgwick concluded, "that capacities, really great capacities like Hall's, can be placed at the caprice of a disordered judgment."

Smith, short of physically spiriting Hall away, was at a loss over what to do. Sedgwick had written to him again, advising against the Skipper's doing anything, and ended the letter: "I have the feeling that he [Hall] is simply sewing himself in a sack." Harrison Smith immediately typed an answer and sent it to Boston:

Personally I feel inclined to wait until we know that the marriage has actually taken place before doing anything and even then I shall not want to do much. I really think that it would have been better if I had done much less—that I have some responsibility for Hall's sewing himself up in a sack. I have removed difficulties which it would have been better to leave for him to solve.

I am not alone in believing that Hall is far from being in love with little Sarah—extraordinary situation of which I will tell you more. So I think if anything should happen to prevent the marriage it would not touch Hall very deeply. I have felt sure that Mrs. Winchester has precipitated matters for she probably considers Hall well fixed in financial matters. She would have reason to think so; when Hall has money he spends liberally. This opinion about Mrs. Winchester is confirmed in Hall's last letter. Speaking of getting the pearl ring made from his stick-pin, he writes, "Sarah, of course, knowing my predicament, didn't give a rap about having a ring, but I didn't want her mother to know." From what little I know of Mrs. Winchester I think the truth would give her quite a different view of the marriage. (Poor old Hall, Sarah I fancy doesn't give a rap about the marriage.)

Hall for his part was trying to be cautious. He had an idea that Mrs. Winchester knew he was barely making a living as a writer, but he didn't want her to know he had only $35 to his name and still wanted to marry her daughter. Nevertheless, despite the protestations against what he wanted to do, Hall married Sarah in the Bethel Church in Papeete. For their honeymoon, the writer Robert Keable, author of *Simon Called Peter*, let them have his home in Papeari, near the isthmus of Taravao and overlooking Port Phaeton.

Hall's marriage to Sarah Winchester was the best thing that could have happened to him. It settled him down, it imposed upon him the necessity for regular work habits, it freed his mind from the immediate mundane considerations for food and drink, clothing and shelter. Sarah, feverishly in love with her man, husbanded her mate, cared for his wants, and coaxed him back into his literary life. But it took time. Sedgwick, still worried, wrote to Nordhoff on December 24, 1925: "I have been very ill at ease about Norman. It is curious how in life there is often a gathering sense of fate. The Greeks had a wonderful sensibility about such things, and I think there really is a sort of prescience in nature which perhaps some day men may learn to read. The immediate difficulty with Norman is that he thinks there is some miraculous cure for his difficulties with writing, and I suspect the truth is that he does not know how to work. Yet he is so capable. . . ."

Slowly, Hall came out of the doldrums, mental, artistic, and financial. In retrospect, the year 1925 had been not too bad a one, literarily. His story on Cridland, "The Forgotten One," for the *Atlantic*, won a citation in The Honor Roll in *O'Brien's Best Short Stories for 1925* and an essay, "Onward, Christian Soldiers" was cited by Odell Shepard for *Best Essays for 1925*. Clearly, he was adjusting to the demands of his craft. More slowly, however, was he adjusting to the demands of his marriage. Again he wrote to Winship: "Well, well, here I am a married man of three months standing, and I haven't yet gotten over the shock. I keep on wondering in a sort of dazed way how the thing happened. Did you feel that way, Jack, after you went over the hurdles? Sometimes, along about midday I hop on my bike and go into town for lunch, and usually, when I'm about halfway through the meal I remember that I have a wife, so I hop on my bike again and hurry home to another lunch which I attack with simulated enthusiasm. That's bad for the digestion.

"I don't want you to think that Sarah isn't a good cook. On the contrary she's a little wonder at cooking. The fact that I run away from her delicious luncheons to abominable ones in Papeete restaurants is merely an evidence of the strength of habit formed through long years of bachelordom. However, I'm breaking it gradually. There's a big tree at a turn in the road about half a mile from my place. I've had a sign put up there where I can't miss seeing it. It reads: Stop! You're Married. Go Back Home to Lunch."

Financially, however, matters had improved hardly at all. Again Smith, through subterfuge with Sedgwick, came to Hall's rescue. On March 31, 1926, Sedgwick suggested to Smith: "In our last chat, you told me to feel quite at liberty to come to you with any financial suggestion, and I do feel now that if you cared to guarantee him [Hall] $100 a month for one year, he could turn his attention to a novel with a clear and comfortable mind." On April 8, Smith replied: "I should have to see Hall before I could convince myself that it will do him any good to stake him again on another long piece of writing. I'm mighty glad however that your latest meeting with him has led you to believe that such a course is prudent. . . . If your plan of advance to Hall is substantially the same as you suggested in your recent letter, and if you wish me to take on half of this liability with you I shall be glad to do so."

Ellery Sedgwick felt that such a plan "would pull Hall together and might well mark an absolute turning point in his fortunes." But the plan had changed somewhat in that, now, the Skipper undertook the full subsistence of his friend. On April 11 he wrote to Sedgwick: "This is my understanding of the plan. I am undertaking to guarantee Hall $100 per month for not more than one year. This is merely a guarantee that he shall receive this amount per month—that he can depend on this income—in case other affairs go wrong. The purpose is to assure Hall $100 per month and not to pay him $100 per month regardless of what else he receives. If he devotes all his time to the novel he will get the $100; if he receives other income, or sells other articles, he is not to call for the guarantee. . . . I hope he will feel that this guarantee places him under obligation to grind away regardless of mood or environment. . . .

"Since I wish to avoid having it known, especially in Tahiti, that I am doing this, would you be willing to make the monthly disbursements, letting me pay you a lump sum to cover the guarantee? There is no convenient way in which I can send money without having [it] known. The Banque de l'Indo-Chine is the local broadcasting station."

On April 14, Sedgwick wrote to Smith: "If he [Hall] can help himself, so much the better. I have, however, advised him very strongly to make no contract for a piece of work so considerable as a novel with me or with anybody else, for cash down. Like another business man in trouble, he had best finance himself by short time security." Smith answered on the seventeenth: "It seems to me important to avoid aiding Hall to go back joyously to Tahiti with the feeling that his troubles are all over for a year. Unquestionably it was partly my own fault that he has previously used money that I gave him with little regard for the purpose for which I gave it.

"Nordy thinks that Hall doesn't know how to concentrate. I think he does. Once he said to me that he could 'concentrate on something that interested him.' In fact he did concentrate on 'The Forgotten One' even after it ceased to interest.

"Since I have known Hall he has always been seeking the ideal lovely spot, on the beach or on the mountain-side—the perfect environment—where he could sit with a pleasant view in front of him while the 'imperishable paragraphs' flowed without effort into his typewriter. ('Imperishable paragraphs' is the way in which Hall & Nordy jokingly refer to their work.)"

In 1926 Hall literally and figuratively came out of the woods. In June his first child, a son, was born. He named him Conrad Lafcadio Hall, at Nordhoff's urging on the night the baby was born, after his two favorite authors: Joseph Conrad and Lafcadio Hearn. Also Houghton Mifflin accepted for publication in book form fifteen of his sketches which had been previously published in *Harper's*, the *Atlantic Monthly*, and *Travel*. It was called *On the Stream of Travel*. Appropriately and gratefully, Hall dedicated the book to Harrison W. Smith. And, most significantly, Hall was established in two homes in the district of Arué, only a few miles up the road from Papeete, and he had a man servant. The main house, off the road and at the base of a hill, was a large frame dwelling with a wide veranda in front, and had a long hallway going straight through to the back. To the right of the hallway were two bedrooms; and to the left two rooms, one Hall's study, and next to it a bedroom for Sarah's mother. Then, behind these rooms abutted a large dining room with built-in cabinets, and from it led a covered breezeway leading to the kitchen and bathroom, both separate from the main house. Hall's other dwelling, his beach house, a smaller native thatched hut with bamboo walls, was across the street from the main house about fifty feet, on the lagoon beach, cool and airy with open sides, a place for Hall to relax from his writing and to listen to music.

Nordhoff, meanwhile, had moved from Taunoa to the district of Punaauia, about twenty miles down the perimeter road from Hall's place. Nordhoff and Vahine now had three children and were planning on having more; accordingly, Nordhoff had built on a large site of some fifty acres between the road and the lagoon, a large frame house with three bedrooms, living room, dining room, kitchen and bath. Nordhoff was working steadily and well. Although his first novel, *Picaro,* had come into the literary world stillborn, his second, a boys' book, *The Pearl Lagoon,* had done very well, and he was now at work on a second juvenile, *The Derelict,* with the same boy hero, Charles Selden, and for it he had already received from Sedgwick a contract and a considerable advance; and he had some sixteen other writing projects, sketches and short stories, for which he was making notes, drawing thumbnail characterizations, and plotting story lines. He worked in the morning from seven to twelve; then, after lunch, from the dock out in front of his house, he took his thirty-six-foot cabin cruiser out to the reef, where he fished with bamboo pole, native line made from twisted coconut cinnet, and hook carved from mother-of-pearl. In an afternoon he could easily catch twenty fish, pulling in dolphin, tuna, bonita, barracuda. He would keep one or two, give some away to native families in his district, and sell the remainder at the market in Papeete. At dusk, Vahine would plant two native torches on the beach, and light them to mark for her husband the way through the pass into the lagoon, and home with his catch. These were happy days for Nordhoff, writing and fishing.

Nordhoff and Hall would often meet at the Aina Paré in Papeete, the halfway point up and down the road for both of them, and discuss their work. While Nordhoff worked on his juvenile, Hall tried for another year writing sketches and once in a while a poem. In 1928 Hall brought together another collection of published pieces, which Houghton Mifflin agreed to publish under the title *Mid-Pacific,* but it, like the earlier collection, did not pay back the cost of publication. Hall was clearly discouraged, and one day at lunch in Papeete with Nordhoff he told his friend he did not see how he could continue as a writer and make much of a living, even in Tahiti.

"Look, Hall," Nordhoff said, "these boys' books go pretty well. I would like to carry Charles Selden on to another adventure—into the World War and the air service. What do you say, would you like to help me write it?"

"What?" Hall was pulled up short by the suggestion. "Write another book together, again?"

"Why not?" Nordhoff said. "We have not had very much success in our literary careers alone."

"It's certainly worth a try!" Hall exclaimed. He reached across the table and shook Nordhoff's hand. "Wonderful!" he said. "We're at it again."

8

Bounty from the Mutiny

"Every writer," Hall wrote in his commonplace book, "however deep his despair, is spurred on again and again in efforts to realize his dreams. He will never succeed, of course, but he will never accept defeat." It was a disease, he knew, that could only be cured by death.

Almost daily for nine months, Nordhoff and Hall met in a rented room at the Aina Paré and worked on their flying book. At first there was indecision and disagreement about who should do what in writing the story; then, at Nordhoff's suggestion, they worked up a rough story line, and arbitrarily assigned chapters. Each having previously recorded and published as nonfiction his war and flying experiences, Hall with *High Adventure* and Nordhoff with *The Fledgling,* it was now a matter of transmuting real-life adventures into fiction. The story line was easy. They began with the call to arms, and flight training at Avord and Pau. These first three chapters Nordhoff did, introducing his boy hero Charles Selden again and having him meet another young man his age, Gordon

Forbes. Now Hall took the young heroes to the front for four chapters, Nordhoff spelled him on one, Hall did three more chapters, and Nordhoff the next four. Hall wrote three chapters on being prisoner of war and the escape, and Nordhoff finished with the last chapter.

The division of labor proved interesting. After one had finished a chapter, he turned it over to the other for editing and criticism; then the first writer rewrote his chapter, sometimes fighting the other's suggestions all the way through. Nordhoff proved the narrative specialist, having the talent to get a story started, keeping it going with the eternal variations of "and then, and then" which every writer must have, and knowing where to end it. Hall, true to his attentive, ruminative nature, was the descriptive specialist and the thoughtful philosophical pauser for the occasional "and yet, on the other hand," meditations. Nordhoff trimmed Hall's romantic excesses to the realistic bone; Hall added body and fullness to Nordhoff's austerity and leanness. Nordhoff, having the better ear, handled the dialogue; Hall, more discursive, did the expository sections. It was a perfect marriage of talent, the one making up for what the other lacked. "Huntsmen of the Clouds"—their working title—was readied for publication as *Falcons of France* by Little, Brown as an Atlantic Press Book. The story was serialized in *Liberty* magazine, for which each received $5,000, and after publication in hard cover it sold twelve thousand copies in the first year. With the re-fusion of their talents, Nordhoff and Hall were a new writing success. Now they could do together again what they could not do alone.

"Why don't we go on writing together?" Nordhoff suggested to Hall, after Sedgwick had hinted to both that they had hit upon the magic formula.

"I'm willing," Hall answered. "But what now?"

"Let's bring Selden back to the South Seas and involve him in some more adventures, like a hurricane?"

"No." Hall rejected the idea flatly. "I'm not greatly interested in any more boys' books."

"They sell!" Nordhoff reminded him.

"I know," Hall admitted. "But I'm still not interested."

Having rejected Nordhoff's idea for continuing the adventures of Charles Selden, Hall now felt a responsibility for coming up with a substitute idea. For a week Hall looked through his commonplace book checking story ideas he had jotted down; then he went to the large biscuit tin which he kept on the top of the bookcase in his study. He pulled down the tin and started looking through it, through memoranda, calling cards, hand-sized notebooks, theater programs, book catalogs, old letters, jottings on backs of envelopes and pieces of paper of all kinds. He flipped through one of the small brown spiral notebooks. "There is no place in civilization for the idler," he read. "No one of us has any right to ease." It was a quote from Henry Ford. Hall had added his comment: "It is not a question of right but of privilege." On another page he read, ". . . that worst of abominations, the automobile." And on another page: "To the hermit crab: 'What is the vilest weed growing in human hearts?' I then asked, 'Is it not the love of Power for the sake of Power?' " He put the tin back on the bookcase; then, he started rearranging his books, solicitously, lovingly. He came upon a small blue volume the size of a little prayer book. He stopped, slipped the book in his side pocket, and rushed out of his house and onto his bicycle to see Nordhoff.

He was breathless and full of enthusiasm when he reached Nordhoff's in Punaauia. He rushed into the house. "Have you ever heard of the *"Bounty* mutiny?" he cried out.

Nordhoff was at work at his typewriter. Beside it stood a half-empty pinch bottle. "Of course," Nordhoff calmly replied. "Who hasn't, who knows anything about the South Seas?"

"Well, what about that for a story?" Hall suggested eagerly.

Nordhoff was unimpressed. "Someone must have written it long since."

"I doubt it," Hall answered, undampened. "The only book I have seen is Sir John Barrow's factual account of the mutiny. Barrow was Secretary of the British Admiralty at that time. And his book was published in 1831!"

Nordhoff brightened. "Eighteen thirty-one? That's almost a hundred years ago!" He smiled slowly and turned in his chair. "By the Lord, Hall!" he said. "Maybe we've got something there! I wish we could get hold of a copy of Barrow's book."

"I have it," Hall said, pulling it out of his pocket. "I bought it in Paris during the war. Here"—he handed it to his friend—"you must read it at once."

The next morning, Nordhoff called on Hall. "Hall, what a story!" he said, pacing up and down on Hall's veranda. "What a story!"

"It's three stories," Hall said. He sat slumped in one of the bamboo chairs, seemingly relaxed, his legs double-crossed. "First, there is the tale of the mutiny; then Bligh's open-boat voyage; and the third adventures of Fletcher Christian and the mutineers who went with him to Pitcairn Island, together with the Tahitian men and women who accompanied them. It's a natural for historical fiction. Who could, possibly, invent a better story? And it has the merit of being true."

Nordhoff was gripped by the idea. "You're right," he said, "it *is* a natural." Then came the cold sprinkle of realistic doubt. "It *must* have been written long since." He soured. "It's incredible that such a tale should have been waiting for a century and a half for someone to see its possibilities."

"We must research it thoroughly and find out for sure," Hall said. "I'll check. And while I'm doing that, why don't you write to Sedgwick, outline the idea to him, and see what he thinks?"

To search the literature, Hall began by writing to the Bishop Museum in Hawaii for a rundown from their card catalog. The tally came in. In addition to Sir John Barrow's *The Mutiny and Piratical Seizure of H.M.S. Bounty*, there were Captain William Bligh's own account of the "mutinous seizure; being his narrative of the voyage to Otaheite [Tahiti], with an account of the mutiny and of his boat journey to Timor," several accounts by British seamen of the episode, and, the most intriguing to Hall, an anonymous account, *Aleck, the Last of the Mutineers, or, The History of Pitcairn Island*, published by J. S. & C. Adams, at Amherst, Massachusetts, in 1845. Hall at once wrote to rare-book dealers in Boston, New York, San Francisco, and Sidney, hoping to find copies of the cited books.

Sedgwick was enthused, as was his young assistant Edward Weeks, who had been the Nordhoff and Hall editor for *Fal-*

cons of France. Sedgwick immediately solicited help from England; on a trip to London he sought out Dr. Leslie Hotson of the British Museum, who located the materials; then he was referred to Commander E. C. Tufnell, RN, Retired, who cooperated grandly. Tufnell sent them all the contemporary published accounts of the voyage, the mutiny, the open-sea voyage, the Pitcairn episode; photostatic copies of the official British Admiralty blueprints of the decks, sail, and rigging of the *Bounty;* and copies of the court-martial proceedings: these came in boxes and bundles and packages to Tahiti. Then, capping his work for them, Commander Tufnell had made for them, by Lieutenant Commander J. A. B. Percy, RN, an exact model of the *Bounty,* made to scale, and sent it to them. Nordhoff and Hall were pleased beyond measure. They had everything they needed to get to work.

"How Melville, Conrad, or Stevenson would have liked to have written this story!" Hall thought, and he plunged into the work as eagerly as any one of them would undoubtedly have. Both Nordhoff and Hall now read widely in eighteenth-century prose, and the clarity and conciseness of its style, the balance and beat of its sentence rhythms, the logical forcefulness of its argument, clearly impinged on their own prose manner for the good.

Edward Weeks at the *Atlantic* was greatly impressed by the manuscript that was delivered in the spring of 1932, after three years of steady and unrelenting work. It was, he said, "a book of exceptional beauty and one which drew a striking contrast between the golden age of Polynesia and the tough brutality of man to man which existed aboard Bligh's ship." And he kept close account of who wrote what chapters. Nordhoff wrote thirteen, Hall fourteen; and, as with *Falcons of France,* Nordhoff had opened and closed the story.

"Nordhoff began," Edward Weeks recalled; "he was to carry the tale through the outward voyage; he would draw the portraits of Captain Bligh with his harsh temper and of Fletcher Christian, the second in command who repeatedly tried to intercede for the men. All this [Chapters 1-8] would be told through the eyes of young Midshipman Byam. Nordhoff would

give the impressions of the seamen as they entered upon the
almost untouched beauty of Polynesia, and of the love affairs
which bound both Christian and Byam to the island. This, of
course, he was perfectly qualified to do, for through his wife
and his father-in-law Nordhoff had come to acquire a word-of-
mouth knowledge of Polynesia before the white occupation.

"Hall took up the story at the outbreak of the mutiny, early
on the homeward voyage [Chapters 9 and 10]. He was responsible for the mutineers' return to Tahiti and the secession
when they began to quarrel among themselves under Christian's leadership; he would describe the arrival of the *Pandora*,
the ship which was sent from London to capture the mutineers; he would tell of its shipwreck and of the eventual court-
martial of the survivors, the execution and the ending [Chap-
ters 14-25].

"But as the book came to be written, these boundaries
tended to disappear. In the Aina Paré, they read aloud the
chapters to each other, and there were frequent interruptions.
Hall kept pausing to describe and to wonder; Nordhoff would
grow impatient to keep the narrative moving, and it was inevitable that they should work in and out of each other's pages as
their spirits prompted.

"Thus in the chapter where Byam surprised Tehani at the
pool [Chapter 12], it was Nordhoff who went too fast, and
Hall interposed. It was not enough that Byam should see her
in her loveliness; they must swim together, and there must be
provocation before the surrender. The scene could not be
taken swiftly, and in the end it was Hall who wrote it three
times the space of Nordhoff's original scene."

The second part of the trilogy, however, the account of the
mutineers under the command of Christian, *Pitcairn's Island*,
did not write easily. Hall and Nordhoff could not find a satisfactory point of view from which to tell the story, although it
seemed at first an easy one to tell. Christian and the mutineers
had returned to Tahiti where they were happy for a while,
until they started fighting among themselves. Then Christian
and eight of the crew, and with them twelve Tahitian women
and six of their men, left on the *Bounty*, leaving the others in

Tahiti, until they eventually reached Pitcairn Island. Here they decided to stay, and gutted and sank the *Bounty*. For eighteen years Christian and his band were thought to be drowned or lost, until quite by accident in 1808 the American ship *Topaz* sent a boat ashore to get water and discovered an island of many English-speaking native women and their children under the rule of Alexander Smith, alias John Adams, the last survivor of the *Bounty* mutiny, who in the bloody battle that eventually developed between the mutineers and the Tahitians over the native women had been wounded, found and secreted away by some of the women, and nursed back to health.

Nordhoff and Hall wrote 65,000 words of the story and quit. They sent the partial manuscript to Weeks and asked for his comments, for a way out of the sea of blood which they felt the story was. "Hall and I agree that it is no good," Nordhoff wrote to Weeks, "though we differ strongly as to why. If you could tell us precisely what is wrong with the story . . . as this is damned important to us."

Fortunately, Weeks found a way out for them. "When I read the fragment," he recalled, "I had to agree. It was much too full of bloodshed for either interest or sympathy. Walking to the office one morning soon after, I had a clue. I had been thinking of the American ship *Topaz*, and of what a surprise it must have been to the boatswain when with his crew he toiled up the path to the plateau, there to be greeted by that incredible colony. There must have been a feast, and while they were eating and afterward the white-bearded patriarch, Alex Smith, would surely have told the American sailors how they got there and of the fighting which almost wiped them out. He would have told only as much of the final tragedy as he could have seen before he was wounded, rolled up in the matting, and hidden by the women, and his telling of it would have been softened by time and by loyalty. If the boys related the story through his eyes it would hold warmth and a certain pathos." The suggestion worked, for that is exactly how Nordhoff and Hall wrote the story, despite Nordhoff's early misgivings.

The third part of the trilogy, the second to be published,

Men Against the Sea, wrote itself. Weeks thought it "a clear, cool little gem." The open-boat voyage of Bligh and eighteen of his loyal crew members was one of the marvels of survival; under the stern discipline and brilliant navigation of Bligh, the boat, eighteen feet at the keel and six at the beam, made it safely 3,600 miles across the South Pacific from Tofua in the Tonga Islands to Timor Island, the beginning of that long stretch of islands that lead toward Java and Sumatra. All that Nordhoff and Hall had to work from was their photostats of Bligh's log which they had from the Admiralty; but, wisely, they chose the surgeon Thomas Ledeward as the person from whose eyes to tell the story, for they felt he would be most aware of the physical and psychical changes in the captain and the crew.

The five years of work on the *Bounty* trilogy from 1929 to 1934 undeniably produced a triple success in the literature of adventure. But they were also a success in other less public, less triumphant, but as significant, ways. And there was also failure, because if Hall had been willing, the failure probably could have been just as well a success. After *Falcons of France,* Nordhoff and Hall decided to write a play on the same story, the same themes of courage, patriotism, and liberty; based on a story, "The Messroom," which Hall had first fashioned, it became *The Empty Chair* as a play. Hall took the play to New York and looked for a producer. Play-readers liked it, but no producer could be found who would gamble on another war play. Then Hall's friend, the "traveling man" who had once tipped him in Grinnell with a volume of Francis Thompson's poems—James Curtis, said he was willing to be the "angel." But Hall turned him down. Hall wrote to Ellery Sedgwick, explaining, "The public appetite for war plays seemed to be jaded, and much as I should like to see our play put on, I could not bring myself to accept Jim Curtis's generous offer to back it. I felt that he would not have an even break for his money, so I talked him out of the business. I had a hard time persuading him to withdraw. It was really an amusing situation: there was he more than willing to go ahead, and actually urging me to let him do it; and there was I talking against my own interests! The worst of it was that I was by no means persuaded that the play would not succeed. Perhaps it would have made a real 'hit.' But my reasoned judgment said 'No,' and I am glad that I remained firm in my decision. If the play had been put on and had failed, Curtis would have stood to lose $15,000 or $20,000, and although he assured me that he could easily afford to lose that amount, I would have felt very badly had he done so, and so, I am sure, would Nordy."

This decision was curiously like Hall. That great prime mover in human affairs—financial and personal gain—did not enter into his life. And, even more curiously, he could have used the money that a hit on Broadway might have brought in. Almost all the money earned on *Falcons* was fast disappearing, draining away like water from a hole in a drinking bag, to medical bills. Conrad Lafcadio Hall, now four years old, had developed a very bad case of amoebic dysentery; Hall had brought him to the Mayo Clinic for observation. The doctors there were skeptical: if the case was not incurable, it would take a long time before it could be cured, and they discouraged the boy's continued living in Tahiti. This blow was crushing to Hall, for now he knew there would always have to be large sums of money readily available to him for Connie. Discouraged, Hall returned with his son to Tahiti.

Perhaps in its inexplicable way, adversity for James Norman Hall put the necessary cutting edge on his craftsmanship, the necessary motivation for a disciplined control of his time. In any case, he was working now as he had never worked before, at his typewriter alone or with Nordhoff at seven o'clock every morning. And honors started accruing to Hall. His short story, "Fame for Mr. Beatty," was selected by O'Brien as one of the *Best Short Stories of 1929;* and two of his manuscripts had been accepted by Houghton Mifflin for publication in the same year, 1930: a story about his prisoner-of-war experience and escape in the war, called *Flying with Chaucer;* and a delightful children's book, *Mother Goose Land.*

Children had always fascinated Hall, and now that he had children of his own he was more fascinated than ever by their wonderful world of play and imagination. Sarah had delivered a stillborn daughter in 1928, to their great grief, but two years later she delivered a fat and lovely daughter, Nancy Ella, who because of her lively and engaging personality forever won her father's heart from the cradle. Hall was the perfect father. He genuinely liked to bathe the children and get them ready for bed; before dinner in the evening, he liked to take them, singing songs the while, for walks to the lagoon beach, to one-tree hill, to the top of the hill behind the Hall house, or take them for rides on his bicycle; and most of all, when they were tucked in bed and ready for sleep, he liked to tell them his own original stories—"Mr. Littlewant and Mr. Troublefinger," "The Heiress," "Captain Nickelmagnet and the Gangsters," and "The Rise of Professor Atwater." His favorite, and the childrens', was his story, in rhyme, about the journey which the little boy Roger Avery took on the back of Mr. Leonard's cow —which was really the cow that jumped over the moon!

Like Hall, Nordhoff also liked children, but in a different way. Although the view of Nordhoff that he liked nature more than human nature had validity, it applied more to adult human nature than to children. And although Nordhoff was naturally aloof and distant, he was nevertheless warm and loving toward children, his children in particular. By 1927 he had four children; his last, a son after three daughters, Charles Bernard, Jr., had been born in late 1927. No boy ever won his father's heart the way young Charles did: in the son Nordhoff saw himself as he had looked as a child: curly blond hair, glowing blue eyes, and golden skin. And further to his credit, the child had the buoyant spirit and lively manner of his Tahitian mother. Little Charles grew up sturdy, healthy, and playful; for his third birthday, Nordhoff bought him a little toy car with a rubber horn, and when he came home from working at Hall's, his son would happily sound the horn and jump up and down greeting his father. When he was three and a half, young Charles developed a pimple high on the bridge of his nose at the base of his forehead. Vahine, thinking nothing of it, simply squeezed it between her fingers and cleaned it with a cloth. Infection soon set in, immediately attacked the brain, and before a doctor could be called, the child was dead. Nordhoff was struck dumb with grief. He hurled recriminations upon his wife, he glowered with anger. He was bent on revenge. He went to his room, closed the door, and in the next four hours, slowly and grimly, he drank. The death of the child had begun the disintegration of the marriage.

Nordhoff never fully recovered from the death of his first son. But, an aristocrat to the end, an impeccable gentleman whose good manners sometimes proceeded, like Scott's Saladin, from "a high sense of what should be expected from himself, rather than what was due to others," he, nevertheless, never revealed his emotions. His trips to Harrison Smith's now were more frequent than before; just the presence of a fellow Harvard man provided solace. Nordhoff, whose imperial manner and psychic distance made him enormously attractive to women, now, like a *seigneur* exercising his *droit,* deigned to return the compliment. And now Hall, anxious to finish an old project, or get started on a new one, would wait for Nordhoff to come to work.

One afternoon toward dusk, Hall came out of his study onto the veranda to find some matches. He carried a book and had inserted a forefinger between its pages to mark his place. He wanted to smoke a cigarette, badly. Sitting in one of the bamboo chairs, with his back to him, was Nordhoff. "This is a happy surprise," Hall said. "When did you come?"

"Two hours ago." Nordhoff was dressed in a suit of white drill.

"And you've been waiting all this time?" Hall asked. He lit his cigarette and pulled deeply at it, inhaling.

"It doesn't matter. I've had a pleasant afternoon on your veranda." A half-empty glass stood on the small end table at his elbow, and beside it a quart of Scotch, almost empty. On Nordhoff's lap an opened book lay, pages down.

Hall saw the bottle of Scotch and said nothing; Nordhoff was always welcome to whatever he had, and as long as he had it. Hall noticed the book. "What have you been reading?"

Nordhoff picked up the book. "Robert Frost's poems. This volume seemed to bow itself into my hand as though it expected to be taken from the shelf."

Hall quoted from memory:

> "My sorrow, when she's here with me,
> Thinks these dark days of autumn rain
> As beautiful as days can be;
> She loves the bare, the withered tree;
> She walks the sodden pasture lane. . . .

Did you read that?" he asked eagerly. "And 'Going for Water,' and 'Storm Fear'?"

"I like 'Mowing' better than the ones you name," Nordhoff said laconically, without enthusiasm.

"Read it aloud, will you?" Hall quashed out his cigarette.

Nordhoff read clearly and distinctly, without a stumble:

> "There was never a sound beside the wood but one,
> And that was my long scythe whispering to the ground.
> What was it it whispered? I knew not well myself;
> Perhaps it was something about the heat of the sun,
> Something, perhaps, about the lack of sound—
> And that was why it whispered and did not speak.
> It was no dream or the gift of idle hours,
> Or easy gold at the hand of fay or elf;
> Anything more than the truth would have seemed too weak
> To the earnest love that laid the swale in rows,
> Not without feeble-pointed spikes of flowers
> (Pale orchises), and scared a bright green snake.
> The fact is the sweetest dream that labour knows.
> My long scythe whispered and left the hay to make."

Hall liked Nordhoff's reading. "Only Frost could have written that," Hall said to his friend. "How well it satisfies his definition of a complete poem: 'Where an emotion has found its thought and the thought has found its words.'"

Nordhoff agreed. "'The fact is the sweetest dream that labour knows.' That is what all scythes whisper to the ground, and all men to themselves, in thought and action, as long as they have breath in their bodies."

"You believe it, then?" Hall wanted to know, for certain.

"Don't you?"

Hall slouched in his chair and crossed his legs. "The perfect saying of it in this case seems to make it valid," he said. "But the facts that labour knows are not the only ones, nor do they necessarily give rise to the sweetest dreams."

"Now what do you mean by that?" Nordhoff asked, a slight scowl on his face.

Hall laughed quietly. "Precisely what the words import," he said. "But men will never see alike in this matter, fortunately so, for us idle ones. Let those who must, mow, and take pleasure at evening in the fact of their labour and its accomplishment. Let the others who wish to—there are not many of them —sit idly by, watch their own fields of uncut grass ruffled to a deeper, richer green by the summer breeze, and dappled by the shadows of clouds. They have their own pleasure and profit, as great, in degree, perhaps, as that of the mowers, in the indisputable fact of their idleness."

"This kind of nonsense is what comes of rambling in the hills so often." Nordhoff frowned. "I suppose that's what you have been doing all day?"

"Yes," Hall admitted. "I went far up the Haapapé plateau to that highest point you can just make out from the road. From there you can see Mount Orofena from base to peak. It is the most beautiful spot on all Tahiti, and except for myself and a few natives who pass that way to gather *fei*, no one goes there from one year's end to another."

Nordhoff admitted a curiosity. "How wide a view do you have from that point?" he asked.

Hall double-crossed his legs and lit another cigarette. "You should visit the place yourself, sometime. Now and then I can make out your boat, and although you are miles offshore, you seem to be creeping along just beyond the barrier reef. I see the rotundity of the earth. In the imagination I visit thousands of islands scattered over the downward slopes of the Pacific."

"How do you occupy your time on these all-day excursions?" Nordhoff seemed impatient about his friend's idleness. "What do you think about?"

"For part of the time, of nothing at all." Hall held out his Camel and stared at its burning tip. "I have acquired the habit of reverie. I can sit for a half hour, even longer, lost in what I can only call a dreamless dream—a waking trance that seems as deep as the sky itself. What passes over the surface of consciousness disturbs it no more than cloud reflections stir the depths of the lagoons. It is sensibility lying somewhere between that of animals and vegetables."

Sitting, listening to Hall, Nordhoff became concerned, paternalistic. "Has it ever occurred to you," he said in a flat straight rhythm, "that the habit of reverie might be a dangerous one to cultivate? Even on an island in the mid-Pacific you must keep some contact with the workaday world. You have your living to earn. The worst possible preparation for that, it seems to me, is to sit on the slope of a mountain dreaming dreamless dreams."

"Dangerous? On the contrary!" Hall countered. "The time is coming, I believe, when men will turn back to a simpler, ampler, more wholesome way of living. They will not fear to do some vegetating. They will seek wisdom from Henry Thoreau rather than Henry Ford, and will refuse to be cheated longer of leisure, the most precious of all gifts."

"Leisure!" Nordhoff stood up from his chair. "How many people want it? Thousands who might have it refuse to accept it on any terms. They travel frantically from one place to another, from one distraction to another, from one war to another, in order to escape this boon. Some have more than is good for them, and so they cultivate the habit of reverie." Nordhoff started slowly pacing the veranda floor.

"I am not alone in thinking it worth cultivating," Hall said. "Let me read you a passage from an article written by a hardheaded professor of economics. How, he asks, is a man to bring order and peace into his own life, however chaotic the spiritual and social conditions around him may be? This is one of the suggestions, and as it is the concluding one it was evidently considered of importance:

And one thing more let him learn: to be still—to sit or walk alone, say, an occasional half-hour, not thinking, not reading, with mind and body as quiet as he can make them. Let him practice this stillness, persevering (for this is difficult) night and morning, until he have its secret. And all for the sake of the adventure, to see what would come of it, with no guarantee that anything would come of it except boredom.

Nordhoff stopped at the wide doorway leading into the veranda from the steps outside. "And boredom is all that would come of it," he said, turning to leave, "in ninety cases out of a hundred." He started down the stairs. "Certainly," he said over his shoulder to Hall, who had got up to see him off, "that would be the result in my own case." Nordhoff waved from the landing. "I'll see you in the morning!" he said, smiling, and walked off into the shadows.

9
Rise and Fall

For every year of his life after he had first read the book on a bench in the Boston Common, James Norman Hall reread Joseph Conrad's *Lord Jim*. In that novel he found himself dissected, laid to view for his full examination. What intrigued him most about Conrad's hero was Lord Jim's inability to distinguish between himself as he was and himself as he imagined that self to be—the eternal dichotomy between appearance and reality—summed up in Jim's answer at the court of inquiry, quoted by Marlow when Jim was asked why he abandoned ship and left hundreds of Moslem passengers deserted on a storm-wracked ship: " 'I had jumped . . .' he checked himself and averted his gaze . . . 'it seems.' "

"Men need to discover themselves," Hall said to Nordhoff one day after working on the first few chapters of *The Hurricane,* as they both drank Bourbon old-fashioneds left for them in the icebox by Sarah. "Nothing could be better as a preparation than to learn to sit quietly, the mind fallow, the habitual nervous tension relaxed."

"How many men want to discover themselves?" Nordhoff asked, falling by habit and disposition into the opposing point of view of any discussion. "We already know too much to wish to make further explorations."

"I disagree," Hall said. "The trouble is that we know too little: that is why we think so meanly of ourselves. If we go far enough . . ."

"Into mysticism, I suppose?" Nordhoff said, cynically.

"Well," Hall replied, unruffled, "even our physicists and astronomers are beginning to acknowledge the necessity for mysticism. It surprises me that they have been so long in making the discovery. It is a pity that there are no secular establishments where the harassed and distracted Protestant man of our day may go into retreat, as the Catholics do. He might learn there how best to meet the soul-killing conditions under which most men have to live. If I had a fortune I would found such houses, and they would be free to all who cared to use them."

Nordhoff smiled at his friend's impracticality. "You would have plenty of applicants for free board and lodging," he said, "but none for spiritual refreshment. . . . But, to come back to Tahiti, is that why you stay on here, year after year: because you love solitude so much?"

"One doesn't have to come so far as this to find solitude," Hall answered calmly. "I love a circumscribed world, small enough to be comprehended at a glance, so to speak, and yet large enough to offer a certain amount of variety. And I like isolation made tangible by thousands of miles of ocean stretching away on every side. Here I have become more and more aware of the 'uncovenanted society' that Mr. Santayana speaks of in one of his essays. Wait—let me find the passage." Hall got up from his desk and walked to the wall of books on the other side of the room.

Nordhoff admired Hall's collection. It ran into the thousands of volumes, neatly stacked on shelves, by author, alphabetically, along the four sides of the room. "I was glancing through your library this afternoon," he commented. "What a picture of yourself these bookshelves offer! A stranger, examining them, would be able to conjure you up: the portrait of a man deduced from his library."

Hall demurred. "It would not be a good likeness. Many volumes that I highly prize are not to be found here."

"Suppose you had to choose ten books to suffice you for the rest of your life?" Nordhoff challenged Hall. "What ones would you select? I mean, from those now on your shelves?"

Hall would not be goaded. "Could you make an offhand choice in such a matter?" He pulled a volume from the shelf.

"Well," Nordhoff said, "put it this way: If you had to make a choice tonight, which ten would you most regret leaving behind?"

"We'll talk of that another time," Hall said. "This is the passage from Santayana. It concludes an essay called 'Cross Lights':

> There is an uncovenanted society of spirits, like that of the morning stars singing together, or of all the larks at once in the sky; it is a happy accident of freedom and a conspiracy of solitudes. When people talk together, they are at once entangled in a mesh of instrumentalities, irrelevance, misunderstanding, vanity and propaganda; and all to no purpose, for why should creatures become alike who are different? But when minds, being naturally akin and each alone in its heaven, soliloquize in harmony, saying compatible things only because their hearts are similar, then society is friendship in the spirit; and the unison of many thoughts twinkles happily in the night across the void of separation.

Nordhoff seemed nettled; it was frequently a rhetorical device he used to provoke discussion. "You are always quoting Santayana, and I am conscious of a feeling of irritation whenever you do. He lacks robustness. Don't you think so, yourself? I wish that he would break out, once in a while, in a bit of good, wholesome, earthy vulgarity."

"If that is wanted"—Hall's Puritanism was unshakable—"there are writers and to spare where it may be found. But what do you think of the idea expressed here?"

"That sort of companionship is too ethereal for my taste," Nordhoff confessed. "I prefer actual companionship, the presence in the flesh of other men I can see and hear and touch with my physical senses; men who emit their forces of attraction or repulsion as I do mine. The communion of spirit with spirit across a void of separation—no, no! Give me two or three companions sitting around a table with a couple of bottles of Scotch before them. What if we do become somewhat entangled in a mesh of vanity and propaganda? That is because we are human. Conversation will only crackle and sparkle the more. Don't you agree?"

"Of course," Hall did agree. "I thoroughly enjoy such conversations, but they are on a different plane from those Mr. Santayana has in mind here. Both kinds are desirable."

"Give me my kind for a steady diet," Nordhoff grumbled.

"And yet"—Hall now took up the offensive—"how many times I have heard you say that you like your friends better at a distance, and that you enjoy their companionship most when you see them least. Have your actual friends ever brought you the pleasure you find through books, or music? I doubt it. They disappoint you and you them. That is why friendship in the spirit is so often to be preferred to such friendship in the flesh as chance puts in one's way. Chance distributes its favors with such a lack of discrimination. In the matter of friendships, more than likely the ones you receive are not at all the ones you should have had, or would have chosen for yourself. Therefore, one falls back gladly, of necessity, upon this uncovenanted society." Hall sat down in one of the easy chairs, in the corner beside a side table and lamp, closed the Santayana and put it on the table.

Nordhoff got up and slowly paced the floor. "But you needn't have come all the way to Tahiti to enjoy its privileges. You might have done that just as well in the U.S.A."

"Perhaps," Hall agreed. "But what of yourself?" he riposted quickly. "If you so greatly enjoy friends within reaching distance, why do you live in a place where there is so little choice?"

"The matter of friendship has nothing to do with it," Nordhoff replied. "A man will, usually, find a few congenial souls wherever he goes. I live here because I like a tropical climate, fishing in tropical waters, and going to seed slowly and pleasantly."

Hall was surprised. "You think one does go to seed here?"

"I know it!" Nordhoff thumped his foot on the floor as he stepped out to turn. "Consider our own cases as examples. We are neither of us anything like as alert, mentally, as we were only a few years back. We used to have quite interesting conversations—do you remember? We discussed everything under the sun and agreed upon nothing. Now when we have a difference of opinion it is usually only a temporary one. We dislike the mental effort necessary to sustain a disagreement; so one or the other of us is sure to say: 'Perhaps . . . yes, I suppose you are right,' and that ends it. More often than not we gossip like a pair of old native women, rather than talk. We discuss island personalities and the small change of island happenings. Or, too lazy to get together, I sit on my veranda in Punaauia, and you on yours, in Arué, each of us in a pleasant stupor, streaked through with sluggish musings. Days pass, each one like the day preceding. We are under the illusion that time is standing still for us, but if you pause to reflect . . ."

Hall interrupted: "And what more agreeable illusion could one be under?" he said. "How many men would envy us the possession of it."

Nordhoff was somewhat peeved. "Allow me to finish," he asked. "If you pause to reflect, you will realize that this is the result of the monotony of our lives. Where there is no variety of happenings from one month to the next, a year slips by before you are aware that it is well begun. You flatter yourself that you have acquired, through effort, the habit of reverie. No effort was needed. You were merely going through the same process of decay experienced by all white men after a certain number of years in such a tropical backwater. It is an inevitable process. The island has put its stamp on both of us. I'm surprised that you haven't the wit to see it."

"Why don't you fly, then?" Hall countered. "Why don't you try to save yourself, before the disintegrating process has been carried too far?"

"I have just said that I enjoy going to seed." Nordhoff would not be put down. "I am clear-sighted enough to realize what is happening, but I don't care; I don't in the least object. I am now in my forty-seventh year. Thus far I have had as wide an experience of life as a man could wish. I have learned many things and unlearned many. I have arrived, by hard thinking, at various conclusions with respect to the meaning of life and man's place in the universe; more particularly, my own place. By hard thinking I have discarded, in turn, these conclusions. I shall form no new ones. I no longer care whether or not there is meaning in life, or whether I am entitled to a place in the cosmical scheme. I have now had the place for a considerable number of years, and in view of that fact I can well afford to be content. Fly from Tahiti? For what reason? And where to?"

Hall spoke softly. "You might go home," he said, reached up, and turned on the light against the encroaching dusk.

Nordhoff became more spirited. "What chance would I have to go to seed there?" he asked. "I should not be permitted to. I should be bribed or forced out of my quite natural inclination to go downhill. I should be driven uphill to the very end, and so cheated out of my birthright to an agreeable old age. And think of the freedom of a special kind one has here: freedom from the influence of the mass mind, with its intolerance, its disregard for minority rights and opinions, its profound belief in material progress, and that science will, ultimately, solve all the riddles of the universe. It is impossible for the individual, living within the scope of this mighty influence, not to be affected by it."

"But," Hall persisted, "have you no desire ever to live at home again?"

"Why do you say 'at home'?" Nordhoff asked. "Isn't Tahiti home to you after all these years?"

"No!" Hall replied flatly. "And that, to me, is the chief disadvantage of living here. All my roots are still in America, in the prairie country of the Middle West. I realize now that it is useless trying to grub them up to transplant on this little island. They won't come up. The other night I wrote some verses on my unfortunate situation. Would you care to hear them?"

"Why are would-be poets always wanting to quote their verses to their friends?" Nordhoff sat down in an easy chair.

"Because they need an audience of at least one person. This poem isn't long, only four stanzas." Hall walked over to his desk and picked up the sheet of manuscript.

"Go ahead, then."

"I have called it 'Thoughts in Exile':

Inclination, Chance, and Need
Demanded that the tree should go.
The stubborn roots would not be freed.
'No!' they said, and always, 'No!'

The tree, to end an argument
That would not, could not be resolved,
Said good-bye to roots, and went,
Careless of the risk involved.

Sap there was in every cell;
Leaves and branches seemed content.
Said trunk, 'I'm doing very well
Without my roots,' and on it went.

But roots had greater hardihood;
Dreams were wafted through the air
To find and nourish, as they could,
A tree with all its branches bare."

"I am surprised that you feel that way about it," Nordhoff said calmly. "I came to Tahiti taproots and all, and they are now comfortably embedded here. Nevertheless, I realize that I am an exotic plant and must suffer the consequences of the change of habitat. My growth here has been sickly, but my decay will, I believe, be luxurious and slow."

Hall was disappointed in his friend, in his pessimism. "You talk as though you were already on the threshold of old age," he said.

"And so I am," Nordhoff quickly replied. "I mean to depart from the practice of most men of our years. They cling to the fiction that they are vigorous youngsters until, at the age of forty-five or thereabout, the fact that they have long been middle-aged is forced upon them. Then they persist in being middle-aged until they are ready to topple into their graves, crowding their old age into a scant year or two."

"Yes," Hall had to agree, "so we do, most of us."

"But consider my happy prospect," Nordhoff continued. "I may have thirty, even forty years to spend in this pleasant old man's garden. I shall have time to enjoy to the full an old man's pleasures. I shall read old books and care nothing about the new ones. I needn't try to keep abreast of the world. My fishing will keep me healthy in body, and the humdrum existence we live here will keep me tranquil in mind. . . . But I'd better be going. It's quite dark already."

"Yes," Hall teased, "old men should keep early hours."

Nordhoff opened the French doors, stepped out on the veranda, and walked over to the open side facing outside. "I never go to bed later than nine thirty," he said, Hall following him out. "What a glorious night! Look at those coconut palms against the sky!"

"Wait till I light the lamp," Hall said. "I will show you down to the road. Mind the second step! There's a board loose."

"Oh, the decay," Nordhoff said, "the decay, in houses and men, in this humid tropical climate!" He shook his head. "Well, good night, my son."

"Good night," Hall replied. "Sleep well, Father."

Hall turned and walked back to his study, there to consider again a chapter he had been working on in the new book. On top of his desk he found some pages of manuscript not his own; they were folded lengthwise in half. He opened them. It was a poem by Nordhoff. When Hall read it—it was called "Saved by the Durian!"—he chuckled and laughed over its humor about a plant that restored sexual potency to old men. There was that side to Nordhoff, he reflected, which few men knew. Hall laughed again. What a delightful poem! And what a wonderful portrait of the Skipper as The Man from Borneo, with his Durian tree! Hall knew about the Durian, having watched it grow at Smith's arboretum; but, even if the plant did have such rejuvenescent properties, he for one could not stand the terrible stink of it.

Hall picked up the first chapter of *The Hurricane* and re-moved the paper clip holding the pages together. He looked again at the first paragraph; Nordhoff had written it. He al-ways wrote the beginning and end of all their stories.

Like the opening of an organ prelude—Lord, how Nordhoff could write!—the paragraph set the magic and enchantment of the story, and the basis for the later violence:

> Scattered over a thousand miles of ocean in the eastern tropical Pacific, below the Equator, lies a vast collection of coral islands extending in a general northwesterly, southeasterly direction across ten degrees of latitude. Seventy-eight atolls, surf-battered dykes of coral, enclosing lagoons, make up this barrier to the steady westward roll of the sea. Some of the lagoons are scarcely more than salt-water ponds; others like *those of* [Hall underlined the words] Rangiroa and Fakarava, are as much as fifty miles long by twenty or thirty across. The *motu,* or islets, composing the land, are threaded at wide inter-vals on the encircling reef. The smaller ones are frequented by sea fowl which nest in the pandanus trees and among the fronds of scattered coconut palms. Others, enchantingly green and restful to sea-weary eyes, follow the curve of the reef for many miles, sloping away over the arc of the world until they are lost to view. But whatever their extent, one feature is com-mon to all: they are mere fringes of land seldom more than a quarter of a mile in width, and rising only a few feet above the sea which seems always on the point of overwhelming them.

Hall chuckled to himself. How they had fought that morn-ing over the words *those of* in the third sentence! Hall had insisted that the two words were necessary for meaning; Nord-hoff, equally adamant, wanted them removed as verbiage. Hall held out, at least for the time being; *those of,* he argued, indicated that Rangiroa and Fakarava were *not* lagoons, but atolls *with lagoons.* "What does it matter?" Nordhoff had said. "Atolls are 99 per cent lagoons anyway." Hall insisted; the two words stayed in.

Hall continued to read what they had written for the first

chapter; that day they had passed it back and forth, crossing out, adding, crossing out again, rewriting entire passages, at least twenty times. He looked at two paragraphs which had been particularly difficult; tomorrow no one would be able to tell who had written what. Remembering now, Hall left Nordhoff's as they were and underlined those he had written:

"Reality!" exclaimed the younger man. "When I leave this place I shall find it hard to believe that the island exists at all. I scarcely know why, but even more than Africa this disquiets me, puts me on the defensive. On such crumbs of land man seems so helpless—so hopelessly, microscopically small. Tropical jungles are bad enough, but nature typified by such an ocean . . . it is too powerful. It numbs the imagination."

"But nature is powerful, my dear Vernier! I know: we try to forget it, and at home, where we herd together, thousands to the square mile, we very nearly succeed. But all our efforts to thwart her, to harness her, must come to nothing in the end."

Hall looked at the results and was immensely pleased. His and Nordhoff's styles, like iron alloyed to steel, had completely fused into one strong distinctive style which was neither one's in particular but belonged to both of them.

After the first chapter, the story went well. And for the next few months Nordhoff wrote eight of them; Hall, seven. And, like the first, they both worked on the last chapter. Then Nordhoff concluded with the epilogue. Interestingly, the idea for the *Hurricane* story had come from a Dr. Williams in Tahiti who had told Hall about a boy who had been imprisoned for stealing a chicken, had escaped, and became a hunted man for most of the rest of his life. When Hall told Nordhoff the story, Nordhoff seemed only slightly interested. "Charles Selden," Nordhoff said, cryptically.

"What?" Hall did not understand.

"Don't you remember?" Nordhoff said. "After *Falcons,* I wanted to put Charles Selden through another adventure—a hurricane."

"Yes. But . . ." Hall was still uncomprehending.

"Let's put this native boy through a hurricane, down in the

Tuamotus. And in it let's have him save someone dear to the police official who is hunting him. The conflict between love and duty."

"Wonderful!" Hall said. "It's a great idea! Let's work up a chapter outline."

They dedicated *The Hurricane* to Edward Weeks, the *Atlantic* editor who had been of so much help to them since they had reactivated their partnership; he, they often admitted between themselves, kept the firm of Nordhoff and Hall going. The book was a great success, and like *Men Against the Sea* and *Pitcairn's Island,* it was serialized in *The Saturday Evening Post.* And, as with *Bounty,* Hollywood was quick to buy it up. With the money, Nordhoff bought more property in Puna-auia and on the isthmus of Taravao; Hall, more cautiously, as he had with the royalties from the *Bounty* trilogy, added to the trust fund he had set up with the New England Trust Company in Boston.

Five best sellers in a row, after so many years of difficulty, firmly established Nordhoff and Hall as writers of the front rank. Now, among the stellar singularities in the literary heavens they had become, like Castor and Pollux, the Gemini of first magnitude. After years of frustration and anxiety, of diffidence and even despair, Hall was now at peace with himself. "Serenity colors his personality," said James McConnaughey, a young newspaperman visiting from the States, of Hall. This serenity went before Hall, announcing him to all who met him, and it made for inner happiness for the rest of his life. He had at last become the writer he had always hoped he was, and he could now live with himself and with others very well indeed.

Hall's wife and children worshiped him, loving him as he loved them, greatly. With part of the royalty money he built a newer and bigger beach house, with wide, open sides and a thatched roof; and he bought the hill behind the main house, from the top of which he could see Matavai Bay where Bligh had first dropped anchor in his search of breadfruit. Hall bought hundreds of more books for the bookshelves in his study, and many more record albums for his music collection in the beach house. At the beach house, after dinner in the evening and on Sunday, he would dance with his loving wife Lala, pumping his arm up and down in the old-fashioned way, and with Nancy Ella—he called her "Midge"—when she was older. One Sunday while they listened to the opening bars of the radio program, "The Firestone Hour," he swept Nancy Ella into his arms, and as they waltzed around the floor, he sang to her:

> "A garden sweet
> A garden small
> A garden just the size
>   for Nancy Hall."

And, often, instead of reading in the afternoon, he would listen to a Beethoven symphony, concerto, or sonata; or a waltz, mazurka, or étude by Chopin. But more often than to Beethoven or Chopin, or to Brahms, Debussy, or Mozart, would he listen to Anton Dvořák's *New World Symphony,* which, like Conrad's *Lord Jim* in literature, said something personal to Hall which he always wanted to hear.

Frequently there were family picnics up on the top of the hill behind the house; and after they ate, the whole family would pitch in to clear away brush and rocks, and to plant grass, coconut and banana trees, and the frangipani flower bushes. Once, on such an outing, Lala asked Hall to get her a green coconut from one of the trees, for she was thirsty and wanted a cool drink of coconut juice. Hall looked at her, amazed at her request. "You know I can't climb a coconut tree!" he said to her. "Of course you can," his wife said to him, as if he were a Tahitian native. The children joined the pleading. "Please, Daddy, try!" cried Nancy Ella, urging him on. Hall retied his sneakers to make them tight on his feet and went to a coconut tree that bent at an angle. He started to shinny up, using hands, arms, elbows, and feet, legs, thighs, and knees; then, getting to the bend in the tree, he went up on his hands and feet, letting them grab either side, just as he had seen the natives do a hundred times, and crawled out to the top end of the tree. Reaching the green nuts, he broke off three. The movement caused him to lose his balance, but he stretched out, grabbed with his two hands one of the palm frond branches, and as it bent down, he swung down with it; when it stopped, leaving him dangling ten feet in the air, he let go and fell to the ground. The children cheered. "You did it! You did it!" they cried. "You see, Jimmy Hall," Lala Hall said as she embraced him, "there are many things you can do that you didn't think you could do!"

Life in Arué for Hall was pleasant. In Punaauia, however, Nordhoff was having trouble of the keenest kind. Vahine, his wife, having known for a long time that her husband had been philandering with Tahitiennes, took on a lover in revenge; and proud and beautiful, to make the revenge sweeter, she selected as her paramour a young Tahitian native whom Nordhoff had recently hired as his chauffeur. Intolerable to Nordhoff was the way in which he discovered what had been going on. One of the children ran up to him to intercept him, one afternoon, for he had left Hall's earlier than expected at home. "Mamma's in bed with the chauffeur," the child told him. Nordhoff rushed home and took out his pistol, which he kept in the dining-room cabinet. He opened the bedroom door and almost fired point-blank, had he not looked and seen that Vahine's lover had fled. Nordhoff desperately fought back the emotions building up in him. "I am getting a divorce," he said to Vahine, speaking tightly and quickly between clenched teeth. He turned and walked out of the house, never to return.

It was a blow from which Nordhoff never recovered. His pride, imperial and aloof, polite and distant, especially where women were concerned, had been irreparably damaged. He immediately moved in with one of the caretakers of Harrison Smith's property. Angry and defiant, he said to the caretaker: "I will get myself a regular bush Kanaka! No more half-castes for me—ever!"

Word of Nordhoff's breakup with Vahine, and the cause, soon reached Hall by the rumor vine, called in Tahiti the "coconut radio." Fortunately, Sarah told it to him. He was shattered by the news. "This could destroy Nordy!" He paused in his thinking, then turned suddenly on Lala: "If you tell anybody about Nordy and Vahine's trouble," he said to her, "I'll beat you—and I've never beaten a woman in my life."

10
By Nordhoff & Hall
and by Hall

The partnership of Nordhoff and Hall was now at a critical turning point. It would either have to disband, or Hall would have to assume its direction. Hall took control. "I think Nordy would wish me to say," Edward Weeks said, referring to this stage in the firm he helped, if not to found, then to maintain, "that in this collaboration after *The Hurricane* he deferred more and more of the work to Hall. Jim never mentioned this to me but I could tell from our correspondence that it was so."

In 1936 Nordhoff and Hall were both forty-nine years old. Success had come late, but it came. Hall had two children; Nordhoff had seven. That year had been a strange one for both of them. It had provided at last the financial security that each needed to be able to work in peace and with equanimity; and at the same time, as if at the provocation of the gods who cannot tolerate human happiness, Nordhoff's life was torn by domestic strife, and Hall's by the ill health of his son and later in the year, his own.

Hall woke up one morning, and as usual washed and shaved, went outside to husk a coconut, scraped its meat, and made some milk for his breakfast. He ate and went into his study. When he sat down at his typewriter and raised his hands to the keys, he was horror-struck at what he saw: his hands had swollen; his fingers were like sausages. His hands started to shake, as if palsied. Hall paled. He thought he had come down with his father's illness—Parkinson's disease. Although frightened, he told no one but Lala and Nordhoff. Fortunately, Nordhoff told the Skipper, and Smith told Sedgwick. Together Hall's family and friends urged him to do something about his condition. Sedgwick wrote to Smith: "I did not know that Hall was in bad health. Of course, I realize that he does not know how to manage his life. He will put his money into some local bank or lose it in some unwise investment. And he will take a chance in regard to a doctor. . . . If there is any real physical trouble with him, we *must* do something about it. He has just won pretty complete terrestrial happiness, and if it is now to be sacrificed by illness it will be something to grieve over." Then referring to both Nordhoff and Hall, he added: "I really care very much for the boys' happiness."

Smith answered: "Hall just has been taking a set of inoculation treatments for the filariasis and slight elephantiasis which he undoubtedly has. For some months he has had occasional swelling of one leg and foot with the fever which here usually precedes the swelling. . . . Anyway Hall is now completing the treatment and seems to have benefited. But he looks thin, and in need of a general physical over-hauling. . . . What a strange man Hall is! Willing to face machine guns but apparently unwilling to face a doctor, to face the facts of his own body. . . .

"After all, I think Hall is really taking better care of himself than he used to. The fact of starting again on the course of inoculations is a good sign; he is now free of financial worries; he is as happily married as anyone I ever knew; he has a very nice house—to my mind the most attractive on the island; he is beginning to protect himself against the mosquitoes outside of his house which is all screened. Our present concern need be only about the beginnings of these preventable diseases, or controllable diseases which could spoil so much of the happiness that Hall deserves."

In April Hall sailed with his son Conrad to America, both of them to seek treatment. Connie for his chronic colitis and Jim for his filariasis. Hall took Conrad to doctors and hospitals for examination and treatment, first in San Diego, then in Los Angeles, leaving him for recuperation with Nordhoff's family in Santa Barbara; then he himself went to Boston, to consult with specialists at the Harvard Medical School. He stayed at the Parker House, visited with his good friends Winship, Greener, and Cushman, and generally enjoyed good health. But on May 26 he had a recurrence of chills and fever. He had lunched with Greener, had come back to the hotel and started to have chills. "I hopped into bed," he wrote to Lala, "and covered myself with blankets. Sure enough my old friend, *mariri*, was back for his fifth visit. My left leg got red, as usual. Dr. Liscoe and Dr. Strong of the Harvard School of Tropical Medicine say I must stay in bed for a week."

Hall in a few days started to feel better, and almost decided to keep traveling east, all the way around the world, to get back to Tahiti. But he soon changed his mind: "I am even more lonesome and homesick this time," he wrote to his wife, "than I was when I went East two years ago."

Also Nordhoff had written to him, telling him he was ready to start on a new book if they could decide on one of several ideas. Harrison Smith had offered them his house to work in, a place where both of them could get away from the infernal tourists with letters of introduction to them. Because of them, Nordhoff said, it would be hopeless to try to work any place else. Then he added that his private affairs were settled to his entire satisfaction. What he dreaded, he said to Hall, was airing the family linen in court. For in that case many things would become matters of record which he would prefer his children never to know.

Early in 1937 Hall returned to Tahiti, inspired to write two books, one with Nordhoff and one by himself. The one he did with Nordhoff was a book they both regretted having done;

and the book he did alone was the most brilliant book he ever wrote. In his research for the *Bounty* story, Hall had done a great deal of reading in eighteenth-century literature and as a result he acquired such a love for the style and the diction that had he had the choice of choosing a period in which to be reborn he would have undoubtedly selected the Age of Johnson. Hall's story, *Doctor Dogbody's Leg,* is without doubt one of the most delightful eighteenth-century stories ever written.

The joint-project story with Nordhoff, however, was one of forced labor. Written in San Diego, Santa Barbara, and San Francisco, it was more of a travelogue of Tahiti than a novel involving credible people in a believable story; it was more melodrama than drama, more pathetic than tragic, more picturesque than a picture of life. Ironically, they wrote the book specifically for the movies, but Hollywood turned it down. Nevertheless the story, called *Dark River,* was serialized in a slick magazine, sold reasonably well between hard covers, and earned them a good year's pay.

In the beginning of the year 1938 and almost immediately after the *Dark River* manuscript was dispatched to Boston, Hall proposed two stories to Nordhoff which he felt were natural for them to write together, one from an idea suggested by the Skipper. "What would happen," Smith had asked, "if a poor Tahiti family suddenly got rich?" The other was a First Fleet story, about the settlement of Botany Bay in Australia by British prisoners. Hall was tremendously enthusiastic and wanted to do the Tahiti story first; but Nordhoff, preoccupied with enervating personal matters, begged for a respite. Agreeing to the vacation, Hall sailed for America to see Conrad in California. Nordhoff, wasting in despair, wallowed in the excesses of drink and sex, and finally took on a full-blooded Tahitian mistress, Teuria, by whom he had three sons in three years, none of whom he legally recognized.

Nordhoff was in a terrible state, and as early as January 26, he was writing to Hall that he couldn't even write his name, let alone a book. Never before, he said, had he been in such a bad mental state. He couldn't sleep at night, hadn't set foot in his boat save twice in six weeks, but just sat in the house all day to sweat and shake. He couldn't even read; thinking the trouble might be drink, he stopped for two months without benefit; then he tried drink for two weeks, but also without benefit.

Trying to decide what was best for his family, Nordhoff sent Sarah, Rita, and Jane to live with his sister Mary in California, and left little daughter Miko, and Charles and James with their mother in Tahiti. Hall urged him to come to California and visit with him and with his family in Santa Barbara. He was in no condition to travel, Nordhoff answered Hall, and he did not want to visit his mother in his present state of depression and nerves. Come down to Tahiti in April, he urged Hall. Maybe by that time, he said, he would be in a better mental state, and able to work.

Hall, friend in affluence and adversity, was patient; he would wait, he told Nordhoff, until he was ready. Nordhoff replied, thanking Hall from the bottom of his heart for the way Hall had stood by him during the months past. Anything, Nordhoff said, he had ever been able to do for Hall in the past was canceled, and Hall now had a credit balance on Nordhoff's books which Hall would never be able to wipe out.

You will recollect the bad state you were in two or three years before your marriage, he reminded Hall; he was now, he said, the same way. He could not read, or write, or sleep soundly at night, or sit still by day. May God, he said, if there is One, bless the House of Hall.

Hall left his family in California and returned to Tahiti in the spring, and at Hall's house in Arué Nordhoff and Hall set up plans to work on *Out of Gas*. "As soon as Nordy and I start writing I won't have time to think about you so much," he wrote to Lala. "But I don't see how I can endure not having Nancy Ella here. And I'm sure that you would feel just as I do if you were here with no little Mischief coming home from school, or coming home from anywhere. Let's give up the plan of leaving her in America until, maybe, next year. If she goes to school there at nine it will be time enough."

The Tuttles of Tahiti story proved to be the most enjoyable and quickest work Nordhoff and Hall ever undertook together.

They took Jonas Tuttle, son of old Enoch Tuttle from New England, mixed in some of Harrison Smith's thrift and frugality, added generations of intermarriage with Tahitian women, and produced lazy but happy Polynesian lotus-eaters. The novel became an enormously successful magazine-movie-book-club package: serialized as "Out of Gas" by *The Saturday Evening Post;* filmed by MGM as "The Tuttles of Tahiti," and selected, but renamed by The Literary Guild as *No More Gas.*

For the Australian *Botany Bay* novel, however, Nordhoff had all but lost interest; he didn't want to do it. Hall, thinking a visit to the scene might change his collaborator's mind, convinced Nordhoff into making a field trip to Sydney to do some on-the-spot research, but Nordhoff returned to Tahiti more dispirited about the project than ever. Sydney, he reported to Hall, covered the whole locale of their story; the modern city buried the old; there was nothing left to interest them. But Nordhoff, knowing what Hall would want, brought back old maps, sketches, books, and articles about the period of the settlement. Hall studied these materials for months, became by them more inspired than ever, and started writing by himself. Then, surprisingly, Hollywood heard about the work in progress, became immediately interested, and started negotiating. Paramount, the highest bidder, bought the movie rights.

Nordhoff, when he heard the news about the Hollywood offer, was recovering from a night at The Lafayette, the night club in Tahiti that opened when the others closed and stayed open until dawn. He had done the tamure with Ina Rapa, the girl with the most beautiful body in Tahiti; Nordhoff in a wild and drunken fury was utterly provoked. Ina, seduced by the music and the rhythm, had ripped off her pareu and danced naked and rippling to the delight of all. The next morning, rising on an elbow and blinking at the message from Hall, Nordhoff decided to help Hall write the story.

At the beginning of the summer the plot outline had been almost worked out and the chapters tentatively assigned. Hall wrote to Lala, "Nordy and I are hard at work. He has his lunches here. We are not ready to start writing but expect to

very soon. We want to be certain that we have the story properly outlined before we set our typewriters to clicking. I feel
very happy just now because Nordy and I are getting on so fast
with our work. I really believe that *Botany Bay* is going to be
our best book yet. Nordy now has little Mary [Miko] and
Charlie at his house and Vahine has Jimmy. Nordy feels much
happier now that he has two of his children with him. Home
seems more like home to him."

To Conrad and Nancy Ella, Hall gave some parental advice:
"Sonny, try not to tease Nancy *too* much. And my sweet Mischief, remember what I said to do if Conrad does tease you.
Pretend that you love teasing more than anything; that you
really dote on being teased. Then you will see how soon Conrad will get tired of it."

Hall was now working steadily with Nordhoff, each turning
out about four pages every day, and by the middle of summer
they had almost finished the new book. Every evening after
work and after Nordhoff had left, Hall would stroll about the
outside of his house, check the grass, shrubbery, and trees. It
was now July and the poinsettias and bougainvillea were all in
bloom; both were very gay and pretty, he thought, against the
green of the house. Then he would go to the woodshed by the
old mango tree out behind the house and start sawing and
chopping wood, adding to the neatly stacked cords of wood
against the house. It was the perfect way for him to relax from
the weariness of mind and soreness of body from writing; he
would work up a fine sweat, then have a shower, dress, and go
sit on the front veranda, there to sip a rum punch and watch
dusk fall. He was content. In the morning mail he had received a statement from the Banque de l'Indo-Chine in Papeete: he had a balance of 45,000 francs. Soon, he knew, he
would get a second advance on royalties of *Dark River;* this
sum would make for an additional 43,000 francs, enough to
carry the Halls through the next year. And, most important,
he would not have to touch his trust fund; the last statement
from the New England Trust in Boston showed $31,000 there,
all invested in blue-ribbon securities.

To make his contentment complete, however, Hall wanted

his family home with him in Arué. Nancy Ella had been teasing her father about not coming home, and when Hall went
out to collect his mail from the *Wairuna* when she docked in
Papeete at the end of July, he talked to Mr. Brewer, the chief
engineer. "Did you see my little Mischief when you were in
San Francisco?" he asked him. "I certainly did," Mr. Brewer
told him, "and her mother, too, and they are both looking in
the best of health." Hall asked him, "Did Nancy give you any
message for me?" "Yes," said the chief, "but I hate to tell you
what it was." "Why should you hate to tell me?" Hall asked.
"Go ahead. I want to know what she said." "Well," said Mr.
Brewer, "Nancy said, 'If you see my daddy in Papeete, I want
you to tell him that I'm *not* coming back.' "

"Midgie Ella Hall!" Hall wrote to his daughter. "What kind
of a message was that to send to your lonesome old dad? I went
back on shore lonesomer than ever. I didn't even care to read
my letters, except Mother's. How in the world am I to get
along here without you? I know that you want to go to school
in America, and I want you to. But I also want you to come
back with Mother for one more year. You'd soon see how lonesome and homesick you'd be if Mother and Irma [a close
friend to the Hall family] came back and left you up there.
Ask our dear Conrad about that. *He* knows how it is. But what
I hope is that, maybe you can *all* come back for one year in
Tahiti—Conrad too. Then, next year, when Nordy and I have
finished our new story, Mother and I could take you and Conrad to California and put you both in the same school. Don't
you think that's a good plan? What a happy time we could
have here in our dear home for a year—all of us together!
That's what I dream about and hope for. Think of what fun it
would be when we have separated for so long. Midge dear, I
wish you would ask Dr. Faber and Doctor Scarborough if they
think it would be safe for Conrad to come home with the rest
of you. [Conrad had had an ileostomy performed.] And if they
say, yes, it would be safe, then please come, all of you, and your
Dad Hall will be the happiest man in the whole world. And
I'll bet that I can make you and Conrad have a better time
here than you would ever have in California. And I will prom-

ise that you can both return to America for school next year."

Then he said to Lala in the same mail: "Nordy and I are getting along rapidly with work. I am now in the midst of my fifth chapter, and Nordy is nearly finished with his fourth. This book, I think, will be one of eighteen chapters, and if we keep on at this rate, will have finished well before the end of September. . . . We are not having nearly as much trouble with this story as we did with *Dark River*."

Arbitrarily, with Nordhoff doing the odd-numbered chapters and Hall the even, they finished the first draft and the revision by October and sent it off to Weeks. Again, as with *Faery Lands* and with the *Bounty*, they had established a fine counterpoint rhythm in working together. And although Nordhoff had not at first shown interest, he was beginning to regain some of his old mettle; his old wiry narrative strength was still there. And, as in his youth and young manhood, Nordhoff turned again for solace and sustenance, not to women or the bottle, but to his aviary full of quail, pheasant, and ducks he had imported to the island—he wished he had thousands of ducks, both woodland and mandarin, to nest and feed on his property. They were not like the damnable frigate birds who ranged the reef, dived on the gannets, and robbed them of the fish they had just caught.

Also, Nordhoff, who it often seemed preferred to fish than to write, could not be coaxed into a fishing party as frequently as before, although he was tempted sometimes right up to the point of going. With friends he would plan a trip to Mooréa or Bora Bora; he would arrange all the details of bait, tackle, fuel, food, accommodations; chart the locations of bonita, marlin, and sailfish; then he would lose interest. "I would like to do it," he would say, "but I can't leave Hall for that long. After this book is finished, though, I'd like to try."

Botany Bay was serialized in the *Post;* but, curiously, although Paramount paid a sizable price for the film option, it did not make a movie of the story. And, despite this recent success, their eighth since the new beginning of their partnership, this last novel marked the end of the Nordhoff and Hall team. The beginning of the end started with the completion of *The Hurricane,* when Edward Weeks had said, "he [Nordy] deferred more and more to Hall." Now, after *Botany Bay,* Weeks said, "the creative imagination which powered their novels was largely Jim's." Actually, the next novel they would do "by Nordhoff and Hall" would be mostly the work of Hall, and the last one, completely the work of Hall.

Before another work, however, whether or not dual in name and solo in work, Hall wanted to have printed another book under his name only. It became one of the great hoaxes in literary history. Under the nom de plume "Fern Gravel," Hall had published by the Prairie Press in Iowa a volume of poems, *Oh Millersville!,* "written in the first half-century by a little girl who lived in an Iowa town which she chose to call Millersville. She was secretive about her poetry, but she had one adult confidant to whom her compositions were sent as they came from her pencil, and who preserved them. Fern Gravel was not her real name; it was her own choice of a pen-name. The verses . . . were written during her ninth, tenth, and eleventh years. . . ."

Hall could not contain himself when he read the reviews. Said *Time* magazine: *"Oh Millersville!* is a collection of juvenilia that no American will want to see pass away. Fern Gravel was the pen-name of a sub-teen authoress whose soul simultaneously exfoliated in and was gripped by her Iowa home town, early in the 1900's. Her verses are as good examples of deadpan lyricism as have ever been printed." "We have found the lost Sappho of Iowa!" praised the *New York Times.* Said the *Washington Post:* "So good it hurts . . . Fern Gravel never dreamed that she was writing social history." Hall's friend, L. L. Winship, who had been let in on the joke, now an editor of the *Boston Globe,* must have chuckled when he read John Holmes's review in the *Boston Transcript:* "The book is amazing, amusing, full of the human scene, and not to be missed because there can't be another like it in the world." Even the Midwest was taken in; no less an authority than Paul Engle, in the *Des Moines Register,* commented: "There is so warm a feeling of validity about these verses, and so accurate a sense of individual character, their final impact is far stronger than a simple amusement at girlish simplicity. . . . This is majestic fooling."

11
Paradise Lost and Found

The early years of the 1940's, before the entry of America into the Second World War, were for Hall the most serene of his life: his work was going extremely well, he was financially at ease, and his health and Conrad's was very good; for Nordhoff, however, the same years marked the beginning of a grim epilogue to his life: he left Tahiti never to return, he tried writing with another partner in California but failed, he remarried in a final attempt at happiness, and at last he reached that point of despair from which there was no return.

One evening in June of 1941, Hall was reading on the veranda of his home in Arué, and in looking up from his book to put out a cigarette he was smoking, he was shocked to see a man standing just inside the entryway to his porch. The man was a native, middle-aged, and though barefoot, he was dressed in blue overalls and a white drill jacket. "May you live!" he said to Hall in Polynesian, walked over to him, and handed him a letter. The letter was from Cridland, "the forgotten one" he had quite literally forgotten about for years. The letter was written in a clumsy scroll, the words starting big and ending small, the lines often crossing one another. "I am ill," the message said, "and as I have grave doubts as to my recovery I must try to put my affairs in order. I have no one with me but an old Chinese servant, Ling Foo, whom you may remember. Could you come to see me? I have chartered a Tuamotuan cutter for the purpose of carrying this letter, and if you find it possible to come this cutter will bring you to the island. I realize that you may not be able to leave at once and I have, therefore, instructed the man who brings this letter—he is the owner of the vessel—to await your orders."

Hall questioned the native messenger. His name, he explained, was Maitua and, one day recently in returning to his home island of Hao from a trip to Mangareva he had been blown off his course by a southerly gale; after the storm, they passed an island which was burning a signal fire. It was Taioro island. They went ashore, were met by Ling Foo, who brought them to the white man, Cridland. The popaa, Maitua said, was very ill and offered them ten thousand francs to deliver the letter and bring Hall to his island.

"What did he tell you to do in case I could not be found?" Hall asked.

"He said we were to return to Taioro as soon as possible to carry his Chinese to some island where he might take passage for Tahiti."

"Did he speak of wanting a doctor?"

"No."

"What do you think of his condition?" Hall inquired. "Is it serious?"

"Unless you can come with me at once," Maitua replied, "I doubt that we shall find him living."

Hall went into his bedroom, told Lala the urgency of Cridland's request, packed a few things into a handbag, and left the house. When they got to Papeete, the ship was ready to sail. The crew, in addition to Hall's escort, were two of Maitua's friends.

Two weeks later, after rotten westerly and southwesterly weather dogging their course, they arrived at Taioro Atoll, and after bringing the cutter to, they went in over the reef into the lagoon and to the shore of the largest islet of the group, Cridland's island. Ling Foo waited for them on the beach and immediately brought Hall to Cridland's house.

When Hall came up the stairs of the veranda and looked in, he thought he was too late. Cridland lay on a sofa, propped up on pillows; his face, white and thin, his eyes, closed in their deep sockets, his arms, pale and folded across his chest, gave the look of a corpse. The Chinese padded across the floor to the couch. At the sound, Cridland opened his eyes, vacantly, wonderingly. "Ling Foo," he asked, "are you there?" In response, his servant touched him on the shoulder. Cridland spoke up. "Go down to the beach," he said. "They must be close inshore by this time."

Hall walked up to the sofa. "We're here, Cridland," he said.

The form came to life, its face brightened. "Please forgive me," Cridland said. "I must have been asleep." He reached out his hand. "I am deeply grateful."

Hall did not answer but looked again at the body on the couch, and grew mad at himself. How had this pitiful wreck of a man, this most inhospitable of hosts, this strangest of strangers, prevailed upon him, Hall, again, to another show of consideration? Why had this man, now a living corpse, thrown his life away on this deserted island, and how could he ask for an act of friendship in his friendless life?

"I had only a faint hope that you would be able to come," Cridland said. "But I clung to that hope."

Changing the subject, Hall asked: "Does the *Toafa* still call here?"

"Yes, once a year," Cridland replied. "But she's not due again until September."

Hall asked to be excused, and went back to the beach. There he found Maitua and his friends and told them they could leave to visit their home island, but would have to come back to get him in ten days to two weeks, depending on the weather. They readily agreed, climbed into the long boat, and left.

When Hall returned to Cridland on the veranda and sat down, he quickly noticed that his host, although he looked directly at him, did not recognize his approach. Puzzled, Hall asked: "Is there anything you want, Cridland?"

The sound startled Cridland. "Oh," he said, "I didn't know you were back. You must have come in very quietly."

"But haven't you seen me sitting here?" Hall said, and as he asked the question he was sorry he had. Obviously, Cridland was blind. Hall's voice softened. "How long have you been like this?" he asked, concerned.

"Nearly three years," Cridland said. "I can still see the faint outline of objects close by, directly in front of me, but nothing more." Then he told Hall how much he missed his books, how he would enjoy again hearing from his old favorites—Thoreau, Milton, Wordsworth. Readily, Hall obliged, and except for the time they took to eat dinner, he read far into the night for him from *Walden, Comus,* and the *Lyrical Ballads.* Cridland was deeply grateful. "Thanks ever so much," he said, at two o'clock in the morning and urging Hall to get some sleep. "I can't tell you what a treat this has been for me."

The next morning and for the next several days Hall helped Cridland to put his personal affairs in order. Objective and orderly, Cridland settled the matter of a will, leaving a considerable fortune to a nephew and niece in England; directed that a balance of five hundred pounds in a Pepeete bank be given to Ling Foo for his long and faithful service; asked that upon his death, Hall would send the official papers of that fact to his attorney in London. Then, in a final request, he asked Hall to go to his desk in his study, remove all the papers, notebooks, and manuscripts, and burn them. "I will feel much better," he said to Hall, "when they are destroyed." Hall complied.

One week later, the business of Cridland's estate settled at last, Hall sat with his host on the back veranda over the lagoon enjoying the cool breeze as night came on. Cridland sat up in his lounge chair. "There is something I have long had on my conscience," he said to Hall. "You will remember, when you were last here, my . . . my strange behavior. What must you have thought of me, leaving you like that? . . . And a guest in my own house, too!"

"Don't speak of it, Cridland," Hall answered. "If apologies are in order let mine come first. I barged in on you without—"

Cridland broke in. "No, please!" he said with emphasis. "You have nothing to reproach yourself for. I was guilty of an unpardonable breach of hospitality. I owe you the fullest explanation of my actions on that occasion. But I don't see how I *can* explain without saying more than . . . than you may care to hear. . . . Would you mind if I were to tell you something that I have never spoken of to anyone?"

Hall was tremendously interested; but with restraint he said: "No, not if you want to tell me."

"I do want to." Cridland was most agreeable. "But whether it will be possible . . . let me ask a question: Have you ever wondered why I came here to live?"

"Many times," Hall replied, matter-of-factly.

"What was your supposition?" Cridland asked, genuinely curious.

"I have never found a satisfactory one," Hall pulled his last cigarette from the package, crumbled the package into a ball, and threw it out into the lagoon. "You have always been a puzzle to me, Cridland," he admitted.

"You're being quite frank?" His host sought an affirmative answer. "You don't know why I have hidden myself away here?"

Hall confessed ignorance. "I haven't the slightest idea," he said.

Cridland became animated. "I believe you. Well, let me get this out, if I can. For some reason I feel a great need to speak, for the first and the last time.

"I am one of those men . . ." He stopped, paused for a moment, and started again. "I am one of those men who . . . who are . . . mistakes of Nature.

"Does this mean anything to you? Do you understand what I am trying to say? Mistakes of Nature . . . tragic, irremediable mistakes. Or experiments, perhaps—who knows? How many there are, of how many kinds! There is one . . . a victim of that blunder in creation is the most unhappy, surely, of all the children of men.

"This sounds maudlin. I am aware of the fact. But I ask you to believe that I am not indulging in self-pity. I gave up that habit long ago. If you like, in this darkness think of me only as a voice, speaking of a man who no longer exists. That," he underscored his observation, "is not far from the truth!"

Then, completely enthralled, Hall listened while Cridland told him the story of his boyhood. It had been completely normal and happy, he said; he had no indication that he was unlike other boys. He studied hard and did well in school, acquiring the tools of language and mathematics in preparation for future scholarship, he hoped in physics. He was oblivious of any eccentricity on his part—until he went to the university.

"In my second year at the university," he said, his voice starting to shake, "I discovered . . . what, it seems, had to be discovered. It was a gradual revelation, but, in the end, complete. My case may have been exceptional, and from what I know I think it was. The fact remains that I was unaware of the existence of such . . . of such abnormality until it was revealed to me by a friend and classmate to whom I was deeply devoted. In the long vacation of my second year I went to Germany for further study. It was the worst move I could have made, it seems. What happened there . . . oh, I'm so mortally tired!"

The last remark struck Hall like the cry of a child in the night. "Cridland," he said, softly and with apology, "you needn't go on. Believe me, I . . ."

"Wait! I beg your pardon," Cridland insisted. His voice became flat and assertive. "Don't misunderstand me. I was not at the point of making any sordid confessions. Allow me to finish. I have a little more to say."

He spoke out, straight ahead, his eyes in a vacant stare, out over the lagoon, to the reef and beyond, out to the sea and to the uncomprehending universe. "In Germany I found myself on the brink of an abyss—so at last I conceived of it. I looked down. I saw unhappy creatures like myself moving about in those depths. I pitied them from my heart, but it was loathing that saved me. I differed from them only in this: they had accepted their fate; many of them, I discovered, gloried in it. I would not accept mine—at least I would not accept the common implications of that fate. I saw what I had to do. I gave up my plans for a career. I cut myself off from family and friends. You see, I didn't trust myself. I didn't know what wretched folly friendship might lead me into. I set out in search of some place, preferably an island, where there could be no question of friendship, not even companionship. When I found that place, I remained . . . as you know."

Three days later Cridland was dead. With the help of Ling Foo, Hall carried the body to a small cove on the lagoon beach, dug a hole, and buried it. There was no headstone, no native rectangle of sea shells, no mark of any kind. It was as Cridland had wished. Over the grave a palm frond waved in the breeze, like a hand outstretched granting peace.

Nordhoff, meanwhile, in California, had remarried. One night at a cocktail party in Santa Barbara he met Laura Grainger Whiley. He was immediately struck by her grace and charm, and by her large smiling eyes. Laura, an interior decorator, born of a Navy family in Manila and raised in France, thought Nordhoff the most attractive man she had ever met. Before the party was over, Nordhoff had asked her to marry him; Laura, overwhelmed by the proposal but flattered and agreeable, accepted.

On June 12, they were married, and they moved into a new house which Nordhoff had bought on the Hope Ranch. Of his new wife, Nordhoff wrote to Hall that she had made him more than happy, after years of a miserable and lonely life; and, he said, he hoped he would be able to make her happy, too.

Often to Nordhoff's home on weekends and for the holidays came young Conrad Hall, now a vibrantly healthy fifteen-year-old, a student at the Cate School. At the Hope Ranch he could ride horseback on twenty-two miles of bridle path, play tennis, or swim at the private beach; or, willingly, visit Nordhoff's three lovely teen-age daughters, who were staying in a rented cottage at Laguna Beach, where, pursued by admiring college boys and young Navy officers, they were closely chaperoned by an old and faithful English maid.

In California, Nordhoff had been working in Hollywood as a scenario writer for the movie "The Tuttles of Tahiti," trying to repair previous playscripts to the satisfaction of Charles Laughton, who found too many of the lines unspeakable. And he had been trying to interest Sol Lesser in making a movie of *Pitcairn's Island*.

After the Japanese attack on Pearl Harbor in December and their continuing months of invasion and conquest in the South Pacific during the first months of 1942, Nordhoff gave up all thought of returning to Tahiti. At one time he had planned on building a house in Mitirapa and living in it; now, with the war and his marriage he instructed Hall to sell his launch for $2,000 if he could get it, and his car for $700; to look after his children, thinking that it would be a good plan for Vahine to live in Punaauia with her children, on condition that the chauffeur who caused his divorce never set foot upon the place.

Just as Hall kept Nordhoff informed about his two sons and daughter in Tahiti, so did Nordhoff keep Hall informed about his son Conrad. He had never seen Connie looking better and stronger and more full of pep than at the present time, Nordhoff reported to Hall. Conrad's character interested him, because Connie possessed the qualities that Hall and Nordhoff lacked so glaringly—scientific and factual pursuits, and mathematics. Conrad, he said, was a thoroughly normal and wholesome boy, and the fact that he was an extrovert would make his life an unusually happy one.

On matters other than children and education, however, there was less agreement between Nordhoff and Hall. Particularly they could not decide on the subject of their next book. Nordhoff wanted them to write a sequel to *Botany Bay;* but Hall proposed a story with the present war in Europe as part of the background, a narrative of five convicts in the penal colony of French Guiana, who, driven with a desire to fight for France, escape in a canoe, are picked up nearly dead by a French freighter, and the whole group make it to England to join the Free French Forces. Hall called it "Sans Patrie," later renaming it *Men Without Country*. Nordhoff could not be stirred to an interest in the story; and although it had all the familiar elements of previous Nordhoff and Hall novels—men against the sea, mutiny, convicts, flying adventures—Nordhoff collaborated desultorily if at all. When Hall submitted the final manuscript to Nordhoff for his editing, Nordhoff objected to the "by Nordhoff and Hall" signature. He said to Hall that it seemed entirely wrong that his name should appear as one of the authors of the story. "You have completely rewritten it," he said to Hall, "rearranged and improved the whole thing so that it is entirely your work. The book," he concluded, "should appear under your name."

Despite these protestations, when the novel was sold to Warner Brothers for $75,000, Nordhoff accepted his half of the proceeds, not entirely on the grounds that his name with Hall's sold books, but that he agreed to rewrite the story for the movie, this time putting a woman in it. Hall objected to this plan; he felt that "men without country" should also be "men without women." Nordhoff insisted that adding a woman would be the only way that a movie could be made. When the film was finally released, as *Passage to Marseilles,* and Hall saw it on the screen, he ran from the theater. "I wanted to vomit," he said.

Hall now turned his attention almost exclusively to the impact of the war upon Polynesia. The attack on Pearl Harbor had shocked him deeply, and he struck back, in verse, with a "savage indignation" worthy of Jonathan Swift. Ellery Sedgwick liked the poem and almost ran it in the *Atlantic,* but at the last minute decided against it. The poem, like most of Hall's better verses, was again occasional, and again spontaneous, written in the white heat of fury. When these emotions had subsided, however, Hall turned to a less highly keyed wartime subject for his next book, a solo venture, a novel based on what was literally happening to the island of Bora Bora in the Society Islands after it was taken over by the United States Navy. From this fact, Hall fashioned his fictional *Lost Island,* a small tragedy in a large tragedy, thinking, Are not continents islands? Said Diana Trilling in the *Nation:* ". . . it is a strange world we have contrived in which we have to destroy civilization in order to try to preserve it." Edward Weeks, in the *Atlantic,* claimed partisanship, but called it ". . . a story of impending doom that breaks upon the mind with the accumulating force of a great comber." The *Springfield Republican* was greatly enthusiastic: "James Norman Hall rises to nostalgic heights in delivering his valedictory to Polynesian life as it was lived on a South Pacific atoll before the Seabees rumbled ashore on a bucking bulldozer. As yet we have read nothing so eloquent of the impact of global war upon native life as Mr. Hall's short novel." In further recognition, the Book-of-the-Month Club selected it, and RKO bought the film rights for $20,000.

Hall reviewed the honors and was heartened. The demon diffidence no longer snapping at him, he now tried another novel. This one, however, was "by Nordhoff and Hall." It was *The High Barbaree,* an autobiographical novel, with some asides to Nordhoff's life and background. It was Hall's most poignantly personalized statement. In the story Alec Brooke from Iowa was James Norman Hall, not in World War I in France, but in World War II in the South Pacific; not a lieutenant in the Air Service flying a Spad, but a lieutenant in the Navy flying a PBY; not a pilot shot down by the Hun behind the lines and imprisoned, but a flier shot down by the Japs and ditched in the Pacific Ocean, a prisoner of his boyhood dreams; not an escape to freedom, but an escape to The High Barbaree, the small Pacific island of his dreams, a dot marked on the maps as "Existence Doubtful," after which he had named his plane; and Hall added his "G-Note Road" from Colfax, and his own Nancy. The book was a marvelous tapestry: the warp and woof of fact and fiction, dream and fantasy, boyhood and manhood, matter-of-fact life as it is and idyllic wish fulfillment. A condensed version appeared in *Cosmopolitan* magazine, and MGM purchased the movie rights for $65,000.

Unlike the occasion of *Men Without Country* when Nordhoff asked Hall to sign only his name to the work, and Hall refused, this time there was no such request. As in the past, Hall continued to share all "by Nordhoff and Hall" royalties on an equal basis. For, Hall knew too, "by Nordhoff and Hall" sold better than "by Hall" alone.

Hall could afford to remember. Nordhoff in California was at loose ends. He tried to get a magazine started, like *La Guerre Aerienne* of the first world war, but failed because of the lack of available paper. He tried to introduce on the market a Polynesian Sauce, but failed because some of the ingredients had to be refrigerated all the way from the South Seas. He tried broadcasting, but failed because he could not get a sustaining program. He tried to write another book, again in collaboration, but this time a spy novel with Tod Ford, an old friend from Pasadena, but he could not find a publisher to accept it.

Nordhoff yearned for the old life in Tahiti and to be reunited with his children there, for he worried about them constantly. He wrote to Hall that he missed his youngsters terribly and often lay awake at night and got in a stew about them. But as things were at present, he thought that they were better off in Tahiti for another year or two. "Your presence," he said to Hall, "and the knowledge that you are keeping an eye on them, is a godsend to me." He would, he said, try to reciprocate by doing everything in his power for Conrad. Nordhoff dreamed of the green and golden days of his youth, and he longed for a return to unspoiled nature.

Notwithstanding Nordhoff's concern for Tahiti and for his children on the island, by the mid-forties and after the end of World War II he had all but lost that concern, that worry which had kept him sleepless and on edge. Hall, patient for as long as he thought practicable, finally spoke out. "This is one of the times," he told Nordhoff, "when plain speaking is necessary." Specifically, the problem was Nordhoff's property and children; both of them needed his immediate attention. Hall wrote to his friend: "You can understand the situation I have been placed in, having to take on the management of your affairs when you yourself should be here to do this. I can't understand why you don't come down, for a month or two at least, to set your Tahiti affairs in order. And, much more important than the land matters, what about the children? When I see two fine boys, Charley and Jimmie, simply vegetating here when they have reached an age when they should be receiving good schooling, I wonder that you can be so indifferent to their future. And then, there are the boys by Teura [Nordhoff's native mistress after he left Vahine]. These boys all deserve a chance in life, and what chance can Tahiti offer them? I realize, of course, that it may not be a question, with you, of what you would like to do for them but of what you can do. Granted that you must let Teura's children 'go bush' as they have already, surely you expect to do something for the others? For Charley and Jimmie, at least? My advice is to give them a break; they well deserve it. Take them to the U.S.A. and give them an education that will fit them for life up there. I can see their future if they have to grow to manhood here with such little education as Tahiti schools can offer. I don't see how you can avoid longer the responsibility you have toward them. . . .

"You may say that all this is none of my business. But neither is it my business to have to take over the management of your land affairs which sorely need your own personal attention. It is no trouble at all for me to pay Teura her small monthly allotment ($12 per month) and to pay Ah You [a Chinese merchant in Papeete] Vahine's monthly bill and to keep your insurance premiums paid. I am glad to take care of these small matters. But when it comes to Mitirapa [after Punaauia, Nordhoff's other property], complicated as it is by your own early promises to Sage [the native whom Nordhoff hired to take care of the property] and by the poisonous relationship between Sage and Vahine . . . well, frankly, I don't think you have the right to stay at a long distance and ask any friend to act for you. It is your affair and your responsibility. If you do what you should do, you will come down here on the first available steamer and put your affairs in order. You wouldn't need to stay any great length of time, but take my word for it, your presence here is needed and badly needed."

Nordhoff never returned to Tahiti. Although he took admirably good care of his four lovely daughters, providing for their education and civilized upbringing, he let his two legal sons and his three natural sons in Tahiti "go bush." Perhaps thinking of his own life in Baja California, one lived happily close to the sea and sky, and to the plains and mountains, the simple one-to-one relationship with nature of the hunter and fisherman, uncomplicated by the requirements of civilization, Nordhoff must have felt he was doing the best possible thing for his sons. For himself, albeit urbane, sophisticated, and polished in appearance, he was never at home in the world of men.

Unable to return to the terrestrial paradise which he had lost, Nordhoff remained in a spiritual hell. Not marriage to a lovely and cultivated woman, not friends and intellectual pursuits, not Scotch or gin in whatever amounts, nor the fretful sleep that followed drink: none of these could halt the final retreat to despair. One night in the spring of 1947, after an evening out with Laura, Nordhoff retired as he always had: he sat up and read for a while, then apparently fell asleep. But on this night, Friday, April 11, Nordhoff read for a while, then fell over dead. His despairing thoughts had turned inward upon himself.

Coincidentally, Hall was in California for his daughter Nancy's wedding, only four days before, which Nordhoff had attended. In less than a week, Hall had lost two of the dearest people under heaven to him. One was a happy loss, Nancy to a Marine Corps veteran, ruggedly handsome Nicholas G. Rutgers, Jr., whose forebears had founded Rutgers University in New Jersey; the other, Nordhoff, a most sorrowful one, for scarcely a day passed during a period of twenty years when they were not together.

For Charles B. Nordhoff, there was no autopsy and a quick burial. It was announced that he had died of a heart attack. His body was cremated and the ashes brought to Redlands for interment. The family was there and a few friends, among them Walter B. Power and James Norman Hall. A hole had been dug. Nordhoff's brother, Franklin, put the casket in. There was no service, no prayers. Hall wept. "It was," Walter Power said, "like burying a dog."

Mournful, with Nordhoff's death fully reminding him of his own mortality, Hall, at sixes and sevens about any future plans, returned to Tahiti with his family, there to find the balm to heal his sadness. Quite by accident two events oc-

curred that provided him with ideas for two books which
would occupy his time for the rest of his life.

A friend came to his house one morning, asking if he could
borrow a trunk for a trip he planned. Hall agreed and went to
look among his many trunks for one which would serve the
purpose. Finding one not too full, Hall started to clean it out,
and was charmed by its contents. He pulled out old diaries,
notebooks, letters he had sent home from Boston and from the
front when he served with Kitchener's Mob and the Escadrille
and from prison camp, old photographs from Colfax, and even
the program from his high school commencement exercises, for
June 1904. Hall was filled with nostalgia and thought he had
enough evidence collected there to begin recollections for writing his memoirs. He would write to Edward Weeks, he decided, for his reaction to such a plan.

And that evening at dusk as he pedaled his bicycle to Papeete to mail off a short-story manuscript to the *Atlantic,* he
heard through the stillness of the night the sound of a native
fisherman chanting on the reef; the melody, though brief, was
haunting and beautiful. Hall had heard it before on other occasions and had inquired about it; it was, he was told, an old
Polynesian call, used from the time of the earliest migrations
eastward across the Pacific. Hearing the call again as he bicy-
cled by, it reminded him that he had often thought of someday
doing the story of Polynesian migration. That night as he slept
he had a curious dream. He dreamed about an island and of a
little thatched hut on a beautiful lagoon. Inside the hut at a
table made from the boards of packing cases sat an old native
writing in a school exercise book and at his elbow was a great
stack of other books already filled. Suddenly, in his dream,
Hall realized that this island was Bikini, and that the man
writing, although unaware of the danger, was trying to finish
his story before the first atom bomb was exploded. When Hall
awoke the next morning, he knew the story had to be told—
before the hell and high water from an atomic bomb came.

The story of his life, the first part of his boyhood and youth
that comprised Volume One, came easily. Weeks liked the
manuscript, except for the too numerous verses of the "wood-

shed poet," most of which he cut out, and he made plans to have it serialized in the *Atlantic* and published in association with Little, Brown. Hall, rather than go on to Volume Two of his memoirs, stopped, and started on "The Call of Maui" story. Often in the past he had worked at two manuscripts at once, one with Nordhoff and one by himself; now he was simply doing both by and for himself. Every morning he would awake at six-thirty, wash, dress, make his breakfast, and be at his typewriter at seven o'clock, and his work progressed most satisfactorily. It was now the summer of 1949. One morning in August, however, he started to wash, and there was no water. Hall cursed the *fonctionnaires,* the Travaux Publiques, and the *gouverneur;* for the past fifteen years he had been trying to get them to pipe water down from a spring not a kilometer away in the hills; there was enough water for the entire district of Arué, but they refused to do it. Hall walked down to the *faréniau,* his beach house, to see if there was any water there. Fortunately, there was enough to fill a bowl for shaving. Indignant, he returned to the main house, sat at the typewriter, and took out his resentment in verse.

Finishing the poem, Hall wanted to send it to the governor; but knew that if he did, he might be kicked off the island. Anyway, the mere act of writing had served its purpose of abating his anger. Yet, he still did not feel like going back to the migration story. He noted on the far right corner of his desk the correspondence of Harrison Smith. In 1945 the Skipper had died of cancer and had made Hall the executor of his estate, leaving Hall his books and papers, and a great ebony table made of one slab of wood. Hall started reading the letters and came upon the correspondence between Smith and Sedgwick in 1925. Hall laughed, nervously; the letters were about him and his marriage to Sarah. Both of his friends had disapproved! He read Smith's letter and was shocked and surprised: "Poor old Hall," the Skipper had written, "sewed up in a sack." Hall could not resist writing a comment in the margin of the letter: *"This is Sept. 8th 1949,"* he wrote and underlined. "I'm still sewed up with Sarah. None of the seams show any evidence of bursting. Hope they hold fast until our silver wedding anniversary, a year from now."

The year 1950 loomed high on the horizon as one of the most important peaks in Hall's life. In April he would celebrate his twenty-fifth wedding anniversary; in June he wanted to return to Grinnell to celebrate the fortieth reunion of his class; and after, from Iowa, he wanted to leave with Sarah on a trip around the world. Toward that end Hall wanted to finish the autobiography and the migration story, both to provide the funds for the three celebrations. In November he went alone to Hawaii to visit Nancy and her husband Nick, and his two grandsons: Nicholas Rutgers III, one and a half years old, and James Norman Rutgers, age three months; and to visit with the librarians at the Bishop Museum to solicit their help in further necessary research for "The Call of Maui," before he could do any more writing on that story.

Nick and Nancy lived on the windward side of the island on Oahu, at Lanikai. Hall, hoping to spend several months, at least until he could finish the novel in the spring, lived in the guest cottage, apart from the main house, where he could work undisturbed.

Working hard against his spring deadline, but perhaps too hard and too anxiously, Hall encountered difficulties in his work, exasperating difficulties that stopped cold any further telling of the story.

He walked over to the main house; he had to tell Nancy about his problem. "Midge," he said to her, "I have to give up. I can't do the love story. Nordy always did the love stories."

Nancy started to mix her father an old-fashioned. "Daddy, you must explain to the reader," she said to him, "that your hero and heroine are actually in love."

"What do you mean, 'actually in love'?"

Nancy handed him his drink. "Sex," she said.

"That has no place in books!"

"Daddy! You don't *know* what's in modern books." She went to the coffee table and picked up a copy of Michener's *Tales of the South Pacific,* which she had been reading. "Sit still and listen!" She read from the love story of the Princeton man for his native sweetheart in Bali-Hi.

Hall blushed. "Did James Michener write that . . . in a book?"

Nancy Ella put down the book. "I could have read from Mailer's *Naked and the Dead,* or some of the others who really get down to cases."

"They ought to be ashamed of themselves! All of them!"

Although only eighteen, Nancy, like her mother, was forceful and determined. Patiently and softly, she explained to her father that sex was the most beautiful and natural wonder in the world, that he must approach it in his story the way the Tahitians did in their lives. "You and Mamma have had the most wonderful love story ever lived," she said. "Why don't you write about it, disguised, in your story?"

"Well." Hall shook his head and finished his drink. "If that's what the public wants."

"If you give up," Nancy told him, "you will admit you are a failure."

Hall put down his glass, looked up at his daughter, and smiled. "Dearest Midge," he said to her, "I won't give up." Hall got up, started to walk, and stumbled.

"What's the matter?" Nancy asked.

"I'm all right," Hall answered. "It's just that my left leg went numb."

On February 10, Hall could see the end of the story. He was writing the last of twenty-five chapters, and would be finished with the epilogue and a rewritten version of the legend in a week. He felt so good about the book, he went into town and made arrangements for his trip around the world with Sarah. They would leave New York on the seventh of July, sailing from New York for Stockholm, Sweden, then to Norway, Denmark, Belgium, perhaps Holland, then France and England— and also Switzerland and Spain if Lala wanted to. They would be gone from the middle of July until October, and they could come home to Tahiti from Australia.

The "Call of Maui" was published as *The Far Lands* by Little, Brown; it was serialized in four issues of the *Atlantic;* and it was chosen by The Literary Guild as one of its selections. Hall was satisfied beyond measure, and went ahead with all plans. Then he remembered: at the same time as his own reunion, his son Conrad would be graduating from the University of Southern California! Hall wrote to his son, explaining how much he wanted to go to Grinnell, and asking if it would be all right if only his mother appeared at his graduation.

"That's OK, Dad," Conrad wrote to him. "I will be only one of seven thousand. I probably won't even go to the ceremonies. And they will have to mail the diploma, anyway."

Hall had decided he wanted to get back to Iowa in time to see the hepaticas when they bloomed, but owing to a delayed wait for Sarah in Hawaii, then a prolonged visit with the Rutgers, and a stop at San Francisco, he missed his wish. Just before leaving Hawaii, he received a letter from the President's Office at Grinnell. Hall guessed it was a formal invitation to the reunion. He read:

> Dear Norman Hall:
>
> I am happy to inform you that the College wishes to confer upon you the honorary degree of Doctor of Literature on your 40th Commencement Anniversary in June. Will you please send us your height, your approximate weight, and the size of your hat so that we can have a suitable cap and gown ready for you? My heartiest congratulations.
>
> > Sincerely yours,
> > SAMUEL N. STEVENS
> > President

Hall was completely taken by surprise. A Doctor of Literature? He couldn't believe it. It was the greatest honor of his life. But wouldn't it ruin his reunion? Wouldn't he have to give an acceptance speech? Wouldn't Chester Davis and Bill Ziegler tease him unmercifully about being up on the stage with all the big shots!

During the last week in May Hall went by train to Iowa and was met in Ames by his nephew Jim, named after him. "Now drive slowly, Jimmy," he said to him. "Not over thirty. I want to look around and smell around." Hall looked and smelled all the way home to Colfax: the rolling plains, the lilacs, the meadowlark, and the great oaks and maples with their thick branches and fans of green leaves. He was driven to the old Hall house on top of Howard Street Hill, where his brother Fred and his family now lived. The first thing he wanted to do, he said, after exchanging greetings, was to visit "his hill."

"Norm, don't," his sister-in-law said. "I wouldn't go out there if I were you."

"Why not?" Hall answered. "They haven't cut off the old timber?"

"Worse than that," she said. "They've straightened the track east of town. You'll be horrified when you see the results."

Hall had to look for himself and he was appalled by what he saw. As from a mound of cake, a thick wedge had been cut from the hill, and from the top had been removed the old linden tree, and from the sides had been cleared all the trees. Hall was horrified. All he could see and hear was from his mind's eye and ear: it was Nordhoff pacing his veranda and saying to him, "Hall, never return to a place where you have known true happiness." Hall quickly turned, his eyes glazed, his ears deaf from the sacrilege. Two days later he was driven on to Grinnell.

On the weekend of June 1st, 2nd, and 3rd, the Class of 1910 held its fortieth reunion at Grinnell College. They were three of the happiest days of Hall's life. Forty-five members of the class, most of whom Hall had not seen since graduation, showed up. There were Chet, Ziggy, Epp, Rube Roberts and their wives. On Sunday afternoon Hall sat on the platform, the president's speech was made, the 250 members of the graduating class were given their degrees, the six other honorary degrees were awarded, and the name of James Norman Hall was called. Hall stood up and stepped forward. President Stevens placed the cape over his head; the cape caught on his ears, then slipped down his neck to his shoulders. At that moment Hall thought: "My Ideal, my companion I used to read poetry with in the library stockroom is here beside me; it's him, not me, the woodshed poet, who's receiving this honorary degree; and that's Old Man Diffidence on my back who was trying to hold off that cape, whispering in my ear: 'It's a certain thing, Norman Hall, no one knows better than yourself how little you deserve this.'" The degree conferred, Hall turned to walk back to his seat, stumbled, and almost fell. The numbness had returned to his left leg.

After the ceremony, Hall blushed as he accepted the congratulations of his classmates, and those of some of his former professors, now retired but still living in Grinnell, among them Professors Pierce and Stoops. Professor Stoops heartened Hall; he greeted him "Doctor." How perfectly appropriate, thought Hall, for it was Stoops who had said of the undergraduates: "They have to learn that a bird in the bush is worth two in the hand!" And this was exactly how Norman Hall had lived his life!

But, Hall decided after the reunion, if he wanted to continue to chase the bird in the bush, he would have to see about the numbness in his leg. Accordingly, he wired Lala: he would go to Boston first, then they could meet in New York for their trip around the world. In Boston Hall consulted the greatest specialist in the East. If the trouble had started around his heart, instead of his leg, the doctor told Hall, he would be dead. "I am mighty lucky to have it where it is," Hall said to Sarah. "As it has happened I am in no danger, but he says that, more than likely I will have the same trouble in my other leg at some time in the future. He wants me to go to the Phillips Hospital, here in Boston, next Wednesday. I shall only have to stay there two days while he gives me a thorough going-over. I will let you know what he says as soon as I have this check-up; but it will, certainly *not* prevent me from going to France if you want to go. I can charter a car for us while we are over there so that we can go wherever we want to . . ."

The Literary Guild Selection, he explained to her, could bring them an extra $20,000 to $25,000 in book sales. "Furthermore," he added, "we are 'sitting pretty' with respect to our savings in the New England Trust Company. I spent part of the morning yesterday with Philip Stocker, and I find that, at the prices stocks are now, our holdings with the New England Trust amount to $108,000. So we are far from being candidates for the poor-house."

Sarah, shrewd and full of insight, read her husband's letter and understood from what she read between his lines that there was great seriousness and concern behind his talk of France and how much money their investments had earned in Boston. She wrote to him and told him she didn't want to go to France, didn't want to make a trip around the world. She wanted, she said, to go home to Tahiti.

"Well, Mamma dear," he replied, "If you don't want to go to France now, then we won't go until later, around the world by the south, from Tahiti. It is, probably, a good thing that we are not going this year on account of my leg. I couldn't do much walking if we went to France this year."

In Boston, the doctors consulted again about Hall, and this time transferred him to the Massachusetts General Hospital for four more days of examination. No operation would be necessary, the specialists at Massachusetts General decided, but they prescribed a strict regimen of leg exercises for Hall, giving him a booklet with illustrations to follow, and, they ordered him, he would have to give up smoking cigarettes. Hall left Massachusetts determined to do both, but had soon relented before he had returned to San Francisco to join his wife. In August Hall and Sarah sailed for Tahiti on board the *Thor*. Sarah suspected, and Hall knew: he was going home to die.

The end came in less than a year. Hall told no one about his predicament, but quietly put his affairs in order. In January 1951, he wrote in his notebook: "My life is not so far different than what I had planned. Looking back over the years of my life I see how little I have changed. Wordsworth never wrote more truly than when he said the boy is father to the man. [I am] still an idealist and a romanticist—and what misery these qualities have caused me!

"Men like myself who have no skill in practical matters are often seized by an almost unbearable sense of anguish thinking how useless their lives have been in comparison to men who build roads, bridges, lay water mains, etc., doing the practical work that has to be done in their time for the benefit of mankind."

Then he mused, almost sadly: "The leisure I have at last attained for myself. I can spend an entire day, or week, read-

ing!" At the end of March, Hall learned that *The Far Lands*
had sold, including the Literary Guild sales, over 250,000 copies. He could not believe it, but he could not deny the facts.
Completely on his own, and with Nordhoff a four-year-old
memory as collaborator, he had now at last established his single reputation as a writer. Thus encouraged, Hall now approached Weeks about bringing out a collection of his better
tales. On the strength of the current popularity of Hall's best
seller, Weeks brought out six of Hall's best stories and sketches
and called the book *The Forgotten One* after one of the stories, updated, about Cridland. Also, Hall started writing the
second volume of his memoirs, and hoped to have it finished in
three more months.

Hall no longer did his exercises: they were too bothersome;
he had tried giving up cigarettes but he could not live without
smoking. On June 2, numbness went over to his right leg and
having to get off his feet because it was too painful to walk,
Hall took to his bed. There he rested peacefully, without complaint, sleeping very restfully. He told Lala that he was having
the most beautiful dreams of his life, as of choirs of angels singing to him while he slept. It must have been very much like
two occasions before in his life when he had been transported
in a kind of apotheosis: once, when he was cycling down the
road from Arué and found himself suddenly "on the high road
to heaven, with everything changed—the trees, the sky, the
mountains, the lagoon, the sea beyond," and the sound of two
men cutting grass by the side of the road seemed like "the music of the spheres"; the other, while he was returning from his
trip to Pitcairn Island, when he was lying on his back on the
deck, staring up at a starlit sky and felt suddenly disembodied,
afloat in the voids of space, "gazing in awe and dismay toward
the sun, as it shrank to the size of an orange, a pea, a grain of
sand, a mote of shining dust. . . . Yet I could still see the
Earth—its oceans, continents, islands, scaling down and down
to infinitely less than microscopic proportions. . . . Having
been shown all this, I was again dropped, with the speed of
thought, into the shell of my body which lay in the same
cramped position on the deck of the *Hinaaro.*"

When the word got around the island about Hall's sickness,

he had many visitors. He smoked and drank with them, often kidding that he would probably have to get his leg amputated before he would be all right again. Lala observed and said nothing, but noted in his eyes the unmistakable signs of pain: the condition, she concluded, must have spread to his body too. "We have had a wonderful life together, Mamma dear," he would say to Sarah. "We showed them all!" Lala would turn quickly, looking to find something to occupy her outside of his room. "When I die," he had said to her a month before, openly and frankly, "I want no mourning or weeping. I want the natives of the district to sing, especially their *himehes*. And give them lots of food and drink."

On Wednesday, the fourth of July, after three painful sieges in his chest, which greatly frightened Sarah, Hall seemed to come back stronger than before, and during the day on the fifth he seemed greatly recovered. But at midnight on that day, Lala ran from his room, screaming for help. Walter Smith, a family friend who lived nearby, heard Sarah, and ran to get a doctor. Dr. Andrea de Balmann came from town in less than a half hour. The doctor, seeing that Hall was having painful difficulty in breathing, gave him an injection to relieve the pain, and took his temperature and blood pressure. As she squeezed the rubber ball for the blood pressure, the doctor noticed that the dial registered nothing. It seemed, she concluded, like a complete coronary collapse. At two o'clock in the morning Hall sat upright in bed and gasped twice. From the far corner of the room Lala rushed to his side. Another moment passed and Hall gasped once more, then again, and died in his wife's arms.

At dawn that morning, the body, having been washed and dressed by Terii, an old family retainer, was brought from the main house, and across the street to the beach house, there laid out on a low couch in the large living room. Before the sun had fully risen, news of Hall's death had circled the island, and mourners started coming to Arué to pay their respects. At the body's feet, on a small table, Terii had laid Hall's medals from his war service, fifteen in all, including the Médaille militaire, the Croix de guerre with five palms, the Legion of

Honor, the Distinguished Service Cross, the Purple Heart, the World War One Victory Medal, the British Victory Medal, and the French and American wings of an aviator.

For the next thirty hours scores of native, European, and American friends came to the beach house, leaving wreaths of frangipani, hibiscus, and poinsettia, and offering their condolences to Sarah, who sat on a chair next to the bier, wracked and shaken with grief. That morning Sarah had tried to get the news to Nick and Nancy, who, unaware that there had been even any illness, were on the high seas, one day out from Hawaii, aboard Cornelius Crane's yacht, the *Vega,* bound for Tahiti for a visit. Conrad could not be reached, but he heard the news on his car radio while he was driving on the Los Angeles freeway, and rushed home to send his mother a telegram.

Late in the morning of Saturday, the seventh, Hall's body, having been placed in a simple wooden coffin, was carried out to the hearse, slowly to the strains of the Andante from Dvořák's *New World Symphony* being played on Hall's record player in the beach house. The funeral cortege stopped first on the peninsula at the temple of Otu-aiai near the tomb of King Pomare V, where a short Protestant service was conducted. Then the procession returned to the perimeter road and moved to the base of the road leading up to Hall's hill behind the main house. Because of the steepness of the climb, the coffin was strapped and placed on the shoulders of six players on the Arué soccer team. They were followed by hundreds of mourners, all dressed in white, winding their way up, through, and under the fronds of the palm trees to the summit of the hill. There facing Matavai Bay in the distance, where Bligh had dropped anchor in thirteen fathoms, Hall was laid to final rest. At the graveside the Protestant minister from Arué recited a prayer, and the native orator, Teriieroo, Chief of the district of Papenoo, delivered a eulogy.

That evening, according to the custom in Tahiti, the mourners returned to the beach house, and for three hours in song and spoken address, they continued to pay their tributes to their dear friend departed, Papa Hall. Of the many Polynesian songs, many were gay and buoyant, as Hall had wished.

And of the many native orations, one in particular most impressed the listeners:

> We all knew and loved Papa Hall. He was one of us in his interest in our sports and our activities. We knew him especially as a *kind* man, a simple man, to whom the interests of the poorest were more important than those of the rich and comfortable. No one ever in vain approached him with a request for aid. These things I knew and we all knew. But today my eyes are opened. When I look upon that cushion upon which are pinned his medals and decorations from the leading governments of the world, I for the first time realize that we have had living amongst us a great man. I know now, but never knew before, that in our midst dwelt a hero.

For the grave, Sarah had struck a simple bronze plaque, and on it inscribed the name, dates, and the first lines written by her beloved woodshed poet:

JAMES NORMAN HALL
April 22, 1887–July 6, 1951
Look to the northward stranger,
Just over the hillside there.
Have you in your travels seen
A land more passing fair.

Bibliography

A. BOOKS BY JAMES NORMAN HALL

Kitchener's Mob: The Adventures of an American in Kitchener's Army, Boston, Houghton Mifflin Company, 1916.

High Adventure: A Narrative of Air Fighting in France, Boston, Houghton Mifflin Company, 1918.

On the Stream of Travel, Boston, Houghton Mifflin Company, 1926.

Mid-Pacific, Boston, Houghton Mifflin Company, 1928.

Flying with Chaucer, Boston, Houghton Mifflin Company, 1930.

Mother Goose Land, Boston, Houghton Mifflin Company, 1930.

The Tale of a Shipwreck, Boston, Houghton Mifflin Company, 1934.

Doctor Dogbody's Leg, Boston, Atlantic Monthly Press–Little, Brown and Company, 1940.

The Friends, Muscatine, Iowa, The Prairie Press, 1939.

Gravel, Fern, *Oh, Millersville!,* Muscatine, Iowa, The Prairie Press, 1940.

Under a Thatched Roof, Boston, Houghton Mifflin Company, 1942.

Lost Island,* Boston, Atlantic Monthly Press–Little, Brown and Company, 1944.

* A Book-of-the-Month Club selection.

A Word for His Sponsor: A Narrative Poem, Boston, Atlantic Monthly Press–Little, Brown and Company, 1949.

*The Far Lands,** Boston, Atlantic Monthly Press–Little, Brown and Company, 1950.

The Forgotten One and Other True Tales of the South Seas, Boston, Atlantic Monthly Press–Little, Brown and Company, 1952.

Her Daddy's Best Ice Cream, Honolulu, Hawaii, privately printed, 1952.

My Island Home, Boston, Atlantic Monthly Press–Little, Brown and Company, 1952.

B. BOOKS BY CHARLES BERNARD NORDHOFF

The Fledgling, Boston, Houghton Mifflin Company, 1919.

The Pearl Lagoon, Boston, Atlantic Monthly Press–Little, Brown and Company, 1924.

Picaro, New York, Harper & Brothers, 1924.

Island Wreck, London, Methuen & Co., Ltd., 1929.

The Derelict: Further Adventures of Charles Selden and His Native Friends in the South Seas, Boston, Atlantic Monthly Press–Little, Brown and Company, 1928.

C. BOOKS BY NORDHOFF AND HALL

The Lafayette Flying Corps (editors), Boston, Houghton Mifflin Company, 1920.

Faery Lands of the South Seas, New York, Harper & Brothers, 1921.

Falcons of France: A Tale of Youth and the Air, Boston, Little, Brown and Company, 1929.

Mutiny on the Bounty,† Boston, Little, Brown and Company, 1932.

Men Against the Sea, Boston, Little, Brown and Company, 1934.

Pitcairn's Island, Boston, Little, Brown and Company, 1934.

The Hurricane, Boston, Atlantic Monthly Press–Litt,e Brown and Company, 1936.

Dark River, Boston, Atlantic Monthly Press–Little, Brown and Company, 1938.

* A Literary Guild selection.
† A Book-of-the-Month Club selection.

*No More Gas,** Boston, Atlantic Monthly Press–Little, Brown and Company, 1940.

Botany Bay, Boston, Atlantic Monthly Press–Little, Brown and Company, 1941.

Men Without Country, Boston, Atlantic Monthly Press–Little, Brown and Company, 1942.

The High Barbaree, Boston, Atlantic Monthly Press–Little, Brown and Company, 1945.

D. BOOKS ABOUT TAHITI AND THE SOUTH SEAS

Barrow, Sir John, *The Mutiny and Piratical Seizure of H.M.S. Bounty,* London, Oxford University Press, 1914.

Bligh, William, *The Mutiny on Board H.M.S. Bounty,* New York, The New American Library of World Literature, Inc., 1962.

Burdick, Eugene, *The Blue of Capricorn,* New York, Fawcett World Library (Crest Book), 1962.

Conrad, Barnaby, *Tahiti,* New York, The Viking Press (A Studio Book), 1962.

Danielsson, Bengt, *Love in the South Seas,* translated by F. H. Lyon, New York, Reynal & Company, Inc., 1956.

Eggleston, George T., *Tahiti: Voyage Through Paradise,* New York, The Devin-Adair Company, 1953.

Furnas, J. C., *Anatomy of Paradise: Hawaii and the Islands of the South Seas,* New York, William Sloane Associates, 1948.

Guild, Caroline, *Rainbow in Tahiti,* London, Hammond, Hammond & Co. Ltd., 1951.

Michener, James A., *Return to Paradise,* New York, Bantam Books, 1964.

Michener, James A., and A. Grove Day, *Rascals in Paradise,* New York, Bantam Books, 1958.

O'Brien, Frederick, *White Shadows in the South Seas,* New York, The Century Company, 1919.

———, *Mystic Isles of the South Seas,* New York, The Century Company, 1921.

Price, Willard, *Adventures in Paradise: Tahiti and Beyond,* New York, The John Day Company, 1955.

Rowe, Newton A., *Voyage to the Amorous Islands: The Discovery of Tahiti,* London, Andre Deutsch Limited, 1955.

* A Literary Guild selection.

Russell, Alexander, *Aristocrats of the South Seas*, New York, Roy
Publishers, Inc., 1961.

E. OTHER BOOKS OF INTEREST

Breit, Harvey, *Writer Observed*, New York, World Publishing Co.,
1956.
Parsons, Edwin C., *The Great Adventure: The Story of the Lafayette
Escadrille*, New York, Doubleday, Doran & Company, Inc.,
1937.
Rickenbacker, Capt. Edward V., *Fighting the Flying Circus*, Phila-
delphia and New York, J. B. Lippincott Company, 1947; New
York, Doubleday & Company, Inc., 1965.
Sedgwick, Ellery, *The Happy Profession*, Boston, Atlantic Monthly
Press–Little, Brown and Company, 1946.
Van Gelder, Robert, *Writers and Writing*, New York, Charles Scrib-
ner's Sons, 1946.
Weeks, Edward, *In Friendly Candor*, Boston, Atlantic Monthly Press–
Little, Brown and Company, 1959.

F. MAGAZINE PIECES BY AND ABOUT JAMES
NORMAN HALL

"Fifth Avenue in Fog," *Century*, 87:622 (February, 1914).
"National Defense," *Outlook*, 111:538-39 (November 3, 1915).
"Kitchener's Mob," *Atlantic*, 117:397-407 (March, 1916); 565-73
(April, 1916); 695-702 (May, 1916).
"August Night," *Survey*, 36:498 (August 12, 1916).
"Out of Flanders," *Atlantic*, 118:478-80 (October, 1916).
"English Opinion as to America," *Outlook*, 114:515-18 (November 1,
1916).
"Poetry Under the Fire Test," *New Republic*, 9:93-96 (November
25, 1916).
"City," *Overland Monthly*, 68:405 (November, 1916).
"A Finger and a Huge, Thick Thumb," *Century*, 93:429-31 (January,
1917).
"From Manhattan," *Overland Monthly*, 69:335 (April, 1917).
"Unromantic English," *Outlook*, 116:443-44 (July 18, 1917).
"Carnot's Story," *Atlantic*, 120:453-62 (October, 1917).
"High Adventure," *Atlantic*, 120:155-62 (August, 1917); 398-405 (Sep-
tember, 1917); 704-14 (November, 1917); 121:256-63 (February,

1918); 682-93 (May, 1918); 823-27 (June, 1918); 122:114-22 (July, 1918).

"Roll of Honor," *Air Power*, Vol. 4, No. 3:102 (June, 1918).

"The Splintered Wing," *U. S. Air Service*, Vol. 2, No. 3:11-12 (October, 1919).

"Sir John, Miss Amy, Joseph and Charles," *Atlantic*, 129:744-54 (June, 1922).

"Land Very Far Away," *Woman's Home Companion*, 49:11-12 (November, 1922).

"Settling Down in Polynesia," *Woman's Home Companion*, 50:12 (May, 1923).

"Reminiscences of a Middle-Western School," *Atlantic*, 131:735-40 (June, 1923).

"Some Polynesian Grandmothers," *Woman's Home Companion*, 50:25 (June, 1923).

"Narrative of a Journey," *Harper's*, 148:85-96 (December, 1923).

"Autumn Sojourn in Iceland," *Harper's*, 148:186-98 (January, 1924).

"The Forgotten One," *Atlantic*, 135:289-306 (March, 1925).

"Snow-Bound," *Atlantic*, 135:447-56 (April, 1925).

"Memoir of a Laundry Slip," *Harper's*, 150:560-70 (April, 1925).

"Onward, Christian Soldiers," *Atlantic*, 136:19-32 (July, 1925).

"Sing: A Song of Sixpence," *Atlantic*, 136:726-36 (December, 1925).

"Enchantment of the Icelandic Wild," *Travel*, 46:26-27 (February, 1926).

"Why I Live in Tahiti," *Atlantic*, 137:461-68 (April, 1926).

"Small Memories," *Atlantic*, 138:460-68 (October, 1926).

"Occupation: Journalist," *Harper's* 153:670-84 (November, 1926).

"On the Island of Happy Indolence," *Travel*, 49:7-11 (July, 1927).

"Cacoethes Scribendi," *Atlantic*, 141:42-46 (January, 1928).

"Winter Sojourn in Iceland," *St. Nicholas*, 55:343-48 (March, 1928).

"To the Ice Mountains," *Atlantic*, 144:20-28 (July, 1929).

"Escape De Luxe," *Harper's*, 160:91-103 (December, 1929).

"Concerning Trains," *Harper's*, 161:154-58 (July, 1930).

"From a Tahitian Commonplace Book," *Virginia Quarterly Review*, 6:557-63 (October, 1930).

"Still Small Voice," *Atlantic*, 146:714-18 (December, 1930).

"Death on an Atoll," *Atlantic*, 147:303-16 (March, 1931).

"Art of Loafing," *Atlantic*, 148:51-63 (July, 1931).

"Youth in These Days," *Harper's*, 163:549 (October, 1931).

"Three Books Re-Read: Don Quixote; Mr. Santayana's Soliloquies in England; Charles Lamb's Letters," *Atlantic*, 148:731-32 (December, 1931).

"Starry Night at Arué," *Atlantic,* 149:561 (May, 1932).

"At Forty-Five," *Atlantic,* 150:350-57 (September, 1932).

"Return to Flanders," *Atlantic,* 150:307 (September, 1932).

"Too Many Books," *Atlantic,* 150:458-60 (October, 1932).

"Coconut Palm," *Atlantic,* 150:510-11 (October, 1932).

"In a Library," *Harper's,* 165:551 (October, 1932).

"Happy Ending," *Harper's,* 166:250-52 (January, 1933).

"Lord of Marutea: The Director's Story," *Atlantic,* 151:12-27 (January, 1933).

"Skip: A Strong Icelandic Noun," *Atlantic,* 151:221-26 (February, 1933).

"Captain Nicklemagnet and the Gangsters," *Harper's,* 166:377-79 (February, 1933).

"Comments for Books: For Ben Jonson's Complete Works, in One Volume; For Haydon's Autobiography; For Wordsworth's Lyrical Poems; For . . . , by J. N. H.," *Bookman,* 76:118-20 (February, 1933).

"Lives That Authors Lead," *Bookman,* 76:219-21 (March, 1933).

"State of Being Bored," *Atlantic,* 151:318-21 (March, 1933).

"Voice," *Atlantic,* 151:578-81 (May, 1933).

"Spirit of Place," *Atlantic,* 152:478-83 (October, 1933).

"Coral Island," *Rotarian,* 43:16-17 (November, 1933).

"From Med to Mum," *Atlantic,* 153:257-68 (March, 1934); 404-14 (April, 1934); 568-78 (May, 1934); 709-18 (June, 1934); 154:96-105 (July, 1934).

"Expatriates," *American Review,* 5:185-90 (May, 1935).

"Wartime Verses and Peacetime Sequel: Airman's Rendezvous: Afterword," *Atlantic,* 155:563-65 (May, 1935).

"In Memoriam: The Old Brown Hen," *Atlantic,* 155:759 (June, 1935).

"December in the Tropics," *Atlantic,* 157:500 (April, 1936).

"Reflections While Worming," *Saturday Review,* 14:12-13 (August 22, 1936).

"Evening on a Coral Island: Comfort That Turned Cold," *Atlantic,* 159:448, 501 (April, 1937).

"In Memoriam: Third Ypres," *Harper's,* 175:595 (November, 1937).

"Happiness," *Atlantic,* 164:696-97 (November, 1939).

"Vulnerary Water: One of the Tall Tales from Doctor Dogbody's Leg," *Scholastic,* 37:29-30 (January 6, 1941; 20-30 (January 13, 1941).

"Tour de l'île," *Atlantic,* 167:614-16 (May, 1941).

"My Conrad," *Atlantic,* 169:583-87 (May, 1942).

"Word for the Essayist," *Yale Review,* Vol. 32, No. 1:50-58 (September, 1942).

"Whistle of the Evening Train," *Reader's Digest,* 42:69-72 (March, 1943).

"Mr. Bolton's Birthday," *Atlantic,* 173:70-72 (June, 1944).

"Reading and Meditating: E. A. Robinson's Poems; S. O. Jewett's Stories; M. Beerbohm's Essays; R. Frost's Poems; When I Am Old," *Atlantic,* 174:57-60 (September, 1944).

"Fern Gravel," *Atlantic,* 178:112-14 (September, 1946).

"Mr. Bolton's Birthday," *Scholastic,* 49:19-20 (October 21, 1946).

"G-Note Road," *Atlantic,* 184:62-65 (July, 1949).

"Frisbie of the South Seas," *Atlantic,* 184:23-32 (August, 1949); 63-71 (September, 1949); 60-66 (October, 1949).

"Far Lands," *Atlantic,* 186:19-31 (August, 1950); 58-68 (September, 1950); 66-74 (October, 1950); 70-79 (November, 1950).

"Haunted Island," *Saturday Evening Post,* 223:40-41 (October 21, 1950).

"My Island Home," *Atlantic,* 190:21-28 (September, 1952); 78-85 (October, 1952); 78-86 (November, 1952); 66-74 (December, 1952).

Welch, Murray D., "James Norman Hall: Poet and Philosopher," *The South Atlantic Quarterly,* Vol. 29, No. 2 (April, 1940).

Stonehill, J., "James Norman Hall," *Saturday Review,* 25:11 (December 12, 1942).

Loveman, Amy, "Everyman's Dilemma," *Saturday Review,* 34:14 (July 21, 1951).

Sedgwick, Ellery, "James Norman Hall," *Atlantic,* 188:19-21 (September, 1951).

Smith, Walter G., "James Norman Hall," *Atlantic,* 188:22 (October, 1951).

Sutton, Horace, "Day on Bounty Bay," *Saturday Review,* 39:25-26 (July 14, 1956).

G. MAGAZINE PIECES BY CHARLES NORDHOFF

"Letters from France," *Atlantic,* 120:565-71 (October, 1917).

"More Letters from France," *Atlantic,* 121:118-27 (January, 1918).

"Flying Thoughts," *Atlantic,* 121:554-62 (April, 1918).

"Winged Words," *Atlantic,* 122:257-64 (August, 1918).

"Aerial Tactics," *Atlantic*, 122:410-16 (September, 1918).
"Squadrons of the Air," *Atlantic*, 123:89-98 (January, 1919).
"The Human Side of Mexico," *Atlantic*, 124:502-09 (October, 1919).
"On the Lagoon," *Atlantic*, 125:763-71 (June, 1920).
"An Island Memory," *Atlantic*, 126:318-24 (September, 1920).
"Rarotonga," *Atlantic*, 126:456-63 (October, 1920).
"Marooned on Mataora," *Atlantic*, 126:587-95 (November, 1920).
"In the Shadow of Faneuhi," *Atlantic*, 128:204-09 (August, 1921).
"South Sea Moonshine," *Atlantic*, 128:492-500 (October, 1921).
"Savagery," *Harper's*, 144:545-59 (April, 1922).
"South Sea Fishermen," *Harper's*, 145:224-33 (July, 1922).
"Man Monday's Fishing," *Harper's*, 153:1-9 (June, 1926).
"Maki's Perfect Day," *Harpers*, 154:421-26 (March, 1927).
"Fishing for the Oil Fish," *Natural History*, 28:40-45 (January, 1928).
"Saved by the Durian!" *Harvard Graduates' Magazine*, 38:146-48 (September, 1929).
"To Sam Pepys, Esq.," *Atlantic*, 161:554 (April, 1938).

H. MAGAZINE PIECES BY AND ABOUT NORDHOFF AND HALL

"Faery Lands of the South Seas," *Harper's* (November, December, 1920; January, February, March, April, May, June, 1921).
"Men Against the Sea," *Saturday Evening Post* (November 18, 25, December 2, 9, 1933).
"Pitcairn's Island," *Saturday Evening Post* (September 22, 29, October, 6, 13, 20, 27, November 3, 1934). Also abridged in *The Reader's Digest* (January 1936).
"The Hurricane," *Saturday Evening Post* (December 28, 1935; January 4, 11, 18, 25, February 1, 1936).
"The Dark River," *Saturday Evening Post* (April 20, May 7, 14, 21, 28, June 4, 11, 18, 25, 1938).
"Out of Gas," *Saturday Evening Post* (November 11, 18, 25, December 2, 9, 1939).
"Botany Bay," *Saturday Evening Post* (September 27, October 4, 11, 18, 25, November 2, 1941).
"Men Without Country," *Atlantic* (June, 1942).
Loveman, Amy, "Modern Damon and Pythias," *Saturday Review*, 10:101-102 (September 9, 1933).
McConnaughey, James, "By Nordhoff and Hall," *Saturday Evening Post*, 210:12-13 (April 23, 1938).

Index

"Tales of the Pacific"

Journey into the watery world of atolls, roaring surf on coral reefs, blue lagoons, volcanoes and hurricanes, Polynesian kingdoms, and exotic brown women. Watch a cast of characters of beachcombers, whalers, missionaries, adventurers, traders, pearl hunters, mutineers, native chiefs, scientists, sun-hungry artists, and American G.I.'s. Read the best of the literature — fiction and nonfiction — from the earthly Paradises of the Pacific — the archipelagoes of Polynesia, Melanesia, and Micronesia. Enjoy dramatic narratives, short stories, and vignettes from a gallery of authors including Herman Melville, Mark Twain, Robert Louis Stevenson, Louis Becke, Jack London, W. Somerset Maugham, James Norman Hall, James Jones, Eugene Burdick, James A. Michener, and others that should be better known. Recall stirring adventures from the days of Captain James Cook and other early explorers through those of Pearl Harbor and the island-hopping campaigns of World War II!

To obtain a full description of "Tales of the Pacific" titles, write to Mutual Publishing, 2055 North King Street, Suite 201, Honolulu, Hawaii 96819.

JACK LONDON

Stories of Hawaii
South Sea Tales
Captain David Grief (originally A Son of the Sun)
The Mutiny of the "Elsinore" ($4.95)

HAWAII

Remember Pearl Harbor by Blake Clark
Kona by Marjorie Sinclair
The Spell of Hawaii, ed. by A. Grove Day and Carl Stroven
A Hawaiian Reader, ed. by A. Grove Day and Carl Stroven
The Golden Cloak by Antoinette Withington
Russian Flag Over Hawaii by Darwin Teilhet
The Wild Wind by Marjorie Sinclair
Teller of Tales by Eric Knudsen
Myths and Legends of Hawaii by W.D. Westervelt, ed. by A. Grove Day

SOUTH SEAS LITERATURE

The Trembling of a Leaf by W. Somerset Maugham
Rogues of the South Seas by A. Grove Day
The Book of Puka-Puka by Robert Dean Frisbie
The Lure of Tahiti, ed. by A. Grove Day
The Blue of Capricorn by Eugene Burdick
Horror in Paradise: Grim and Uncanny Tales from Hawaii and The South Seas, ed. by A. Grove Day and Bacil F. Kirtley
Best South Sea Stories, ed. by A. Grove Day
The Forgotten One by James Norman Hall

TRAVEL, BIOGRAPHY, ANTHROPOLOGY

Manga Reva by Robert Lee Eskridge
Coronado's Quest: The Discovery of the American Southwest by A. Grove Day
Love in the South Seas by Bengt Danielsson
Road My Body Goes by Clifford Gessler
The House in the Rain Forest by Charis Crockett
My Tahiti by Robert Dean Frisbie
Home from the Sea: Robert Louis Stevenson in Samoa by Richard A. Bermann
The Nordhoff-Hall Story: In Search of Paradise by Paul L. Briand, Jr. ($4.95)